"DOWN WE GO, FOR A CERTAINTY"

The Pathfinder

BY

J. FENIMORE COOPER

Author of "The Last of the Mohicans" "Deerslayer" "Ned Myers" &c.

"Here the heart
May give a useful lesson to the head,
And Learning wiser grow without his books."
—COWPER.

BLACKIE & SON LIMITED
LONDON AND GLASGOW

BLACKIE & SON LIMITED
50 Old Bailey, London
17 Stanhope Street, Glasgow

BLACKIE & SON (INDIA) LIMITED
Warwick House, Fort Street, Bombay

BLACKIE & SON (CANADA) LIMITED
Toronto

Printed in Great Britain by Blackie & Son, Ltd., Glasgow

BIOGRAPHICAL NOTE

James Fenimore Cooper was born at Burlington, New Jersey, in the United States, in 1789. After completing his education, he served before the mast on a merchantman, and in 1808 entered the American navy. He married at the beginning of 1811, and resigned his commission in the navy a few months later. He began his literary career in 1820 with an unimportant novel, but with *The Spy* (1821) he started the series of stories of adventure that have given him an assured fame. The most notable of these are the following: *The Pioneers* (1823), *The Pilot* (1823), *The Last of the Mohicans* (1826), *The Prairie* (1827), *The Red Rover* (1828), *Homeward Bound* (1838), *The Pathfinder* (1840), *Deerslayer* (1841), *The Two Admirals* (1842), *The Wing-and-Wing* (1842), *Ned Myers* (1843), *Afloat and Ashore* (1844), *The Crater* (1847), and *The Sea Lions* (1849). He died at his mansion of Cooperstown, in the state of New York, in 1851.

THE PATHFINDER

CHAPTER I

THE sublimity connected with vastness is familiar to every eye.
The most abstruse, the most far-reaching, perhaps the most
chastened of the poet's thoughts, crowd on the imagination as
he gazes into the depths of the illimitable void. The expanse of
the ocean is seldom seen by the novice with indifference; and
the mind, even in the obscurity of night, finds a parallel to that
grandeur, which seems inseparable from images that the senses
cannot compass. With feelings akin to this admiration and awe
—the offspring of sublimity—were the different characters with
which the action of this tale must open gazing on the scene before
them. Four persons in all—two of each sex—they had managed
to ascend a pile of trees, that had been uptorn by a tempest, to
catch a view of the objects that surrounded them. By letting in
the light of heaven upon the dark and damp recesses of the wood,
these trees, called windrows, form a sort of oasis in the solemn
obscurity of the virgin forests of America. They lay on the
brow of a gentle acclivity; and, though small, it had opened the
way for an extensive view to those who might occupy its upper
margin, a rare occurrence to the traveller in the woods. The
viewless influence had piled tree on tree, in such a manner as
had not only enabled the two males of the party to ascend to an
elevation of some thirty feet above the level of the earth, but,
with a little care and encouragement, to induce their more timid
companions to accompany them. The vast trunks which had
been broken and driven by the force of the gust lay blended like
jack-straws; while their branches, still exhaling the fragrance of
withering leaves, were interlaced in a manner to afford sufficient
support to the hands. One tree had been completely uprooted,
and its lower end, filled with earth, had been cast uppermost, in
a way to supply a sort of staging for the four adventurers, when
they had gained the desired distance from the ground.

Two of the party, a male and female, belonged to the native owners of the soil, being Indians of the well-known tribe of the Tuscaroras; while their companions were—a man, who bore about him the peculiarities of one who had passed his days on the ocean, and was, too, in a station little, if any, above that of a common mariner; and his female associate, who was a maiden of a class in no great degree superior to his own; though her youth, sweetness of countenance, and a modest, but spirited mien, lent that character of intellect and refinement which adds so much to the charm of beauty in the sex. On the present occasion, her full blue eye reflected the feeling of sublimity that the scene excited, and her pleasant face was beaming with the pensive expression with which all deep emotions, even though they bring the most grateful pleasure, shadow the countenances of the ingenuous and thoughtful.

Towards the west, in which direction the faces of the party were turned, the eye ranged over an ocean of leaves, glorious and rich in the varied and lively verdure of a generous vegetation, and shaded by the luxuriant tints which belong to the forty-second degree of latitude. The elm with its graceful and weeping top, the rich varieties of the maple, most of the noble oaks of the American forest, with the broad-leaved linden known in the parlance of the country as the basswood, mingled their uppermost branches, forming one broad and seemingly interminable carpet of foliage, which stretched away towards the setting sun, until it bounded the horizon, by blending with the clouds, as the waves and the sky meet at the base of the vault of heaven.

"Uncle," said the wondering, but pleased girl, addressing her male companion, whose arm she rather touched than leaned on, to steady her own light but firm footing, "this is like a view of the ocean you so much love!"

"So much for ignorance, and a girl's fancy, Magnet,"—a term of affection the sailor often used in allusion to his niece's personal attractions; "no one but a child would think of likening this handful of leaves to a look at the real Atlantic. You might size all these treetops to Neptune's jacket, and they would make no more than a nosegay for his bosom."

"More fanciful than true, I think, Uncle. Look thither; it must be miles on miles, and yet we see nothing but leaves! what more could one behold, if looking at the ocean?"

"More!" returned the uncle, giving an impatient gesture with the elbow the other touched, for his arms were crossed, and the hands were thrust into the bosom of a vest of red cloth, a fashion of the times,—"more, Magnet! say, rather, what less? Where are your combing seas, your blue water, your rollers, your breakers, your whales, or your waterspouts, and your endless motion, in this bit of a forest, child?"

"And where are your treetops, your solemn silence, your fragrant leaves, and your beautiful green, Uncle, on the ocean?"

"Tut, Magnet! if you understood the thing, you would know that green water is a sailor's bane."

"But green trees are a different thing. Hist! that sound is the air breathing among the leaves!"

"You should hear a nor'wester breathe, girl, if you fancy wind aloft. Now, where are your gales, and hurricanes, and trades, and levanters, and such like incidents, in this bit of a forest? and what fishes have you swimming beneath yonder tame surface?"

"That there have been tempests here, these signs around us plainly show; and beasts, if not fishes, are beneath those leaves."

"I do not know that," returned the uncle, with a sailor's dogmatism. "They told us many stories at Albany of the wild animals we should fall in with, and yet we have seen nothing to frighten a seal. I doubt if any of your inland animals will compare with a low-latitude shark."

"See!" exclaimed the niece, who was more occupied with the sublimity and beauty of the "boundless wood" than with her uncle's arguments; "yonder is a smoke curling over the tops of the trees—can it come from a house?"

"Ay, ay; there is a look of humanity in that smoke," returned the old seaman, "which is worth a thousand trees. I must show it to Arrowhead, who may be running past a port without knowing it. It is probable there is a caboose where there is a smoke."

As he concluded, the uncle drew a hand from his bosom, touched the male Indian, who was standing near him, lightly on the shoulder, and pointed out a thin line of vapour which was stealing slowly out of the wilderness of leaves, at a distance of about a mile, and was diffusing itself in almost imperceptible threads of humidity in the quivering atmosphere. The Tuscarora was one of those noble-looking warriors oftener met with among the aborigines of this continent a century since than to-day; and, while he had mingled sufficiently with the colonists to be familiar with their habits and even with their language, he had lost little, if any, of the wild grandeur and simple dignity of a chief.

Between him and the old seaman the intercourse had been friendly, but distant; for the Indian had been too much accustomed to mingle with the officers of the different military posts he had frequented not to understand that his present companion was only a subordinate. So imposing, indeed, had been the quiet superiority of the Tuscarora's reserve, that Charles Cap, for so was the seaman named, in his most dogmatical or facetious moments, had not ventured on familiarity in an intercourse which had now lasted more than a week. The sight of the curling smoke, however, had struck the latter like the sudden appearance of a sail at sea; and, for the first time since they met, he ventured to touch the warrior, as has been related.

The quick eye of the Tuscarora instantly caught a sight of the smoke; and for full a minute he stood, slightly raised on tiptoe, with distended nostrils, like the buck that scents a taint in the air, and a gaze as riveted as that of the trained pointer while he waits his master's aim. Then, falling back on his feet, a low exclamation, in the soft tones that form so singular a contrast to its harsher cries in the Indian warrior's voice, was barely audible; otherwise, he was undisturbed. His countenance was calm, and his quick, dark, eagle eye moved over the leafy panorama, as if to take in at a glance every circumstance that might enlighten his mind. That the long journey they had attempted to make through a broad belt of wilderness was necessarily attended with danger, both uncle and niece well knew; though neither could at once determine whether the sign that others were in their vicinity was the harbinger of good or evil.

"There must be Oneidas or Tuscaroras near us, Arrowhead," said Cap, addressing his Indian companion by his conventional English name; "will it not be well to join company with them, and get a comfortable berth for the night in their wigwam?"

"No wigwam there," Arrowhead answered in his unmoved manner—"too much tree."

"But Indians must be there; perhaps some old messmates of your own, Master Arrowhead."

"No Tuscarora—no Oneida—no Mohawk—paleface fire."

"Is it? Well, Magnet, this surpasses a seaman's philosophy: we old seadogs can tell a lubber's nest from a mate's hammock; but I do not think the oldest admiral in his Majesty's fleet can tell a king's smoke from a collier's."

The idea that human beings were in their vicinity, in that ocean of wilderness, had deepened the flush on the blooming cheek and brightened the eye of the fair creature at his side; but she soon turned with a look of surprise to her relative, and said hesitatingly, for both had often admired the Tuscarora's knowledge, or, we might almost say, instinct:

"A paleface's fire! Surely, Uncle, he cannot know *that*?"

"Ten days since, child, I would have sworn to it; but now I hardly know what to believe. May I take the liberty of asking, Arrowhead, why you fancy that smoke, now, a paleface's smoke, and not a redskin's?"

"Wet wood," returned the warrior, with the calmness with which the pedagogue might point out an arithmetical demonstration to his puzzled pupil. "Much wet—much smoke; much water—black smoke."

"But, begging your pardon, Master Arrowhead, the smoke is not black, nor is there much of it. To my eye, now, it is as light and fanciful a smoke as ever rose from a captain's teakettle, when nothing was left to make the fire but a few chips from the dunnage."

"Too much water," returned Arrowhead, with a slight nod of the head; "Tuscarora too cunning to make fire with water!"

"Well, that's reasonable, I allow," said Cap. "How far, now, Arrowhead, do you make us, by your calculation, from the bit of a pond that you call the Great Lake, and towards which we have been so many days shaping our course?"

The Tuscarora looked at the seaman with quiet superiority as he answered, "Ontario, like heaven; one sun, and the great traveller will know it."

"Well, I have been a great traveller, I cannot deny; but of all my v'y'ges this has been the longest, the least profitable, and the farthest inland. If this body of fresh water is so nigh, Arrowhead, and so large, one might think a pair of good eyes would find it out; for apparently everything within thirty miles is to be seen from this lookout."

"Look," said Arrowhead, stretching an arm before him with quiet grace; "Ontario!"

"Uncle, you are accustomed to cry 'Land ho!' but not 'Water ho!' and you do not see it," cried the niece, laughing.

"How now, Magnet! dost suppose that I shouldn't know my native element, if it were in sight?"

"But Ontario is not your native element, dear Uncle; for you come from the salt water, while this is fresh."

"That might make some difference to your young mariner, but

none to the old one. I should know water, child, were I to see it in China."

"Ontario," repeated Arrowhead with emphasis, again stretching his hand towards the north-west.

Cap looked at the Tuscarora, for the first time since their acquaintance, with something like an air of contempt, though he did not fail to follow the direction of the chief's eye and arm, both of which were directed towards a vacant point in the heavens, a short distance above the plain of leaves.

"Ay, ay; this is much as I expected, when I left the coast in search of a freshwater pond," resumed Cap, shrugging his shoulders like one whose mind was made up, and who thought no more need be said. "Ontario may be there, or, for that matter, it may be in my pocket. Well, I suppose there will be room enough, when we reach it, to work our canoe. But, Arrowhead, if there be palefaces in our neighbourhood, I confess I should like to get within hail of them."

The Tuscarora now gave a quiet inclination of his head, and the whole party descended from the tree in silence. When they had reached the ground, Arrowhead intimated his intention to go towards the fire, and ascertain who had lighted it; while he advised his wife and the two others to return to a canoe, which they had left in the adjacent stream, and await his return.

"Why, chief, this might do on soundings, and in an offing where one knew the channel," returned old Cap; "but in an unknown region like this, I think it unsafe to trust the pilot alone too far from the ship; so, with your leave, we will not part company."

"What my brother want?" asked the Indian gravely.

"Your company, Master Arrowhead, and no more. I will go with you and speak these strangers."

The Tuscarora assented without difficulty, and again he directed his patient and submissive little wife, who seldom turned her full rich black eye on him but to express equally her respect, her dread, and her love, to proceed to the boat. But here Magnet raised a difficulty. Although spirited, and of unusual energy under circumstances of trial, she was but woman; and the idea of being entirely deserted by her two male protectors, in the midst of a wilderness that her senses had just told her was seemingly illimitable, became so keenly painful, that she expressed a wish to accompany her uncle.

"The exercise will be a relief after sitting so long in the canoe," she added, as the rich blood slowly returned to a cheek that had paled in spite of her efforts to be calm; "and there may be females with the strangers."

"Come, then, child; it is but a cable's length, and we shall return an hour before the sun sets."

With this permission, the girl, whose real name was Mabel Dunham, prepared to be of the party; while the Dew-of-June, as the wife of Arrowhead was called, passively went her way towards the canoe.

The three who remained in the windrow now picked their way around its tangled maze, and gained the margin of the woods. A few glances of the eye sufficed for Arrowhead; but old Cap deliberately set the smoke by a pocket compass, before he trusted himself within the shadows of the trees.

"This steering by the nose, Magnet, may do well enough for an Indian, but your thoroughbred knows the virtue of the needle," said the uncle, as he trudged at the heels of the light-stepping Tuscarora. "Friend Arrowhead, didst ever see a machine like this?"

The Indian turned, cast a glance at the compass, and gravely answered, "A paleface eye. The Tuscarora see in his head. The Saltwater (for so the Indian styled his companion) all eye now; no tongue."

"He means, Uncle, that we had needs be silent; perhaps he distrusts the persons we are about to meet."

"Ay, 'tis an Indian's fashion of going to quarters. You perceive he has examined the priming of his rifle, and it may be as well if I look to that of my own pistols."

Without betraying alarm at these preparations, to which she had become accustomed by her long journey in the wilderness, Mabel followed with a step as elastic as that of the Indian, keeping close in the rear of her companions. For the first half-mile no other caution beyond a rigid silence was observed; but as the party drew nearer to the spot where the fire was known to be, much greater care became necessary.

The forest, as usual, had little to intercept the view below the branches but the tall straight trunks of trees. These trees, however, often served to conceal the adventurer, or the foe; and, as Arrowhead swiftly approached the spot where his unerring senses told him the strangers ought to be, his footstep gradually became lighter, his eye more vigilant, and his person was more carefully concealed.

"See, Saltwater," said he exultingly, pointing through the vista of trees; "paleface fire!"

"The fellow is right!" muttered Cap; "there they are, sure enough, and eating their grub as quietly as if they were in the cabin of a three-decker."

"Arrowhead is but half right," whispered Mabel; "for there are two Indians and only one white man."

"Palefaces," said the Tuscarora, holding up two fingers; "red man," holding up one.

"Well," rejoined Cap, "it is hard to say which is right and which is wrong. One is entirely white, and a fine comely lad he is, with an air of respectability about him; one is a redskin as plain as paint and nature can make him; but the third chap is half-rigged, being neither brig nor schooner."

"Palefaces," repeated Arrowhead, again raising two fingers; "red man," showing but one.

"He must be right, Uncle; for his eye seems never to fail. But it is now urgent to know whether we meet as friends or foes. They may be French."

"One hail will soon satisfy us on that head," returned Cap. "Stand you behind this tree, Magnet, lest the knaves take it into their heads to fire a broadside without a parley, and I will soon learn what colours they sail under."

The uncle had placed his two hands to his mouth to form a trumpet, and was about to give the promised hail, when a rapid movement from the hand of Arrowhead defeated the intention by deranging the instrument.

"Red man, Mohican," said the Tuscarora; "good; palefaces, Yengeese."

"These are heavenly tidings," murmured Mabel, who little relished the prospect of a deadly fray in that remote wilderness. "Let us approach at once, dear Uncle, and proclaim ourselves friends."

"Good!" said the Tuscarora; "red man cool, and know; paleface hurried, and fire. Let the squaw go."

"What!" said Cap in astonishment; "send little Magnet ahead as a lookout, while two lubbers, like you and me, lie-to to see what sort of a landfall she will make. If I do, I——"

"It is wisest, Uncle," interrupted the generous girl, "and I have no fear. No Christian, seeing a woman approach alone, would fire upon her; and my presence will be a pledge of peace. Let me go forward, as Arrowhead wishes, and all will be well. We are, as yet, unseen, and the surprise of the strangers will not partake of alarm."

"Good!" returned Arrowhead, who did not conceal his approbation of Mabel's spirit.

"It has an unseamanlike look," answered Cap; "but, being in the woods, no one will know it. If you think, Mabel——"

"Uncle, I know. There is no cause to fear for me; and you are always nigh to protect me."

"Well, take one of the pistols, then——"

"Nay, I had better rely on my youth and feebleness," said the girl, smiling. "Among Christian men, a woman's best guard is her claim to their protection."

The uncle desisted; and, after receiving a few cautious instructions from the Tuscarora, Mabel rallied all her spirit, and advanced alone towards the group seated near the fire. Although the heart of the girl beat quick, her step was firm, and her movements, seemingly, were without reluctance. A deathlike silence reigned in the forest, for they towards whom she approached were too much occupied in appeasing their hunger to avert their looks for an instant from the important business in which they were all engaged. When Mabel, however, had got within a hundred feet of the fire, she trod upon a dried stick, and the trifling noise produced by her light footstep caused the Mohican, as Arrowhead had pronounced the Indian to be, and his companion, whose character had been thought so equivocal, to rise to their feet as quick as thought. Both glanced at the rifles that leaned against a tree; and then each stood without stretching out an arm, as his eye fell on the form of the girl. The Indian uttered a few words to his companion, and resumed his seat and his meal as calmly as if no interruption had occurred. On the contrary, the white man left the fire and came forward to meet Mabel.

The latter saw, as the stranger approached, that she was about to be addressed by one of her own colour, though his dress was so strange a mixture of the habits of the two races that it required a near look to be certain of the fact. He was of middle age; but there was an open honesty, a total absence of guile, in his face, which otherwise would not have been thought handsome, that at once assured Magnet she was in no danger. Still she paused.

"Fear nothing, young woman," said the hunter; "you have met Christian men in the wilderness, and such as know how to treat all kindly who are disposed to peace and justice. I am a man well known in all these parts, and perhaps my name may have reached your ears. The troops and rangers along this side of the water call me Pathfinder, inasmuch as I have never been known to miss one end of the trail when there was a Mingo, or a friend who stood in need of me, at the other."

This was not uttered boastfully, but with the honest confidence of one who well knew that by whatever name others might have heard of him, he had no reason to blush at the reports. The effect on Mabel was instantaneous. The moment she heard the last *sobriquet*, she clasped her hands eagerly and repeated the word "Pathfinder!"

"Then you are the friend my father promised to send to meet us?"

"If you are Sergeant Dunham's daughter, the great Prophet of the Delawares never uttered more truth."

"I am Mabel; and yonder, hid by the trees, are my uncle, whose name is Cap, and a Tuscarora called Arrowhead. We did not hope to meet you until we had nearly reached the shores of the lake."

"I wish a juster - minded Indian had been your guide," said Pathfinder; "for I am no lover of the Tuscaroras. Is the Dew-of-June with him?"

"His wife accompanies us, and a mild, gentle creature she is."

"Ay, and true-hearted; which is more than any who know him will say of Arrowhead. Well, I suppose worse guides might have been found than the Tuscarora; though he has too much Mingo blood for one who consorts altogether with the Delawares."

"It is, then, perhaps, fortunate we have met," said Mabel.

"It is not misfortunate, at any rate; for I promised the Sergeant I would see his child safe to tne garrison. We expected to meet you before you reached the Falls, where we have left our own canoe; while we thought it might do no harm to come up a few miles, in order to be of service if wanted. It is lucky we did, for I doubt if Arrowhead be the man to shoot the current."

"Here come my uncle and the Tuscarora." As Mabel concluded, Cap and Arrowhead drew nigh; and a few words sufficed to let them know as much as the girl herself had learned from the strangers. As soon as this was done, the party proceeded towards the two who still remained near the fire.

CHAPTER II

THE Mohican continued to eat, though the second white man rose and courteously took off his cap to Mabel Dunham. He was young, healthful, and manly in appearance; and he wore a dress which, while it was less rigidly professional than that of the uncle, also denoted one accustomed to the water. Although the Pathfinder was scarcely in the prime of life, Mabel had met him with a steadiness that may have been the consequence of having braced her nerves for the interview; but when her eyes encountered those of the young man at the fire, they fell before the gaze of admiration with which she saw, or fancied she saw, he greeted her. Each, in truth, felt that interest in the other which similarity of age, condition, mutual comeliness, and their novel situation would be likely to inspire in the young and ingenuous.

"Here," said Pathfinder, with an honest smile bestowed on Mabel, "are the friends your worthy father has sent to meet you. This is a great Delaware; we call him the Big Sarpent."

While the Pathfinder was delivering this address, the two Indians gazed on each other steadily, and the Tuscarora advanced and spoke to the other in an apparently friendly manner.

"I like to see this," continued Pathfinder; "the salutes of two redskins in the woods, Master Cap, are like the hailing of friendly vessels on the ocean. But speaking of water, it reminds me of my young friend, Jasper Western here, who can claim to know something of these matters, seeing that he has passed his days on Ontario."

"I am glad to see you, friend," said Cap, giving the young fresh-water sailor a cordial gripe. "This is my niece Mabel; I call her Magnet, for a reason she never dreams of, though you may possibly have education enough to guess at it, having some pretensions to understand the compass, I suppose."

"The reason is easily comprehended," said the young man, involuntarily fastening his keen dark eye, at the same time, on the suffused face of the girl; "and I feel sure that the sailor who steers by your Magnet will never make a bad landfall."

"Ha! you do make use of some of the terms, I find, and that with propriety; though, on the whole, I fear you have seen more green than blue water."

"It is not surprising that we should get some of the phrases which belong to the land, for we are seldom out of sight of it twenty-four hours at a time."

"More's the pity, boy! A very little land ought to go a great way with a seafaring man. Now, if the truth were known, Master Western, I suppose there is more or less land all round your lake."

"And, Uncle, is there not more or less land around the ocean?" said Magnet.

"No, child, there is more or less ocean all round the land; that's what I tell the people ashore, youngster."

Young Western had a profound deference for a mariner of the ocean, on which he had often pined to sail; but he had also a natural regard for the broad sheet on which he had passed his life, and which was not without its beauties in his eyes.

"What you say, sir," he answered modestly, "may be true as to the Atlantic; but we have a respect for the land up here on Ontario."

"That is because you are always landlocked," returned Cap, laughing; "but yonder is the Pathfinder with some smoking platters, inviting us to share in his mess; and I will confess that one gets no venison at sea. Master Western, civility to girls, at your time of life, comes as easy as taking in the slack of the ensign halyards; and if you will just keep an eye to her kid and can, while I join the mess of the Pathfinder and our Indian friends, I make no doubt she will remember it."

Master Cap uttered more than he was aware of at the time. Jasper Western did attend to the wants of Mabel, and she long remembered the kind, manly attention of the young sailor at this their first interview. He placed the end of a log for a seat, obtained for her a delicious morsel of the venison, gave her a draught of pure water from the spring, and as he sat near her, fast won his way to her esteem by his gentle but frank manner of manifesting his care.

The remainder of the party had taken their places around a platter of venison steaks, which served for the common use, and the discourse naturally partook of the characters of the different individuals which composed it.

"There must be satisfaction in this life of yours, no doubt, Mr. Pathfinder," said Cap; "it has some of the chances and luck that we seamen like; and if ours is all water, yours is all land."

"Nay, we have water too in our journeyings," returned his white companion. "We border men handle the paddle and the spear almost as much as the hunting-knife."

"Ay; but do you handle the brace and the bow-line, the wheel and the lead-line, the reef-point and the top-rope? The paddle is a good thing, out of doubt, in a canoe, but of what use is it in the ship?"

"Nay, I respect all men in their callings, and I can believe the things you mention have their uses. I am not very old, but I have lived in the woods, and have some acquaintance with human natur'. I never believe much in the learning of them that dwell in towns, for I never yet met with one that had an eye for a rifle or a trail."

"That's my manner of reasoning, Master Pathfinder, to a yarn. Walking about streets, going to church of Sundays, and hearing sermons never yet made a man of a human being. Now, there is my brother-in-law, the Sergeant: he is as good a fellow as ever broke a biscuit, in his way; but what is he, after all? Why, nothing but a soldier. A sergeant, to be sure, but that is a sort of a soldier, you know. When he wished to marry poor Bridget, my sister, I told the girl what he was, as in duty bound, and what she might expect from such a husband; but you know how it is with girls when their minds are jammed by an inclination. It is true, the Sergeant has risen in his calling, and they say he is an important man at the fort; but his poor wife has not lived to see it all, for she has now been dead these fourteen years."

"A soldier's calling is honourable, provided he has fi't only on the side of right," returned the Pathfinder. "The Sarpent, here, has his fashions, and I have mine; and yet have we fi't side by side these many years without either thinking a hard thought consarning the other's ways. I tell him there is but one heaven and one hell, notwithstanding his traditions, though there are many paths to both."

"That is rational; and he is bound to believe you, though, I fancy, most of the roads to the last are on dry land. The sea is what my sister Bridget used to call a 'purifying place', and one is out of the way of temptation when out of sight of land."

"That towns and settlements lead to sin, I will allow; but our lakes are bordered by the forests, and one is every day called upon to worship God in such a temple. That men are not always the same, even in the wilderness, I must admit, for the difference between a Mingo and a Delaware is as plain to be seen as the difference between the sun and the moon. I am glad, friend Cap, that we have met, however, if it be only that you may tell the Big Sarpent here that there are lakes in which the water is salt. We have been pretty much of one mind since our acquaintance began, and if the Mohican has only half the faith in me than

(M 5)

I have in him, he believes all that I have told him touching the white men's ways and natur's laws; but it has always seemed to me that none of the redskins have given as free a belief as an honest man likes to the accounts of the Big Salt Lakes, and to that of there being rivers that flow up stream."

"This comes of getting things wrong end foremost," answered Cap, with a condescending nod. "You have thought of your lakes and rifts as the ship; and of the ocean and the tides as the boat. Neither Arrowhead nor the Serpent need doubt what you have said concerning both, though I confess myself to some difficulty in swallowing the tale about there being inland seas at all, and still more that there is any sea of fresh water. I have come this long journey as much to satisfy my own eyes concerning these facts as to oblige the Sergeant and Magnet, though the first was my sister's husband and I love the last like a child."

"You are wrong, friend Cap, very wrong, to distrust the power of God in anything," returned Pathfinder earnestly. "There are matters which belong altogether to the ordering of God's providence; and these salt and freshwater lakes are some of them. I do not pretend to account for these things, but I think it the duty of all to believe in them."

"Hold on there, Master Pathfinder," interrupted Cap, not without some heat. "In the way of a proper and manly faith, I will turn my back on no one when afloat. All I mean to say is this, that, being accustomed to see water in large bodies salt, I should like to taste it before I can believe it to be fresh."

"God has given the salt lick to the deer; and He has given to man, redskin and white, the delicious spring at which to slake his thirst. It is unreasonable to think that He may not have given lakes of pure water to the west, and lakes of impure water to the east."

"Well, well, friend Pathfinder," said Cap, "we will leave the argument where it is; and we can try the water when we once reach it."

The guide seemed content to let the matter rest, and the conversation changed.

"We are not over-conceited consarning our gifts," observed the Pathfinder, after a short pause, "and well know that such as live in the towns, and near the sea——"

"On the sea," interrupted Cap.

"On the sea, if you wish it, friend—have opportunities which do not befall us of the wilderness. Still, we know our own callings, and they are what I consider natural callings, and are not parvarted by vanity and wantonness. Now, my gifts are with the rifle, and on a trail, and in the way of game and scouting. The youth Jasper, there, is a different creetur'; for he may be said to breathe the water, as it might be, like a fish. The Frenchers of the north shore call him Eau-douce, on account of his gifts in this particular. He is better at the oar, and the rope too, than in making fires on a trail."

"There must be something about these gifts of which you speak after all," said Cap. "Now this fire, I will acknowledge, has overlaid all my seamanship. Arrowhead, there, said the smoke came from a paleface's fire, and that is a piece of philosophy which I hold to be equal to steering in a dark night by the edges of the sand."

"It's no great secret," returned Pathfinder, laughing with great inward glee. "Nothing is easier to us who pass our time in the great school of Providence than to larn its lessons. We should be as useless on a trail, or in carrying tidings through the wilderness, as so many woodchucks, did we not soon come to a knowledge of these niceties. Eau-douce is so fond of the water that he gathered a damp stick or two for our fire; and wet will bring dark smoke."

"That must be a keen eye of Arrowhead's to see so slight a difference."

"He would be but a poor Indian if he didn't. No, no; it is wartime, and no redskin is outlying without using his senses. It was many years before I could master all these higher branches of a forest education."

"You have been a ready scholar, Master Pathfinder, as is seen by your understanding these things so well. I suppose it would be no great matter for a man regularly brought up to the sea to catch these trifles, if he could only bring his mind fairly to bear upon them."

"I don't know that. The white man has his difficulties in getting redskin habits, quite as much as the Indian in getting whiteskin ways. Still, without the edication I have received, I should think it, at this very moment, a risky journey to go over the very ground that lies between us and the garrison, in the present state of the frontier. There are about as many Iroquois on this side of Ontario as there are on the other. It is for this reason, friend Cap, that the Sergeant has engaged us to come out and show you the path."

"What! do the knaves dare to cruise so near the guns of one of his Majesty's works?"

"Do not the ravens resort near the carcass of the deer, though the fowler is at hand? They come this-a-way, as it might be, naturally. There are more or less whites passing between the forts and the settlements, and they are sure to be on their trails. The Sarpent has come up one side of the river, and I have come up the other, in order to scout for the outlying rascals, while Jasper brought up the canoe, like a bold-hearted sailor as he is. The Sergeant told him, with tears in his eyes, all about his child, and how his heart yearned for her, and how gentle and obedient she was, until I think the lad would have dashed into a Mingo camp single-handed rather than not a-come."

"We thank him, and shall think the better of him for his readiness; though I suppose the boy has run no great risk."

"Only the risk of being shot from a cover as he forced the canoe up a swift rift, or turned an elbow in the stream, with his eyes fastened on the eddies. Of all the risky journeys, that on an ambushed river is the most risky, in my judgment, and that risk has Jasper run."

"And why has the Sergeant sent for me to travel a hundred and fifty miles in this outlandish manner? If it were not for little Magnet there, I would tack ship this instant, make the best of my way back to York, and let Ontario take care of itself, salt water or fresh."

"That wouldn't mend the matter much, friend mariner, as the road to return is much longer, and almost as bad as the road to go on. Trust to us, and we will carry you through safely, or lose our scalps."

Cap wore a tight solid queue, done up in eelskin, while the top of his head was nearly bald; and he mechanically passed his hand over both, as if to make certain that each was in its right place.

"I make no doubt, Master Pathfinder," he answered, "that we shall reach port in safety. What distance may we now be from the fort?"

"Little more than fifteen miles; and swift miles too, as the river runs, if the Mingos let us go clear."

"And I suppose the woods will stretch along starboard and larboard, as heretofore?"

"Anan?"

"I mean that we shall have to pick our way through these trees."

"Nay, you will go in the canoe, and the Oswego has been cleared of its floodwood by the troops. It will be floating down stream, and that, too, with a swift current."

"And what is to prevent these minks of which you speak from shooting us as we double a headland, or are busy in steering clear of the rocks?"

"The Lord!—He who has so often helped others in greater difficulties. Many and many is the time that my head would have been stripped of hair, skin, and all, hadn't the Lord fi't of my side. I never go into a scrimmage, friend mariner, without thinking of this great ally, who can do more in battle than all the battalions of the 60th, were they brought into a single line."

"Ay, ay, this may do well enough for a scouter; but we seamen like our offing, and to go into action with nothing in our minds but the business before us—plain broadside and broadside work, and no trees or rocks to thicken the water."

"And no Lord too, I dare to say, if the truth were known. Take my word for it, Master Cap, that no battle is the worse fi't for having the Lord on your side."

"Well, Pathfinder, we have but a few hours of sun, and had better be drifting down this said current of yours while we may. Magnet, dear, are you not ready to get under way?"

Magnet started, blushed brightly, and made her preparations for immediate departure. Not a syllable of the discourse just related had she heard; for Eau-douce had been filling her ears with a description of the yet distant part towards which she was journeying, with accounts of her father, whom she had not seen since a child, and with the manner of life of those who lived in the frontier garrisons. Unconsciously she had become deeply interested, and her thoughts had been too intently directed to these matters to allow any of the less agreeable subjects discussed by those so near to reach her ears. The bustle of departure put an end to the conversation, and, the baggage of the scouts or guides being trifling, in a few minutes the whole party was ready to proceed. As they were about to quit the spot, however, to the surprise of even his fellow guides, Pathfinder collected a quantity of branches and threw them upon the embers of the fire, taking care even to see that some of the wood was damp, in order to raise as dark and dense a smoke as possible.

"When you can hide your trail, Jasper," said he, "a smoke at leaving an encampment may do good instead of harm. If there are a dozen Mingos within ten miles of us, some on 'em are on the heights, or in the trees, looking out for smokes; let them see this, and much good may it do them."

"But may they not strike and follow on our trail?" asked the youth. "We shall leave a broad path to the river."

"The broader the better; when there, it will surpass Mingo cunning even to say which way the canoe has gone—up stream or down. Do you not see, Eau-douce, that if any Mingos have seen our path below the falls, they will strike off towards this smoke, and that they will naturally conclude that they who began by going up stream will end by going up stream. If they know anything, they now know a party is out from the fort, and it will exceed even Mingo wit to fancy that we have come up here just for the pleasure of going back again, and that, too, the same day, and at the risk of our scalps."

"Certainly," added Jasper, who was talking apart with the Pathfinder; "they cannot know anything about the Sergeant's daughter, for the greatest secrecy has been observed on her account."

"And they will learn nothing here," returned Pathfinder, causing his companion to see that he trod with the utmost care on the impression left on the leaves by the little foot of Mabel; "unless this old saltwater fish has been taking his niece about in the windrow, like a fa'n playing by the side of the old doe."

"Buck, you mean, Pathfinder."

"Isn't he a queerity? Now I can consort with such a sailor as yourself, Eau-douce, and find nothing very contrary in our gifts, though yours belong to the lakes and mine to the woods. Hark'e, Jasper," continued the scout, laughing, "suppose we try the temper of his blade, and run him over the falls?"

"And what would be done with the pretty niece in the meanwhile?"

"Nay, no harm shall come to her; she must walk round the portage, at any rate; but you and I can try this Atlantic oceaner, and then all parties will become better acquainted. We shall find out whether his flint will strike fire; and he may come to know something of frontier tricks."

Young Jasper smiled, for he was not averse to fun, and had been a little touched by Cap's superciliousness; but Mabel's fair face, light, agile form, and winning smiles, stood like a shield between her uncle and the intended experiment.

"Perhaps the Sergeant's daughter will be frightened," said he.

"Not she, if she has any of the Sergeant's spirit in her. She doesn't look like a skeery thing. Leave it to me then, Eau-douce, and I will manage the affair alone."

"Not you, Pathfinder; you would only drown both. If the canoe goes over, I must go in it."

"Well, have it so, then."

Jasper laughed, nodded his head by way of consent, and then the subject was dropped, as the party had reached the canoe so often mentioned.

CHAPTER III

It is generally known that the waters which flow into the southern side of Ontario are, in general, narrow, sluggish, and deep. There are some exceptions to this rule, for many of the rivers have rapids, and some have falls. Among the latter was the Oswego, formed by the junction of the Oneida and the Onondaga, both of which flow from lakes. It pursues its way some eight or ten miles, until it reaches the margin of a sort of natural terrace, down which it tumbles some ten or fifteen feet to another level, across which it glides with the silent, stealthy progress of deep water, until it throws its tribute into the Ontario. The canoe in which Cap and his party had travelled from Fort Stanwix, the last military station on the Mohawk, lay by the side of this river, and into it the whole party now entered, with the exception of Pathfinder, who remained on the land in order to shove the light vessel off.

"Let her starn drift down stream, Jasper," said the man of the woods to the young mariner of the lake, who had dispossessed Arrowhead of his paddle and taken his own station as steersman. "Should any of these Mingos strike our trail, or follow it to this point, they will not fail to look for the signs in the mud; and if they discover that we have left the shore with the nose of the canoe up stream, it is a natural belief to think we went up stream."

This direction was followed; and, giving a vigorous shove, the Pathfinder, who was in the flower of his strength and activity, made a leap, landing lightly, and without disturbing its equilibrium, in the bow of the canoe. As soon as it had reached the centre of the river or the strength of the current, the boat was turned, and it began to glide noiselessly down stream.

Cap was seated on a low thwart, in the centre of the canoe; the Big Serpent knelt near him. Arrowhead and his wife occupied places forward of both, the former having relinquished his post aft. Mabel was half reclining behind her uncle, while Pathfinder and Eau-douce stood erect, the one in the bow and the other in the stern, each using a paddle, with a long, steady, noiseless sweep. The conversation was carried on in low tones, all the party beginning to feel the necessity of prudence, as they drew nearer to the outskirts of the fort, and had no longer the cover of the woods.

The Oswego, just at that place, was a deep, dark stream of no great width, its still, gloomy-looking current winding its way among overhanging trees, which, in particular spots, almost shut out the light of the heavens. Here and there some half-fallen giant of the forest lay nearly across its surface, rendering care necessary to avoid the limbs; and most of the distance the lower branches and leaves of the trees of smaller growth were laved by its waters. It will be remembered that this was in the year 175-, or long before even speculation had brought any portion of western New York within the bounds of civilization. At that distant day there were two great channels of military communication between the inhabited portion of the colony of New York and the frontiers which lay adjacent to the Canadas—that by Lakes Champlain and George, and that by means of the Mohawk, Wood Creek, the Oneida, and the rivers we have been describing. Along both these lines of communication military posts had been established, though there existed a blank space of a hundred miles between the last fort at the head of the Mohawk and the outlet of the Oswego, which embraced most of the distance that Cap and Mabel had journeyed under the protection of Arrowhead."

"I sometimes wish for peace again," said the Pathfinder, "when one can range the forest without searching for any other enemy than the beasts and fishes. I sometimes wish that them blessed days might come back, for it is not my real gift to slay my own kind. I'm sartin the Sergeant's daughter don't think me a wretch that takes pleasure in preying on human natur'?"

As this remark, a sort of half interrogatory, was made, Pathfinder looked behind him; and, though the most partial friend could scarcely term his sunburnt and hard features handsome, even Mabel thought his smile attractive, by its simple ingenuousness and the uprightness that beamed in every lineament of his honest countenance.

"I do not think my father would have sent one like those you mention to see his daughter through the wilderness," the young woman answered.

"That he wouldn't; the Sergeant is a man of feeling, and many is the march and the fight that we have had—stood shoulder to shoulder in, as *he* would call it."

"You are, then, the young friend of whom my father has spoken so often in his letters?"

"His *young* friend—the Sergeant has the advantage of me by thirty years; yes, he is thirty years my senior, and as many my better."

"Not in the eyes of the daughter, perhaps, friend Pathfinder," put in Cap, whose spirits began to revive when he found the water once more flowing around him. "The thirty years that you mention are not often thought to be an advantage in the eyes of girls of nineteen."

Mabel coloured; and, in turning aside her face to avoid the looks of those in the bow of the canoe, she encountered the admiring gaze of the young man in the stern. As a last resource, her spirited but soft blue eyes sought refuge in the water. Just at this moment a dull, heavy sound swept up the avenue formed by the trees, borne along by a light air that hardly produced a ripple on the water.

"That sounds pleasantly," said Cap, pricking up his ears like a dog that hears a distant baying; "it is the surf on the shores of your lake, I suppose?"

"Not so," answered the Pathfinder; "it is merely this river tumbling over some rocks half a mile below us."

"Is there a fall in the stream?" demanded Mabel, a still brighter flush glowing in her face.

"Master Pathfinder, or you, Mr. Eau-douce, had you not better give the canoe a sheer, and get nearer to the shore? These water-falls have generally rapids above them, and one might as well get into the Maelstrom at once as to run into their suction."

"Trust to us, friend Cap," answered Pathfinder; "we are but freshwater sailors, it is true, and I cannot boast of being much even of that; but we understand rifts and rapids and cataracts; and in going down these we shall do our endeavours not to disgrace our edication."

"In going down!" exclaimed Cap. "You do not dream of going down a waterfall in this eggshell of a bark!"

"Sartain; the path lies over the falls, and it is much easier to shoot them than to unload the canoe and to carry that and all it contains around a portage of a mile by hand."

Mabel turned her pallid countenance towards the young man in the stern of the canoe, for just at that moment a fresh roar of the fall was borne to her ears by a new current of the air.

"We thought that, by landing the females and the two Indians," Jasper quietly observed, "we three white men, all of whom are used to the water, might carry the canoe over in safety, for we often shoot these falls."

"And we counted on you, friend mariner, as a mainstay," said Pathfinder, winking to Jasper over his shoulder; "for you are accustomed to see waves tumbling about; and without someone to steady the cargo, all the finery of the Sergeant's daughter might be washed into the river and be lost."

Cap was puzzled. The idea of going over a waterfall was, perhaps, more serious in his eyes than it would have been in those of one totally ignorant of all that pertained to boats, for he understood the power of the element, and the total feebleness of man when exposed to its fury. Still his pride revolted at the thought of deserting the boat, while others not only steadily, but coolly, proposed to continue in it.

"What is to be done with Magnet?" he demanded, affection for his niece raising another qualm in his conscience. "We cannot allow Magnet to land if there are enemy's Indians near?"

"Nay, no Mingo will be near the portage; for that is a spot too public for their dark works," answered the Pathfinder. "Natur' is natur', and it is an Indian's natur' to be found where he is least expected. Sheer in, Eau-douce, and we will land the Sergeant's daughter on the end of that log, where she can reach the shore with a dry foot."

The injunction was obeyed, and in a few minutes the whole party had left the canoe, with the exception of Pathfinder and the two sailors. Notwithstanding his professional pride, Cap would have gladly followed; but he did not like to exhibit so unequivocal a weakness in the presence of a freshwater sailor.

"I call all hands to witness," said he, as those who had landed moved away, "that I do not look on this affair as anything more than canoeing in the woods. There is no seamanship in tumbling over a waterfall, which is a feat the greatest lubber can perform as well as the oldest mariner."

"Nay, you needn't despise the Oswego Falls, neither," put in Pathfinder; "for, though they may not be Niagara, they are narvous enough for a new beginner. Now, Eau-douce, a steady hand and a true eye, for all rests on you, seeing that we can count Master Cap for no more than a passenger."

The canoe was leaving the shore as he concluded, while Mabel went hurriedly to the rock that had been pointed out, while her eyes were riveted on the agile and vigorous form of Eau-douce, as he stood erect in the stern of the light boat, governing its movements. As soon, however, as she reached a point where she got a view of the fall, she gave an involuntary but suppressed scream, and covered her eyes. At the next instant, the latter were again free, and the entranced girl stood immovable as a statue, a scarcely breathing observer of all that passed, while the wife of Arrowhead came near Mabel, and appeared to watch the motions of the canoe with some such interest as a child regards the leaps of a tumbler.

As soon as the boat was in the stream, Pathfinder sank on his knees, continuing to use the paddle, though in a manner not to interfere with the efforts of his companion. The latter still stood erect; and, as he kept his eye on some object beyond the fall, it was evident that he was carefully looking for the spot proper for their passage.

"Farther west, boy," muttered Pathfinder; "where you see the water foam."

Eau-douce made no answer; for the canoe was in the centre of the stream, with its head pointed towards the fall, and it had already begun to quicken its motion by the increased force of the current. At that moment Cap would cheerfully have renounced every claim to glory that could possibly be acquired by the feat, to have been safe again on shore. He heard the roar of the water, thundering, as it might be, behind a screen, but becoming more and more distinct, louder and louder, and before him he saw its line cutting the forest below, along which the green and angry element seemed stretched and shining, as if the particles were about to lose their principle of cohesion.

"Down with your helm, man!" he exclaimed, unable any longer to suppress his anxiety, as the canoe glided towards the edge of the fall.

"Ay, down it is sure enough," answered Pathfinder, looking behind him for a single instant, with his silent laugh,—"down we go, of a sartainty! Heave her starn up, boy!"

The rest was like the passage of the viewless wind. Eau-douce gave the required sweep with his paddle, the canoe glanced into the channel, and for a few seconds it seemed to Cap that he was tossing in a caldron. He felt the bow of the canoe tip, saw the raging, foaming water careering madly by his side, was sensible that the light fabric in which he floated was tossed about like an eggshell, and then, not less to his great joy than to his surprise, he discovered that it was gliding across the basin of still water below the fall, under the steady impulse of Jasper's paddle.

The Pathfinder continued to laugh; but he arose from his knees, and, searching for a tin pot and a horn spoon, he began deliberately to measure the water that had been taken in the passage.

"Fourteen spoonfuls, Eau-douce; fourteen fairly measured spoonfuls. I have known you to go down with only ten."

"Master Cap leaned so hard up stream," returned Jasper, "that I had difficulty in trimming the canoe."

"It may be so; but I have known you go over with only ten."

Cap now gave a tremendous hem, felt for his queue as if to ascertain its safety, and then looked back in order to examine the danger he had gone through. His safety is easily explained. Most of the river fell perpendicularly ten or twelve feet; but near its centre the force of the current had so far worn away the rock as to permit the water to shoot through a narrow passage, at an angle of about forty or forty-five degrees. Down this ticklish descent the canoe had glanced, amid fragments of broken rock, whirlpools, foam, and furious tossings of the element, which an uninstructed eye would believe menaced inevitable destruction to an object so fragile.

To say that Cap was astonished would not be expressing half his feelings; he felt awed: for the profound dread of rocks which most seamen entertain came in aid of his admiration of the boldness of the exploit. Still he was indisposed to express all he felt, lest it might be conceding too much in favour of fresh water and inland navigation; and no sooner had he cleared his throat with the aforesaid hem, than he loosened his tongue in the usual strain of superiority.

"I do not gainsay your knowledge of the channel, Master Eau-douce, and, after all, to know the channel in such a place is the main point. I have had cockswains with me who could come down that shoot too, if they only knew the channel."

"It isn't enough to know the channel," said Pathfinder; "it needs narves and skill to keep the canoe straight, and to keep her clear of the rocks too. There isn't another boatman in all this region that can shoot the Oswego, but Eau-douce there, with any sar-tainty; though, now and then, one has blundered through. I can't do it myself unless by means of Providence, and it needs Jasper's hand and eye to make sure of a dry passage."

"I think little of this affair, sir; nothing at all, to speak my mind freely. It's a mere wash of spray to shooting London Bridge, which is done every day by hundreds of persons, and often by the most delicate ladies in the land. The king's majesty has shot the bridge in his royal person."

"Well, I want no delicate ladies or king's majesties (God bless em!) in the canoe, in going over these falls; for a boat's breadth, either way, may make a drowning matter of it."

By this time the party had reached the place where Jasper had left his own canoe, concealed in the bushes, and they all re-embarked; Cap, Jasper, and his niece in one boat, and Pathfinder, Arrowhead, and the wife of the latter in the other. The Mohican had already passed down the banks of the river by land, looking cautiously and with the skill of his people for the signs of an enemy.

The cheek of Mabel did not recover all its bloom until the canoe was again in the current, down which it floated swiftly, occasionally impelled by the paddle of Jasper. She witnessed the descent of the falls with a degree of terror which had rendered her mute; but her fright had not been so great as to prevent admiration of the steadiness of the youth who directed the movement from blending with the passing terror. In truth, one much less sensitive might have had her feelings awakened by the cool and gallant air with which Eau-douce had accomplished this clever exploit. He had stood firmly erect, notwithstanding the plunge; and to those on shore it was evident that, by a timely application of his skill and strength, the canoe had received a sheer which alone carried it clear of a rock over which the boiling water was leaping in *jets d'eau*,—now leaving the brown stone visible, and now covering it with a limpid sheet, as if machinery controlled the play of the element. The tongue cannot always express what the eyes view; but Mabel saw enough, even in that moment of fear, to blend for ever in her mind the picture presented by the plunging canoe and the unmoved steersman. She admitted that insidious feeling which binds woman so strongly to man, by feeling additional security in finding herself under his care; and, for the first time since leaving Fort Stanwix, she was entirely at her ease in the frail bark in which she travelled. As the other canoe kept quite near her own, however, and the Pathfinder, by floating at her side, was most in view, the conversation was principally maintained with that person; Jasper seldom speaking unless addressed, and constantly exhibiting a wariness in the management of his own boat, which might have been remarked by one accustomed to his ordinarily confident, careless manner.

"We know too well a woman's gifts to think of carrying the Sergeant's daughter over the falls," said Pathfinder, looking at Mabel, while he addressed her uncle; "though I've been acquainted with some of her sex that would think but little of doing the thing."

"Mabel is faint-hearted, like her mother," returned Cap; "and you did well, friend, to humour her weakness. You will remember the child has never been at sea."

"No, no, it was easy to discover that; by your own fearlessness, anyone might have seen how little you cared about the matter. I went over once with a raw hand, and he jumped out of the canoe just as it tipped, and you may judge what a time he had of it."

"What became of the poor fellow?" asked Cap. "One who has passed the place knows how to feel for him."

"He was a *poor* fellow, as you say; and a poor frontier man too, though he came out to show his skill among us ignoranters. What became of him? Why, he went down the falls, topsy-turvy like, as would have happened to a courthouse or a fort."

"If it should jump out of a canoe," interrupted Jasper, smiling.

"The boy is right," rejoined Pathfinder, laughing in Mabel's face, "he is sartainly right. But you have not told us what you think of the leap we took?"

"It was perilous and bold," said Mabel; "while looking at it, I could have wished that it had not been attempted, though, now it is over, I can admire its boldness and the steadiness with which it was made."

"We did it for the best," Pathfinder continued; "'twas all for the best. Had we waited to carry the canoe across the portage, time would have been lost, and nothing is so precious as time when you are mistrustful of Mingos."

"But we can have little to fear now. The canoes move swiftly, and two hours, you have said, will carry us down to the fort."

"It shall be a cunning Iroquois who hurts a hair of your head, pretty one; for all here are bound to the Sergeant, and most, I think, to yourself, to see you safe from harm. Ha, Eau-douce! what is that in the river, in the lower turn, yonder, beneath the bushes,—I mean standing on the rock?"

" 'Tis the Big Sarpent, Pathfinder; he is making signs to us in a way I don't understand."

" 'Tis the Sarpent, as sure as I'm a white man, and he wishes us to drop in nearer to his shore. Mischief is brewing, or one of his deliberation and steadiness would never take this trouble. Courage, all! we are men, and must meet danger as becomes our colour and our callings."

CHAPTER IV

THE Pathfinder had no sooner recognized the form of his red friend, than, with a strong sweep of his paddles, he threw the head of his own canoe towards the shore, motioning for Jasper to follow. In a minute both boats were silently drifting down the stream, within reach of the bushes that overhung the water, all observing a profound silence; some from alarm, and others from habitual caution. As the travellers drew nearer the Indian, he made a sign for them to stop; and then he and Pathfinder had a short but earnest conference.

"The chief is not apt to see enemies in a dead log," observed the white man to his red associate; "why does he tell us to stop?"

"Mingos are in the woods."

"That we have believed these two days; does the chief know it?"

The Mohican held up the head of a pipe formed of stone.

"It lay on a fresh trail that led towards the garrison."

"That may be the bowl of a pipe belonging to a soldier. Many use the redskin pipes."

"See," said the Big Serpent, again holding the thing he had found up to the view of his friend.

The bowl of the pipe was of soapstone, and was carved with great care and with a very respectable degree of skill; in its centre was a small Latin cross, made with an accuracy which permitted no doubt of its meaning.

"That does foretell wickedness," said the Pathfinder, who had all the provincial horror of the holy symbol in question which then pervaded the country, and which became so incorporated with its prejudices, by confounding men with things, as to have left its traces strong enough on the moral feeling of the community to be discovered even at the present hour. "No Indian who had not been parvarted by the cunning priests of the Canadas would dream of carving a thing like that on his pipe. I'll warrant ye, the knave prays to the image every time he wishes to sarcumvent the innocent, and work his fearful wickedness. It looks fresh too, Chingachgook?"

"The tobacco was burning when I found it."

"That is close work, chief. Where was the trail?"

The Mohican pointed to a spot not a hundred yards from that where they stood.

The matter now began to look very serious, and the two principal guides conferred apart for several minutes, when both ascended the bank, approached the indicated spot, and examined the trail with the utmost care. After this investigation had lasted a quarter of an hour, the white man returned alone, his red friend having disappeared in the forest.

The ordinary expression of the countenance of the Pathfinder was that of simplicity, integrity, and sincerity, blended in an air of self-reliance which usually gave great confidence to those who found themselves under his care; but now a look of concern cast a shade over his honest face that struck the whole party.

"What cheer, Master Pathfinder?" demanded Cap. "Has the enemy got between us and our port?"

"I know nothing of ports; but there is a direful Mingo trail within a hundred yards of this very spot, and as fresh as venison without salt. If one of the wretches has passed, so have a dozen; and, what is worse, they have gone down towards the garrison, and not a soul crosses the clearing around it that some of their piercing eyes will not discover, when sartain bullets will follow."

"Cannot this said fort deliver a broadside, and clear everything within the sweep of its hawse?"

"Nay, the forts this-a-way are not like forts in the settlements, and two or three light cannon are all they have down at the mouth of the river; and then, broadsides fired at a dozen outlying Mingos, lying behind logs and in a forest, would be powder spent in vain. We have but one course, and that is a very nice one. We are judgmatically placed here, both canoes being hid by the high bank and the bushes, from all eyes, except those of any lurker directly opposite. Here, then, we may stay without much present fear; but how to get the bloodthirsty thieves up the stream again? Ha! I have it? if it does no good, it can do no harm. Do you see the wide-topped chestnut here, Jasper, at the last turn in the river—on our own side of the stream, I mean?"

"That near the fallen pine?"

"The very same. Take the flint and tinder-box, creep along the bank, and light a fire at that spot; maybe the smoke will draw them above us. In the meanwhile, we will drop the canoes carefully down beyond the point below, and find another shelter. Bushes are plenty, and covers are easily to be had in this region."

"I will do it, Pathfinder," said Jasper, springing to the shore.

"And, Eau-douce, use plenty of damp wood this time," half whispered the other. "When smoke is wanted, water helps to thicken it."

The young man was soon off, making his way rapidly towards the desired point. A slight attempt of Mabel to object to the risk was disregarded, and the party immediately prepared to change its position, as it could be seen from the place where Jasper intended to light his fire. The canoes were got clear of the bushes, then suffered to drop down with the stream until they reached the spot where the chestnut, at the foot of which Jasper was to light the fire, was almost shut out from view, when they stopped, and every eye was turned in the direction of the adventurer.

"There goes the smoke!" exclaimed the Pathfinder, as a current of air whirled a little column of the vapour from the land, allowing it to rise spirally above the bed of the river. "I hope Eau-douce will have the wit to bethink him of the damp wood now when it may serve us all a good turn."

"Too much smoke—too much cunning," said Arrowhead.

"That is gospel truth, Tuscarora, if the Mingos didn't know that they are near soldiers; but soldiers commonly think more of their dinner at a halt than of their danger. No, let the boy pile on his logs, and smoke them well, too; it will all be laid to the stupidity of some Scotch or Irish blunderer, who is thinking more of his oatmeal or his potatoes than of Indian sarcumventions."

"And yet I should think, from all we have heard in the towns, that the soldiers on this frontier are used to the artifices of their enemies," said Mabel, "and become almost as wily as the red men themselves."

"Not they. Experience makes them but little wiser; and they wheel, and platoon, and battalion it about, here in the forest, just as they did in their parks at home, of which they are all so fond of talking. But there is smoke enough, of all conscience, and we had better drop into another cover. The lad has thrown the river on his fire, and there is danger that the Mingos will believe a whole regiment is out."

While speaking, the Pathfinder permitted his canoe to drift away from the bush by which it had been retained, and in a couple of minutes the bend in the river concealed the smoke and the tree. Fortunately a small indentation in the shore presented itself, within a few yards of the point they had just passed; and the two canoes glided into it, under the impulsion of the paddles.

A better spot could not have been found for the purpose. The bushes were thick, and overhung the water, forming a complete canopy of leaves. There was a small gravelly strand at the bottom of the little bay, where most of the party landed to be more at their ease, and the only position from which they could possibly be seen was a point on the river directly opposite. There was little danger, however, of discovery from that quarter, as the thicket there was even denser than common, and the land beyond it was so wet and marshy as to render it difficult to be trodden.

"This is a safe cover," said the Pathfinder, after he had surveyed his position; "but it may be necessary to make it safer. Master Cap, I ask nothing of you but silence, and a quieting of such gifts as you may have got at sea, while the Tuscarora and I make provision for the evil hour."

The guide then went a short distance into the bushes, accompanied by the Indian, where the two cut off the larger stems of several alders and other bushes, using the utmost care not to make a noise. The ends of these little trees were forced into the mud, outside of the canoes, the depth of the water being very trifling; and in the course of ten minutes a very effectual screen was interposed between them and the principal point of danger.

"This is the best cover I ever yet got into," said the Pathfinder, with his quiet laugh, after having been on the outside to reconnoitre. "The leaves of our new trees fairly touch those of the bushes over our heads. Hist!—yonder comes Eau-douce, wading, like a sensible boy, as he is, to leave his trail in the water; and we shall soon see whether our covering is good for anything or not."

Jasper had indeed returned from his duty above; and missing the canoes, he at once inferred that they had dropped round the next bend in the river, in order to get out of sight of the fire. His habits of caution immediately suggested the expediency of stepping into the water, in order that there might exist no visible communication between the marks left on the shore by the party and the place where he believed them to have taken refuge below. Should the Canadian Indians return on their own trail, and discover that made by the Pathfinder and the Serpent in their ascent from and descent to the river, the clue to their movements would cease at the shore, water leaving no prints of footsteps. The young man had therefore waded, knee-deep, as far as the point, and was now seen making his way slowly down the margin of the stream, searching curiously for the spot in which the canoes were hid.

To those who watched his motions from behind their cover, and they were all in the canoes, it was evident that Jasper was totally at a loss to imagine where the Pathfinder had secreted himself. When fairly round the curvature in the shore, and out of sight of the fire he had lighted above, the young man stopped and began examining the bank deliberately and with great care. Occasionally he advanced eight or ten paces, and then halted again, to renew the search. The water being much shallower than common, he stepped aside, in order to walk with greater ease to himself, and came so near the artificial plantation that he might have touched it with his hand. Still he detected nothing, and was actually passing the spot when Pathfinder made an opening beneath the branches, and called to him in a low voice to enter.

"This is pretty well," said the Pathfinder, laughing; "though paleface eyes and redskin eyes are as different as human spy-glasses."

"Don't you think, Master Pathfinder, that it would be wisest, after all," said Cap, "to get under way at once, and carry sail hard down stream, as soon as we are satisfied that these rascals are fairly astern of us? We seamen call a stern chase a long chase."

"I wouldn't move from this spot until we hear from the Sarpent, with the Sergeant's pretty daughter here in our company, for all the powder in the magazine of the fort below. Sartain captivity or sartain death would follow. If a tender fa'n, such as the maiden we have in charge, could thread the forest like old deer, it might, indeed, do to quit the canoes; for by making a circuit we could reach the garrison before morning."

"Then let it be done," said Mabel, springing to her feet under the sudden impulse of awakened energy. "I am young, active, used to exercise, and could easily outwalk my dear uncle. Let no one think me a hindrance. I cannot bear that all your lives should be exposed on my account."

"No, no, pretty one; we think you anything but a hindrance

or anything that is unbecoming, and would willingly run twice this risk to do you and the honest Sergeant a service. Do I not speak your mind, Eau-douce?"

"To do *her* a service?" said Jasper with emphasis. "Nothing shall tempt me to desert Mabel Dunham until she is safe in her father's arms."

"Well said, lad; bravely and honestly said, too; and I join in it, heart and hand. No, no! you are not the first of your sex I have led through the wilderness, and never but once did any harm befall any of them."

Mabel looked from one of her protectors to the other, and her fine eyes swam in tears. Frankly placing a hand in that of each, she answered them, though at first her voice was choked: "I have no right to expose you on my account. My dear father will thank you, God will reward you; but let there be no unnecessary risk. I can walk far, and have often gone miles on some girlish fancy; why not now exert myself for my life?—nay, for your precious lives?"

"She is a true dove, Jasper," said the Pathfinder, neither relinquishing the hand he held until the girl herself, in native modesty, saw fit to withdraw it, "and wonderfully winning! We get to be rough, and sometimes even hard-hearted, in the woods, Mabel; but the sight of one like you brings us back again to our young feelings, and does us good for the remainder of our days. I dare say Jasper here will tell you the same. Speak out now, Jasper, and say if it is not so?"

"I question if many like Mabel Dunham are to be found anywhere," returned the young man gallantly, an honest sincerity glowing in his face, that spoke more eloquently than his tongue.

"We had better leave the canoes," Mabel hurriedly rejoined; "for I feel it is no longer safe to be here."

"You can never do it. It would be a march of more than twenty miles, and that, too, of tramping over brush and roots, and through swamps, in the dark; the trail of such a party would be wide, and we might have to fight our way into the garrison after all. We will wait for the Mohican."

Such appearing to be the decision of him to whom all, in their present strait, looked up for counsel, no more was said on the subject. Pathfinder and Cap occupied one canoe, chatting of their different adventures by sea and land; while Jasper and Mabel sat in the other, making greater progress in intimacy in a single hour than might have been effected under other circumstances in a twelvemonth. Notwithstanding their situation as regards the enemy, the time flew by swiftly, and the young people, in particular, were astonished when Cap informed them how long they had been thus occupied.

"If one could smoke, Master Pathfinder," observed the old sailor, "this berth would be snug enough. The only hardship is the denial of the pipe."

"The scent of the tobacco would betray us; and where is the use of taking all these precautions against the Mingo's eyes, if we are to tell him where the cover is to be found through the nose? Did you hear nothing, Jasper?"

"The Serpent is coming."

"Then let us see if Mohican eyes are better than them of a lad who follows the water."

The Mohican had indeed made his appearance in the same direction as that by which Jasper had rejoined his friends. Instead of coming directly on, however, no sooner did he pass the bend, where he was concealed from any who might be higher up stream, than he moved close under the bank; and, using the utmost caution, got a position where he could look back, with his person sufficiently concealed by the bushes to prevent its being seen by any in that quarter.

"The Sarpent sees the knaves!" whispered Pathfinder. "As I'm a Christian white man, they have bit at the bait, and have ambushed the smoke!"

Here a hearty but silent laugh interrupted his words, and nudging Cap with his elbow, they all continued to watch the movements of Chingachgook in profound stillness. The Mohican remained stationary as the rock on which he stood full ten minutes; and then it was apparent that something of interest had occurred within his view, for he drew back with a hurried manner, looked anxiously and keenly along the margin of the stream, and moved quickly down it, taking care to lose his trail in the shallow water. He was evidently in a hurry and concerned, now looking behind him, and then casting eager glances towards every spot on the shore where he thought a canoe might be concealed.

"Call him in," whispered Jasper, scarcely able to restrain his impatience,—"call him in, or it will be too late? See! he is actually passing us."

"Not so, not so, lad; nothing presses, depend on it," returned his companion, "or the Sarpent would begin to creep. The Lord help us and teach us wisdom! I *do* believe even Chingachgook, whose sight is as faithful as the hound's scent, overlooks us, and will not find out the ambushment we have made."

This exultation was untimely; for the words were no sooner spoken than the Indian, who had actually got several feet lower down the stream than the artificial cover, suddenly stopped; fastened a keen-riveted glance among the transplanted bushes; made a few hasty steps backward; and, bending his body and carefully separating the branches, he appeared among them.

"The accursed Mingos!" said Pathfinder.

"Iroquois," returned the Indian.

"No matter; Iroquois, Mingo, Mengwes, or furies—all are pretty much the same. Come hither, chief, and let us converse rationally."

When their private communication was over, Pathfinder rejoined the rest, and made them acquainted with all he had learned.

The Mohican had followed the trail of their enemies some distance towards the fort, until the latter caught sight of the smoke of Jasper's fire, when they instantly retraced their steps. It now became necessary for Chingachgook, who ran the greatest risk of detection, to find a cover where he could secrete himself until the party might pass. It was perhaps fortunate for him that the savages were so intent on this recent discovery, that they did not bestow the ordinary attention on the signs of the forest. At all events, they passed him swiftly, fifteen in number, treading lightly in each other's footsteps; and he was enabled again to get into their rear. After proceeding to the place where the footsteps of Pathfinder and the Mohican had joined the principal trail, the Iroquois had struck off to the river, which they reached just as Jasper had disappeared behind the bend below. The smoke being now in plain view, the savages plunged into the woods and endeavoured to approach the fire unseen. Chingachgook profited by this occasion to descend to the water, and to gain the bend in the river also, which he thought had been effected undiscovered. Here he paused, as has been stated, until he saw his enemies at the fire, where their stay, however, was very short.

Of the motives of the Iroquois the Mohican could judge only by their acts. He thought they had detected the artifice of the fire, and were aware that it had been kindled with a view to mislead them; for, after a hasty examination of the spot, they had separated, some plunging again into the woods, while six or eight had followed the footsteps of Jasper along the shore, and come down the stream towards the place where the canoes had landed. What course they might take on reaching that spot was only to be conjectured; for the Serpent had felt the emergency to be too pressing to delay looking for his friends any longer. From some indications that were to be gathered from their gestures, however, he thought it probable that their enemies might follow down in the margin of the stream, but could not be certain.

As the Pathfinder related these facts to his companions, the professional feelings of the two other white men came uppermost and both naturally reverted to their habits, in quest of the means of escape.

"Let us run out the canoes at once," said Jasper eagerly; "the current is strong, and by using the paddles vigorously we shall soon be beyond the reach of these scoundrels!"

"And this poor flower, shall it wither in the forest?" objected his friend.

"We must all die first," answered the youth, a generous colour mounting to his temples; "Mabel and Arrowhead's wife may lie down in the canoes, while we do our duty, like men, on our feet."

"Ay, you are active at the paddle and the oar, Eau-douce, I will allow, but an accursed Mingo is more active at his mischief; the canoes are swift, but a rifle bullet is swifter."

"It is the business of men, engaged as we have been by a confiding father, to run this risk——"

"But it is not their business to overlook prudence."

"Prudence! A man may carry his prudence so far as to forget his courage."

The group was standing on the narrow strand, the Pathfinder leaning on his rifle, the butt of which rested on the gravelly beach, while both his hands clasped the barrel, at the height of his own shoulders. As Jasper threw out this severe and unmerited imputation, the deep red of his comrade's face maintained its hue unchanged, though the young man perceived that the fingers grasped the iron of the gun with the tenacity of a vice. Here all betrayal of emotion ceased.

"You are young and hot-headed," returned Pathfinder, with a dignity that impressed his listeners with a keen sense of his moral superiority; "but my life has been passed among dangers of this sort, and my experience and gifts are not to be mastered by the impatience of a boy. As for courage, Jasper, I will not send back an angry and unmeaning word to meet an angry and an unmean-

ing word; for I know that you are true in your station and
according to your knowledge; but take the advice of one who
has faced the Mingos when you were a child, and know that
their cunning is easier sarcumvented by prudence than outwitted
by foolishness."

"I ask your pardon, Pathfinder," said the repentant Jasper.
"'Twas a foolish as well as wicked thing to hint of a man whose
heart, in a good cause, is known to be as firm as the rocks on the
lake shore."

For the first time the colour deepened on the cheek of the
Pathfinder, and the solemn dignity which he had assumed, under
a purely natural impulse, disappeared in the expression of the
earnest simplicity inherent in all his feelings.

"'Tis well, Jasper," he answered, laughing; "I bear no ill will,
nor shall anyone on my behalf. My natur' is that of a white
man, and that is to bear no malice. It might have been ticklish
work to have said half as much to the Sarpent here, though he is
a Delaware, for colour will have its way——"

A touch on his shoulder caused the speaker to cease. Mabel
was standing erect in the canoe, her light but swelling form bent
forward in an attitude of graceful earnestness, her finger on her
lips, her head averted, her spirited eyes riveted on an opening in
the bushes, and one arm extended with a fishing-rod, the end of
which had touched the Pathfinder. The latter bowed his head to
a level with a lookout near which he had intentionally kept himself, and then whispered to Jasper:

"The Mingos! Stand to your arms, my men, but lay quiet as
the corpses of dead trees!"

Jasper advanced rapidly, but noiselessly, to the canoe, and with
a gentle violence induced Mabel to place herself in such an attitude as concealed her entire body, though it would have probably
exceeded his means to induce the girl so far to lower her head
that she could not keep her gaze fastened on their enemies. He
then took his own post near her, with his rifle cocked and poised,
in readiness to fire. Arrowhead and Chingachgook crawled to the
cover, and lay in wait like snakes, with their arms prepared for
service, while the wife of the former bowed her head between her
knees, covered it with her calico robe, and remained passive and
immovable. Cap loosened both his pistols in their belt, but seemed
quite at a loss what course to pursue. The Pathfinder did not
stir. He had originally got a position where he might aim with
deadly effect through the leaves, and where he could watch the

movements of his enemies; and he was far too steady to be disconcerted at a moment so critical.

Just as Mabel touched the shoulder of her guide, three of the Iroquois had appeared in the water, at the bend of the river, within a hundred yards of the cover, and halted to examine the stream below. They were all naked to the waist, armed, and in their warpaint.

CHAPTER V

IT was a breathless moment. The only clue the fugitives possessed to the intentions of their pursuers was in their gestures and the indications which escaped them in the fury of disappointment. That a party had returned already, on their own footsteps, by land, was pretty certain; and all the benefit expected from the artifice of the fire was necessarily lost. But that consideration became of little moment just then; for the party was menaced with an immediate discovery by those who had kept on a level with the river. All the facts presented themselves clearly, and as it might be by intuition, to the mind of Pathfinder, who perceived the necessity of immediate decision and of being in readiness to act in concert. Without making any noise, therefore, he managed to get the two Indians and Jasper near him, when he opened his communications in a whisper.

"We must be ready," he said. "There are but three of the scalping fiends, and we are five, four of whom may be set down as manful warriors for such a skrimmage. Eau-douce, do you take the fellow that is painted like death; Chingachgook, I give you the chief; and Arrowhead must keep his eye on the young one. There must be no mistake, for two bullets in the same body would be sinful waste, with one like the Sergeant's daughter in danger. I shall hold myself in resarve against accident, lest a fourth reptile appear, for one of your hands may prove unsteady. By no means fire until I give the word; we must not let the crack of the rifle be heard except in the last resort, since all the rest of the miscreants are still within hearing. Jasper, boy, in case of any movement behind us on the bank, I trust to you to run out the canoe with the Sergeant's daughter, and to pull for the garrison, by God's leave."

The Pathfinder had no sooner given these directions than the near approach of their enemies rendered profound silence necessary. The Iroquois in the river were slowly descending the stream, keeping of necessity near the bushes which overhung the water, while the rustling of leaves and the snapping of twigs soon gave fearful evidence that another party was moving along the bank, at an equally graduated pace, and directly abreast of them. In consequence of the distance between the bushes planted by the fugitives and the true shore, the two parties became visible to each other when opposite that precise point. Both stopped, and a conversation ensued, that may be said to have passed directly over the heads of those who were concealed. Indeed, nothing sheltered the travellers but the branches and leaves of plants, so pliant that they yielded to every current of air, and which a puff of wind a little stronger than common would have blown away. Fortunately the line of sight carried the eyes of the two parties of savages, whether they stood in the water or on the land, above the bushes, and the leaves appeared blended in a way to excite no suspicion. Perhaps the very boldness of the expedient alone prevented an immediate exposure. The conversation which took place was conducted earnestly, but in guarded tones, as if those who spoke wished to defeat the intentions of any listeners. It was in a dialect that both the Indian warriors beneath, as well as the Pathfinder, understood. Even Jasper comprehended a portion of what was said.

"The trail is washed away by the water!" said one from below, who stood so near the artificial cover of the fugitives, that he might have been struck by the salmon-spear that lay in the bottom of Jasper's canoe. "Water has washed it so clear that a Yengeese hound could not follow."

"The palefaces have left the shore in their canoes," answered the speaker on the bank.

"It cannot be. The rifles of our warriors below are certain."

The Pathfinder gave a significant glance at Jasper, and he clenched his teeth in order to suppress the sound of his own breathing.

"Let my young men look as if their eyes were eagles'," said the eldest warrior among those who were wading in the river. "We have been a whole moon on the warpath, and have found but one scalp. There is a maiden among them, and some of our braves want wives."

Happily these words were lost on Mabel; but Jasper's frown became deeper, and his face fiercely flushed.

The savages now ceased speaking, and the party which was concealed heard the slow and guarded movements of those who were on the bank, as they pushed the bushes aside in their wary progress. It was soon evident that the latter had passed the cover; but the group in the water still remained, scanning the shore with eyes that glared through their warpaint like coals of living fire. After a pause of two or three minutes, these three began also to descend the stream, though it was step by step, as men move who look for an object that has been lost. In this manner they passed the artificial screen, and Pathfinder opened his mouth in that hearty but noiseless laugh that nature and habit had contributed to render a peculiarity of the man. His triumph, however, was premature; for the last of the retiring party, just at this moment casting a look behind him, suddenly stopped; and his fixed attitude and steady gaze at once betrayed the appalling fact that some neglected bush had awakened his suspicions.

It was perhaps fortunate for the concealed that the warrior who manifested these fearful signs of distrust was young, and had still a reputation to acquire. He knew the importance of discretion and modesty in one of his years, and most of all did he dread the ridicule and contempt that would certainly follow a false alarm. Without recalling any of his companions, therefore, he turned on his own footsteps; and, while the others continued to descend the river, he cautiously approached the bushes, on which his looks were still fastened, as by a charm. Some of the leaves which were exposed to the sun had drooped a little, and this slight departure from the usual natural laws had caught the quick eyes of the Indian; for so practised and acute do the senses of the savage become, more especially when he is on the warpath, that trifles apparently of the most insignificant sort often prove to be clues to lead him to his object.

The trifling nature of the change which had aroused the suspicion of this youth was an additional motive for not acquainting his companions with his discovery. Should he really detect anything, his glory would be the greater for being unshared; and should he not, he might hope to escape that derision which the young Indian so much dreads. Then there were the dangers of an ambush and a surprise, to which every warrior of the woods is keenly alive, to render his approach slow and cautious. In consequence of the delay that proceed from these combined causes, the two parties had descended some fifty or sixty yards before the

young savage was again near enough to the bushes of the Pathfinder to touch them with his hand.

Nothwithstanding their critical situation, the whole party behind the cover had their eyes fastened on the working countenance
of the young Iroquois, who was agitated by conflicting feelings.
First came the eager hope of obtaining success where some of the
most experienced of his tribe had failed, and with it a degree of
glory that had seldom fallen to the share of one of his years or a
brave on his first warpath; then followed doubts, as the drooping
leaves seemed to rise again and to revive in the currents of air;
and distrust of hidden danger lent its exciting feeling to keep the
eloquent features in play. So very slight, however, had been the
alteration produced by the heat on the bushes of which the stems
were in the water, that when the Iroquois actually laid his hand
on the leaves, he fancied that he had been deceived. As no man
ever distrusts strongly without using all convenient means of satis-
fying his doubts, however, the young warrior cautiously pushed
aside the branches and advanced a step within the hiding-place,
when the forms of the concealed party met his gaze, resembling so
many breathless statues. The low exclamation, the slight start,
and the glaring eye, were hardly seen and heard before the arm
of Chingachgook was raised, and the tomahawk of the Delaware
descended on the shaven head of his foe. The Iroquois raised his
hands frantically, bounded backward, and fell into the water, at a
spot where the current swept the body, the struggling limbs still
tossing and writhing in the agony of death. The Delaware made
a vigorous but unsuccessful attempt to seize an arm, with the hope
of securing the scalp, but the blood-stained waters whirled down
the current, carrying with them their quivering burthen.

All this passed in less than a minute, and the events were so
sudden and unexpected, that men less accustomed than the Pathfinder and his associates to forest warfare, would have been at a
loss how to act.

"There is not a moment to lose," said Jasper, tearing aside the
bushes as he spoke earnestly, but in a suppressed voice. "Do as
I do, Master Cap, if you would save your niece; and you, Mabel,
lie at your length in the canoe."

The words were scarcely uttered when, seizing the bow of the
light boat, he dragged it along the shore, wading himself, while
Cap aided behind, keeping so near the bank as to avoid being
seen by the savages below, and striving to gain the turn in the
river above him, which would effectually conceal the party from

the enemy. The Pathfinder's canoe lay nearest to the bank, and was necessarily the last to quit the shore. The Delaware leaped on the narrow strand and plunged into the forest, it being his assigned duty to watch the foe in that quarter, while Arrowhead motioned to his white companion to seize the bow of the boat and to follow Jasper. All this was the work of an instant; but when the Pathfinder reached the current that was sweeping round the turn, he felt a sudden change in the weight he was dragging, and, looking back, he found that both the Tuscarora and his wife had deserted him. The thought of treachery flashed upon his mind, but there was no time to pause, for the wailing shout that arose from the party below proclaimed that the body of the young Iroquois had floated as low as the spot reached by his friends. The report of a rifle followed; and then the guide saw that Jasper, having doubled the bend in the river, was crossing the stream, standing erect in the stern of the canoe, while Cap was seated forward, both propelling the light boat with vigorous strokes of the paddles. A glance, a thought, and an expedient followed each other quickly in one so trained in the vicissitudes of the frontier warfare. Springing into the stern of his own canoe, he urged it by a vigorous shove into the current, and commenced crossing the stream himself, at a point so much lower than that of his companions as to offer his own person for a target to the enemy, well knowing that their keen desire to secure a scalp would control all other feelings.

"Keep well up the current, Jasper," shouted the gallant guide, as he swept the water with long, steady, vigorous strokes of the paddle; "keep well up the current, and pull for the alder bushes opposite. Presarve the Sergeant's daughter before all things, and leave these Mingo knaves to the Sarpent and me."

Jasper flourished his paddle as a signal of understanding, while shot succeeded shot in quick succession, all now being aimed at the solitary man in the nearest canoe.

"Ay, empty your rifles like simpletons as you are," said the Pathfinder; "empty your rifles with an unsteady aim, and give me time to put yard upon yard of river between us. That was well meant," throwing back his head, as a rifle bullet cut a lock of hair from his temple; "but the lead that misses by an inch is as useless as the lead that never quits the barrel. Bravely done, Jasper! the Sergeant's sweet child must be saved, even if we go in without our own scalps."

By this time the Pathfinder was in the centre of the river, and almost abreast of his enemies, while the other canoe, impelled by the vigorous arms of Cap and Jasper, had nearly gained the opposite shore at the precise spot that had been pointed out to them. The old mariner now played his part manfully, for he was on his proper element, loved his niece sincerely, had a proper regard for his own person, and was not unused to fire, though his experience certainly lay in a very different species of warfare. A few strokes of the paddles were given, and the canoe shot into the bushes, Mabel was hurried to land by Jasper, and for the present all three of the fugitives were safe.

Not so with the Pathfinder; his hardy self-devotion had brought him into a situation of unusual exposure, the hazards of which were much increased by the fact that, just as he drifted nearest to the enemy, the party on the shore rushed down the bank and joined their friends who still stood in the water. The Oswego was about a cable's length in width at this point, and, the canoe being in the centre, the object was only a hundred yards from the rifles that were constantly discharged at it; or, at the usual target distance for that weapon.

In this extremity the steadiness and skill of the Pathfinder did him good service. He knew that his safety depended altogether on keeping in motion, for a stationary object, at that distance, would have been hit nearly every shot. Nor was motion of itself sufficient; for, accustomed to kill the bounding deer, his enemies probably knew how to vary the line of aim so as to strike him, should he continue to move in any one direction. He was consequently compelled to change the course of the canoe—at one moment shooting down with the current, with the swiftness of an arrow, and at the next checking its progress in that direction, to glance athwart the stream. Luckily the Iroquois could not reload their pieces in the water, and the bushes that everywhere fringed the shore rendered it difficult to keep the fugitive in view when on the land. Aided by these circumstances, and having received the fire of all his foes, the Pathfinder was gaining fast in distance, both downwards and across the current, when a new danger suddenly, if not unexpectedly, presented itself, by the appearance of the party that had been left in ambush below with a view to watch the river.

They were no less than ten in number; and, understanding all the advantages of their bloody occupation, they had posted themselves at a spot where the water dashed among rocks and over shallows, in a way to form a rapid which, in the language of the country, is called a rift. The Pathfinder saw that, if he entered this rift, he should be compelled to approach a point where the Iroquois had posted themselves, for the current was irresistible, and the rocks allowed no other safe passage, while death or captivity would be the probable result of the attempt. All his efforts, therefore, were turned towards reaching the western shore, the foe being all on the eastern side of the river; but the exploit surpassed human power, and to attempt to stem the stream would at once have so far diminished the motion of the canoe as to render aim certain. In this exigency the guide came to a decision with his usual cool promptitude, making his preparations accordingly. Instead of endeavouring to gain the channel, he steered towards the shallowest part of the stream, on reaching which he seized his rifle and pack, leaped into the water, and began to wade from rock to rock, taking the direction of the western shore. The canoe whirled about in the furious current, now rolling over some slippery stone, now filling, and then emptying itself, until it lodged on the shore, within a few yards of the spot where the Iroquois had posted themselves.

In the meantime the Pathfinder was far from being out of danger. For the first minute, admiration of his promptitude and daring, which are so high virtues in the mind of an Indian, kept his enemies motionless; but the desire of revenge, and the cravings for the much-prized trophy, soon overcame this transient feeling, and aroused them from their stupor. Rifle flashed after rifle, and the bullets whistled around the head of the fugitive, amid the roar of the waters. Still he proceeded like one who bore a charmed life; for, while his rude frontier garments were more than once cut, his skin was not razed.

As the Pathfinder, in several instances, was compelled to wade in water which rose nearly to his arms, while he kept his rifle and ammunition elevated above the raging current, the toil soon fatigued him, and he was glad to stop at a large stone, or a small rock, which rose so high above the river that its upper surface was dry. On this stone he placed his powder-horn, getting behind it himself, so as to have the advantage of a partial cover for his body. The western shore was only fifty feet distant, but the quiet, swift, dark current that glanced through the interval sufficiently showed that here he would be compelled to swim.

A short cessation in the firing now took place on the part of the Indians, who gathered about the canoe, and, having found the paddles, were preparing to cross the river.

"Pathfinder," called a voice from among the bushes, at the point nearest to the person addressed, on the western shore.

"What would you have, Jasper?"

"Be of good heart—friends are at hand, and not a single Mingo shall cross without suffering for his boldness. Had you not better leave the rifle on the rock, and swim to us before the rascals can get afloat!"

"A true woodsman never quits his piece while he has any powder in his horn or a bullet in his pouch. I have not drawn a trigger this day, Eau-douce, and shouldn't relish the idea of parting with those reptiles without causing them to remember my name. A little water will not harm my legs; and I see that blackguard, Arrowhead, among the scamps, and wish to send him the wages he has so faithfully earned. You have not brought the Sergeant's daughter down here in a range with their bullets, I hope, Jasper?"

"She is safe for the present at least; though all depends on our keeping the river between us and the enemy. They must know our weakness now; and should they cross, no doubt some of their party will be left on the other side."

"This canoeing touches your gifts rather than mine, boy, though I will handle a paddle with the best Mingo that ever struck a salmon. If they cross below the rift, why can't we cross in the still water above, and keep playing at dodge and turn with the wolves?"

"Because, as I have said, they will leave a party on the other shore ; and then, Pathfinder, would you expose Mabel to the rifles of the Iroquois?"

"The Sergeant's daughter must be saved," returned the guide, with calm energy. "You are right, Jasper. What can be done, then? They must be kept from crossing for an hour or two, if possible, when we must do our best in the darkness."

"I agree with you, Pathfinder, if it can be effected; but are we strong enough for such a purpose?"

"The Lord is with us, boy. There is not a boat between the falls and the garrison, except these two canoes, to my sartain knowledge; and I think it will go beyond redskin gifts to cross in the face of two rifles like these of yourn and mine. I will not vaunt, Jasper, but it is well known on all this frontier that Killdeer seldom fails."

"Your skill is admitted by all, far and near, Pathfinder; but a rifle takes time to be loaded; nor are you on the land, aided by a good cover, where you can work to the advantage you are used to. If you had our canoe, might you not pass to the shore with a dry rifle?"

"Can an eagle fly, Jasper?" returned the other, laughing and looking back as he spoke. "But it would be unwise to expose yourself on the water; for them miscreants are beginning to bethink them again of powder and bullets."

"It can be done without any such chances. Master Cap has gone up to the canoe, and will cast the branch of a tree into the river to try the current. See, there it comes already; if it float fairly, you must raise your arm, when the canoe will follow. At all events, if the boat should pass you, the eddy below will bring it up, and I can recover it."

While Jasper was still speaking, the floating branch came in sight; and, quickening its progress with the increasing velocity of the current, it swept swiftly down towards the Pathfinder, who seized it as it was passing, and held it in the air as a sign of success. Cap understood the signal, and presently the canoe was launched into the stream. It floated in the same direction as the branch, and in a minute was arrested by the Pathfinder.

"This has been done with a frontier man's judgment, Jasper," said the guide; "but you have your gifts, which incline most to the water, as mine incline to the woods. Now let them Mingo knaves cock their rifles and get rests, for this is the last chance they are likely to have at a man without a cover."

"Nay, shove the canoe towards the shore, quartering the current, and throw yourself into it as it goes off," said Jasper eagerly. "There is little use in running any risk."

"I love to stand up face to face with my enemies like a man, while they set me the example," returned the Pathfinder proudly. I am not a redskin born, and it is more a white man's gifts to fight openly than to lie in ambushment."

"And Mabel?"

"True, boy, true; the Sergeant's daughter must be saved; and, as you say, foolish risks only become boys. Think you that you can catch the canoe where you stand?"

"There can be no doubt, if you give a vigorous push."

Pathfinder made the necessary effort; the light bark shot across the intervening space, and Jasper seized it as it came to land. To secure the canoe, and to take proper positions in the cover, occupied the friends but a moment, when they shook hands cordially, like those who had met after a long separation.

"Now, Jasper, we shall see if a Mingo of them all dares cross the Oswego in the teeth of Killdeer! You are handier with the oar and the paddle and the sail than with the rifle, perhaps; but you have a stout heart and a steady hand, and them are things that count in a fight."

"Mabel will find me between her and her enemies," said Jasper calmly.

"Yes, the Sergeant's daughter must be protected. See, Jasper! three of the knaves are actually getting into the canoe! They must believe we have fled, or they would not surely venture so much."

Sure enough the Iroquois did appear bent on venturing across the stream; for, as the Pathfinder and his friends now kept their persons strictly concealed, their enemies began to think that the latter had taken to flight. Such a course was that which most white men would have followed; but Mabel was under the care of those who were much too well skilled in forest warfare to neglect to defend the only pass that, in truth, now offered even a probable chance for protection.

As the Pathfinder had said, three warriors were in the canoe, two holding their rifles at a poise, as they knelt in readiness to aim the deadly weapons, and the other standing erect in the stern to wield the paddle. In this manner they left the shore, having had the precaution to haul the canoe, previously to entering it, so far up the stream as to have got into the comparatively still water above the rift. It was apparent at a glance that the savage who guided the boat was skilled in the art; for the long, steady sweep of his paddle sent the light bark over the glassy surface of the tranquil river as if it were a feather floating in the air.

"Shall I fire?" demanded Jasper in a whisper, trembling with eagerness to engage.

"Not yet, boy, not yet. There are but three of them, and if Master Cap yonder knows how to use the popguns he carries in his belt, we may even let them land, and then we shall recover the canoe."

"But Mabel——?"

"No fear for the Sergeant's daughter. She is safe in the hollow stump, you say, with the opening judgmatically hid by the brambles. If what you tell me of the manner in which you concealed the trail be true, the sweet one might lie there a month and laugh at the Mingos."

"We are never certain. I wish we had brought her nearer to our own cover!"

"What for, Eau-douce? To place her pretty little head and leaping heart among flying bullets? No; she is better where she is, because she is safer,"

"We are never certain. We thought ourselves safe behind the bushes, and yet you saw that we were discovered."

"And the Mingo imp paid for his curiosity, as these knaves are about to do."

The Pathfinder ceased speaking; for at that instant the sharp report of a rifle was heard, when the Indian in the stern of the canoe leaped high in the air, and fell into the water, holding the paddle in his hand. A small wreath of smoke floated out from among the bushes of the eastern shore, and was soon absorbed by the atmosphere.

"That is the Sarpent hissing!" exclaimed the Pathfinder exultingly. "A bolder or a truer heart never beat in the breast of a Delaware. I am sorry that he interfered; but he could not have known our condition."

The canoe had no sooner lost its guide than it floated with the stream, and was soon sucked into the rapids of the rift. Perfectly helpless, the two remaining savages gazed wildly about them, but could offer no resistance to the power of the element. It was perhaps fortunate for Chingachgook that the attention of most of the Iroquois was intently given to the situation of those in the boat, else would his escape have been to the last degree difficult, if not totally impracticable. But not a foe moved, except to conceal his person behind some cover; and every eye was riveted on the two remaining adventurers. Immediately the canoe was whirling and tossing in the rift, while both the savages had stretched themselves in its bottom, as the only means of preserving the equilibrium. This natural expedient soon failed them; for, striking a rock, the light craft rolled over, and the two warriors were thrown into the river. The water is seldom deep on a rift, except in particular places where it may have worn channels; and there was little to be apprehended from drowning, though their arms were lost; and the two savages were fain to make the best of their way to the friendly shore, swimming and wading as circumstances required. The canoe itself lodged on a rock in the centre of the stream, where for the moment it became useless to both parties.

"Now is our time, Pathfinder," cried Jasper, as the two Iroquois exposed most of their persons while wading in the shallowest part of the rapids. "The fellow up stream is mine, and you can take the lower."

So excited had the young man become by all the incidents of the stirring scene that the bullet sped from his rifle as he spoke, but uselessly, as it would seem, for both the fugitives tossed their arms in disdain. The Pathfinder did not fire.

"No, no, Eau-douce," he answered. "I do not seek blood without a cause; and my bullet is well leathered and carefully driven down for the time of need. One life is sufficient for our present wants; and there may yet be occasion to use Killdeer in behalf of the Sarpent, who has done an untimorsome thing to let them so plainly know that he is in their neighbourhood. As I'm a wicked sinner, there is one of them prowling along the bank this very moment, like one of the boys of the garrison skulking behind a fallen tree to get a shot at a squirrel!"

As the Pathfinder pointed with his finger while speaking, the quick eye of Jasper soon caught the object towards which it was directed. One of the young warriors of the enemy, burning with a desire to distinguish himself, had stolen from his party towards the cover in which Chingachgook had concealed himself; and as the latter was deceived by the apparent apathy of his foes, as well as engaged in some further preparations of his own, he had evidently obtained a position where he got a sight of the Delaware. This circumstance was apparent by the arrangements the Iroquois was making to fire, for Chingachgook himself was not visible from the western side of the river. The rift was at a bend in the Oswego, and the sweep of the eastern shore formed a curve so wide that Chingachgook was quite near to his enemies in a straight direction, though separated by several hundred feet on the land, owing to which fact air lines brought both parties nearly equidistant from the Pathfinder and Jasper. The general width of the river being a little less than two hundred yards, such necessarily was about the distance between his two observers and the skulking Iroquois.

"The Sarpent must be thereabouts," observed Pathfinder, who never turned his eye for an instant from the young warrior; "and yet he must be strangely off his guard to allow a Mingo to get his stand so near, with manifest signs of bloodshed in his heart."

"See!" interrupted Jasper—"there is the body of the Indian the Delaware shot! It has drifted on a rock, and the current has forced the head and face above the water."

"Quite likely, boy, quite likely. Human natur' is little better than a log of driftwood when the life that was breathed into its nostrils has departed. That Iroquois will never harm anyone more; but yonder skulking savage is bent on taking the scalp of my best and most tried friend."

The Pathfinder suddenly interrupted himself by raising his rifle, a weapon of unusual length, with admirable precision, and firing the instant it had got its level. The Iroquois on the opposite shore was in the act of aiming when the fatal messenger from Killdeer arrived. His rifle was discharged, it is true, but it was with the muzzle in the air, while the man himself plunged into the bushes, quite evidently hurt, if not slain.

"The skulking reptyle brought it on himself," muttered Pathfinder sternly, as, dropping the butt of his rifle, he carefully commenced reloading it.

"We have served the Serpent as good a turn as he served us. Those rascals are troubled, Pathfinder, and are falling back into their covers, since they find we can reach them across the river."

"The shot is no great matter, Jasper, no great matter. Ask any of the 60th, and they can tell you what Killdeer can do. No, no! this is no great matter, and the unthoughtful vagabond drew it down on himself."

"Is that a dog, or a deer, swimming towards this shore?"

Pathfinder started, for sure enough an object was crossing the stream, above the rift, towards which, however, it was gradually setting by the force of the current. A second look satisfied both the observers that it was a man, and an Indian, though so concealed as at first to render it doubtful. Some stratagem was apprehended, and the closest attention was given to the movements of the stranger.

"He is pushing something before him as he swims, and his head resembles a drifting bush," said Jasper.

"'Tis Indian trickery, boy; but we will sarcumvent their arts."

As the man slowly approached, the observers began to doubt the accuracy of their first impressions, and it was only when two-thirds of the stream were passed that the truth was really known.

"The Big Sarpent, as I live!" exclaimed Pathfinder, looking at his companion, and laughing until the tears came into his eyes with pure delight at the success of the artifice. "He has tied bushes to his head, so as to hide it, put the horn on top, lashed the rifle to that bit of log he is pushing before him, and has come over to join his friends."

"It may not be the Serpent after all, Pathfinder; I can see no feature that I can remember."

"Feature! Who looks for features in an Indian? No, no, boy; 'tis the paint that speaks, and none but a Delaware would wear that paint. Them are his colours, Jasper, just as your craft on the lake wears St. George's Cross. Now, you see the eye, lad, and it is the eye of a chief. There is a soul and a heart under that red skin, rely on it; although they are a soul and a heart with gifts different from our own."

"No one who is acquainted with the chief ever doubted that."

The Serpent now reached the shore, directly in the front of his two comrades, with whose precise position he must have been acquainted before leaving the eastern side of the river, and rising from the water he shook himself like a dog, and made the usual exclamation—"Hugh!"

CHAPTER VI

As the chief landed he was met by the Pathfinder, who addressed him in the language of the warrior's people: "Was it well done, Chingachgook," said he reproachfully, "to ambush a dozen Mingos alone!"

"The Great Serpent is a Mohican warrior—he sees only his enemies when he is on the warpath."

"I know your gifts, I know your gifts, and respect them too. No man shall hear me complain that a redskin observed redskin natur'. But prudence as much becomes a warrior as valour; and had not the Iroquois been looking after their friends who were in the water, a hot trail they would have made of yourn."

"What is the Delaware about to do?" exclaimed Jasper, who observed at that moment that the chief had suddenly left the Pathfinder and advanced to the water's edge, apparently with an intention of again entering the river. "He will not be so mad as to return to the other shore for any trifle he may have forgotten?"

"Not he, not he; he is as prudent as he is brave, in the main, though so forgetful of himself in the late ambushment. Hark'e, Jasper," leading the other a little aside, just as they heard the

Indian's plunge in the water—"hark'e, lad, Chingachgook is not a Christian white man, like ourselves, but a Mohican chief, who has his gifts and traditions to tell him what he ought to do; and he who consorts with them that are not strictly and altogether of his own kind had better leave natur' and use to govern his comrades. A king's soldier will swear and he will drink, and it is of little use to try to prevent him; a gentleman likes his delicacies, and a lady her feathers, and it does not avail much to struggle against either; whereas an Indian's natur' and gifts are much stronger than these, and no doubt were bestowed by the Lord for wise ends, though neither you nor me can follow them in all their windings."

"What does this mean? See, the Delaware is swimming towards the body that is lodged on the rock. Why does he risk this?"

"For honour and glory and renown, as great gentlemen quit their quiet homes beyond seas — where, as they tell me, heart has nothing left to wish for; that is, such hearts as can be satisfied in a clearing—to come hither to live on game and fight the Frenchers."

"I understand you — your friend has gone to secure the scalp."

"'Tis his gift, and let him enjoy it. We are white men, and cannot mangle a dead enemy; but it is honour in the eyes of a redskin to do so."

"A savage will be a savage, Pathfinder, let him keep what company he may."

"It is well for us to say so, lad; but, as I tell you, white honour will not always conform to reason or to the will of God. I have passed days thinking of these matters, out in the silent woods, and I have come to the opinion, boy, that, as Providence rules all things, no gift is bestowed without some wise and reasonable end."

"The Serpent greatly exposes himself to the enemy, in order to get his scalp! This may lose us the day."

"Not in his mind, Jasper. That one scalp has more honour in it, according to the Sarpent's notions of warfare, than a field covered with slain, that kept the hair on their heads."

Here a great outcry from among the Iroquois was succeeded by the quick reports of their rifles, and so eager did the enemy become, in the desire to drive the Delaware back from his victim, that a dozen rushed into the river, several of whom even advanced near a hundred feet into the foaming current, as if they actually meditated a serious sortie. But Chingachgook continued un-moved, as he remained unhurt by the missiles, accomplishing his task with the dexterity of long habit. Flourishing his reeking trophy, he gave the warwhoop in its most frightful intonations, and for a minute the arches of the silent woods and the deep vista formed by the course of the river echoed with cries so terrific that Mabel bowed her head in irrepressible fear.

"This surpasses all I have heard from the wretches," Jasper exclaimed.

"'Tis their music, boy, their drum and fife, their trumpets and clarions. No doubt they love those sounds, for they stir up in them fierce feelings and a desire for blood," returned the Path-finder, totally unmoved. "I hope the Sarpent is now satisfied, for here he comes with the scalp at his belt."

The Pathfinder regarded his friend with the philosophical indif-ference of one who has made up his mind to be indifferent to things he deemed immaterial. As the Delaware passed deeper into the bushes, with a view to wring his trifling calico dress and to prepare his rifle for service, he gave one glance of triumph at his companions, and then all emotion connected with the recent exploit seemed to cease.

"Jasper," resumed the guide, "step to Master Cap, and ask him to join us. Our plans must be laid quickly, for it will not be long before them Mingos will be plotting our ruin."

The young men complied; and in a few minutes the four were assembled near the shore, completely concealed from the view of their enemies, in order to consult on their own future move-ments.

By this time the day had so far advanced as to leave but a few minutes between the passing light and an obscurity that promised to be even deeper than common. The sun had already set, and the twilight of a low latitude would soon pass into the darkness of deep night. Most of the hopes of the party rested on this favourable circumstance, though it was not without its dangers also, as the very obscurity which would favour their escape would be as likely to conceal the movements of their wily enemies.

"The moment has come," Pathfinder announced, "when our plans must be coolly laid. In an hour's time these woods will be as dark as midnight; and if we are ever to gain the garrison, it must be done under favour of this advantage. What say you, Master Cap?"

"Well, in my judgment, all we have to do is to go on board the canoe when it gets to be so dark the enemy's lookouts can't see us, and run for the haven, as wind and tide will allow."

"That is easily said, but not so easily done," returned the guide. "We shall be more exposed in the river than by following the woods; and then there is the Oswego rift below us, and I am far from sartain that Jasper himself can carry a boat safely through it in the dark. What say you, lad?"

"I am of Master Cap's opinion about using the canoe. Mabel is too tender to walk through swamps and among roots of trees in such a night as this promises to be, and then I always feel myself stouter of heart and truer of eye when afloat than when ashore."

"Stout of heart you always be, lad, and I think tolerably true of eye, too. As to your opinion, friends, there is much for and much against it. For it, it may be said water leaves no trail. Then a canoe is both swift and easy when it floats with the current, and the tender limbs of the Sergeant's daughter will be favoured by its motion. But, on the other hand, the river will have no cover but the clouds in the heavens; the rift is a ticklish thing for boats to venture into, even by daylight; and it is six fairly measured miles, by water, from this spot to the garrison. Then a trail on land is not easy to be found in the dark. I am troubled, Jasper, to say which way we ought to counsel and advise."

"If the Serpent and myself could swim into the river and bring off the other canoe," the young sailor replied, "it would seem to me that our safest course would be the water."

"If, indeed! and yet it might easily be done, as soon as it is a little darker. Well, I am not certain it will not be the best, Jasper," continued the guide. "Will you undertake to bring in the canoe?"

"I will undertake anything that will serve and protect Mabel, Pathfinder."

"The Sarpent, who is nearly naked already, can help you; and this will be cutting off one of the means of the wretches to work their harm."

This material point being settled, the different members of the party prepared themselves to put the project in execution. The shades of evening fell fast upon the forest; and by the time all was ready for the attempt, it was found impossible to discern objects on the opposite shore. Time now pressed; for Indian cunning could devise so many expedients for passing so narrow a stream, that the Pathfinder was getting impatient to quit the spot. While Jasper and his companion entered the river, armed with nothing but their knives and the Delaware's tomahawk, observing the greatest caution not to betray their movements, the guide brought Mabel from her place of concealment, and, bidding her and Cap proceed along the shore to the foot of the rapids, he got into the canoe that remained in his possession, in order to carry it to the same place.

This was easily effected. The canoe was laid against the bank, and Mabel and her uncle entered it, taking their seats as usual, while the Pathfinder, erect in the stern, held by a bush, in order to prevent the swift stream from sweeping them down its current. Several minutes of intense and breathless expectation followed, while they awaited the result of the bold attempt of their comrades.

It will be understood that the two adventurers were compelled to swim across a deep and rapid channel before they could reach a part of the rift that admitted of wading. This portion of the enterprise was soon effected. Having secured firm footing, they took hold of each other's hands, and waded slowly and with extreme caution in the supposed direction of the canoe. But the darkness was already so deep that they soon ascertained they were to be but little aided by the sense of sight, and that their search must be conducted on that species of instinct which enables the woodman to find his way when the sun is hid, no stars appear, and all would seem chaos to one less accustomed to the mazes of the forest. Once or twice the wanderers altered their course, in consequence of unexpectedly stepping into deep water, for they knew that the boat had lodged on the shallowest part of the rift. In short, with this fact for their compass, Jasper and his companion wandered about in the water for nearly a quarter of an hour; and at the end of that period they found themselves apparently no nearer the object of their search than they had been at its commencement. Just as the Delaware was about to stop to inform his associate that they would do well to return to the land, in order to take a fresh departure, he saw the form of a man moving about in the water, almost within reach of his arm. Jasper was at his side, and he at once understood that the Iroquois were engaged on the same errand as he was himself.

"Mingo!" he uttered in Jasper's ear. "The Serpent will show his brother how to be cunning."

The young sailor caught a glimpse of the figure at that instant, and the startling truth also flashed on his mind. Understanding the necessity of trusting all to the Delaware chief, he kept back, while his friend moved cautiously in the direction in which the strange form had vanished. In another moment it was seen again, evidently moving towards themselves.

"Hugh!" exclaimed the strange savage, adding, in the language of his people, "The canoe is found, but there were none to help me. Come, let us raise it from the rock."

"Willingly," answered Chingachgook, who understood the dialect. "Lead; we will follow."

The stranger, unable to distinguish between voices and accents amid the raging of the rapid, led the way in the necessary direction; and, the two others keeping close at his heels, all three speedily reached the canoe. The Iroquois laid hold of one end, Chingachgook placed himself in the centre, and Jasper went to the opposite extremity, as it was important that the stranger should not detect the presence of a paleface, a discovery that might be made by the parts of the dress the young man still wore, as well as by the general appearance of his head.

"Lift," said the Iroquois, and by a trifling effort the canoe was raised from the rock, and then placed carefully on the water in its proper position. All three held it firmly, lest it should escape from their hands under the pressure of the violent current, while the Iroquois, who led, of course, being at the upper end of the boat, took the direction of the eastern shore.

As the Delaware and Jasper well knew there must be several more of the Iroquois on the rift, from the circumstance that their own appearance had occasioned no surprise in the individual they had met, both felt the necessity of extreme caution. So all-important to the safety of Mabel, indeed, did Jasper deem the possession or the destruction of this canoe, that he had drawn his knife, and stood ready to rip up the bark, in order to render the boat temporarily unserviceable, should anything occur to compel the Delaware and himself to abandon their prize.

In the meantime, the Iroquois, who led the way, proceeded slowly through the water in the direction of his own party, still grasping the canoe, and dragging his reluctant followers in his train. Once Chingachgook raised his tomahawk, and was about to bury it in the brain of his confiding and unsuspicious neighbour; but the probability that the deathcry or the floating body might give the alarm induced that wary chief to change his purpose. At the next moment he regretted this indecision, for the three who clung to the canoe suddenly found themselves in the centre of a party of no less than four others who were in quest of it.

After the usual brief characteristic exclamation of satisfaction, the savages eagerly laid hold of the canoe, for all seemed impressed with the necessity of securing this important boat, the one side in order to assail their foes, and the other to secure their retreat. The addition to the party, however, was so unlooked-for, and so completely gave the enemy the superiority, that for a few moments the ingenuity and address of even the Delaware were at fault. The five Iroquois, who seemed perfectly to understand their errand, pressed forward towards their own shore, without pausing to converse.

In this manner, the body of friends and foes united reached the margin of the eastern channel, where, as in the case of the western, the river was too deep to be waded. Here a short pause succeeded, it being necessary to determine the manner in which the canoe was to be carried across. One of the four who had just reached the boat was a chief: and the habitual deference which the American Indian pays to station kept the others silent until this individual had spoken.

The halt greatly added to the danger of discovering the presence of Jasper in particular, who, however, had the precaution to throw the cap he wore into the bottom of the canoe. His position, too, at the stern of the canoe a little favoured his concealment, the Iroquois naturally keeping their looks directed the other way. Not so with Chingachgook. This warrior was literally in the midst of his most deadly foes, and he could scarcely move without touching one of them. Yet he was apparently unmoved, though he kept all his senses on the alert, in readiness to escape, or to strike a blow at the proper moment. By carefully abstaining from looking towards those behind him, he lessened the chances of discovery, and waited with the indomitable patience of an Indian for the instant when he should be required to act.

"Let all my young men but two, one at each end of the canoe, cross and get their arms," said the Iroquois chief. "Let the two push over the boat."

The Indians quietly obeyed, leaving Jasper at the stern, and the Iroquois who had found the canoe at the bow of the light craft, Chingachgook burying himself so deep in the river as to be passed by the others without detection. The splashing in the water, and the calls of one to another soon announced that the four who had last joined the party were already swimming. As soon as this fact was certain, the Delaware rose, resumed his former station, and began to think the moment for action was come.

One less habitually under self-restraint than this warrior would probably have now aimed his meditated blow, but Chingachgook was a warrior much too trained and experienced to risk anything unnecessarily. He suffered the Indian at the bow of the canoe to push off into the deep water, and then all three were swimming in the direction of the eastern shore. Instead, however, of helping the canoe across the swift current, no sooner did the Delaware and Jasper find themselves within the influence of its greatest force than both began to swim in a way to check their farther progress across the stream; but this was done so warily, and so gradually that the Iroquois at the bow fancied at first he was merely struggling against the strength of the current. Of course, while acted on by these opposing efforts, the canoe drifted down stream, and in about a minute it was floating in still deeper water at the foot of the rift. Here, however, the Iroquois was not slow in finding that something unusual retarded their advance, and, looking back, he first learned that he was resisted by the efforts of his companions.

That second nature which grows up through habit instantly told the young Iroquois that he was alone with enemies. Dashing the water aside, he sprang at the throat of Chingachgook, and the two Indians relinquishing their hold of the canoe, seized each other like tigers. In the midst of the darkness of that gloomy night, and floating in an element so dangerous to man when engaged in deadly strife, they appeared to forget everything but their fell animosity and their mutual desire to conquer.

Jasper had now complete command of the canoe, which flew off like a feather impelled by the breath under the violent reaction of the struggles of the two combatants. The first impulse of the youth was to swim to the aid of the Delaware, but the importance of securing the boat presented itself with tenfold force, while he listened to the heavy breathings of the warriors as they throttled each other, and he proceeded as fast as possible towards the western shore. This he soon reached; and after a short search he succeeded in discovering the remainder of the party and in procuring his clothes. A few words sufficed to explain the situation in which he had left the Delaware and the manner in which the canoe had been obtained.

When those who had been left behind had heard the explanations of Jasper, a profound stillness reigned among them, each listening intently in the vain hope of catching some clue to the result of the fearful struggle that had just taken place, if it were not still going on in the water. Nothing was audible beyond the steady roar of the rushing river; it being a part of the policy of their enemies on the opposite shore to observe the most deathlike stillness.

"Take this paddle, Jasper," said Pathfinder calmly, "and follow with your own canoe. It is unsafe for us to remain here longer."

"But the Serpent?"

"The Great Sarpent is in the hands of his own Deity, and will live or die, according to the intentions of Providence. We can do him no good, and may risk too much by remaining here in idleness. This darkness is very precious."

A loud, long, piercing yell came from the shore, and cut short the words of the guide.

"What is the meaning of that uproar, Master Pathfinder?" demanded Cap. "It sounds more like the outcries of fiends than anything that can come from the throats of Christians and men?"

"Christians they are not, and do not pretend to be; and in calling them fiends you have scarcely misnamed them. That yell is one of rejoicing, and it is as conquerors they have given it. The body of the Sarpent, no doubt, dead or alive is in their power."

"And we!" exclaimed Jasper, who felt a pang of generous regret, as the idea that he might have averted the calamity presented itself to his mind, had he not deserted his comrade.

"We can do the chief no good, lad, and must quit this spot as fast as possible."

"Without one attempt to rescue him?—without even knowing whether he be dead or living!"

"Tut! Tut!" returned the impatient guide, forcing the canoe into the stream as he spoke; "ye know nothing and ye fear nothing. If ye value your lives, think of reaching the garrison, and leave the Delaware in the hands of Providence."

CHAPTER VII

THE darkness of the night had lessened, by the dispersion of the clouds; but the overhanging woods rendered the shore so obscure, that the boats floated down the current in a belt of gloom that effectually secured them from detection. Still, there was necessarily a strong feeling of insecurity in all on board them; and even Jasper, who by this time began to tremble, in behalf of the girl, at every unusual sound that arose from the forest, kept casting uneasy glances around him, as he drifted on in company. The paddle was used lightly, and only with exceeding care; for the slightest sound in the breathing stillness of that hour and place might apprise the watchful ears of the Iroquois of the position.

"Mabel!" said the suppressed voice of Jasper, as the two canoes floated so near each other that the hand of the young man held them together; "you have no dread? you trust freely to our care and willingness to protect you?"

"I am a soldier's daughter, as you know, Jasper Western, and ought to be ashamed to confess fear."

"Rely on me—on us all. Your uncle, Pathfinder, I myself, will risk everything rather than harm should reach you."

"I believe you, Jasper," returned the girl, her hand unconsciously playing in the water. "I know that my uncle loves me, and will never think of himself until he has first thought of me; and I believe you are all my father's friends, and would willingly assist his child. But though only a girl from the towns, and like most of that class, a little disposed to see danger where there is none, I promise you, Jasper, no foolish fears of mine shall stand in the way of your doing your duty."

"The Sergeant's daughter is right, and she is worthy of being honest Thomas Dunham's child," put in the Pathfinder. "Ah's me, pretty one! many is the time that your father and I have scouted and marched together on the flanks and rear of the enemy, in nights darker than this, and that, too, when we did not know but the next moment would lead us into a bloody ambushment. I was at his side when he got the wound in his shoulder; and the honest fellow will tell you the manner in which we contrived to cross the river which lay in our rear, in order to save his scalp."

"He *has* told me," said Mabel. "I have his letters, in which he has mentioned all that, and I thank you from the bottom of my heart for the service. There is no gratitude that you can ask of the daughter which she will not cheerfully repay for her father's life."

"Ay, that is the way with all your gentle and pure-hearted creatures. The Sergeant himself has talked to me of his own young days, and of your mother, and of the manner in which he courted her, and of all the crossings and disappointments, until he succeeded at last."

"My mother did not live long to repay him for what he did to win her," said Mabel, with a trembling lip.

"So he tells me. For, being so many years my senior, he has looked on me, in our many scoutings together, as a sort of son."

"Perhaps, Pathfinder," observed Jasper, with a huskiness in his voice, "he would be glad to have you for one in reality."

"And if he did, Eau-douce, where would be the sin of it? He knows what I am on a trail or a scout, and he has seen me often face to face with the Frenchers. I have sometimes thought, lad, that we all ought to seek for wives; for the man that lives altogether in the woods, and in company with his enemies or his prey, gets to lose some of the feeling of kind in the end. It is not easy to dwell always in the presence of God and not feel the power of his goodness. The woods are the true temple after all, for there the thoughts are free to mount higher even than the clouds."

"You speak the truth, Master Pathfinder," said Cap, "and a truth that all who live much in solitude know. What, for instance, is the reason that seafaring men in general are so religious and conscientious in all they do, but the fact that they are so often alone with Providence, and have so little to do with the wickedness of the land. I agree with you, Master Pathfinder, in saying, if you want a truly religious man, go to sea, or go into the woods."

"Uncle, I thought seamen had little credit generally for their respect for religion?"

"All slander, girl; for all the essentials of Christianity the seaman beats the landsman hand-over-hand."

"I will not answer for all this, Master Cap," returned Pathfinder; "but I dare say some of it may be true. How is it with you, Eau-douce? you face the tempests as well as Master Cap, and ought to know something of the feelings of storms."

"I fear that I am too young and too inexperienced to be able to say much on such a subject," modestly answered Jasper.

"But you have your feelings!" said Mabel quickly. "You cannot—no one can live among such scenes without feeling how much they ought to trust in God!"

"I shall not belie my training so much as to say I do not sometimes think of these things, but I fear it is not so often or so much as I ought."

While this desultory conversation was being carried on in subdued voices, the canoes were dropping slowly down with the current within the deep shadows of the western shore, the paddles being used merely to preserve the desired direction and proper positions. The strength of the stream varied materially, the water being seemingly still in places, while in other reaches it flowed at a rate exceeding two or even three miles in the hour. Jasper was of opinion that they might drift down with the current to the mouth of the river in two hours from the time they left the shore, and he and the Pathfinder had agreed on the expediency of suffering the canoes to float of themselves for a time, or at least until they had passed the first dangers of their new movement. The dialogue had been carried on in voices, too, guardedly low; for though the quiet of deep solitude reigned in that vast forest, nature was speaking with her thousand tongues in the eloquent language of night in a wilderness. All living sounds had ceased. Once, it is true, the Pathfinder fancied he heard the howl of a distant wolf, of which a few prowled through these woods; but it was a transient and doubtful cry, that might possibly have been attributed to the imagination. When he desired his companions, however, to cease talking, his vigilant ear had caught the peculiar sound which is made by the parting of a dried branch of a tree, and which, if his senses did not deceive him, came from the western shore.

"There is the footstep of a man on the bank," said Pathfinder to Jasper. "Can the Iroquois have crossed the river already, with their arms, and without a boat?"

"It may be the Delaware. He would follow us, of course, down this bank, and would know where to look for us. Let me draw closer in to the shore, and reconnoitre."

"Go, boy, but be light with the paddle, and on no account venture ashore on an onsartainty."

"Is this prudent?" demanded Mabel, with an impetuosity that rendered her incautious in modulating her sweet voice.

"Very imprudent, if you speak so loud, fair one. I like your

(M5) 5

voice, which is soft and pleasing; but it must not be heard too much, or too freely, just now. Go, Jasper, and do justice to your own character for prudence."

Ten anxious minutes succeeded the disappearance of the canoe of Jasper. During this time the party continued to float with the current, no one speaking, and, it might almost be said, no one breathing, so strong was the general desire to catch the minutest sound that should come from the shore. But the same solemn, we might, indeed, say sublime, quiet reigned as before; the wash-ing of the water, as it piled up against some slight obstruction, and the sighing of the trees, alone interrupting the slumbers of the forest. Then the snapping of dried branches was again faintly heard, and the Pathfinder fancied that the sound of smothered voices reached him.

"I may be mistaken," he said, "for the thoughts often fancy what the heart wishes; but these were notes like the low tones of the Delaware."

"Do the dead of the savages ever walk?" demanded Cap.

"Ay, and run too, in their happy hunting grounds, but nowhere else. A redskin finishes with the 'arth, after the breath quits the body."

"I see some object on the water," whispered Mabel, whose eye had not ceased to dwell on the body of gloom, with close inten-sity, since the disappearance of Jasper.

"It is the canoe," returned the guide, greatly relieved. "All must be safe, or we should have heard from the lad."

In another minute the two canoes, which became visible to those they carried only as they drew near each other, again floated side by side, and the form of Jasper was recognized at the stern of his own boat. The figure of a second man was seated in the bow; and, as the young sailor so wielded his paddle as to bring the face of his companion near the eyes of the Pathfinder and Mabel, they both recognized the person of the Delaware.

"Chingachgook—my brother!" said the guide in the dialect of the other's people, a tremor shaking his voice that betrayed the strength of his feelings. ' My heart is very glad. Often have we passed through blood and strife together, but I was afraid it was never to be so again."

"Hugh! The Mingos are squaws! Three of their scalps hang at my girdle. Their hearts have no blood; and their thoughts are on their return path, across the waters of the Great Lake."

"Have you been among them, chief; and what has become of the warrior who was in the river?"

"He has turned into a fish, and lies at the bottom with the eels! Pathfinder, I have counted the enemy, and have touched their rifles."

"Ah, I thought he would be venturesome!" exclaimed the guide in English. "The risky fellow has been in the midst of them, and has brought us back their whole history. Speak, Chingachgook."

The Delaware now related in a low voice the substance of all his discoveries, since he was last seen struggling with his foe in the river. Of the fate of his antagonist he said no more, it not being usual for a warrior to boast in his more direct and useful narratives. As soon as he had conquered in that fearful strife, however, he swam to the eastern shore, landed with caution, and wound his way in amongst the Iroquois, concealed by the darkness, undetected, and, in the main, even unsuspected. By the passing remarks, he soon ascertained that the party was out expressly to intercept Mabel and her uncle, concerning whose rank, however, they had evidently been deceived. He also ascertained enough to justify the suspicion that Arrowhead had betrayed them to their enemies, for some motive that it was not now easy to reach, as he had not yet received the reward of his services.

Pathfinder communicated no more of this intelligence to his companions than he thought might relieve their apprehensions, intimating, at the same time, that now was the moment for exertion, the Iroquois not having yet entirely recovered from the confusion created by their losses.

"We shall find them at the rift, I make no manner of doubt," continued he; "and there it will be our fate to pass them, or to fall into their hands. The distance to the garrison will then be so short, that I have been thinking of the plan of landing with Mabel myself, that I may take her in, by some of the by-ways, and leave the canoes to their chances in the rapids."

"It will never succeed, Pathfinder," eagerly interrupted Jasper. "Mabel is not strong enough to tramp the woods in a night like this. Put her in my skiff, and I will lose my life, or carry her through the rift safely, dark as it is."

"No doubt you will, lad; no one doubts your willingness to do anything to serve the Sergeant's daughter; but it must be the eye of Providence, and not your own, that will take you safely through the Oswego rift in a night like this."

"And who will lead her safely to the garrison if she land? Is not the night as dark on shore as on the water? or do you think I know less of my calling than you know of yours?"

"Spiritedly said, lad; but if I should lose my way in the dark, no other harm would come of it than to pass a night in the forest; whereas a false turn of the paddle, or a broad sheer of the canoe, would put you and the young woman into the river, out of which it is more than probable the Sergeant's daughter would never come alive."

"I will leave it to Mabel herself; I am certain that she will feel more secure in the canoe."

"I have great confidence in you both," answered the girl; "and have no doubts that either will do all he can to prove to my father how much he values him; but I confess I should not like to quit the canoe, with the certainty we have of there being enemies like those we have seen in the forest. But my uncle can decide for me in this matter."

"I have no liking for the woods," said Cap, "while one has a clear drift like this on the river. Besides, Master Pathfinder, to say nothing of the savages, you overlook the sharks."

"Sharks! who ever heard of sharks in the wilderness!"

"Ay, sharks, or bears, or wolves—no matter what you call a thing, so it has the mind and power to bite."

"Bless me, man! do you dread any creetur' that is to be found in the American forest? A catamount is a skeary animal, I will allow, but then it is nothing in the hands of a practised hunter. Talk of the Mingos and their practices if you will; but do not raise a false alarm about bears and wolves."

"Ay, ay, Master Pathfinder, this is all well enough for you, who probably know the name of every creature you would meet. But Mabel and I had better stick to the canoe."

"Mabel would do well to change canoes," added Jasper. "This of mine is empty, and even Pathfinder will allow that my eye is surer than his own on the water."

"That I will, cheerfully, boy. The water belongs to your gifts, and no one will deny that you have improved them to the utmost. You are right enough in believing that the Sergeant's daughter will be safer in your canoe than in this; and though I would gladly keep her near myself, I have her welfare too much at heart not to give her honest advice. Bring your canoe close alongside, Jasper, and I will give you what you must consider as a precious treasure."

"I do so consider it," returned the youth, not losing a moment in complying with the request; when Mabel passed from one canoe to the other.

As soon as this arrangement was made, the canoes separated a short distance, and the paddles were used, though with great care to avoid making any noise. The conversation gradually ceased; and as the dreaded rift was approached, all became impressed with the gravity of the moment. That their enemies would endeavour to reach this point before them was almost certain; and it seemed so little probable anyone should attempt to pass it, in the profound obscurity which reigned, that Pathfinder was confident parties were on both sides of the river, in the hope of intercepting them when they might land. He would not have made the proposal he did had he not felt sure of his own ability to convert this very anticipation of success into a means of defeating the plans of the Iroquois. As the arrangement now stood, however, everything depended on the skill of those who guided the canoes; for should either hit a rock, if not split asunder, it would almost certainly be upset, and then would come not only all the hazards of the river itself, but for Mabel, the certainty of falling into the hands of her pursuers.

As the canoes stole silently along, the roar of the rift became audible, and it required all the fortitude of Cap to keep his seat, while these boding sounds were approached, amid a darkness which scarcely permitted a view of the outlines of the wooded shore and of the gloomy vault above his head.

Mabel certainly felt distrust and apprehension; but her entire situation was so novel, and her reliance on her guide so great, that she retained a self-command which might not have existed had she had clearer perceptions of the truth, or been better acquainted with the helplessness of men when placed in opposition to the power and majesty of Nature.

"Is that the spot you have mentioned?" she said to Jasper, when the roar of the rift first came distinctly on her ear.

"It is; and I beg you to have confidence in me. We are not old acquaintances, Mabel; but we live many days in one in this wilderness. I think, already, that I have known you years!"

"And I do not feel as if you were a stranger to me, Jasper. I have every reliance on your skill, as well as on your disposition to serve me."

"We shall see. Pathfinder is striking the rapids too near the centre of the river; the bed of the water is closer to the eastern shore; but I cannot make him hear me now. Hold firmly to the canoe, Mabel, and fear nothing."

At the next moment the swift current had sucked them into the rift, and for three or four minutes the awestruck girl saw nothing around her but sheets of glancing foam, heard nothing but the roar of waters. Twenty times did the canoe appear about to dash against some curling and bright wave that showed itself even amid that obscurity; and as often did it glide away again unharmed, impelled by the vigorous arm of him who governed its movements. Once, and once only, did Jasper seem to lose command of his frail bark, during which brief space it fairly whirled entirely round; but by a desperate effort he brought it again under control, recovered the lost channel, and was soon rewarded for all his anxiety by finding himself floating quietly in the deep water below the rapids, secure from every danger, and without having taken in enough of the element to serve for a draught.

"All is over, Mabel," the young man cried cheerfully. "The danger is past, and you may now indeed hope to meet your father this very night."

"God be praised! Jasper, we shall owe this great happiness to you."

"The Pathfinder may claim a full share in the merit; but what has become of the other canoe?"

"I see something near us on the water; is it not the boat of our friends?"

A few strokes of the paddle brought Jasper to the side of the object in question; it was the other canoe, empty and bottom upwards. No sooner did the young man ascertain this fact than he began to search for the swimmers, and, to his great joy, Cap was soon discovered drifting down with the current; the old seaman preferring the chances of drowning to those of landing among savages. He was hauled into the canoe, though not without difficulty, and then the search ended; for Jasper was persuaded that the Pathfinder would wade to the shore, the water being shallow, in preference to abandoning his beloved rifle.

The remainder of the passage was short, though made amid darkness and doubt. After a short pause, a dull roaring sound was heard, which at times resembled the mutterings of distant thunder, and then again brought with it the washing of waters. Jasper announced to his companions that they now heard the surf of the lake. Low curved spits of land lay before them, into the bay formed by one of which the canoe glided. and then it shot up noiselessly upon a gravelly beach. In the course of a few minutes sentinels had been passed, a gate was opened, and the agitated girl found herself in the arms of a parent who was almost a stranger to her.

CHAPTER VIII

THE rest that succeeds fatigue, and which attends a newly awakened sense of security, is generally sweet and deep. Such was the fact with Mabel, who did not rise from her humble pallet until long after the garrison had obeyed the usual summons of the drums, and had assembled at the morning parade. Sergeant Dunham, on whose shoulders fell the task of attending to these ordinary and daily duties, had got through all his morning avocations, and was beginning to think of his breakfast, before his child left her room, and came into the fresh air, equally bewildered, delighted, and grateful, at the novelty and security of her new situation.

At the time of which we are writing, Oswego was one of the extreme frontier posts of the British possessions on this continent. It had not been long occupied, and was garrisoned by a battalion of a regiment which had been originally Scotch, but into which many Americans had been received since its arrival in this country; an innovation that had led the way to Mabel's father filling the humble but responsible situation of the oldest sergeant. A few young officers also, who were natives of the colonies, were to be found in the corps. The fort itself, like most works of that character, was better adapted to resist an attack of savages than to withstand a regular siege; but the great difficulty of transporting heavy artillery and other necessaries rendered the occurrence of the latter a probability so remote as scarcely to enter into the estimate of the engineers who had planned the defences. There were bastions of earth and logs, a dry ditch, a stockade, a parade of considerable extent, and barracks of logs, that answered the double purpose of dwellings and fortifications. A few light field-pieces stood in the area of the fort, ready to be conveyed to any point where they might be wanted, and one or two heavy iron guns looked out from the summits of the advanced angles, as so many admonitions to the audacious to respect their power.

When Mabel, quitting the convenient but comparatively retired hut where her father had been permitted to place her, issued into the pure air of the morning, she found herself at the foot of a bastion, which lay invitingly before her, with a promise of giving a *coup d'œil* of all that had been concealed in the darkness of the preceding night. Tripping up the grassy ascent, the light-hearted as well as light-footed girl found herself at once on a point where the sight, at a few varying glances, could take in all the external novelties of her new situation.

To the southward lay the forest, through which she had been journeying so many weary days, and which had proved so full of dangers. It was separated from the stockade by a belt of open land, that had been principally cleared of its woods to form the martial constructions around her. This glacis, for such in fact was its military uses, might have covered a hundred acres; but with it every sign of civilization ceased. All beyond was forest; that dense, interminable forest which Mabel could now picture to herself, through her recollections, with its hidden glassy lakes, its dark rolling stream, and its world of nature.

Turning from this view, our heroine felt her cheek fanned by a fresh and grateful breeze, such as she had not experienced since quitting the far-distant coast. Here a new scene presented itself; although expected, it was not without a start, and a low exclamation indicative of pleasure, that the eager eyes of the girl drank in its beauties. To the north, and east, and west, in every direction, in short, over one entire half of the novel panorama, lay a field of rolling waters. The element was neither of that glassy green which distinguishes the American waters in general, nor yet of the deep blue of the ocean, the colour being of a slightly amber hue, which scarcely affected its limpidity. No land was to be seen, with the exception of the adjacent coast, which stretched to the right and left in an unbroken outline of forest with wide bays and low headlands or points; still, much of the shore was rocky, and into its caverns the sluggish waters occasionally rolled, producing a hollow sound, which resembled the concussions of a distant gun. No sail whitened the surface, no whale or other fish gambolled on its bosom, no sign of use or service rewarded the longest and most minute gaze at its boundless expanse. It was a scene, on one side, of apparently endless forests, while a waste of seemingly interminable water spread itself on the other.

Mabel Dunham, though unsophisticated, was not altogether without a feeling for the poetry of this beautiful earth of ours. Although she could scarcely be said to be educated at all, still she had been taught much more than was usual for young women in

her own station in life; and, in one sense certainly, she did credit
to her teaching. The widow of a field-officer, who formerly belonged to the same regiment as her father, had taken the child in
charge at the death of its mother; and under the care of this lady
Mabel had acquired some tastes and many ideas which otherwise
might always have remained strangers to her. Her situation in
the family had been that of a humble companion, and the results
were quite apparent in her attire, her language, her sentiments,
and even in her feelings. She had lost the less refined habits
and manners of one in her original position, without having quite
reached a point that disqualified her for the situation in life that
the accidents of birth and fortune would probably compel her to
fill.

With such antecedents it will occasion the reader no wonder
if he learns that Mabel viewed the novel scene before her with
a pleasure far superior to that produced by vulgar surprise. She
felt its ordinary beauties as most would have felt them, but she
had also a feeling for its sublimity—for that softened solitude,
that calm grandeur, and eloquent repose, which ever pervades
broad views of natural objects yet undisturbed by the labours
and struggles of man.

"How beautiful!" she exclaimed, unconscious of speaking, as
she stood on the solitary bastion, facing the air from the lake,
and experiencing the genial influence of its freshness pervading
both her body and her mind. "How very beautiful! and yet how
singular!"

The words, and the train of her ideas, were interrupted by a
touch of a finger on her shoulder, and turning, in the expectation
of seeing her father, Mabel found Pathfinder at her side. He was
leaning quietly on his long rifle, while, with an outstretched arm,
he swept over the whole panorama of land and water.

"Here you have both our domains," said he,—"Jasper's and
mine. The lake is for him, and the woods are for me. The lad
sometimes boasts of the breadth of his dominions; but I tell him
my trees make as broad a plain on the face of this 'arth as all his
water. Well, Mabel, you are fit for either; for I do not see that
fear of the Mingos, or night-marches, can destroy your pretty looks."

"It is a new character for the Pathfinder to appear in, to compliment a silly girl."

"Not silly, Mabel. The Sergeant's daughter would do discredit
to her worthy father, were she to do or say anything that could be
called silly."

"Then she must take care and not put too much faith in flattering words. But, Pathfinder, I rejoice to see you among us again; for, though Jasper did not seem to feel much uneasiness, I was afraid some accident might have happened to you and your friend on that frightful rift."

"The lad knows us both, and was sartain that we should not drown. It would have been hard swimming of a sartainty, with a long-barrelled rifle in the hand; and what between the game, and the savages and the French, Killdeer and I have gone through too much in company to part very easily. No, no; we waded ashore, the rift being shallow enough for that with small exceptions, and we landed with our arms in our hands. We had to take our time for it, on account of the Iroquois, I will own; but, as soon as the skulking vagabonds saw the lights that the Sergeant sent down to your canoe, we well understood they would decamp, since a visit might have been expected from some of the garrison. So it was only sitting patiently on the stones for an hour, and all the danger was over. Patience is the greatest of virtues in a woodsman."

"I rejoice to hear this, for fatigue itself could scarcely make me sleep, for thinking of what might befall you."

"Lord bless your little heart, Mabel! But this is the way with all you gentle ones. I must say, on my part, however, that I was right glad to see the lanterns come down to the waterside, which I knew to be a sure sign of *your* safety. We hunters and guides are rude beings; but both Jasper and I would have died before you should have come to harm—we would."

"I thank you for all you did for me, Pathfinder; from the bottom of my heart, I thank you; and, depend on it, my father shall know it. I have already told him much, but have still a duty to perform on this subject."

"Tush, Mabel! The Sergeant knows what the woods be, and what red men be, too. There is little need to tell him anything about it. Well, now you have met your father, do you find the honest old soldier the sort of person you expected to find."

"He is my own dear father, and received me as a soldier and a father should receive a child. Have you known him long, Pathfinder?"

"I was just twelve when the Sergeant took me on my first scouting, and that is now more than twenty years ago. As it was before your day you would have had no father, had not the rifle been one of my natural gifts."

"Explain yourself."

"We were ambushed, and the Sergeant got a bad hurt, and would have lost his scalp, but for a sort of inbred turn I took to the weapon. We brought him off, however, all right."

"You saved my father's life, Pathfinder?" exclaimed Mabel, unconsciously, though warmly, taking one of his hands into both her own. "God bless you for this too, among your other good acts!"

"Nay, I did not say that much, though I believe I did save his scalp. A man might live without a scalp, and so I cannot say I saved his life. Jasper may say that much consarning you; for without his eye and arm the canoe would never have passed the rift in safety on a night like the last. The gifts of the lad are for the water, while mine are for the hunt and the trail. He is yonder, in the cove there, looking after the canoes, and keeping his eye on his beloved little craft."

Mabel now turned her eyes beneath her, and got a view of what might be called the foreground of the remarkable picture she had been studying with so much pleasure. The Oswego threw its dark waters into the lake, between banks of some height; that on its eastern side being bolder and projecting farther north than that on its western. The fort was on the latter, and immediately beneath it were a few huts of logs, which, as they could not interfere with the defence of the place, had been erected along the strand for the purpose of receiving and containing such stores as were landed, or were intended to be embarked, in the communications between the different ports on the shores of Ontario. Two low, curved, gravelly points had been formed with surprising regularity by the counteracting forces of the northerly winds and the swift current, and, inclining from the storms of the lake, formed two coves within the river: that on the western side was the most deeply indented; and, as it also had the most water, it formed a sort of picturesque little port for the post. It was along the narrow strand that lay between the low height of the fort and the water of this cove, that the rude buildings just mentioned had been erected.

Several skiffs, bateaux, and canoes were hauled up on the shore, and in the cove itself lay the little craft from which Jasper obtained his claim to be considered a sailor. She was cutter-rigged, might have been of forty tons burthen, was so neatly constructed and painted as to have something of the air of a vessel of war, though entirely without quarters, and rigged and sparred with so scrupulous a regard to proportions and beauty, as well as fitness and judgment, as to give her an appearance that even Mabel at once distinguished to be gallant and trim. Her mould was admirable, for a wright of great skill had sent her drafts from England, at the express request of the officer who had caused her to be constructed; her paint dark, warlike, and neat; and the long coach-whip pennant that she wore at once proclaimed her to be the property of the king. Her name was the *Scud*.

"That, then, is the vessel of Jasper!" said Mabel, who associated the master of the little craft very naturally with the cutter itself. "Are there many others on this lake?"

"The Frenchers have three: one of which, they tell me, is a real ship, such as are used on the ocean; another a brig; and a third is a cutter, like the *Scud* here, which they call the *Squirrel*, in their own tongue, however; and which seems to have a natural hatred of our own pretty boat, for Jasper seldom goes out that the *Squirrel* is not at his heels."

"And is Jasper one to run from a Frenchman, though he appears in the shape of a squirrel, and that, too, on the water?"

"Of what use would valour be without the means of turning it to account? Jasper is a brave boy, as all on this frontier know; but he has no gun except a little howitzer, and then his crew consists only of two men besides himself, and a boy. I was with him in one of his trampooses, and the youngster was risky enough, for he brought us so near the enemy that rifles began to talk; but the Frenchers carry cannon and ports, and never show their faces outside of Frontenac, without having some twenty men, besides their *Squirrel*, in their cutter. No, no; this *Scud* was built for flying, and the major says he will not put her in a fighting humour by giving her men and arms, lest she should take him at his word, and get her wings clipped."

"Ah! here is my uncle, none the worse for his swim, coming to look at this inland sea."

Sure enough, Cap, who had announced his approach by a couple of lusty hems, now made his appearance on the bastion, where, after nodding to his niece and her companion, he made a deliberate survey of the expanse of water before him.

"Well, Master Cap," asked the Pathfinder, "is it not a beautiful sheet, and fit to be named a sea?"

"Just as I expected. A pond in dimensions, and a scuttle-butt in taste. I knew it would turn out just in this way. But what is this thing anchored here under the hill?"

"That is the cutter of Jasper, Uncle," said Mabel hurriedly; "and a very pretty vessel I think it is."

"Ay, it will do well enough for a lake, perhaps, but it's no great affair. The lad has got a standing bowsprit, and who ever saw a cutter with a standing bowsprit before?"

"But may there not be some good reason for it, on a lake like this, Uncle?"

"Sure enough—I must remember this is not the ocean, though it does look so much like it."

"Ah, Uncle! then Ontario does look like the ocean after all?"

"In your eyes, I mean, and those of Pathfinder; not in the least in mine, Magnet. Now you might set me down out yonder, in the middle of this bit of a pond, and that, too, in the darkest night that ever fell from the heavens, and in the smallest canoe, and I could tell you it was only a lake. For that matter, the *Dorothy* would find it out as quick as I could myself. And Jasper sails that boat? I must have a cruise with the lad, Magnet, before I quit you, just for the name of the thing. It would never do to say I got in sight of this pond, and went away without taking a trip on it."

"Well, you needn't wait long for that," returned Pathfinder; "for the Sergeant is about to embark with a party, to relieve a post among the Thousand Islands; and as I heard him say he intended that Mabel should go along, you can join company too."

"Is this true, Magnet?"

"I believe it is," returned the girl, a flush so imperceptible as to escape the observation of her companions glowing on her cheeks; "but here comes Father, and you can enquire of himself."

Notwithstanding his humble rank, there was something in the mien and character of Sergeant Dunham that commanded respect: of a tall, imposing figure, grave and saturnine disposition, and accurate and precise in his acts and manner of thinking, even Cap, dogmatical and supercilious as he usually was with landsmen, did not presume to take the same liberties with the old soldier as he did with his other friends. It is no wonder, then, that the announcement of Mabel put a sudden termination to the singular dialogue we have just related, though it had been often observed that the Pathfinder was the only man on that frontier, beneath the condition of a gentleman, who presumed to treat the Sergeant at all as an equal, or even with the cordial familiarity of a friend.

"Good morrow, brother Cap," said the Sergeant, giving the
military salute, as he walked, in a grave, stately manner, on
the bastion. "My morning duty has made me seem forgetful
of you and Mabel, but we have now an hour or two to spare,
and to get acquainted. Do you not perceive, brother, a strong
likeness in the girl to her we have so long lost?"

"Mabel is the image of her mother, Sergeant, as I have always
said, with a little of your firmer figure; though, for that matter,
the Caps were never wanting in spring and activity."

"You have taken a long and troublesome journey, brother,
on my account; and we will try to make you comfortable while
you stay among us."

"I hear you are likely to receive orders to lift your anchor,
Sergeant, and to shift your berth into a part of the world where
they say there are a thousand islands!"

"We shall embark a relief party," replied the Sergeant, "shortly
for a post on the lake, though I do not say it is for the Thousand
Islands, and I may have to go with it; in which case I intend to
take Mabel to make my broth for me; and I hope, brother, you
will not despise a soldier's fare for a month or so."

"That will depend on the manner of marching. I have no love
for woods and swamps."

"We shall sail in the *Scud*; and, indeed, the whole service,
which is no stranger to us, is likely enough to please one accustomed to the water."

"Ay, to salt water if you will, but not to lake water. If you
have no person to handle that bit of a cutter for you, I have no
objection to ship for the v'y'ge, notwithstanding; though I shall
look on the whole affair as so much time thrown away, for I
consider it an imposition to call sailing about this pond going
to sea."

"Jasper is every way able to manage the *Scud*, brother Cap;
and in that light I cannot say that we have need of your services,
though we shall be glad of your company. You cannot return to
the settlements until a party is sent in, and that is not likely
to happen until after my return. Well, Pathfinder, this is the
first time I ever knew men on the trail of the Mingos, and
you not at their head."

"To be honest with you, Sergeant," returned the guide, not
without a little awkwardness of manner, and a perceptible difference in the hue of a face that had become so uniformly red by
exposure, "I have not felt that it was my gift this morning.

In the first place, I very well know that the soldiers of the 55th are not the lads to overtake Iroquois in the woods; and the knaves did not wait to be surrounded when they knew that Jasper had reached the garrison. Besides, the Sarpent is out with them; and if the miscreants are to be found at all, you may trust to his inmity and sight. He loves the skulking vagabonds as little as myself; and so I thought I would play idler once in my life."

"And no one has a better right, if long and faithful service entitles a man to a furlough," returned the Sergeant kindly "Mabel will think none the worse of you for preferring her company to the trail of the savages; and, I dare say, will be happy to give you a part of her breakfast if you are inclined to eat. You must not think, girl, however, that the Pathfinder is in the habit of letting prowlers around the fort beat a retreat without hearing the crack of his rifle."

"If I thought she did, Sergeant, I would shoulder Killdeer and quit the garrison before her pretty eyes had time to frown. No, Mabel knows me better, for there has been no want of Mingos to enliven the short march we have already made in company."

"It would need a great deal of testimony, Pathfinder, to make me think ill of you in any way, and more than all in the way you mention," returned Mabel. "Both father and daughter, I believe, owe you their lives, and believe me, that neither will ever forget it."

"Thank you, Mabel. But I will not take advantage of your ignorance neither, girl, and therefore shall say, I do not think the Mingos would have hurt a hair of your head, had they succeeded by their contrivances in getting you into their hands."

"And why should I suppose that enemies, known to spare neither women nor children, would have shown more mercy to me than to another? I feel, Pathfinder, that I owe you my life."

"I say nay, Mabel; they wouldn't have had the heart to hurt you. Bad as I suspect the vampires to be, I do not suspect them of anything so wicked as that. They might have wished you, nay, forced you to become the wife of one of their chiefs, and that would be torment enough to a Christian young woman; but beyond that I do not think even the Mingos themselves would have gone."

"Well, then, I shall owe my escape from this great misfortune to you," said Mabel, taking his hard hand into her own frankly and cordially. "To me it would be a lighter evil to be killed than to become the wife of an Indian."

"That is her gift, Sergeant," exclaimed Pathfinder, turning to his old comrade with gratification written on every lineament of his honest countenance, "and it will have its way. That is the gift of a young woman born of Christian parents, and it ought to be maintained."

"You are right, Pathfinder; and so far as Mabel Dunham is concerned it *shall* be maintained. But it is time to break your fasts; and if you will follow me, brother Cap, I will show you how we poor soldiers live here on a distant frontier."

CHAPTER IX

THE table of Sergeant Dunham, as a matter of course, partook of the abundance and luxuries of the frontier, as well as of its privations. A delicious broiled salmon smoked on a homely platter, hot venison steaks sent up their appetizing odours, and several dishes of cold meats, all of which were composed of game, had been set before the guests, in honour of the newly-arrived visitors, and in vindication of the old soldier's hospitality.

"You do not seem to be on short allowance in this quarter of the world, Sergeant," said Cap; "your salmon might satisfy a Scotsman."

"It fails to do it, notwithstanding, brother Cap; for among two or three hundred of the fellows that we have in this garrison, there are not half a dozen who will not swear that the fish is unfit to be eaten."

"Ay, that is Christian natur'," put in Pathfinder; "and I must say it is none to its credit. Now, a redskin never repines, but is always thankful for the food he gets, whether it be fat or lean, venison or bear, wild turkey's breast or wild goose's wing."

"It is so with the 55th, as I can answer, though I cannot say as much for their Christianity," returned the Sergeant. "Even the major himself, old Duncan of Lundie, will sometimes swear that an oatmeal cake is better fare than the Oswego bass. "I hope, brother Cap, that bit of a cold roasted pig is to your mind; you seem to fancy the food."

"Ay, ay; give me civilized grub if I must eat," returned the seaman. "Venison is well enough for your inland sailors, but we of the ocean like a little of that which we understand."

Here Pathfinder laid down his knife and fork, and indulged in a hearty laugh; then he asked, with a little curiosity in his manner:

"Don't you miss the skin, Master Cap?"

"It would have been better for its jacket, I think myself, Pathfinder; but I suppose it is a fashion of the woods to serve up shoats in this style."

"Well, a man may go round the 'arth and not know everything. If you had had the skinning of that pig, Master Cap, it would have left you sore hands. The creetur' is a hedgehog."

"Hang me, if I thought it wholesome natural pork!" returned Cap. "But then I believed even a pig might lose some of its good qualities up in the woods."

"If the skinning of it, brother, does not fall to my duty. Pathfinder, I hope you didn't find Mabel disobedient on the march?"

"Not she. If Mabel is only half as well satisfied with Jasper and Pathfinder as the Pathfinder and Jasper are satisfied with her, Sergeant, we shall be friends for the remainder of our days."

As the guide spoke, he turned his eyes towards the blushing girl, with a sort of innocent desire to know her opinion; and then, with an inborn delicacy, which proved he was far superior to the vulgar desire to invade the sanctity of feminine feeling, he looked at his plate, and seemed to regret his own boldness.

"Well, we must remember that women are not men, my friend," resumed the Sergeant, "and make proper allowances for nature and education."

"Uncle," said Mabel, "if you have breakfasted, I will thank you to go out upon the bastion with me again. We have neither of us half seen the lake, and it would be hardly seemly for a young woman to be walking about the fort, the first day of her arrival, quite alone."

Cap understood the motive of Mabel; and accordingly accompanied his niece, leaving Sergeant Dunham and his friend, the Pathfinder, alone together. As soon as the sailor had beat a retreat, the Sergeant turned to his companion, and, with a smile, remarked:

"Well, my friend, how do you like the girl?"

"You have reason to be proud of her, Sergeant. I have seen many of her sex, and some that were great and beautiful; but never before did I meet with one in whom I thought Providence had so well balanced the different gifts."

"And the good opinion, I can tell you, Pathfinder, is mutual. She told me last night all about your coolness, and spirit, and kindness—particularly the last, for kindness counts for more than half with females, my friend—and the first inspection seems to give satisfaction on both sides. Brush up the uniform, and pay a little more attention to the outside, Pathfinder, and you will have the girl heart and hand."

"Nay, Sergeant, I've forgotten nothing that you have told me, and grudge no reasonable pains to make myself as pleasant in the eyes of Mabel as she is getting to be in mine. I cleaned and brightened up Killdeer this morning as soon as the sun rose; and, in my judgment, the piece never looked better than it does at this very moment."

"That is according to your hunting notions, Pathfinder; but firearms should sparkle and glitter in the sun, and I never yet could see any beauty in a clouded barrel."

"Lord Howe thought otherwise, Sergeant; and he was accounted a good soldier."

"Very true; his lordship had all the barrels of his regiment darkened, and what good came of it? You can see his 'scutcheon hanging in the English Church at Albany. Had you much discourse with Mabel, Pathfinder, as you came along in the canoe?"

"There was not much opportunity, Sergeant, and then I found myself so much beneath her in idees, that I was afraid to speak of much beyond what belonged to my own gifts."

"Therein you are partly right and partly wrong, my friend. Women love trifling discourse, though they like to have most of it to themselves. Dignity is commanding and useful, and there is no getting on without it, as respects the men; but if you would be thoroughly esteemed by a woman, it is necessary to condescend a little on occasions."

"Ah's me, Sergeant, I sometimes fear it will never do."

"Why do you think so discouragingly of a matter on which I thought both our minds were made up?"

"We did agree, if Mabel should prove what you told me she was, and if the girl could fancy a rude hunter and guide, that I should quit some of my wandering ways, and try to humanize my mind down to a wife and children. But since I have seen the girl, I will own that many misgivings have come over me."

"How's this?" interrupted the Sergeant sternly; "did I not

understand you to say that you were pleased?—and is Mabel a young woman to disappoint expectation?"

"Ah, Sergeant, it is not Mabel that I distrust, but myself. I am but a poor ignorant woodsman, after all; and perhaps I'm not, in truth, as good as even you and I may think me."

"If you doubt your own judgment of yourself, Pathfinder, I beg you will not doubt mine. Am I not accustomed to judge men's character? and am I often deceived? Ask Major Duncan, sir, if you desire any assurances in this particular."

"But, Sergeant, we have long been friends; have fi't side by side a dozen times, and have done each other many services. When this is the case, men are apt to think over kindly of each other; and I fear me that the daughter may not be so likely to view a plain ignorant hunter as favourably as the father does."

"Tut, tut, Pathfinder; you don't know yourself, man, and may put all faith in my judgment. In the first place you have experience; and, as all girls must want that, no prudent young woman would overlook such a qualification. Then you are not one of the coxcombs that strut about when they first join a regiment; but a man who has seen service, and who carries the marks of it on his person and countenance. I dare say you have been under fire some thirty or forty times, counting all the skirmishes and ambushes that you've seen."

"All of that, Sergeant, all of that; but what will it avail in gaining the goodwill of a tender-hearted young female?"

"It will gain the day. Experience in the field is as good in love as in war. But you are as honest-hearted and as loyal a subject as the king can boast of—God bless him!"

"That may be too; but I'm afeard I'm too rude and too old and too wild like to suit the fancy of such a young and delicate girl as Mabel, who has been unused to our wilderness ways, and may think the settlements better suited to her gifts and inclinations."

"These are new misgivings for you, my friend; and I wonder they were never paraded before."

"Because I never knew my own worthlessness, perhaps, until I saw Mabel. I do wish, Sergeant, that I was ten years younger, more comely to look at, and better suited to please a handsome young woman's fancy."

"Cheer up, my brave friend, and trust to a father's knowledge of womankind. Mabel half loves you already, and a fortnight's intercourse and kindness, down among the islands yonder, will close ranks with the other half. The girl as much as told me this herself last night."

"Can this be so, Sergeant?" said the guide, whose meek and modest nature shrank from viewing himself in colours so favourable. "Can this be truly so? Do you think the girl will consent to quit all her beloved settlement usages, and her visitings and church-goings, to dwell with a plain guide and hunter up hereaway in the woods? Will she not, in the end, crave her old ways, and a better man."

"A better man, Pathfinder, would be hard to find," returned the father. "As for town usages, they are soon forgotten in the freedom of the forest, and Mabel has just spirit enough to dwell on a frontier. I've not planned the marriage, my friend, without thinking it over, as a general does his campaign. At first I thought of bringing you into the regiment, that you might succeed me when I retire, which must be sooner or later; but on reflection, Pathfinder, I think you are scarcely fitted for the office. Still, if not a soldier in all the meanings of the word, you are a soldier in its best meaning, and I know that you have the goodwill of every officer in the corps. As long as I live Mabel can dwell with me, and you will always have a home when you return from your scoutings and marches."

"This is very pleasant to think of, Sergeant, if the girl can only come into our wishes with goodwill. But it does not seem that one like myself can ever be agreeable in her handsome eyes. If I were younger, and more comely, now, as Jasper Western is, for instance, there might be a chance."

"That for Jasper Eau-douce, and every younker of them in or about the fort!" returned the Sergeant, snapping his fingers. "If not actually younger, you are a younger-looking, ay, and a better-looking man than the *Scud's* master——"

"Anan?" said Pathfinder, looking up at his companion with an expression of doubt, as if he did not understand his meaning.

"I say if not actually younger in days and years, you look more hardy and like whipcord than Jasper, or any of them; and there will be more of you, thirty years hence, than of all of them put together. A good conscience will keep one like you a mere boy all his life."

"Jasper has as clear a conscience as any youth I know, Sergeant, and is as likely to wear on that account as any man in the colony."

"Then you are my friend," squeezing the other's hand,—"my tried, sworn, and constant friend."

"Yes, we have been friends, Sergeant, near twenty years, before Mabel was born."

"True enough; before Mabel was born we were well-tried friends; and the hussy would never dream of refusing to marry a man who was her father's friend before she was born."

"We don't know, Sergeant. Like loves like. The young prefer the young for companions, and the old the old."

"Not for wives, Pathfinder; I never knew an old man who had an objection to a young wife. Then you are respected and esteemed by every officer of the fort, and it will please her fancy to like a man that everyone else likes."

"I hope I have no enemies but the Mingos," returned the guide. "I've *tried* to do right, and that ought to make friends, though it sometimes fails."

"And you may be said to keep the best company; for even old Duncan of Lundie is glad to see you, and you pass hours in his society."

"Ay, even greater than he is have marched by my side for days, and have conversed with me as if I were their brother; but the woods often bring men to a level who would not be so in the settlements."

"And you are known to be the greatest rifle shot that ever pulled trigger in all this region."

"If Mabel could fancy a man for that, I might have no great reason to despair; and yet, Sergeant, I sometimes think that it is all as much owing to Killdeer as to any skill of my own."

"That is your own humble opinion of yourself, Pathfinder; but we have seen too many fail with the same weapon, and you succeed too often with the rifles of other men to allow me to agree with you. We will get up a shooting match in a day or two, when you can show your skill, and when Mabel will form some judgment concerning your true character."

"Will that be fair, Sergeant? Everybody knows that Killdeer seldom misses; and ought we to make a trial of this sort when we all know what must be the result?"

"Tut, tut, man! I foresee I must do half this courting for you. For one who is always inside of the smoke in a skirmish, you are the faintest-hearted suitor I ever met with."

Here the Sergeant arose, and proceeded to attend to his never-ceasing duties, without apology; the terms on which the guide

stood with all in the garrison rendering the freedom quite a
matter of course.

The reader will have gathered from the conversation just related, one of the plans that Sergeant Dunham had in view in
causing his daughter to be brought to the frontier. In making
this choice, he had not been as much governed by a clear and
judicious view of the merits of the individual, perhaps, as by
his own likings; still no one knew the Pathfinder so intimately
as himself, without always conceding to the honest guide a high
place in his esteem on account of his many virtues. That his
daughter could find any serious objections to the match the old
soldier did not apprehend; while, on the other hand, he saw
many advantages to himself in dim perspective, connected with
the decline of his days, and an evening of life passed among
descendants who were equally dear to him through both parents.
He had first made the proposition to his friend, who had listened
to it kindly, but who, the Sergeant was now pleased to find,
already betrayed a willingness to come into his own views that
was proportioned to the doubts and misgivings proceeding from
his humble distrust of himself.

CHAPTER X

A week passed in the usual routine of a garrison. Mabel was
becoming used to a situation that, at first, she had found not
only novel, but a little irksome; and the officers and men in
their turn, gradually familiarized to the presence of a young and
blooming girl, whose attire and carriage had that air of modest
gentility about them which she had obtained in the family of
her patroness, annoyed her less by their ill-concealed admiration,
while they gratified her by the respect which, she was fain to
think, they paid her on account of her father; but which, in
truth, was more to be attributed to her own modest but spirited
deportment, than to any deference for the worthy Sergeant.

Acquaintances made in a forest, or in any circumstances of
unusual excitement, soon attain their limits. Mabel found one
week's residence at Oswego sufficient to determine her as to those
with whom she might be intimate and those whom she ought
to avoid. The sort of neutral position occupied by her father,
who was not an officer, while he was so much more than a

common soldier, by keeping her aloof from the two great classes of military life, lessened the number of those whom she was compelled to know, and made the duty of decision comparatively easy. Still she soon discovered that there were a few, even among those that could aspire to a seat at the Commandant's table, who were disposed to overlook the halbert for the novelty of a well-turned figure and of a pretty winning face; and by the end of the first two or three days she had admirers even among the gentlemen. The Quartermaster, in particular, a middle-aged soldier, who had more than once tried the blessings of matrimony already, but was now a widower, was evidently disposed to increase his intimacy with the Sergeant, though their duties often brought them together; and the youngsters among his messmates did not fail to note that this man of method, who was a Scotsman of the name of Muir, was much more frequent in his visits to the quarters of his subordinate than had formerly been his wont. A laugh, or a joke, in honour of the "Sergeant's daughter", however, limited their strictures; though "Mabel Dunham" was soon a toast that even the ensign, or the lieutenant, did not disdain to give.

At the end of the week Duncan of Lundie sent for Sergeant Dunham, after evening rollcall, on business of a nature that, it was understood, required a personal conference. The old veteran dwelt in a movable hut, which, being placed on trucks, he could order to be wheeled about at pleasure, sometimes living in one part of the area within the fort, and sometimes in another. On the present occasion he had made a halt near the centre; and there he was found by his subordinate, who was admitted to his presence without any delay or dancing attendance in an antechamber. In point of fact, there was very little difference in the quality of the accommodations allowed to the officers and those allowed to the men, the former being merely granted the most room.

"Walk in, Sergeant, walk in," said old Lundie heartily, as his inferior stood in a respectful attitude at the door;—"walk in, and take a seat on that stool. I have sent for you, man, to discuss anything but rosters and pay-rolls this evening. It is now many years since we have been comrades, and 'auld lang syne' should count for something, even between a major and his orderly, a Scot and a Yankee. Sit ye down, man, and just put yourself at your ease. It has been a fine day, Sergeant."

"It has indeed, Major Duncan," returned the other, who, though he complied so far as to take the seat, was much too practised not to understand the degree of respect it was necessary to maintain in his manner; "a very fine day, sir, it has been, and we may look for more of them at this season."

"I hope so with all my heart. The crops look well as it is, man, and you'll be finding that the 55th make almost as good farmers as soldiers. I never saw better potatoes in Scotland than we are likely to have in that new patch of ours."

"They promise a good yield, Major Duncan; and, in that light, a more comfortable winter than the last."

"Life is progressive, Sergeant, in its comforts as well as in its need of them. We grow old, and I begin to think it time to retire and settle in life. I feel that my working days are nearly over."

"The king, God bless him! sir, has much good service in your honour yet."

"It may be so, Sergeant Dunham, especially if he should happen to have a spare lieutenant-colonelcy left."

"The 55th will be honoured the day that commission is given to Duncan of Lundie, sir."

"And Duncan of Lundie will be honoured the day he receives it. But, Sergeant, if you have never had a lieutenant-colonelcy, you have had a good wife, and that is the next think to rank in making a man happy."

"I have been married, Major Duncan; but it is now a long time since I have had no drawback on the love I bear his majesty and my duty."

"What, man! not even the love you bear that active, little, round-limbed, rosy-cheeked daughter that I have seen in the fort these last few days? Out upon you, Sergeant! old fellow as I am, I could almost love that little lassie myself, and send the lieutenant-colonelcy to the devil."

"We all know where Major Duncan's heart is, and that is in Scotland, where a beautiful lady is ready and willing to make him happy, as soon as his own sense of duty shall permit."

"Ay, hope is ever a far-off thing, Sergeant," returned the superior, a shade of melancholy passing over his hard Scottish features as he spoke; "and bonnie Scotland is a far-off country. Well, if we have no heather and oatmeal in this region, we have venison for the killing of it and salmon as plenty as at Berwick-upon-Tweed. Is it true, Sergeant, that the men complain of having been over-venisoned and over-pigeoned of late?"

"Not for some weeks, Major Duncan, for neither deer nor birds are so plenty at this season as they have been. They begin to throw their remarks about concerning the salmon, but I trust we shall get through the summer without any serious disturbance on the score of food. The Scotch in the battalion do, indeed, talk more than is prudent of their want of oatmeal, grumbling occasionally of our wheaten bread."

"Ah, that is human nature, Sergeant! pure, unadulterated Scotch human nature. A cake, man, to say the truth, is an agreeable morsel, and I often see the time when I pine for a bite myself."

"If the feeling gets to be troublesome, Major Duncan, I would humbly recommend that some oatmeal be imported, or prepared in this country for them, and I think we shall hear no more of it. A very little would answer for a cure, sir."

"You are a wag, Sergeant; but hang me if I am sure you are not right. There may be sweeter things in this world, after all, than oatmeal. You have a sweet daughter, Dunham, for one."

"The girl is like her mother, Major Duncan, and will pass inspection," said the Sergeant proudly.

"That would she, I'll answer for it. Well, I may as well come to the point at once, man, and bring up my reserve into the front of the battle. Here is Davy Muir, the quartermaster, disposed to make your daughter his wife, and he has just got me to open the matter to you, being fearful of compromising his own dignity; and I may as well add that half the youngsters in the fort toast her, and talk of her from morning till night."

"She is much honoured, sir," returned the father stiffly; "but I trust the gentlemen will find something more worthy of them to talk about ere long. I hope to see her the wife of an honest man before many weeks, sir."

"Yes, Davy is an honest man, and that is more than can be said for all in the quartermaster's department, I'm thinking, Sergeant," returned Lundie, with a slight smile. "Well, then, may I tell the Cupid-stricken youth that the matter is as good as settled?"

"I thank your honour; but Mabel is betrothed to another."

"What? Already! That will produce a stir in the fort; though I'm not sorry to hear it either, for, to be frank with you, Sergeant, I'm no great admirer of unequal matches."

"I think with your honour, and have no desire to see my daughter an officer's lady. If she can get as high as her mother was before her, it ought to satisfy any reasonable woman."

"And may I ask, Sergeant, who is the lucky man that you intend to call son-in-law?"

"The Pathfinder, your honour."

"Pathfinder!"

"The same, Major Duncan; and in naming him to you I give you his whole history. No one is better known on this frontier than my honest, brave, true-hearted friend."

"All that is true enough; but is he, after all, the sort of person to make a girl of twenty happy?"

"Why not, your honour? The man is at the head of his calling. There is no other guide or scout connected with the army who has half the reputation of Pathfinder, or who deserves to have it half as well."

"Very true, Sergeant; but is the reputation of a scout exactly the sort of renown to captivate a girl's fancy?"

"Talking of girls' fancies, sir, is in my humble opinion much like talking of a recruit's judgment. If we were to take the movements of the awkward squad, sir, as a guide, we should never form a decent line in battalion, Major Duncan."

"But your daughter has nothing awkward about her; for a genteeler girl of her class could not be found in old Albion itself. Is she of your way of thinking in this matter?—though I suppose she must be, as you say she is betrothed."

"We have not yet conversed on the subject, your honour; but I consider her mind as good as made up, from several little circumstances which might be named."

"And what are these circumstances, Sergeant?" asked the Major, who began to take more interest than he had at first felt on the subject. "I confess a little curiosity to know something about a woman's mind, being, as you know, a bachelor myself."

"Why, your honour, when I speak of the Pathfinder to the girl, she always looks me full in the face; chimes in with everything I say in his favour, and has a frank, open way with her, which says as much as if she half considered him already as a husband."

"Hum! and these signs, you think, Dunham, are faithful tokens of your daughter's feelings?"

"I do, your honour, for they strike me as natural."

"Is there not some material difference in the age of the intended bridegroom and that of his pretty bride, Sergeant?"

"You are quite right, sir; Pathfinder is well advanced towards forty, and Mabel has every prospect of happiness that a young woman can derive from the certainty of possessing an experienced husband. I was quite forty myself, your honour, when I married her mother."

"But will your daughter be as likely to admire a green hunting-shirt, such as that our worthy guide wears, with a fox-skin cap, as the smart uniform of the 55th?"

"Perhaps not, sir; and therefore she will have the merit of self-denial, which always makes a young woman wiser and better."

"And are you not afraid that she may be left a widow while still a young woman? What between wild beasts, and wilder savages, Pathfinder may be said to carry his life in his hand."

"'Every bullet has its billet', Lundie," for so the Major was fond of being called in his moments of condescension, and when not engaged in military affairs; "and no man in the 55th can call himself beyond or above the chances of sudden death. In that particular, Mabel would gain nothing by a change. Besides, sir, if I may speak freely on such a subject, I much doubt if ever Pathfinder dies in battle, or by any of the sudden chances of the wilderness."

"And why so, Sergeant?" asked the Major. "He is a soldier, so far as danger is concerned, and one that is much more than usually exposed; and, being free of his person, why should he expect to escape when others do not?"

"I do not believe, your honour, that the Pathfinder considers his own chances better than anyone's else, but the man will never die by a bullet. I have seen him so often handling his rifle with as much composure as if it were a shepherd's crook, in the midst of the heaviest showers of bullets, and under so many extraordinary circumstances, that I do not think Providence means he should ever fall in that manner. And yet, if there be a man in his Majesty's dominions who really deserves such a death, it is Pathfinder."

"We never know, Sergeant," returned Lundie, with a countenance grave with thought; "and the less we say about it, perhaps, the better. But will your daughter be as willing to accept one who, after all, is a mere hanger-on of the army, as to take one from the service itself? There is no hope of promotion for the guide, Sergeant?"

"He is at the head of his corps already, your honour. In short, Mabel has made up her mind on this subject; and, as your honour has had the condescension to speak to me about Mr Muir, I trust you will be kind enough to say that the girl is as good as billeted for life."

"Well, this is your own matter, and now—Sergeant Dunham!"

"Your honour," said the other, rising, and giving the customary salute.

"You have been told it is my intention to send you down among the Thousand Islands for the next month. All the old subalterns have had their tours of duty in that quarter—all that I like to trust at least; and it has at length come to your turn. Lieutenant Muir, it is true, claims his right; but being quartermaster I do not like to break up well-established arrangements. Are the men drafted?"

"Everything is ready, your honour. The draft is made, and I understood that the canoe which got in last night brought a message to say that the party already below is looking out for the relief."

"It did; and you must sail the day after to-morrow, if not to-morrow night. It will be wise, perhaps, to sail in the dark."

"So Jasper thinks, Major Duncan; and I know no one more to be depended on in such an affair than young Western."

"Young Jasper Eau-douce!" said Lundie, a slight smile gathering around his usually stern mouth. "Will that lad be of your party, Sergeant?"

"Your honour will remember that the *Scud* never quits port without him."

"True; but all general rules have their exceptions. Have I not seen a seafaring person about the fort within the last few days?"

"No doubt, your honour; it is Master Cap, a brother-in-law of mine, who brought my daughter from below."

"Why not put him in the *Scud* for this cruise, Sergeant, and leave Jasper behind? Your brother-in-law would like the variety of a freshwater cruise, and you would enjoy more of his company."

"I intended to ask your honour's permission to take him along; but he must go as a volunteer. Jasper is too brave a lad to be turned out of his command without a reason, Major Duncan; and I'm afraid brother Cap despises fresh water too much to do duty on it."

"Quite right, Sergeant, and I leave all this to your own discretion. Eau-douce must retain his command, on second thoughts. You intend that Pathfinder shall also be of the party?"

"If your honour approves of it. There will be service for both the guides, the Indian as well as the white man."

"I think you are right. Remember, the post is to be destroyed and abandoned when your command is withdrawn. It will have done its work by that time, or we shall have failed entirely, and it is too ticklish a position to be maintained unnecessarily."

Sergeant Dunham gave the customary salute, turned on his heels as if they had been pivots, and had got the door nearly drawn to after him, when he was suddenly recalled.

"I had forgotten, Sergeant, the young officers have begged for a shooting-match, and to-morrow has been named for the day. All competitors will be admitted, and the prizes will be a silver-mounted powder-horn, a leathern flask ditto," reading from a piece of paper, "as I see by the professional jargon of this bill, and a silk calash for a lady. The latter is to enable the victor to show his gallantry by making an offering of it to her he best loves."

"All very agreeable, your honour, at least to him that succeeds. Is the Pathfinder to be permitted to enter?"

"I do not see how he can be excluded, if he choose to come forward. Latterly, I have observed that he takes no share in these sports, probably from a conviction of his own unequalled skill."

"That's it, Major Duncan; the honest fellow knows there is not a man on the frontier who can equal him, and he does not wish to spoil the pleasure of others. I think we may trust to his delicacy in anything, sir. Perhaps it may be as well to let him have his own way?"

"In this instance we must, Sergeant. Whether he will be as successful in all others remains to be seen. I wish you good evening, Dunham."

The Sergeant now withdrew, leaving Duncan of Lundie to his own thoughts. Half an hour might have passed, when a tap at the door was answered by a direction to enter. A middle-aged man, in the dress of an officer, but whose uniform wanted the usual smartness of the profession, made his appearance, and was saluted as "Mr. Muir".

"I have come, sir, at your bidding, to know my fortune," said the Quartermaster in a strong Scotch accent, as soon as he had taken the seat which was proffered to him. "To say the truth to you, Major Duncan, this girl is making as much havoc in the garrison as the French did before Ty: I never witnessed so general a rout in so short a time."

"Surely, Davy, you don't mean to persuade me that your young and unsophisticated heart is in such a flame, after one week's ignition? Why, man, this is worse than the affair in Scotland, where it was said the heat within was so intense that it just burnt a hole through your own precious body, and left a place for all the lassies to peer in at, to see what the combustible material was worth."

"Ye'll have your own way, Major Duncan; and your father and mother would have theirs before ye, even if the enemy were in the camp. But I will just ask if you did me the favour to speak to the Sergeant on the trifling affair?"

"I did, David; and am sorry to say, for your hopes, that I see no great chance of your succeeding."

"Not succeeding! An officer, and a quartermaster in the bargain, and not succeed with a sergeant's daughter!"

"It's just that, Davy."

"And why not, Lundie? Will ye have the goodness to answer just that?"

"The girl is betrothed. Hand plighted, word passed, love pledged—no, hang me if I believe that either; but she is betrothed."

"Well, that's an obstacle, it must be avowed, Major, though it counts for little if the heart is free."

"Quite true; and I think it probable the heart is free in this case; for the intended husband appears to be the choice of the father rather than of the daughter."

"And who may it be, Major?" asked the Quartermaster. "I do not recollect any plausible suitor that is likely to stand in my way."

"No, *you* are the only *plausible* suitor on the frontier, Davy. The happy man is Pathfinder."

"Pathfinder, Major Duncan!"

"No more, nor any less, David Muir. Pathfinder is the man."

"I thought as much!" exclaimed the Quartermaster, drawing a long breath. "But I do not think it possible I can be deceived as to the young woman's inclinations, which I think I may boldly pronounce to be altogether above the condition of Pathfinder. As for the individual himself—why, time will show."

"Now, tell me frankly, Davy Muir," said Lundie, stopping short in his walk, "do you really suppose a girl like the daughter of Sergeant Dunham can take a serious fancy to a man of your years and appearance, and experience, I might add?"

"Hout, awa', Lundie! ye dinna know the sax, and that's the reason yer unmarried in yer forty-fifth year."

"And what may be *your* age, Lieutenant Muir, if I may presume to ask so delicate a question?"

"Forty-seven; and if I get Mabel, there'll be just a wife for every twa lustrums. But I didna think Sergeant Dunham would be so humble-minded as to dream of giving that sweet lass of his to one like the Pathfinder."

"There's no dream about it, Davy; the man is as serious as a soldier about to be flogged."

"Well, Major, we are auld friends, and ought to know how to take and give a joke, off duty. It is possible the worthy man has not understood my hints, or he never would have thought of such a thing. The difference between an officer's consort and a guide's woman is as vast as that between the antiquity of Scotland and the antiquity of America. I'm auld blood too, Lundie."

"Take my word for it, Davy, your antiquity will do you no good in this affair; and as for your blood it is not older than your bones. Well, ye know the Sergeant's answer; and so ye perceive that my influence, on which ye counted so much, can do nought for ye."

"I'm infinitely obliged to you, Major, for this and all your other acts of friendship; and if you could but add another, I should think you had not altogether forgotten the playfellow of your boyhood."

"Well, Davy, if the request be reasonable, and such as a superior ought to grant, out with it, man."

"If ye could only contrive a little service for me, down among the Thousand Isles, for a fortnight or so, I think this matter might be settled to the satisfaction of all parties. Remember, Lundie, the lassie is the only marriageable white female on this frontier."

"There is always duty for one in your line at a post, however small; but this below can be done by the Sergeant as well as by the Quartermaster-general, and better, too."

"But not better than by a regimental officer. There is great waste, in common, among the orderlies."

"I'll think of it, Muir," said the Major, laughing, "and you shall have my answer in the morning. Here will be a fine occasion, man, the morrow, to show yourself off before the lady; you are expert with the rifle, and prizes are to be won. Make up your mind to display your skill, and who knows what may yet happen before the *Scud* sails."

"I'm thinking most of the young men will try their hands in this sport, Major!"

"That will they, and some of the old ones too, if you appear. To keep you in countenance, I'll try a shot or two myself, Davy; and you know I have some name that way."

"It might, indeed, do good. The female heart, Major Duncan, is susceptible in many different modes, and sometimes in a way that the rules of philosophy might reject. Some require a suitor to sit down before them, as it might be, in a regular siege, and only capitulate when the place can hold out no longer; others, again, like to be carried by storm; while there are hussies who can only be caught by leading them into an ambush. The first is the most creditable and officerlike process, perhaps; but I must say I think the last the most pleasing."

"An opinion formed from experience, out of all question. And what of the storming parties?"

"They may do for younger men, Lundie," returned the Quartermaster, rising; "every period of life has its necessities, and at forty-seven it's just as well to trust a little to the head. I wish you a very good even, Major, and freedom from gout, with a sweet and refreshing sleep."

"The same to yourself, Mr. Muir, with many thanks."

The Quartermaster withdrew, leaving Lundie to reflect on what had just passed. Use had so accustomed Major Duncan to Lieutenant Muir and all his traits and humours, that the conduct of the latter did not strike the former with the same force as it will probably the reader.

CHAPTER XI

IT was now September, a month in which the strong gales of the coast often appear to force themselves across the country as far as the great lakes, where the inland sailor sometimes feels that genial influence which characterizes the winds of the ocean invigorating his frame, cheering his spirits, and arousing his moral force. Such a day was that on which the garrison of Oswego assembled to witness what its commander had jocularly called "a passage of arms". While so earnestly bent on pleasure, however, they on whom that duty devolved did not neglect the safety of the garrison. One standing on the ramparts of the fort, and gazing on the waste of glittering water that bounded the view all along the northern horizon, and on the slumbering and seemingly boundless forest which filled the other half of the panorama, would have fancied the spot the very abode of peacefulness and security; but Duncan of Lundie too well knew that the woods might, at any moment, give up their hundreds, bent on the destruction of the fort and all it contained; and that even the treacherous lake offered a highway of easy approach by which his more civilized and scarcely less wily foes, the French, could come upon him at an unguarded moment. Parties were sent out under old and vigilant officers to scour the forest; and one entire company held the fort, under arms, with orders to maintain a vigilance as strict as if an enemy of superior force was known to be near.

The spot selected for the sports was a sort of esplanade a little west of the fort, and on the immediate bank of the lake. It had been cleared of its trees and stumps, that it might answer the purpose of a parade-ground, as it possessed the advantages of having its rear protected by the water, and one of its flanks by the works. Men drilling on it could be attacked, consequently, on two sides only; and as the cleared space beyond it, in the direction of the west and south, was large, any assailants would be compelled to quit the cover of the woods before they could make an approach sufficiently near to render them dangerous.

Although the regular arms of the regiment were muskets, some fifty rifles were produced on the present occasion. Every officer had one as a part of his private provision for amusement; many belonged to the scouts and friendly Indians, of whom more or less were always hanging about the fort; and there was a public provision of them for the use of those who followed the game with the express object of obtaining supplies. Among those who carried the weapon were some five or six who had reputation for knowing how to use it particularly well—so well, indeed, as to have given them a celebrity on the frontier; twice that number who were believed to be much better than common; and many who would have been thought expert in almost any situation but the precise one in which they now happened to be placed.

The distance was a hundred yards, and the weapon was to be used without a rest; the target, a board, with the customary circular lines in white paint, having the bull's-eye in the centre.

Most of the soldiers were Scotch, the regiment having been raised at Stirling and its vicinity not many years before, though, as in the case of Sergeant Dunham, many Americans had joined

it since its arrival in the colonies.   The provincials were generally
the most expert marksmen; and after a desultory trial of half an
hour it was necessarily conceded that a youth who had been born
in the colony of New York, and who came of Dutch extraction,
was the most expert of all who had yet tried their skill.   It was
just as this opinion prevailed that the oldest captain, accompanied
by most of the gentlemen and ladies of the fort, appeared on the
parade.   A train of some twenty females of humbler condition
followed, among whom was seen the well-turned form, intelligent,
blooming, animated countenance, and neat, becoming attire of
Mabel Dunham.

Of females who were officially recognized as belonging to the
class of ladies, there were but three in the fort, all of whom were
officers' wives; Mabel being strictly, as had been stated by the
Quartermaster, the only real candidate for matrimony among her
sex.

Some little preparation had been made for the proper reception
of the females, who were placed on a low staging of planks near
the immediate bank of the lake.   In this vicinity the prizes were
suspended from a post.   Great care was taken to reserve the front
seat of the stage for the three ladies and their children; while
Mabel and those who belonged to the non-commissioned officers
of the regiment, occupied the second.   The wives and daughters
of the privates were huddled together in the rear.   Mabel, who
had already been admitted to the society of the officers' wives on
the footing of a humble companion, was a good deal noticed by
the ladies in front.

As soon as this important portion of the spectators had got
into their places, Lundie gave orders for the trial of skill to
proceed in the manner that had been prescribed in his previous orders.   Some eight or ten of the best marksmen of the
garrison now took possession of the stand, and began to fire in
succession.   Among them were officers and men indiscriminately
placed, nor were the casual visitors in the fort excluded from the
competition.   As might have been expected of men whose amuse-
ments and comfortable subsistence equally depended on skill in
the use of their weapons, it was soon found that they were all
sufficiently expert to hit the bull's-eye, or the white spot in the
centre of the target.   Others who succeeded them, it is true, were
less sure, their bullets striking in the different circles that surrounded the centre of the target without touching it.

According to the rules of the day, none could proceed to the second trial who had failed in the first, and the adjutant of the place, who acted as marshal of the day, called upon the successful adventurers by name to get ready for the next effort, while he gave notice that those who failed to present themselves for the shot at the bull's-eye would necessarily be excluded from all the higher trials. Just at this moment Lundie, the Quartermaster, and Jasper Eau-douce appeared in the group at the stand, while the Pathfinder walked leisurely on the ground without his rifle, for him a measure so unusual as to be understood by all present as a proof that he did not consider himself a competitor for the honours of the day. All made way for Major Duncan, who, as he approached the stand in a good-humoured way, took his station, levelled his rifle carelessly, and fired. The bullet missed the required mark by several inches.

"Major Duncan is excluded from the other trials!" proclaimed the Adjutant, in a voice so strong and confident that all the elder officers and the sergeants well understood that this failure was preconcerted, while all the younger gentlemen and the privates felt new encouragement to proceed on account of the evident impartiality with which the laws of the sports were administered.

"Now, Master Eau-douce, comes your turn," said Muir; "and if you do not beat the Major, I shall say that your hand is better skilled with the oar than with the rifle."

Jasper's handsome face flushed, he stepped upon the stand, cast a hasty glance at Mabel, whose pretty form he ascertained was bending eagerly forward as if to note the result, dropped the barrel of his rifle with but little apparent care into the palm of his left hand, raised the muzzle for a single instant with exceeding steadiness, and fired. The bullet passed directly through the centre of the bull's-eye, much the best shot of the morning, since the others had merely touched the paint.

"Well performed, Master Jasper," said Muir, as soon as the result was declared; "and a shot that might have done credit to an older head and a more experienced eye. Now, Sergeant Dunham, I'll thank you to request the ladies to give a closer attention than common; for I'm about to make that use of the rifle which may be called the intellectual. Jasper would have killed, I allow; but then there would not have been half the satisfaction in receiving such a shot as in receiving one that is discharged scientifically."

All this time the Quartermaster was preparing himself for the scientific trial; but he delayed his aim until he saw that the eye

of Mabel, in common with those of her companions, was fastened
on him with curiosity. As the others left him room, out of respect
to his rank, no one stood near the competitor but his commanding
officer, to whom he now said in his familiar manner :

"Ye see, Lundie, that something is to be gained by exciting a
female's curiosity. It's an active sentiment is curiosity, and properly improved may lead to gentler innovations in the end."

"Very true, Davy; but ye keep us all waiting while ye make
your preparations; and here is Pathfinder drawing near to catch
a lesson from your greater experience."

"Well, Pathfinder, and so *you* have come to get an idea, too,
concerning the philosophy of shooting? I do not wish to hide my
light under a bushel, and yer welcome to all ye'll learn. Do ye
no' mean to try a shot yersel', man ?"

"Why should I, Quartermaster? I want none of the prizes;
and as for honour, I have had enough of that, if it's any honour
to shoot better than yourself. I'm not a woman to wear a calash."

"Very true, but ye might find a woman that is precious in your
eyes to wear it for ye, as——"

"Come, Davy," interrupted the Major, "your shot or a retreat.
The Adjutant is getting impatient."

"The Quartermaster's department and the Adjutant's department are seldom compliable, Lundie, but I'm ready. Stand a
little aside, Pathfinder, and give the ladies an opportunity."

Lieutenant Muir now took his attitude with a good deal of
studied elegance, raised his rifle slowly, lowered it, raised it again,
repeated the manœuvres, and fired.

"Missed the target altogether!" shouted the man whose duty it
was to mark the bullets, and who had little relish for the Quartermaster's tedious science. "Missed the target!"

"It cannot be!" cried Muir, his face flushing equally with
indignation and shame; "it cannot be, Adjutant; for I never did
so awkward a thing in my life. I appeal to the ladies for a juster
judgment."

"The ladies shut their eyes when you fired!" exclaimed the
regimental wags. "Your preparations alarmed them."

"I will na believe such calumny of the leddies, nor sic' a reproach
on my own skill," returned the Quartermaster; "it's a conspiracy
to rob a meritorious man of his dues."

"It's a dead miss, Muir," said the laughing Lundie, "and ye'll
jist sit down quietly with the disgrace."

"No, Major," Pathfinder observed, "the Quartermaster *is* a good shot for a slow one and a measured distance, though nothing extr'ornary for real service. He has covered Jasper's bullet, as will be seen, if anyone will take the trouble to examine the target."

The respect for Pathfinder's skill and for his quickness and accuracy of sight was so profound and general, that, the instant he made this declaration, the spectators began to distrust their own opinions, and a dozen rushed to the target in order to ascertain the fact. There, sure enough, it was found that the Quartermaster's bullet had gone through the hole made by Jasper's, and that, too, so accurately as to require a minute examination to be certain of the circumstance.

"I told ye, ladies, ye were about to witness the influence of science on gunnery," said the Quartermaster, advancing towards the staging occupied by the females. "Major Duncan derides the idea of mathematics entering into target-shooting; but I tell him philosophy colours, and improves, and explains everything that belongs to human life, whether it be a shooting-match or a sermon. In a word, philosophy is philosophy, and that is saying all that the subject requires."

"I trust you exclude love from the catalogue," observed the wife of a captain who knew the history of the Quartermaster's marriages; "it seems that philosophy has little in common with love."

"You wouldn't say that, madam, if your heart had experienced many trials. It's the man or the woman that has had many occasions to improve the affections that can best speak of such matters; and, believe me, of all love, philosophical is the most lasting, as it is the most rational."

"You would then recommend experience as an improvement on the passion?"

"Your quick mind has conceived the idea at a glance. The happiest marriages are those in which youth and beauty and confidence on one side, rely on the sagacity, moderation, and prudence of years—middle age, I mean, madam, for I'll no' deny that there is such a thing as a husband's being too old for a wife. Here is Sergeant Dunham's charming daughter now, to approve of such sentiments, I am certain."

"Sergeant Dunham's daughter is scarcely a fitting interlocutor in a discourse between you and me, Lieutenant Muir," rejoined the captain's lady; "and yonder is the Pathfinder about to take his chance, by way of changing the subject,"

"I protest, Major Duncan," cried Muir, hurrying back towards the stand, with both arms elevated by way of enforcing his words— "I protest in the strongest terms, gentlemen, against Pathfinder's being admitted into these sports with Killdeer, which is a piece, to say nothing of long habit, that is altogether out of proportion, for a trial of skill against Government rifles."

"Killdeer is taking its rest, Quartermaster," returned Pathfinder calmly, "and no one here thinks of disturbing it. I did not think, myself, of pulling a trigger to-day; but Sergeant Dunham has been persuading me that I shall not do proper honour to his handsome daughter, who came in under my care, if I am backward on such an occasion. I'm using Jasper's rifle, Quartermaster, as you may see, and that is no better than your own."

Lieutenant Muir was now obliged to acquiesce, and every eye turned towards the Pathfinder, as he took the required station. The air and attitude of this celebrated guide and hunter were extremely fine, as he raised his tall form and levelled the piece. Pathfinder was not what is usually termed a handsome man, though his appearance excited so much confidence and commanded respect. Tall, and even muscular, his frame might have been esteemed nearly perfect, were it not for the total absence of everything like flesh. Although no one perceived any of those gentler or more insinuating qualities which are apt to win upon a woman's affections, as he raised his rifle not a female eye was fastened on him without a silent approbation of the freedom of his movements and the manliness of his air. Thought was scarcely quicker than his aim; and, as the smoke floated above his head, the butt-end of the rifle was seen on the ground, the hand of the Pathfinder was leaning on the barrel, and his honest countenance was illuminated by his usual silent, hearty laugh.

"If one dared to hint at such a thing," cried Major Duncan, "I should say that the Pathfinder had also missed the target."

"No, no, Major," returned the guide confidently, "that *would* be a risky declaration. I didn't load the piece, and can't say what was in it; but if it was lead, you will find the bullet driving down those of the Quartermaster and Jasper, else is not my name Pathfinder."

A shout from the target announced the truth of this assertion.

"That's not all, that's not all, boys," called out the guide, who was now slowly advancing towards the stage occupied by the females; "if you find the target touched at all, I'll own to a miss.

The Quartermaster cut the wood, but you'll find no wood cut by that last messenger."

"Very true, Pathfinder, very true," answered Muir, who was lingering near Mabel, though ashamed to address her particularly in the presence of the officers' wives. "The Quartermaster did cut the wood, and by that means he opened a passage for your bullet, which went through the hole he had made."

"Well, Quartermaster, there goes the nail, and we'll see who can drive it closer, you or I; for, though I did not think of showing what a rifle can do to-day, now my hand is in, I'll turn my back to no man that carries King George's commission. Chingachgook is outlying, or he might force me into some of the niceties of the art; but, as for you, Quartermaster, if the nail don't stop you, the potato will."

"You're over boastful this morning, Pathfinder; but you'll find you've no green boy fresh from the settlements and the towns to deal with, I will assure ye!"

"I know that well, Quartermaster; I know that well, and shall not deny your experience. You've lived many years on the frontiers, and I've heard of you in the colonies, and among the Indians, too, quite a human life ago."

"Na, na," interrupted Muir in his broadest Scotch, "this is injustice, man. I've no' lived so very long, neither."

"I'll do you justice, Lieutenant, even if you get the best in the potato trial. I say you've passed a good human life, for a soldier, in places where the rifle is daily used, and I know you are a creditable and ingenious marksman; but then you are not a true rifle-shooter. As for boasting, I hope I'm not a vain talker about my own exploits; but a man's gifts are his gifts, and it's flying in the face of Providence to deny them. The Sergeant's daughter, here, shall judge between us, if you have the stomach to submit to so pretty a judge."

The Pathfinder had named Mabel as the arbiter because he admired her, and because, in his eyes, rank had little or no value; but Lieutenant Muir shrank at such a reference in the presence of the wives of the officers. Notwithstanding these doubts and misgivings, Mabel looked so prettily, blushed so charmingly, smiled so sweetly, and altogether presented so winning a picture of youth, spirit, modesty, and beauty, that he found it exceedingly tempting to be kept so prominently before her imagination, and to be able to address her freely.

"You shall have it your own way, Pathfinder," he answered;

"let the Sergeant's charming daughter be the umpire then; and to her we will both dedicate the prize, that one or the other must certainly win. Pathfinder must be humoured, ladies, as you perceive, else, no doubt, we should have had the honour to submit ourselves to one of your charming society."

A call for the competitors now drew the Quartermaster and his adversary away, and in a few moments the second trial of skill commenced. A common wrought nail was driven lightly into the target, its head having been first touched with paint, and the marksman was required to hit it, or he lost his chances in the succeeding trials. No one was permitted to enter who had already failed in the essay against the bull's-eye.

There might have been half a dozen aspirants for the honours of this trial; one or two, who had barely succeeded in touching the spot of paint in the previous strife, preferring to rest their reputations there, feeling certain that they could not succeed in the greater effort that was now exacted of them. The first three adventurers failed, all coming very near the mark, but neither touching it. The fourth person who presented himself was the Quartermaster, who, after going through his usual attitudes, so far succeeded as to carry away a small portion of the head of the nail, planting his bullet by the side of its point. This was not considered an extraordinary shot, though it brought the adventurer within the category.

"You've saved your bacon, Quartermaster, as they say in the settlements," cried Pathfinder; "but it would take a long time to build a house with a hammer no better than yours. Jasper, here, will show you how a nail is to be started, or the lad has lost some of his steadiness of hand and sartainty of eye."

"We shall see, Pathfinder; I call that a pretty attempt at a nail; and I doubt if the 55th has another hammer, as you call it, that can do just the same thing over again."

"Jasper is not in the 55th, but there goes his rap."

As the Pathfinder spoke, the bullet of Eau-douce hit the nail square, and drove it into the target, within an inch of the head.

"Be all ready to clench it, boys!" cried Pathfinder, stepping into his friend's tracks the instant they were vacant. "Never mind a new nail; I can see that, though the paint is gone, and what I can see I can hit, at a hundred yards, though it were only a mosquito's eye. Be ready to clench!"

The rifle cracked, the bullet sped its way, and the head of the nail was buried in the wood, covered by the piece of flattened lead.

"Well, Jasper lad," continued Pathfinder, dropping the butt-end of his rifle to the ground, "you improve daily. The Quartermaster is respectable, but he will never get any farther; whereas you, Jasper, have the gift, and may one day defy any who pull trigger."

"Hoot, hoot!" exclaimed Muir, "do you call hitting the head of the nail respectable only, when it's the perfection of the art? Anyone the least refined and elevated in sentiment knows that the delicate touches denote the master; whereas your sledge-hammer blows come from the rude and uninstructed."

"The surest way of settling this rivalry will be to make another trial," observed Lundie, "and that will be of the potato."

As Major Duncan manifested some impatience of manner, Muir had too much tact to delay the sports any longer with his discursive remarks, but judiciously prepared himself for the next appeal. To say the truth, the Quartermaster had little or no faith in his own success in the trial of skill that was to follow, nor would he have been so free in presenting himself as a competitor at all had he anticipated it would have been made; but Major Duncan, who was somewhat of a humorist in his own quiet Scotch way, had secretly ordered it to be introduced expressly to mortify him; for, a laird himself, Lundie did not relish the notion that one who might claim to be a gentleman should bring discredit on his caste by forming an unequal alliance. As soon as everything was prepared, Muir was summoned to the stand, and the potato was held in readiness to be thrown. At the word "heave!" which was given by the marksman, the tuber was thrown with a gentle toss into the air, and it was the business of the adventurer to cause a ball to pass through it before it reached the ground.

The Quartermaster, in a hundred experiments, had once succeeded in accomplishing this difficult feat; but he now essayed to perform it again, with a sort of blind hope that was fated to be disappointed. The potato was thrown in the usual manner, the rifle was discharged, but the flying target was untouched.

"To the rightabout, and fall out, Quartermaster," said Lundie, smiling at the success of the artifice. "The honour of the silken calash will lie between Jasper Eau-douce and Pathfinder."

"And how is the trial to end, Major?" enquired the latter. "Are we to have the two-potato trial, or is it to be settled by centre and skin?"

"By centre and skin, if there is any perceptible difference, otherwise the double shot must follow."

"This is an awful moment to me, Pathfinder," observed Jasper, as he moved towards the stand, his face actually losing its colour in intensity of feeling.

Pathfinder gazed earnestly at the young man; and then, begging Major Duncan to have patience for a moment, he led his friend out of the hearing of all near him before he spoke.

"You seem to take this matter to heart, Jasper!" the hunter remarked, keeping his eyes fastened on those of the youth.

"I must own, Pathfinder, that my feelings were never before so much bound up in success."

"And do you so much crave to outdo me, an old and tried friend?—and that, as it might be, in my own way? Shooting is my gift, boy, and no common hand can equal mine."

"I know it—I know it, Pathfinder, but yet——"

"But what, Jasper, boy?—speak freely, you talk to a friend."

The young man compressed his lips, dashed a hand across his eye, and flushed and paled alternately, like a girl confessing her love. Then, squeezing the other's hand, he said calmly, like one whose manhood has overcome all other sensations, "I would lose an arm, Pathfinder, to be able to make an offering of that calash to Mabel Dunham."

The hunter dropped his eyes to the ground, and as he walked slowly back towards the stand he seemed to ponder deeply on what he had just heard.

"You never could succeed in the double trial, Jasper!" he suddenly remarked.

"Of that I am certain, and it troubles me."

"What a creetur' is mortal man! he pines for things which are not of his gift, and treats the bounties of Providence lightly. No matter, no matter. Take your station, Jasper, for the Major is waiting; and hark'ee, lad—I must touch the skin, for I could not show my face in the garrison with less than that."

"I suppose I must submit to my fate," returned Jasper, flushing and losing his colour as before; "but I will make the effort, if I die."

"What a thing is mortal man!" repeated Pathfinder, falling back to allow his friend room to take his aim; he overlooks his own gifts, and craves those of another!"

The potato was thrown, Jasper fired, and the shout that followed preceded the announcement of the fact that he had driven his bullet through its centre, or so nearly so as to merit that award.

"Here is a competitor worthy of you, Pathfinder," cried Major

Duncan with delight, as the former took his station; "and we may look to some fine shooting in the double trial."

"What a thing is mortal man?" repeated the hunter, scarcely seeming to notice what was passing around him, so much were his thoughts absorbed in his own reflections. "Toss!"

The potato was tossed, the rifle cracked—it was remarked just as the little black ball seemed stationary in the air, for the marksman evidently took unusual heed to his aim,—and then a look of disappointment and wonder succeeded among those who caught the falling target.

"Two holes in one?" called out the Major.

"The skin, the skin!" was the answer; "only the skin!"

"How's this, Pathfinder? Is Jasper Eau-douce to carry off the honours of the day?"

"The calash is his," returned the other, shaking his head and walking quietly away from the stand. "What a creature is mortal man! never satisfied with his own gifts, but for ever craving that which Providence denies!"

As Pathfinder had not buried his bullet in the potato, but had cut through the skin, the prize was immediately adjudged to Jasper. The calash was in the hands of the latter when the Quartermaster approached, and with a polite air of cordiality he wished his successful rival joy of his victory.

"But now you've got the calash, lad, it's of no use to you," he added; "it will never make a sail, nor even an ensign. I'm thinking, Eau-douce, you'd no' be sorry to see its value in good siller of the king?"

"Money cannot buy it, Lieutenant," returned Jasper, whose eye lighted with all the fire of success and joy. "I would rather have won this calash than have obtained fifty new suits of sails for the *Scud*!"

"Hoot, hoot, lad! you are going mad like all the rest of them. I'd even venture to offer half a guinea for the trifle rather than it should lie kicking about in the cabin of your cutter, and in the end become an ornament for the head of a squaw."

Although Jasper did not know that the wary Quartermaster had not offered half the actual cost of the prize, he heard the proposition with indifference. Shaking his head in the negative, he advanced towards the stage, where his approach excited a little commotion, the officers' ladies, one and all, having determined to accept the present, should the gallantry of the young sailor induce him to offer it. But Jasper's diffidence, no less than admiration for another, would have prevented him from aspiring to the honour of complimenting any whom he thought so much his superiors.

"Mabel," said he, " this prize is for you, unless——"

"Unless what, Jasper?" answered the girl, losing her own bashfulness in the natural and generous wish to relieve his embarrassment, though both reddened in a way to betray strong feeling.

"Unless you may think too indifferently of it, because it is offered by one who may have no right to believe his gift will be accepted."

"I do accept it, Jasper; and it shall be a sign of the danger I have passed in your company, and of the gratitude I feel for your care of me—your care, and that of the Pathfinder."

"Never mind me!" exclaimed the latter; "this is Jasper's luck, and Jasper's gift: give him full credit for both. My turn may come another day; mine and the Quartermaster's."

The remainder of the sports offered nothing of interest. The shooting was reasonably good; but the trials were all of a scale lower than those related, and the competitors were soon left to themselves. The ladies and most of the officers withdrew, and the remainder of the females soon followed their example. Mabel was returning along the low flat rocks that line the shore of the lake, dangling her pretty calash from a prettier finger, when Pathfinder met her. He carried the rifle which he had used that day; but his manner had less of the frank ease of the hunter about it than usual, while his eye seemed roving and uneasy. After a few unmeaning words concerning the noble sheet of water before them, he turned towards his companion with strong interest in his countenance, and said:

"Jasper earned that calash for you, Mabel, without much trial of his gifts."

"It was fairly done, Pathfinder."

"No doubt. The bullet passed neatly through the potato, and no man could have done more; though others might have done as much."

"But no one did as much!" exclaimed Mabel, with an animation that she instantly regretted; for she saw by the pained look of the guide that he was mortified equally by the remark and by the feeling with which it was uttered.

"It is true, Mabel, no one did as much then; but—yet there is no reason I should deny my gifts which come from Providence—yes; no one did as much there, but you shall know what *can* be done here. Do you observe the gulls that are flying over our heads?"

"Certainly, Pathfinder; there are too many to escape notice."

"Here, where they cross each other in sailing about," he added, cocking and raising his rifle; "the two—the two. Now look!"

The piece was presented quick as thought, as two of the birds came in a line, though distant from each other many yards; the report followed, and the bullet passed through the bodies of both the victims. No sooner had the gulls fallen into the lake, than Pathfinder dropped the butt-end of the rifle, and laughed in his peculiar manner, every shade of dissatisfaction and mortified pride having left his honest face.

"That is something, Mabel, that is something; although I have no calash to give you! But ask Jasper himself; I'll leave it all to Jasper, for a truer tongue and heart are not in America."

"Then it was not Jasper's fault that he gained the prize?"

"Not it. He did his best, and he did well. For one that has water gifts, rather than land gifts, Jasper is uncommonly expert, and a better backer no one need wish, ashore or afloat. But it was my fault, Mabel, that he got the calash; though it makes no difference, for the thing has gone to the right person.'

"I believe I understand you, Pathfinder," said Mabel, blushing in spite of herself, "and I look upon the calash as the joint gift of yourself and Jasper."

"That would not be doing justice to the lad, neither. He won the garment, and had a right to give it away. The most you may think, Mabel, is to believe that, had I won it, it would have gone to the same person."

"I will remember that, Pathfinder, and take care that others know your skill, as it has been proved upon the poor gulls in my presence."

"Lord bless you, Mabel! there is no more need of your talking in favour of my shooting on this frontier than of your talking about the water in the lake or the sun in the heavens. Everybody knows what I can do in that way, and your words would be thrown away."

"Then you think that Jasper knew you were giving him this advantage, of which he had so unhandsomely availed himself?" said Mabel, the colour which has imparted so much lustre to her eyes gradually leaving her face, which became grave and thoughtful.

"I do not say that, but very far from it. We all forget things that we have known, when eager after our wishes. Jasper is satisfied that I can pass one bullet through two potatoes, as I sent my bullet through the gulls; and he knows no other man on the frontier can do the same thing. But with the calash before his eyes, and the hope of giving it to you, the lad was inclined to think better of himself, just at that moment, perhaps, than he ought. No, there's nothing mean or distrustful about Jasper Eau-douce, though it is a gift natural to all young men to wish to appear well in the eyes of handsome young women."

"I'll try to forget all, but the kindness you've both shown to a poor motherless girl," said Mabel, struggling to keep down emotions she scarcely knew how to account for herself. "Believe me, Pathfinder, I can never forget all you have already done for me—you and Jasper; and this new proof of your regard is not thrown away. Here, here is a brooch that is of silver, and I offer it as a token that I owe you life or liberty."

"What shall I do with this, Mabel?" asked the hunter, holding the trinket in his hand. "I have neither buckle nor button about me, for I wear nothing but leathern strings. It's pretty to the eye, but it is prettier far on the spot it came from than it can be about me."

"Nay, put it in your hunting-shirt; it will become it well. Remember, Pathfinder, that it is a token of friendship between us, and a sign that I can never forget you or your services."

Mabel then smiled an adieu; and, bounding up the bank, she was soon lost to view behind the mound of the fort.

CHAPTER XII

A FEW hours later Mabel Dunham was on the bastion that over-looked the river and the lake, seemingly in deep thought. The evening was calm and soft, and the question had arisen whether the party for the Thousand Islands would be able to get out that night or not, on account of the total absence of wind. The stores, arms, and ammunition were already shipped, and even Mabel's effects were on board; but the small draft of men that was to go was still ashore, there being no apparent prospect of the cutter's getting under way. Jasper had warped the *Scud* out of the cove, and so far up the stream as to enable him to pass through the outlet of the river whenever he chose; but there he still lay, riding at single anchor. The drafted men were lounging about the shore of the cove, undecided whether or not to pull off.

Everything near appeared lovely and soothing, while the solemn grandeur of the silent forest and placid expanse of the lake lent a sublimity that other scenes might have wanted. For the first time, Mabel felt the hold that the towns and civilization had gained on her habits sensibly weakened; and the warm-hearted girl began to think that a life passed amid objects such as those around her might be happy. How far the experience of the last ten days came in aid of the calm and holy eventide, and contributed towards producing that young conviction, may be suspected, rather than affirmed, in this early portion of our legend.

"A charming sunset, Mabel?" said the hearty voice of her uncle, so close to the ear of our heroine as to cause her to start—"a charming sunset, girl, for a freshwater concern, though we should think but little of it at sea."

"And is not nature the same on shore or at sea—on a lake like this or on the ocean? Does not the sun shine on all alike, dear Uncle; and can we not feel gratitude for the blessings of Providence as strongly on this remote frontier as in our own Manhattan?"

"The girl has fallen in with some of her mother's books. Is not nature the same, indeed! Now, Mabel, do you imagine that the nature of a soldier is the same as that of a seafaring man? You've relations in both callings, and ought to be able to answer."

"But, Uncle, I mean human nature."

"So do I, girl; the human nature of a seaman, and the human nature of one of these fellows of the 55th, not even excepting your own father. But here is Pathfinder."

Cap nodded his head, and then ceased to speak, while the hunter approached, not with his usual frank and easy manner, but in a way to show that he was slightly embarrassed, if not distrustful of his reception.

"Uncle and niece make a family party," said Pathfinder, when near the two, "and a stranger may not prove a welcome companion?"

"You are no stranger, Master Pathfinder," returned Cap, "and no one can be more welcome than yourself. We were talking of you not so long ago, and when friends speak of an absent man, he can guess what they have said."

"I ask no secrets. Every man has his enemies, and I have mine, though I count neither you, Master Cap, nor pretty Mabel here among the number. As for the Mingos, I will say nothing, though they have no just cause to hate me."

"That I'll answer for, Pathfinder! for you strike my fancy as being well-disposed and upright. There is a method, however, of getting away from the enmity of even these Mingos; and if you choose to take it, no one will more willingly point it out than myself, without a charge for my advice either."

"I wish no enemies, Saltwater," for so the Pathfinder had begun to call Cap,—"I wish no enemies. I'm as ready to bury the hatchet with the Mingos as with the French, though you know that it depends on One greater than either of us so to turn the heart as to leave a man without enemies."

"By lifting your anchor, and accompanying me down to the coast, friend Pathfinder, when we get back from this short cruise on which we are bound, you will find yourself beyond the sound of the warwhoop, and safe enough from any Indian bullet."

"And what should I do on the salt water? Hunt in your towns? Follow the trails of people going and coming from market, and ambush dogs and poultry! You are no friend to my happiness, Master Cap, if you would lead me out of the shades of the woods to put me in the sun of the clearings."

"I did not propose to leave you in the settlements, Pathfinder, but to carry you out to sea, where a man can only be said to breathe freely. Mabel will tell you that such was my intention, before a word was said on the subject."

"And what does Mabel think would come of such a change? She knows that a man has his gifts, and that it is as useless to pretend to others as to withstand them that come from Providence. I am a hunter, and a scout, or a guide, Saltwater, and it is not in me to fly so much in the face of Heaven as to try to become anything else. Am I right, Mabel, or are you so much a woman as to wish to see a natur' altered?"

"I would wish to see no change in you, Pathfinder," Mabel answered, with cordial sincerity; "and much as my uncle admires the sea, and great as is all the good that he thinks may come of it, I could not wish to see the best and noblest hunter of the woods transformed into an admiral. Remain what you are, my brave friend, and you need fear nothing short of the anger of God."

"Do you hear this, Saltwater? So long as the Sergeant's daughter is satisfied with me as I am, I shall not fly in the face of the gifts of Providence, by striving to become anything else. I may seem useless here in a garrison; but when we get down among the Thousand Islands, there may be an opportunity to prove that a sure rifle is sometimes a Godsend."

"You are then to be of our party!" said Mabel, smiling so frankly and so sweetly on the guide that he would have followed her to the end of the earth. "I shall be the only female, with the exception of one soldier's wife, and shall feel none the less secure, Pathfinder, because you will be among our protectors."

"The Sergeant would do that, Mabel, though you were not of his kin. I should think your uncle here would like an expedition of this sort, where we shall go with sails, and have a look at an inland sea?"

"Your inland sea is no great matter, Master Pathfinder, and I expect nothing from it."

"You don't know the lakes, Master Cap, or you would not say that. Before we get to the Thousand Islands, you will have other notions of what natur' has done in this wilderness."

"I have my doubts whether you have such a thing as a real island in all this region."

"We'll show you hundreds of them; not exactly a thousand, perhaps, but so many that eye cannot see them all, nor tongue count them."

"I'll engage, when the truth comes to be known, they'll turn out to be nothing but peninsulas, or promontories; though these are matters, I dare say, of which you know little or nothing. But, islands or no island, what is the object of the cruise, Master Pathfinder?"

"There can be no harm in giving you some idea of what we are going to do. Being so old a sailor, Master Cap, you've heard, no doubt, of such a port as Frontenac?"

"Who hasn't? I will not say I've ever been inside the harbour, but I've frequently been off the place."

"Then you are about to go upon ground with which you are acquainted. These great lakes, you must know, make a chain, the water passing out of one into the other, until it reaches Erie, which is a sheet off here to the westward, as large as Ontario itself. Well, out of Erie the water comes, until it reaches a low mountain like, over the edge of which it passes."

"I should like to know how it can do that?"

"Why, easy enough, Master Cap," returned Pathfinder, laughing, "seeing that it has only to fall downhill. Had I said the water went *up* the mountain, there would have been natur' ag'in it; but we hold it no great matter for water to run downhill—that is, *fresh* water."

"Ay, ay; but you speak of the water of a lake's coming down the side of a mountain; it's in the teeth of reason."

"Well, we will not dispute the point; but what I've seen I've seen. After getting into Ontario, all the water of *all* the lakes passes down into the sea by a river; and in the narrow part of the sheet, where it is neither river nor lake, lie the islands spoken of. Now Frontenac is a post of the Frenchers above these same islands; and, as they hold the garrison below, their stores and ammunition are sent up the river to Frontenac, to be forwarded along the shores of this and the other lakes, in order to enable the enemy to do his mischief among the savages, and to take Christian scalps."

"And will our presence prevent these horrible acts?" demanded Mabel, with interest.

"It may or it may not. as Providence wills. Lundie sent a party down to take a station among the islands, to cut off some of the French boats; and this expedition of ours will be the second relief. As yet they've not done much, though two bateaux loaded with Indian goods have been taken; but a runner came in last week. and brought such tidings that the Major is about to make a last effort to sarcumvent the knaves. Jasper knows the way, and we shall be in good hands, for the Sergeant is prudent, and of the first quality at an ambushment."

"Is this all?" said Cap contemptuously.

"Jasper is bringing the cutter out," observed the guide, whose look was drawn in that direction by the fall of some heavy article on the deck. "The lad sees the signs of wind, no doubt, and wishes to be ready for it."

"Ay, now we shall have an opportunity of learning seamanship," returned Cap, with a sneer. "There is a nicety in getting a craft under her canvas that shows the thoroughbred mariner as much as anything else."

"I will not say that Jasper is equal to your seafarers below," observed Pathfinder; "but he is a bold boy, and manages his cutter as skilfully as any man can desire, on this lake at least."

Cap made no other answer than a dissatisfied ejaculation, and then a general silence followed, all on the bastion studying the movements of the cutter with interest. It was still a dead calm, the surface of the lake literally glittering with the last rays of the sun. The *Scud* had been warped up to a kedge that lay a hundred yards above the points of the outlet, where she had room to manœuvre in the river which then formed the harbour of Oswego. But the total want of air prevented any such attempt, and it was soon evident that the light craft was to be taken through the passage under her sweeps. Not a sail was loosened; but as soon as the kedge was tripped, the heavy fall of the sweeps was heard, when the cutter, with her head up stream, began to sheer towards the centre of the current; on reaching which the efforts of the men ceased, and she drifted towards the outlet. In the narrow pass itself her movement was rapid, and in less than five minute the *Scud* was floating outside of the two low gravelly points which intercepted the waves of the lake. No anchor was let go, but the vessel continued to set off from the land, until her dark hull was seen resting on the glossy surface of the lake, full a quarter of a mile beyond the low bluff which formed the eastern extremity of what might be called the outer harbour or roadstead. Here the influence of the river current ceased, and she became virtually stationary.

"She seems very beautiful to me, Uncle," said Mabel, whose gaze had not been averted from the cutter for a single moment while it had thus been changing its position. "I dare say you can find faults in her appearance, and in the way she is managed; but to my ignorance both are perfect."

"Ay, ay; she drops down with the current well enough, girl, and so would a chip. But when you come to niceties, an old tar like myself has no need of spectacles to find fault."

"Well, Master Cap," put in the guide, "I've heard old and experienced saltwater mariners confess that the *Scud* is as pretty a craft as floats. I know nothing of such matters myself; but one may have his own notions about a ship, even though they be wrong notions; and it would take more than one witness to persuade me Jasper does not keep his boat in good order."

"I do not say that the cutter is downright lubberly, Master Pathfinder; but she has great faults."

By this time the cutter had begun to drift at the mercy of the currents of the lake, her head turning in all directions, though slowly, and not in a way to attract particular attention. Just at this moment the jib was loosened and hoisted, and presently the canvas swelled towards the land, though no evidences of air were yet to be seen on the surface of the water. Slight, however, as was the impulsion, the light hull yielded; and in another minute the *Scud* was seen standing across the current of the river with a movement so easy and moderate as to be scarcely perceptible. When out of the stream she struck an eddy, and shot up towards the land, under the eminence where the fort stood, when Jasper dropped his kedge.

"Not lubberly done," muttered Cap in a sort of soliloquy,— "not over lubberly, though he should have put his helm a-starboard instead of a-port; for a vessel ought always to come-to with her head off shore, whether she is a league from the land or only a cable's length, since it has a careful look, and looks are something in this world."

"Jasper is a handy lad," suddenly observed Sergeant Dunham at his brother-in-law's elbow; "and we place great reliance on his skill in our expeditions. But come, one and all, we have but half an hour more of daylight to embark in, and the boats will be ready for us by the time we are ready for them."

On this intimation the whole party separated, each to find those trifles which had not been shipped already. A few taps of the drum gave the necessary signal to the soldiers, and in a minute all were in motion.

CHAPTER XIII

THE embarkation of so small a party was a matter of no great delay or embarrassment. The whole force confided to the care of Sergeant Dunham consisted of but ten privates and two noncommissioned officers, though it was soon positively known that Mr. Muir was to accompany the expedition. The Quartermaster, however, went as a volunteer, while some duty connected with his own department, as had been arranged between him and his commander, was the avowed object. To these must be added the Pathfinder and Cap, with Jasper and his subordinates, one of whom was a boy. The party, consequently, consisted of less than twenty men, and a lad of fourteen. Mabel and the wife of a common soldier were the only females.

Sergeant Dunham carried off his command in a large bateau, and then returned for his final orders, and to see that his brother-in-law and daughter were properly attended to. Having pointed out to Cap the boat that he and Mabel were to use, he ascended the hill to seek his last interview with Lundie.

It was nearly dark when Mabel found herself in the boat that was to carry her off to the cutter. So very smooth was the surface of the lake, that it was not found necessary to bring the bateaux into the river to receive their freights; but the beach outside being totally without surf, and the water as tranquil as that of a pond, everybody embarked there.

Jasper was in readiness to receive his passengers; and, as the deck of the *Scud* was but two or three feet above the water, no difficulty was experienced in getting on board her. As soon as this was effected, the young man pointed out to Mabel and her companion the accommodations prepared for their reception. The little vessel contained four apartments below, all between decks having been expressly constructed with a view to the transportation of officers and men, with their wives and families. First in rank was what was called the after-cabin, a small apartment that contained four berths, and which enjoyed the advantage of possessing small windows, for the admission of air and light. This was uniformly devoted to females whenever any were on board; and as Mabel and her companion were alone, they had ample accommodation. The main-cabin was larger, and lighted from above. It was now appropriated to the Quartermaster, the Sergeant, Cap, and Jasper, the Pathfinder roaming through any part of the cutter he pleased. The corporals and common soldiers occupied the space beneath the main hatch, which had a deck for such a purpose, while the crew were berthed, as usual, in the forecastle.

As soon as Mabel had taken possession of her own really comfortable cabin she went on deck again. Here all was momentarily in motion; the men were roving to and fro in quest of their knapsacks and other effects; but method and habit soon reduced things to order, when the stillness on board became even imposing, for it was connected with the idea of future adventure and ominous preparation.

Darkness was now beginning to render objects on shore indistinct, the whole of the land forming one shapeless black outline of even forest summits, to be distinguished from the impending heavens only by the greater light of the sky. The stars, however, soon began to appear, one after another, in their usual mild, placid lustre, bringing with them that sense of quiet which ordinarily accompanies night. There was something soothing, as well as exciting, in such a scene; and Mabel, who was seated on the quarterdeck, sensibly felt both influences. The Pathfinder was

standing near her, and she fancied that, through the growing
darkness of the hour, she could trace even stronger lines of
thought than usual in his rugged countenance.

"To you, Pathfinder, expeditions like this can be no great
novelty," said she; "though I am surprised to find how silent
and thoughtful the men appear to be."

"We learn this by making war ag'in Indians. A silent army, in
the woods, is doubly strong; and a noisy one, doubly weak."

"But we are neither an army, nor in the woods. There can be
no danger of Mingos in the *Scud*."

"No one is safe from a Mingo, who does not understand his
very natur'; and even then he must act up to his own knowledge,
and that closely. Ask Jasper how he got command of this very
cutter."

"And how *did* he get the command?" enquired Mabel, with an
earnestness and interest that quite delighted her simple-minded
companion, who was never better pleased than when he had an
opportunity of saying aught in favour of a friend. "It is honourable to him that he has reached this station while yet so
young."

"That is it; but he deserved it all, and more. A frigate
wouldn't have been too much to pay for so much spirit and
coolness, had there been such a thing on Ontario."

"But Jasper—you have not yet told me how he got the command of the schooner."

"It is a long story, Mabel, and one your father can tell much
better than I; for he was present, while I was off on a distant
scouting. Jasper is not good at a story; I have heard him questioned about this affair, and he never made a good tale of it.
The *Scud* had near fallen into the hands of the French and the
Mingos, when Jasper saved her, in a way which none but a
quick-witted mind and a bold heart would have attempted."

Mabel determined to ask her father to repeat the incidents of
the affair that very night; for it struck her young fancy that
nothing better could well offer, than to listen to the praises of
one who was a bad historian of his own exploits.

"Will the *Scud* remain with us when we reach the island?" she
asked, after a little hesitation about the propriety of the question;
"or shall we be left to ourselves?"

"That's as may be: Jasper does not often keep the cutter idle
when anything is to be done; and we may expect activity on his
part. We shall have all right under Jasper, I make no doubt,

who can find a trail on Ontario as well as a Delaware can find one on the land."

"And our own Delaware, Pathfinder—the big Serpent—why is he not with us to-night?"

"The Sarpent is out, with two or three more, scouting the lake shores, and will join us down among the islands, with the tidings he may gather. The Sergeant is too good a soldier to forget his rear while he is facing the enemy in front."

"Shall we have enemies to face in front?" asked Mabel, smiling, and for the first time feeling a slight apprehension about the dangers of the expedition. "Are we likely to have an engagement?"

"If we have, Mabel, there will be men enough ready and willing to stand between you and harm. But you are a soldier's daughter, and, we all know, have the spirit of one. Don't let the fear of a battle keep your pretty eyes from sleeping."

"I do feel braver out here in the woods, Pathfinder, than I ever felt before amid the weaknesses of the town, although I have always tried to remember what I owe to my dear father."

"Ay, your mother was so before you. 'You will find Mabel, like her mother, no screamer, or faint-hearted girl, to trouble a man in his need; but one who would encourage her mate, and help to keep his heart up when sorest prest by danger,' said the Sergeant to me, before I ever laid eyes on that sweet countenance of yours."

"And why should my father have told you this, Pathfinder?" the girl demanded a little earnestly. "Perhaps he fancied you would think the better of me if you did not believe me a silly coward, as so many of my sex love to make themselves appear."

Deception, unless it were at the expense of his enemies in the field—nay, concealment of even a thought—was so little in accordance with the Pathfinder's very nature, that he was not a little embarrassed by this simple question. In such a strait he involuntarily took refuge in a middle course, not revealing that which he fancied ought not to be told, nor yet absolutely concealing it.

"You must know, Mabel," said he, "that the Sergeant and I are old friends, and have stood side by side on many a hard fi't and bloody day. It's the way of us skirmishers to think little of the fight when the rifle has done cracking; and at night around our fires, or on our marches, we talk of the things we love. Now it was natural that the Sergeant, having such a daughter as you, should love her better than anything else, and that he should talk of her oftener than of anything else,—while I, having neither daughter, nor sister, nor mother, nor kith, nor kin to love, I naturally chimed in, as it were, and got to love you, Mabel, before I ever saw you—yes I did—just by talking about you so much."

"And now you *have* seen me," returned the smiling girl, "you are beginning to see the folly of forming friendships for people before you know anything about them, except by hearsay."

"It wasn't friendship—it isn't friendship, Mabel, that I feel for you. I am the friend of the Delawares, and have been so from boyhood; but my feelings for them are not the same as those I got from the Sergeant for you; and, especially, now that I begin to know you better. I'm sometimes afeard it isn't wholesome for one who is much occupied in a very manly calling, like that of a guide or scout, to form friendships for women, as they seem to me to lessen the love of enterprise, and to turn the feelings away from their gifts and natural occupations."

"You surely do not mean, Pathfinder, that a friendship for a girl like me would make you less bold, and more unwilling to meet the French than you were before?"

"Not so. With you in danger, for instance, I fear I might become foolhardy; but before we became so intimate, as I may say, I loved to think of my scoutings, and of my marches, and outlyings, and fights, and other adventures: but now my mind cares less about them; I think more of the barracks, and of evenings passed in discourse, of feelings in which there are no wranglings and bloodshed, and of young women, and of their laughs and their cheerful, soft voices, their pleasant looks and their winning ways. I sometimes tell the Sergeant that he and his daughter will be the spoiling of one of the best and most experienced scouts on the lines."

"Not they, Pathfinder; they will try to make that which is already so excellent perfect. You do not know us, if you think that either wishes to see you in the least changed. Remain as at present, the same honest, upright, fearless, trustworthy guide that you are, and neither my dear father nor myself can ever think of you differently from what we now do."

It was too dark for Mabel to note the workings of the countenance of her listener; but her own sweet face was turned towards him, as she spoke with an energy equal to her frankness, in a way to show how little embarrassed were her thoughts, and how sincere were her words.

The Pathfinder's humble nature was encouraged by the direct-ness and strength of the words he had just heard. Unwilling, if not unable, to say any more, he walked away, and stood leaning on his rifle and looking up at the stars for full ten minutes in profound silence.

Meanwhile an interview on the bastion took place between Lundie and the Sergeant.

"Have the men's knapsacks been examined?" demanded Major Duncan.

"All, your honour; and all are right."

"The ammunition—arms?"

"All in order, Major Duncan, and fit for any service."

"You have the men named in my own draft, Dunham?"

"Without an exception, sir. Better men could not be found in the regiment."

"You have need of the best of our men, Sergeant. This experi-ment has now been tried three times; always under one of the ensigns, who have flattered me with success, but have as often failed. After so much preparation and expense, I do not like to abandon the project entirely; but this will be the last effort; and the result will mainly depend on you and on the Pathfinder."

"You may count on us both, Major Duncan. The duty you have given us is not above our habits and experience, and I think it will be well done. I know that the Pathfinder will not be wanting."

"On that, indeed, it will be safe to rely. He is a most extra-ordinary man, Dunham—one who long puzzled me; but who, now that I understand him, commands as much of my respect as any general in his majesty's service."

"I was in hopes, sir, that you would come to look at the pro-posed marriage with Mabel as a thing I ought to wish and for-ward."

"As for that, Sergeant, time will show," returned Lundie, smiling; "one woman is sometimes more difficult to manage than a whole regiment of men. By the way, you know that your would-be son-in-law, the Quartermaster, will be of the party: and I trust you will at least give him an equal chance in the trial for your daughter's smiles."

"If respect for his rank, sir, did not cause me to do this, your honour's wish would be sufficient."

"I thank you, Sergeant. We have served much together, and ought to value each other in our several stations. Understand me, however, I ask no more for Davy Muir than a clear field and no favour. Are you certain that the rations have been properly calculated?"

"I'll answer for it, Major Duncan; but if they were not, we cannot suffer with two such hunters as Pathfinder and the Serpent in company."

"That will never do, Dunham," interrupted Lundie sharply; "and it comes of your American birth and training. No thorough soldier ever relies on anything but his commissary for supplies; and I beg that no part of my regiment may be the first to set an example to the contrary."

"You have only to command, Major Duncan, to be obeyed; and yet, if I might presume, sir——"

"Speak freely, Sergeant; you are talking with a friend."

"I was merely about to say that I find even the Scotch soldiers like venison and birds quite as well as pork, when they are difficult to be had."

"That may be very true; but likes and dislikes have nothing to do with system. An army can rely on nothing but its commissaries. You have no doubt of the skill of this Jasper Eau-douce?"

"The boy has been tried, sir, and found equal to all that can be required of him."

"He has a French name, and has passed much of his boyhood in the French colonies; has he French blood in his veins?"

"Not a drop, your honour. Jasper's father was an old comrade of my own, and his mother came of an honest and loyal family in this very province."

"How came he then so much among the French, and whence his name? He speaks the language of the Canadas, too, I find."

"The boy was left under the care of one of our mariners in the old war, and he took to the water like a duck, passing most of his time on the other side of the lake, where the French have had a few vessels these fifty years. He learned to speak their language, as a matter of course, and got his name from the Indians and Canadians."

"A French master is but a poor instructor for a British sailor, notwithstanding."

"I beg your pardon, sir: Jasper Eau-douce was brought up under a real English seaman, one that had sailed under the king's pennant, and may be called a thorough-bred; that is to say, a subject born in the colonies."

"He behaved well when I gave him the command of the *Scud*; no lad could have conducted himself more loyally or better."

"Or more bravely, Major Duncan. I am sorry to see, sir, that you have doubts as to the fidelity of Jasper."

"It is the duty of the soldier who is entrusted with the care of a distant and important post like this, Dunham, never to relax in his vigilance. We have two of the most artful enemies that the world has ever produced, in their several ways, to contend with, and nothing should be overlooked that can lead to injury."

"I hope your honour considers me fit to be entrusted with any particular reason that may exist for doubting Jasper, since you have seen fit to trust me with this command."

"It is not that I doubt you, Dunham, that I hesitate to reveal all I may happen to know; but from a strong reluctance to circulate an evil report concerning one of whom I have hitherto thought well. You must think well of the Pathfinder, or you would not wish to give him your daughter?"

"For the Pathfinder's honesty I will answer with my life, sir," returned the Sergeant firmly, and not without a dignity of manner that struck his superior. "Such a man doesn't know how to be false."

"I believe you are right, Dunham; and yet this last information has unsettled all my old opinions. I have received an anonymous communication, Sergeant, advising me to be on my guard against Jasper Western, who, it alleges, has been bought by the enemy, and giving me reason to expect that further and more precise information will soon be sent."

"Letters without signatures to them, sir, are scarcely to be regarded in war."

"Or in peace, Dunham. No one can entertain a lower opinion of the writer of an anonymous letter, in ordinary matters, than myself; the very act denotes cowardice, meanness, and baseness; and it usually is a token of falsehood, as well as of other vices. But in matters of war it is not exactly the same thing. Besides, several suspicious circumstances have been pointed out to me."

"Such as is fit for an orderly to hear, your honour?"

"Certainly, one in whom I confide as much as in yourself, Dunham. It is said, for instance, that your daughter and her party were permitted to escape the Iroquois, when they came in, merely to give Jasper credit with me. I am told that the gentry at Frontenac will care more for the capture of the *Scud*, with Sergeant Dunham and a party of men, together with the defeat of our favourite plan, than for the capture of a girl and the scalp of her uncle."

"I understand the hint, sir, but I do not give it credit. Jasper can hardly be true, and Pathfinder false; and, as for the last, I would as soon distrust your honour as distrust him."

"It would seem so, Sergeant. But Jasper is not the Pathfinder, after all; and I will own, Dunham, I should put more faith in the lad if he didn't speak French."

"It's no recommendation in my eyes, I assure your honour; but the boy learned it by compulsion, as it were, and ought not to be condemned too hastily for the circumstance."

"I should have much more faith in this Jasper, did he know nothing of their language. This letter has made me uneasy; and, were there another to whom I could trust the cutter, I would devise some means to detain him here. I have spoken to you already of a brother-in-law who goes with you, Sergeant, and who is a sailor?"

"A real seafaring man, your honour, and somewhat prejudiced against fresh water. I doubt if he could be induced to risk his character on a lake, and I'm certain he never could find the station."

"The last is probably true, and then, the man cannot know enough of this treacherous lake to be fit for the employment. You will have to be doubly vigilant, Dunham. I give you full powers; and should you detect this Jasper in any treachery, make him a sacrifice at once to offended justice."

"Being in the service of the crown, your honour, he is amenable to martial law."

"Very true; then iron him, from head to heels, and send him up here in his own cutter. That brother-in-law of yours must be able to find the way back after he has once travelled the road."

"I make no doubt, Major Duncan, we shall be able to do all that will be necessary, should Jasper turn out as you seem to anticipate; though I think I would risk my life on his truth."

"I like your confidence—it speaks well for the fellow; but that letter! there is such an air of truth about it; nay, there is so much truth in it, touching other matters."

"I think your honour said it wanted the name at the bottom; a great omission for an honest man to make."

"Quite right, Dunham, and no one but a cowardly rascal would write an anonymous letter on private affairs. It *is* different, however, in war; dispatches are feigned, and artifice is generally allowed to be justifiable."

"Military manly artifices, sir, if you will; such as ambushes, surprises, feints, false attacks, and even spies; but I never heard of a true soldier who could wish to undermine the character of an honest young man by such means as these."

"I have met with many strange events, and some stranger people, in the course of my experience. But fare you well, Sergeant; I must detain you no longer. You are now on your guard, and I recommend to you untiring vigilance. I think Muir means shortly to retire; and, should you fully succeed in this enterprise, my influence will not be wanting in endeavouring to put you in the vacancy, to which you have many claims."

"I humbly thank your honour," returned the Sergeant, "and hope I shall never disgrace my station, whatever it may be. I am what nature and Providence have made me, and hope I'm satisfied."

"You have not forgotten the howitzer?"

"Jasper took it on board this morning, sir."

"Be wary, and do not trust that man unnecessarily. Make a confidant of Pathfinder at once; he may be of service in detecting any villainy that may be stirring. His simple honesty will favour his observation by concealing it. *He must* be true."

"For him, sir, my own head shall answer, or even my rank in the regiment. I have seen him too often tried to doubt him."

"Of all wretched sensations, Dunham, distrust, where one is compelled to confide, is the most painful. You have bethought you of the spare flints?"

"A sergeant is a safe commander for all such details, your honour."

"Well, then, give me your hand, Dunham. God bless you! and may you be successful! Have all the ammunition carefully examined and dried as soon as you arrive; the damp of the lake may affect it. And now, farewell, Sergeant. Beware of that Jasper, and consult with Muir in any difficulty. I shall expect you to return, triumphant, this day month."

"God bless your honour! If anything should happen to me, I trust to you, Major, to care for an old soldier's character."

"Rely on me, Dunham—you will rely on a friend. Be vigilant: remember you will be in the very jaws of the lion, and beyond support. Have the flints counted and examined in the morning—and—farewell, Dunham, farewell!"

The Sergeant took the extended hand of his superior with proper respect, and they finally parted; Lundie hastening into his own movable abode, while the other left the fort, and got into a boat.

The *Scud's* kedge was lifted as soon as the boat with the Sergeant, who was the last person expected, was seen to quit the shore, and the head of the cutter was cast to the eastward by means of the sweeps. A few vigorous strokes of the latter, in which the soldiers aided, now sent the light craft into the line of the current that flowed from the river, when she was suffered to drift into the offing again. As yet there was no wind, the light and almost imperceptible air from the lake, that had existed previously to the setting of the sun, having entirely failed.

All this time an unusual quiet prevailed in the cutter. It appeared as if those on board of her felt that they were entering upon an uncertain enterprise, in the obscurity of night; and that their duty, the hour, and the manner of their departure lent a solemnity to their movements. The cutter set slowly out into the lake, until she had got as far as the river current would carry her, when she became stationary, waiting for the usual land breeze. An interval of half an hour followed, during the whole of which time the *Scud* lay as motionless as a log. Sergeant Dunham, having first ascertained that both his daughter and her female companion were on the quarterdeck, led the Pathfinder to the after-cabin, where, closing the door with great caution, and otherwise making certain that he was beyond the reach of eavesdroppers, he commenced as follows:—

"It is now many years, my friend, since you began to experience the hardships and dangers of the woods in my company."

"It is, Sergeant. I sometimes fear I am too old for Mabel, who was not born until you and I had fought the Frenchers as comrades."

"No fear on that account, Pathfinder. I was near your age before I prevailed on the mind of her mother; and Mabel is a steady, thoughtful girl, who will regard character more than anything else. A lad like Jasper Eau-douce, for instance, will have no chance with her, though he is both young and comely."

"Does Jasper think of marrying?" enquired the guide.

"I should hope not—at least, not until he has satisfied everyone of his fitness to possess a wife."

"Jasper is a gallant boy, and may claim a wife as well as another."

"To be frank with you, Pathfinder, I brought you here to talk about this very youngster. Major Duncan has received some information which has led him to suspect that Eau-douce is false, and in the pay of the enemy; I wish to hear your opinion on the subject."

"Anan?"

"I say, the Major suspects Jasper of being a traitor—a French spy—or, what is worse, of being bought to betray us. He has received a letter to this effect, and has been charging me to keep an eye on the boy's movements; for he fears we shall meet with enemies when we least suspect it, and by his means."

"Duncan of Lundie has told you this, Sergeant Dunham?"

"He has indeed, Pathfinder; and, though I have been loath to believe anything to the injury of Jasper, I have a feeling which tells me I ought to distrust him. Do you believe in presentiments, my friend?"

"In what, Sergeant?"

"Presentiments,—a sort of secret foreknowledge of events that are about to happen. The Scotch of our regiment are great sticklers for such things; and my opinion of Jasper is changing so fast, that I begin to fear there must be some truth in their doctrines."

"But you've been talking with Duncan of Lundie concerning Jasper, and his words have raised misgivings."

"Not it, not so in the least; for, while conversing with the Major, my feelings were altogether the other way; and I endeavoured to convince him all I could that he did the boy injustice. But there is no use in holding out against a presentiment; and I fear there is something in the suspicion after all."

"I know nothing of presentiments, Sergeant; but I have known Jasper Eau-douce since he was a boy, and I have as much faith in his honesty as I have in my own or of the Sarpent himself."

"But the Serpent, Pathfinder, has his tricks and ambushes in war as well as another."

"Ay, them are his nat'ral gifts, and are such as belong to his people. Neither redskin nor paleface can deny natur'."

"That I believe; nor should I have thought ill of Jasper this very morning. It seems to me, Pathfinder, since I've taken up this presentiment, that the lad does not bustle about his deck naturally, as he used to do; but that he is moody and thoughtful, like a man who has a load on his conscience."

"Jasper is never noisy; and he tells me noisy ships are generally ill-worked ships. No, I will believe naught against Jasper until I see it. Send for your brother, Sergeant, and let us question him in this matter; for to sleep with distrust of one's friend in the heart is like sleeping with lead there."

The Sergeant, although he scarcely knew with what object, complied, and Cap was summoned to join in the consultation. As Pathfinder was more collected than his companion, he assumed the office of spokesman.

"We have asked you to come down, Master Cap," he commenced, "in order to enquire if you have remarked anything out of the common way in the movements of Eau-douce this evening."

"His movements are common enough, I dare say, for fresh water, Master Pathfinder, though we should think most of his proceedings irregular down on the coast."

"Yes, we know you will never agree with the lad about the manner the cutter ought to be managed; but it is on another point we wish your opinion."

The Pathfinder then explained to Cap the nature of the suspicions which the Sergeant entertained, and the reasons why they had been excited, so far as the latter had been communicated by Major Duncan.

"The youngster talks French, does he?" said Cap.

"They say he speaks it better than common," returned the Sergeant gravely.

"I'll not gainsay it," answered the guide. "But this would prove nothing ag'in a Mississagua, and, least of all, ag'in one like Jasper. I speak the Mingo dialect myself, having learnt it while a prisoner among the reptyles; but who will say I am their friend? Not that I am an enemy, either, according to Indian notions; though I am their enemy, I will admit, agreeable to Christianity."

"Ay, Pathfinder; but Jasper did not get his French as a prisoner: he took it in boyhood, when the mind is easily impressed, and gets its permanent notions; when nature has a presentiment, as it were, which way the character is likely to incline."

"A very just remark," added Cap, "for that is the time of life when we all learn the catechism, and other moral improvements. The Sergeant's observation shows that he understands human nature, and I agree with him perfectly; it *is* a suspicious thing for a youngster, up here, to talk French. If it were down on the

Atlantic, now, where a seafaring man has occasion sometimes to converse with a pilot, or a linguister, in that language, I should not think so much of it; but up here, on Ontario, I hold it to be a most suspicious circumstance."

"But Jasper must talk in French to the people on the other shore," said Pathfinder, " or hold his tongue, as there are none but French to speak to."

"You don't mean to tell me, Pathfinder, that France lies here-away on the opposite coast?" cried Cap; "that one side of this bit of fresh water is York, and the other France?"

"I mean to tell you this is York, and that is Upper Canada; and that English and Dutch and Indian are spoken in the first, and French and Indian in the last. Even the Mingos have got many of the French words in their dialect."

"Very true: and what sort of people are the Mingos, my friend?" enquired the Sergeant: "no one knows them better than yourself, and I ask you what sort of a tribe are they?"

"Jasper is no Mingo, Sergeant."

"He speaks French, and he might as well be, in that particular. Brother Cap, can you recollect no movement of this young man, in the way of his calling, that would seem to denote treachery?"

"Not distinctly, Sergeant, though he has gone to work wrong-end foremost half his time. It is true that one of his hands coiled a rope against the sun, and he called it *querling* a rope, too, when I asked him what he was about; but I am not certain that any-thing was meant by it; though, I dare say, the French coil half their running rigging the wrong way, and may call it 'querling it down', too, for that matter. Then Jasper himself belayed the end of the jib-halyards to a stretcher in the rigging, instead of bringing in to the mast, where they belong, at least among British sailors."

"I dare say Jasper may have got some Canada notions about working his craft, from being so much on the other side," Path-finder interposed; " but catching an idee, or a word, isn't treachery and bad faith. I sometimes get an idee from the Mingos them-selves; but my heart has always been with the Delawares. No, no, Jasper is true; and the king might trust him with his crown, just as he would trust his eldest son, who, as he is to wear it one day, ought to be the last man to wish to steal it."

"Fine talking!" said Cap; "all fine talking, Master Pathfinder, but little logic. In the first place, the king's majesty cannot lend his crown, it being contrary to the laws of the realm, which require
(M 5)   9

him to wear it at all times, in order that his sacred person may be known. Thus you see, friend Pathfinder, that in order to reason truly, one must get under way, as it might be, on the right tack. Law is reason, and reason is philosophy, and philosophy is a steady drag; whence it follows that crowns are regulated by law, reason, and philosophy."

"I know little of all this, Master Cap; but nothing short of seeing and feeling will make me think Jasper Western a traitor."

"There you are wrong again, Pathfinder; for there is a way of proving a thing much more conclusively than by either seeing or feeling, or by both together; and that is by a circumstance."

"It may be so in the settlements; but it is not so here on the lines."

"It is so in nature, which is monarch over all. There was a circumstance, just after we came on board this evening, that is extremely suspicious, and which may be set down at once as a makeweight against this lad. Jasper bent on the king's ensign with his own hands; and, while he pretended to be looking at Mabel and the soldier's wife, giving directions about showing them below here, and all that, he got the flag union down!"

"That might have been an accident," returned the Sergeant, "for such a thing has happened to myself; besides, the halyards lead to a pulley, and the flag would have come right, or not, according to the manner in which the lad hoisted it."

"A pulley!" exclaimed Cap, with strong disgust; "I wish, Sergeant Dunham, I could prevail on you to use proper terms. An ensign-halyard-block is no more a pulley than your halbert is a boarding-pike. It is true that by hoisting on one part, another part would go uppermost; but I look upon that affair of the ensign as a circumstance, and shall bear it in mind. I trust supper is not to be overlooked, however, even if we have a hold full of traitors."

"It will be duly attended to, brother Cap; but I shall count on you for aid in managing the *Scud* should anything occur to induce me to arrest Jasper."

"I'll not fail you, Sergeant; and in such an event you'll probably learn what this cutter can really perform; for, as yet, I fancy it is pretty much matter of guesswork."

"Well, for my part," said Pathfinder, "I shall cling to the hope of Jasper's innocence, and recommend plain dealing, by asking the lad himself, without further delay, whether he is or is not a traitor. I'll put Jasper Western against all the presentiments and circumstances in the colony."

"That will never do," rejoined the Sergeant. "The responsibility of this affair rests with me, and I request and enjoin that nothing be said to anyone without my knowledge. We will all keep watchful eyes about us, and take proper note of circumstances."

"Ay, ay! circumstances are the things after all," returned Cap. "One circumstance is worth fifty facts. Many a man has been hanged on circumstances."

The conversation now ceased, and, after a short delay, the whole party returned to the deck.

CHAPTER XIV

ALL this time matters were elsewhere passing in their usual train. Jasper, like the weather and his vessel, seemed to be waiting for the land breeze; while the soldiers, accustomed to early rising, had, to a man, sought their pallets in the main hold. None remained on deck but the people of the cutter, Mr. Muir, and the two females. The Quartermaster was endeavouring to render himself agreeable to Mabel, while our heroine herself, little affected by his assiduities, was enjoying the peculiarities of a scene and situation which, to her, were full of the charms of novelty.

The sails had been hoisted, but as yet not a breath of air was in motion; and so still and placid was the lake, that not the smallest motion was perceptible in the cutter. She had drifted in the river current to a distance a little exceeding a quarter of a mile from the land, and there she lay like a fixture. Young Jasper was on the quarterdeck, near enough to hear occasionally the conversation which passed; but too diffident of his own claim, and too intent on his duties, to attempt to mingle in it. The fine blue eyes of Mabel followed his motions in curious expectation, and more than once the Quartermaster had to repeat his compliments before she heard them, so intent was she on the little occurrences of the vessel, and, we might add, so indifferent to the eloquence of her companion. Presently an oar-blade fell in a boat beneath the fort, and the sound reached the cutter as distinctly as if it had been produced on her deck. Then came a murmur, like a sigh of the night, a fluttering of the canvas, the creaking of the boom, and the flap of the jib. These well-known sounds were followed by a slight heel in the cutter, and by the bellying of all the sails.

"Here's the wind, Anderson," called out Jasper to the oldest of his sailors; "take the helm."

This brief order was obeyed; the helm was put up, the cutter's bows fell off, and in a few minutes the water was heard murmuring under her head, as the *Scud* glanced through the lake at the rate of five miles in the hour. Then Jasper gave the order to "ease off the sheets a little, and keep her along the land."

It was at this instant that the party from the after-cabin re-appeared on the quarterdeck.

"You've no inclination, Jasper lad, to trust yourself too near our neighbours the French," observed Muir, who took that occasion to recommence the discourse. "Well, well, your prudence will never be questioned by me, for I like the Canadas as little as you can possibly like them yourself."

"I hug this shore, Mr. Muir, on account of the wind. The land breeze is always freshest close in, provided you are not so near as to make a lee of the trees. We have Mexico Bay to cross; and that, on the present course, will give us quite offing enough."

"I'm right glad it's not the Bay of Mexico," put in Cap, "which is a part of the world I would rather not visit in one of your inland craft. Does your cutter bear a weather helm, Master Eau-douce?"

"She is easy on her rudder, Master Cap; but likes looking up at the breeze as well as another, when in lively motion."

"I suppose you have such things as reefs, though you can hardly have occasion to use them?"

Mabel's bright eye detected the smile that gleamed for an instant on Jasper's handsome face; but no one else saw that momentary exhibition of surprise and contempt.

"We have reefs, and often have occasion to use them," quietly returned the young man. "Before we get in, Master Cap, an opportunity may offer to show you the manner in which we do so; for there is easterly weather brewing, and the wind cannot chop, even on the ocean itself, more readily than it flies round on Lake Ontario."

"So much for knowing no better! I have seen the wind in the Atlantic fly round like a coach wheel, in a way to keep your sails shaking for an hour, and the ship would become perfectly motion-less from not knowing which way to turn."

"We have no such sudden changes here, certainly," Jasper mildly answered; "though we think ourselves liable to unexpected shifts of wind. I hope, however, to carry this land breeze as far as the first islands; after which there will be less danger of our being seen and followed by any of the lookout boats from Frontenac."

"Do you think the French keep spies out on the broad lake, Jasper?" enquired the Pathfinder.

"We know they do; one was off Oswego during the night of Monday last. A bark canoe came close in with the eastern point, and landed an Indian and an officer. Had you been outlying that night as usual, we should have secured one, if not both of them."

It was too dark to betray the colour that deepened on the weather-burnt features of the guide; for he felt the consciousness of having lingered in the fort that night, listening to the sweet tones of Mabel's voice as she sang ballads to her father, and gazing at the countenance which, to him, was radiant with charms.

"I confess it, Jasper, I confess it," said he humbly. "Had I been out that night—and I now recollect no sufficient reason why I was not—it might, indeed, have turned out as you say."

"It was the evening you passed with us, Pathfinder," Mabel innocently remarked; "surely one who lives so much of his time in the forest, in front of the enemy, may be excused for giving a few hours of his time to an old friend and his daughter."

"Nay, I've done little else but idle since we reached the garrison," returned the other, sighing; "and it is well that the lad should tell me of it: the idler needs a rebuke."

"Rebuke, Pathfinder! I never dreamt of saying anything disagreeable, and least of all would I think of rebuking you, because a solitary spy and an Indian or two have escaped us. Now I know where you were, I think your absence the most natural thing in the world."

"I think nothing of what you said, Jasper, since it was deserved. We are all human, and all do wrong."

"This is unkind, Pathfinder."

"Give me your hand, lad, give me your hand. It wasn't you that gave the lesson; it was conscience."

"Well, well," interrupted Cap; "now this latter matter is settled to the satisfaction of all parties, perhaps you will tell us how it happened to be known that there were spies near us so lately."

As the mariner uttered the last sentence, he pressed a foot slily on that of the Sergeant, and nudged the guide with his elbow.

"It is known, because their trail was found next day by the Serpent, and it was that of a military boot and a moccasin. One of our hunters, moreover, saw the canoe crossing towards Frontenac next morning."

"Did the trail lead near the garrison, Jasper?" Pathfinder asked.

"We thought not; though, of course, it did not cross the river. It was followed down to the eastern point, at the river's mouth, where what was doing in port might be seen; but it did not cross, as we could discover."

"And why didn't you get under weigh, Master Jasper," Cap demanded, "and give chase? On Tuesday morning it blew a good breeze; one in which this cutter might have run nine knots."

"That may do on the ocean, Master Cap," put in Pathfinder, "but it would not do here. Water leaves no trail, and a Mingo and a Frenchman are a match for the evil one in a pursuit."

"Who wants a trail when the chase can be seen from the deck, as Jasper here said was the case with this canoe? and it mattered nothing if there were twenty of your Mingos and Frenchmen, with a good British-built bottom in their wake. I'll engage, Master Eau-douce, had you given me a call that said Tuesday morning, that we should have overhauled the blackguards."

"I dare say, Master Cap, that the advice of as old a seaman as you might have done no harm to as young a sailor as myself, but it is a long and a hopeless chase that has a bark canoe in it."

"You would have had only to press it hard, to drive it ashore."

"Ashore, Master Cap! You do not understand our lake navigation at all, if you suppose it an easy matter to force a bark canoe ashore. As soon as they find themselves pressed, these bubbles paddle right into the wind's eye, and before you know it, you find yourself a mile or two dead under their lee."

"You don't wish me to believe, Master Jasper, that anyone is so heedless of drowning as to put off into this lake in one of them eggshells when there is any wind?"

"I have often crossed Ontario in a bark canoe, even when there has been a good deal of sea on. Well managed, they are the driest boats of which we have any knowledge."

Cap now led his brother-in-law and Pathfinder aside, when he assured him that the admission of Jasper concerning the spies was "a circumstance", and "a strong circumstance", and as such it deserved his deliberate investigation; while his account of the canoes was so improbable as to wear the appearance of browbeating the listeners. Jasper spoke confidently of the character oi the two individuals who had landed, and this Cap deemed pretty strong proof that he knew more about them than was to be gathered from a mere trail. As for moccasins, he said that they were worn in that part of the world by white men as well as by Indians. Although much of this logic was thrown away on the Sergeant, still it produced some effect. He thought it a little singular himself, that there should have been spies detected so near the fort and he know nothing of it; nor did he believe that this was a branch of knowledge that fell particularly within the sphere of Jasper. It was true that the *Scud* had, once or twice, been sent across the lake to land men of this character, or to bring them off; but then the part played by Jasper, to his own certain knowledge, was very secondary, the master of the cutter remaining as ignorant as anyone else of the purport of the visits of those whom he had carried to and fro; nor did he see why he alone, of all present, should know anything of the late visit. Pathfinder viewed the matter differently. With his habitual diffidence, he reproached himself with a neglect of duty, and that knowledge, of which the want struck him as a fault in one whose business it was to possess it, appeared a merit in the young man. He saw nothing extraordinary in Jasper's knowing the facts he had related; while he did feel it was unusual, not to say disgraceful, that he himself now heard of them for the first time.

"As for moccasins, Master Cap," said he, when a short pause invited him to speak, "they may be worn by palefaces as well as by redskins, it is true, though they never leave the same trail on the foot of one as on the foot of the other. Anyone who is used to the woods can tell the footstep of an Indian from the footstep of a white man, whether it be made by a boot or a moccasin. It will need better evidence than this to persuade me into the belief that Jasper is false."

"You will allow, Pathfinder, that there are such things in the world as traitors?" put in Cap logically.

"I never knew an honest-minded Mingo—one that you could put faith in, if he had a temptation to deceive you."

"Then why not believe that this Jasper may have the same weakness? A man is a man, and human nature is sometimes but a poor concern, as I know by experience."

This was the opening of another long and desultory conversation, in which the probability of Jasper's guilt or innocence was argued *pro* and *con*, until both the Sergeant and his brother-in-law had nearly reasoned themselves into settled convictions in favour of the first, while their companion grew sturdier and sturdier in his defence of the accused, and still more fixed in his opinion of his being unjustly charged with treachery.

By this time the Sergeant had reached a state of mind that disposed him to view every act of the young sailor with distrust, and he soon got to coincide with his relative in deeming the peculiar knowledge of Jasper, in reference to the spies, a branch of information that certainly did not come within the circle of his regular duties, as "a circumstance".

While this matter was thus discussed near the taffrail, Mabel sat silently by the companionway, Mr. Muir having gone below to look after his personal comforts, and Jasper standing a little aloof, with his arms crossed, and his eyes wandering from the sails to the clouds, from the clouds to the dusky outline of the shore, from the shore to the lake, and from the lake back again to the sails. Our heroine, too, began to commune with her own thoughts.

The season and the night, to represent them truly, were of a nature to stimulate the sensations which youth, health, and happiness are wont to associate with novelty. The weather was warm, while the air that came off the land, in breathing currents, brought with it the coolness and fragrance of the forest. The wind was far from being fresh, though there was enough of it to drive the *Scud* merrily ahead, and, perhaps, to keep attention alive, in the uncertainty that more or less accompanies darkness. Jasper, however, appeared to regard it with complacency, as was apparent by what he said in a short dialogue that now occurred between him and Mabel.

" At this rate, Eau-douce,"—for so Mabel had already learned to style the young sailor,—" we cannot be long in reaching our place of destination."

" Has your father then told you what that is, Mabel?"

" He has told me nothing; my father is too much of a soldier, and too little used to have a family around him, to talk of such matters. Is it forbidden to say whither we are bound?"

" It cannot be far, while we steer in this direction, for sixty or seventy miles will take us into the St. Lawrence, which the French might make too hot for us; and no voyage on this lake can be very long."

" So says my Uncle Cap; but to me, Jasper, Ontario and the ocean appear very much the same."

"You have then been on the ocean; while I, who pretend to be a sailor, have never yet seen salt water. You must have a great contempt for such a mariner as myself, Mabel Dunham?"

"Then I have no such thing, Jasper Eau-douce. What right have I, a girl without experience or knowledge, to despise any, much less one like you, who are trusted by the Major, and who command a vessel like this? I have never been on the ocean, though I have seen it; and I repeat, I see no difference between this lake and the Atlantic."

"Nor in them that sail on both? I was afraid, Mabel, your uncle had said so much against us freshwater sailors, that you had begun to look upon us as little better than pretenders?"

"Give yourself no uneasiness on that account, Jasper; for I know my uncle. No, no, neither my father nor myself think anything of such opinions."

"But your father, Mabel, has a better opinion of soldiers than of anyone else? he wishes you to be the wife of a soldier?"

"I the wife of a soldier! My father wishes it! Why should he wish any such thing? What soldier is there in the garrison that I could marry—that he could wish me to marry?"

"One may love a calling so well as to fancy it will cover a thousand imperfections."

"But one is not likely to love his own calling so well as to cause him to overlook everything else. You say my father wishes me to marry a soldier; and yet there is no soldier at Oswego that he would be likely to give me to; for while I am not good enough to be the wife of one of the gentlemen of the garrison, I think even you will admit, Jasper, I am too good to be the wife of one of the common soldiers."

As Mabel spoke thus frankly she blushed, she knew not why, though the obscurity concealed the fact from her companion; and she laughed faintly, like one who felt that the subject, however embarrassing it might be, deserved to be treated fairly. Jasper, it would seem, viewed her position differently from herself.

"It is true, Mabel," said he, "you are not what is called a lady, in the common meaning of the word."

"Not in any meaning, Jasper," the generous girl eagerly interrupted: "on that head I have no vanities. Providence has made me the daughter of a sergeant, and I am content to remain in the station in which I was born."

"But all do not remain in the stations in which they were born, Mabel; for some rise above them, and some fall below them

Many sergeants have become officers—even generals; and why may not sergeants' daughters become officers' ladies?"

"In the case of Sergeant Dunham's daughter, I know no better reason than the fact that no officer is likely to wish to make her his wife," returned Mabel, laughing.

"*You* may think so; but there are some in the 55th that know better. There is certainly one officer in that regiment, Mabel, who *does* wish to make you his wife."

"I know no officer in the 55th, or any other regiment, who would be likely to do so foolish a thing; nor do I think I myself would do so foolish a thing as to marry an officer."

"Foolish, Mabel?"

"Yes, foolish, Jasper. You know, as well as I can know, what the world would think of such matters; and I should be very sorry to find that my husband ever regretted that he had so far yielded to a fancy for a face or figure as to have married the daughter of one so much his inferior as a sergeant."

"*Your* husband, Mabel, will not be so likely to think of the father as to think of the daughter."

The girl continued, in a manner less playful, and one critically attentive might have fancied in a manner slightly melancholy:

"Parent and child ought so to live as not to have two hearts, or two modes of feeling and thinking. A common interest in all things I should think as necessary to happiness in man and wife, as between the other members of the same family. Most of all ought neither the man nor the woman to have any unusual cause for unhappiness. the world furnishing so many of itself."

"Am I to understand, then, Mabel, you would refuse to marry an officer, merely because he was an officer?"

"Have you a right to ask such a question, Jasper?" said Mabel, smiling.

"No other right than what a strong desire to see you happy can give. My anxiety has been increased from happening to know that it is your father's intention to persuade you to marry Lieutenant Muir."

"My dear father can entertain no notion so ridiculous—no notion so cruel!"

"Would it, then, be cruel to wish you the wife of a quartermaster?"

"I have told you what I think on that subject, and cannot make my words stronger. Having answered you so frankly,

Jasper, I have a right to ask how you know that my father thinks of any such thing?"

"That he has chosen a husband for you, I know from his own mouth; for he has told me this much during our frequent conversations while he has been superintending the shipment of the stores; and that Mr. Muir is to offer for you, I know from the officer himself, who has told me as much. By putting the two things together, I have come to the opinion mentioned."

"May not my dear father"—Mabel's face glowed like fire while she spoke—"have been thinking of another? It does not follow, from what you say, that Mr. Muir was in his mind."

"Is it not probable from all that has passed? What brings the quartermaster here? He thinks of you for his wife; and your father has made up his own mind that you shall be so. You must see, Mabel, that Mr. Muir follows you?"

Mabel made no answer. Her feminine instinct had, indeed, told her that she was an object of admiration with the Quartermaster, though she had hardly supposed to the extent that Jasper believed; and she, too, had even gathered from the discourse of her father that he thought seriously of having her disposed of in marriage; but by no process of reasoning could she ever have arrived at the inference that Mr. Muir was to be the man. She did not believe it now, though she was far from suspecting the truth. By way of changing the conversation, after the pause had lasted long enough to be embarrassing to both parties, she said: "Of one thing you may be certain, Jasper—and that is all I wish to say on the subject—Lieutenant Muir, though he were a colonel, will never be the husband of Mabel Dunham. And now, tell me of your voyage; when will it end?"

"That is uncertain. Once afloat, we are at the mercy of the winds and waves. Pathfinder will tell you that he who begins to chase the deer in the morning cannot tell where he will sleep at night."

"But we are not chasing a deer; nor is it morning; so Pathfinder's moral is thrown away."

"I can tell you no more than I have said already; for it is our duty to be close-mouthed, whether anything depends on it or not. I am afraid, however, I shall not keep you long enough in the *Scud* to show you what she can do at need."

"I think a woman unwise who ever marries a sailor," said Mabel abruptly, and almost involuntarily.

"This is a strange opinion; why do you hold it?"

"Because a sailor's wife is certain to have a rival in his vessel. Uncle Cap, too, says that a sailor should never marry."

"He means saltwater sailors," returned Jasper, laughing. "If he thinks wives not good enough for those who sail on the ocean, he will fancy them just suited to those who sail on the lakes."

"Sail, ho!" exclaimed the very individual of whom they were conversing; "or boat, ho! would be nearer the truth."

Jasper ran forward; and, sure enough, a small object was discernible about a hundred yards ahead of the cutter, and nearly on her lee bow. At the first glance he saw it was a bark canoe; for, though the darkness prevented hues from being distinguished, the eye that had become accustomed to the night might discern forms at some little distance; and the eye which, like Jasper's, had long been familiar with things aquatic, could not be at a loss in discovering the outlines necessary to come to the conclusion he did.

"This may be an enemy," the young man remarked; "and it may be well to overhaul him."

"He is paddling with all his might, lad," observed the Pathfinder, "and means to cross your bows and get to windward."

"Let her luff," cried Jasper to the man at the helm. "Luff up, till she shakes. There, steady, and hold all that."

The helmsman complied; and, as the *Scud* was now dashing the water aside merrily, a minute or two put the canoe so far to leeward as to render escape impracticable. Jasper now sprang to the helm himself; and, by judicious and careful handling, he got so near his chase that it was secured by a boathook. On receiving an order, the two persons who were in the canoe left it, and no sooner had they reached the deck of the cutter than they were found to be Arrowhead and his wife.

CHAPTER XV

THE meeting with the Indian and his wife excited no surprise in the majority of those who witnessed the occurrence; but Mabel, and all who knew of the manner in which this chief had been separated from the party of Cap, simultaneously entertained suspicions, which it was far easier to feel than to follow out by any plausible clue to certainty. Pathfinder, who alone could converse freely with the prisoners, took Arrowhead aside, and held a long conversation with him concerning the reasons of the latter for having deserted his charge, and the manner in which he had been since employed.

As respects the separation, his excuses were very simply made, and they seemed to be sufficiently plausible. When he found that the party was discovered in its place of concealment, he naturally sought his own safety, which he secured by plunging into the woods.

"This is well," returned Pathfinder, affecting to believe the other's apologies; "my brother did very wisely; but his woman followed?"

"Do not the palefaces' women follow their husbands? Would not Pathfinder have looked back to see if one he loved was coming?"

This appeal was made to the guide while he was in a most fortunate frame of mind to admit its force; for Mabel and her blandishments and constancy were becoming images familiar to his thoughts. The Tuscarora, though he could not trace the reason, saw that his excuse was admitted, and he stood with quiet dignity awaiting the next enquiry.

"This is reasonable and natural," returned Pathfinder; "this is natural, and may be so. A woman would be likely to follow the man to whom she had plighted faith, and husband and wife are one flesh. Your words are honest, Tuscarora, and very pleasant and just. But why has my brother been so long from the fort? His friends have thought of him often, but have never seen him."

"If the doe follows the buck, ought not the buck to follow the doe!" answered the Tuscarora, smiling, as he laid a finger significantly on the shoulder of his interrogator. "Arrowhead's wife followed Arrowhead; it was right in Arrowhead to follow his wife. She lost her way, and they made her cook in a strange wigwam."

"I understand you, Tuscarora. The woman fell into the hands of the Mingos, and you kept upon their trail."

"Pathfinder can see a reason as easily as he can see the moss on the trees. It is so."

"And how long have you got the woman back, and in what manner has it been done?"

"Two suns. The Dew-of-June was not long in coming when her husband whispered to her the path."

"Well, all this seems natural, and according to matrimony. But, Tuscarora, how did you get that canoe, and why are you paddling towards the St. Lawrence instead of the garrison?"

"Arrowhead can tell his own from that of another. This canoe is mine; I found it on the shore near the fort."

"That sounds reasonable, too, for the canoe does belong to the man, and an Indian would make few words about taking it. Still, it is extraordinary that we saw nothing of the fellow and his wife, for the canoe must have left the river before we did ourselves."

This idea, which passed rapidly through the mind of the guide, was now put to the Indian in the shape of a question.

"Pathfinder knows that a warrior can have shame. The father would have asked me for his daughter, and I could not give her to him. I sent the Dew-of-June for the canoe, and no one spoke to the woman."

All this, too, was plausible, and in conformity with Indian character and customs. As was usual, Arrowhead had received one half of his compensation previously to quitting the Mohawk; and his refraining to demand the residue was a proof of that conscientious consideration of mutual rights that quite as often distinguishes the morality of a savage as that of a Christian.

"You would not look upon the grief of the girl's father?" said Pathfinder.

Arrowhead made a quiet inclination of the body as if to assent.

"One thing more my brother will tell me," continued Pathfinder, "and there will be no cloud between his wigwam and the strong-house of the Yengeese. Why was the head of Arrowhead's canoe looking towards the St. Lawrence, where there are none but enemies to be found?"

"Why were the Pathfinder and his friends looking the same way?" asked the Tuscarora calmly.

"Why, to own the truth, Arrowhead, we are out scouting, in other words we are on the king's business, and we have a right to be here, though we may not have a right to say why we are here."

"Arrowhead saw the big canoe, and he loves to look on the face of Eau-douce. He was going towards the sun at evening in order to seek his wigwam; but, finding that the young sailor was going the other way, he turned that he might look in the same direction."

Pathfinder now returned to the others, and repeated the result of his examination. He appeared himself to believe that the account of Arrowhead might be true; but his auditors, Jasper excepted, seemed less disposed to put faith in the explanations.

"This chap must be ironed at once, brother Dunham," said

Cap; "he must be turned over to the master-at-arms, and a court-martial ought to be ordered as soon as we reach port."

"I think it wisest to detain the fellow," the Sergeant answered. "In the morning the matter shall be enquired into."

Arrowhead was now summoned and told the decision. The Indian listened gravely, and made no objection; and he stood apart, an attentive but calm observer of what was passing. Jasper caused the cutter's sails to be filled, and the *Scud* resumed her course.

It was now getting near the hour to set the watch, and when it was usual to retire for the night. Most of the party went below, leaving no one on deck but Cap, the Sergeant, Jasper, and two of the crew. Arrowhead and his wife also remained.

"You will find a place for your wife below, Arrowhead, where my daughter will attend to her wants," said the Sergeant kindly, who was himself on the point of quitting the deck; "yonder is a sail where you may sleep yourself."

"I thank my father. The woman will look for my blankets in the canoe."

"As you wish, my friend. We think it necessary to detain you; but not necessary to confine or to maltreat you. Send your squaw into the canoe for the blankets, and you may follow her yourself, and hand us up the paddles. As there may be some sleepy heads in the *Scud*, Eau-douce," added the Sergeant in a lower tone, "it may be well to secure the paddles."

Jasper assented, and Arrowhead and his wife silently complied with the directions. A few expressions of sharp rebuke passed from the Indian to his wife while both were employed in the canoe, which the latter received with submissive quiet, immediately repairing an error she had made by laying aside the blanket she had taken and searching for another that was more to her tyrant's mind.

"Come, bear a hand, Arrowhead," said the Sergeant, who stood on the gunwale overlooking the movements of the two, which were proceeding too slowly for the impatience of a drowsy man; "it is getting late."

"Arrowhead is coming," was the answer, as the Tuscarora stepped towards the head of his canoe.

One blow of his keen knife severed the rope which held the boat, and then the cutter glanced ahead, leaving the light bubble of bark almost stationary. So suddenly and dexterously was the manoeuvre performed, that the canoe was on the lee quarter of the *Scud* before the Sergeant was aware of the artifice, and quite in her wake ere he had time to announce it to his companions.

"Hard-a-lee!" shouted Jasper, letting fly the jib-sheet with his own hands, when the cutter came swiftly up to the breeze, with all her canvas flapping, or was running into the wind's eye, as seamen term it, until the light craft was a hundred feet to windward of her former position. Quick and dexterous as was this movement, and ready as had been the expedient, it was not quicker or more ready than that of the Tuscarora. With an intelligence that denoted some familiarity with vessels, he had seized his paddle and was already skimming the water, aided by the efforts of his wife. The direction he took was south-westerly, or on a line that led him equally towards the wind and the shore, while it also kept him so far aloof from the cutter as to avoid the danger of the latter falling on board of him when she filled on the other tack. Swiftly as the *Scud* had shot into the wind, and far as she had forced ahead, Jasper knew it was necessary to cast her ere she had lost all her way; and it was not two minutes from the time the helm had been put down before the lively little craft was aback forward, and rapidly falling off, in order to allow her sails to fill on the opposite tack.

"He will escape!" said Jasper the instant he caught a glimpse of the relative bearings of the cutter and the canoe. "The cunning knave is paddling dead to windward, and the *Scud* can never overtake him!"

"You have a canoe!" exclaimed the Sergeant, manifesting the eagerness of a boy to join in the pursuit; "let us launch it and give chase."

"It will be useless. If Pathfinder had been on deck, there might have been a chance; but there is none now. To launch the canoe would have taken three or four minutes, and the time lost would be sufficient for the purposes of Arrowhead."

Both Cap and the Sergeant saw the truth of this, which would have been nearly self-evident even to one unaccustomed to vessels. The shore was distant less than half a mile, and the canoe was already glancing into its shadows, at a rate to show that it would reach the land before its pursuers could probably get half the distance. The helm of the *Scud* was reluctantly put up again, and the cutter wore short round on her heel, coming up to her course on the other tack, as if acting on an instinct. All this was done by Jasper in profound silence, his assistants understanding what was necessary, and lending their aid in a sort of mechanical imitation. While these manœuvres were in the course of execution, Cap took the Sergeant by a button and led him towards the cabin door, where he was out of earshot, and began to unlock his stores of thought.

"Hark'e, brother Dunham," said he, with an ominous face, "this is a matter that requires mature thought and much circumspection."

"The life of a soldier, brother Cap, is one of constant thought and circumspection. On this frontier, were we to overlook either, our scalps might be taken from our heads in the first nap."

"But I consider this capture of Arrowhead as a circumstance; and I might add his escape as another. This Jasper Freshwater must look to it."

"They are both circumstances truly, brother; but they tell different ways. If it is a circumstance against the lad that the Indian has escaped, it is a circumstance in his favour that he was first taken."

"Ay, ay, but two circumstances do not contradict each other like two negatives. If you will follow the advice of an old seaman, Sergeant, not a moment is to be lost in taking the steps necessary for the security of the vessel and all on board of her. The cutter is now slipping through the water at the rate of six knots, and as the distances are so short on this bit of a pond, we may all find ourselves in a French port before morning, and in a French prison before night."

"This may be true enough. What would you advise me to do, brother?"

"In my opinion you should put this Master Freshwater under arrest on the spot; send him below under the charge of a sentinel, and transfer the command of the cutter to me. All this you have power to perform, the craft belonging to the army, and you being the commanding officer of the troops present."

Sergeant Dunham deliberated more than an hour on the propriety of this proposal. The habit of superintending the personal police of the garrison had made him acquainted with character, and he had long been disposed to think well of Jasper. Still that subtle poison, suspicion, had entered his soul; and so much were the artifices and intrigues of the French dreaded, that, especially warned as he had been by his commander, it is not to be wondered that the recollection of years of good conduct should vanish under the influence of a distrust so keen, and seemingly so plausible. In this embarrassment the Sergeant consulted the Quartermaster, whose opinion, as his superior, he felt bound to respect, though at the moment independent of his control. In the present instance it was unfortunate, as respects a candid consideration of the subject, that Cap, instead of the Sergeant himself, made the statement of the case; for the earnest old sailor was not backward in letting his listener perceive to which side he was desirous that the Quartermaster should lean. Lieutenant Muir was much too politic to offend the uncle and father of the woman he hoped and expected to win, had he really thought the case admitted of doubt; but in the manner in which the facts were submitted to him, he was seriously inclined to think that it would be well to put the control of the *Scud* temporarily into the management of Cap, as a precaution against treachery. This opinion then decided the Sergeant, who forthwith set about the execution of the necessary measures.

Without entering into any explanations, Sergeant Dunham simply informed Jasper that he felt it to be his duty to deprive him temporarily of the command of the cutter, and to confer it on his own brother-in-law. A natural and involuntary burst of surprise, which escaped the young man, was met by a quiet remark, reminding him that military service was often of a nature that required concealment, and a declaration that the present duty was of such a character that this particular arrangement had become indispensable. Although Jasper's astonishment remained undiminished, the young man was accustomed to obey with military submission; and he quietly acquiesced, with his own mouth directing the little crew to receive their further orders from Cap until another change should be effected. When, however, he was told the case required that not only he himself, but his principal assistant, who, on account of his long acquaintance with the lake, was usually termed the pilot, were to remain below, there was an alteration in his countenance and manner that denoted strong feeling, though it was so well mastered as to leave even the distrustful Cap in doubt as to its meaning.

Jasper and his assistant both threw themselves silently on their pallets, which neither quitted again that night.

"And now, Sergeant," said Cap, as soon as he found himself master of the deck, "you will just have the goodness to give me the courses and distance, that I may see the boat keeps her head the right way."

"I know nothing of either, brother Cap," returned Dunham, not a little embarrassed at the question. "We must make the best of our way to the station among the Thousand Islands, where 'we shall land, relieve the party that is already out, and get information for our future government'. That's it, nearly word for word, as it stands in the written orders."

"But you can muster a chart—something in the way of bearings and distances, that I may see the road !"

"I do not think Jasper ever had anything of the sort to go by."

"No chart, Sergeant Dunham!"

"Not a scrap of a pen even. Our sailors navigate this lake without any aid from maps."

"They do! They must be regular Yahoos. And do you suppose, Sergeant Dunham, that I can find one island out of a thousand without knowing its name or its position, without even a course or a distance?"

"As for the *name*, brother Cap, you need not be particular, for not one of the whole thousand *has* a name, and so a mistake can never be made on that score. As for the position, never having been there myself, I can tell you nothing about it, nor do I think its position of any particular consequence, provided we find the spot. Perhaps one of the hands on deck can tell us the way."

"Hold on, Sergeant—hold on a moment, if you please. If I am to command this craft, it must be done, if you please, without holding any councils of war with the cook and cabin-boy. A shipmaster is a shipmaster, and he must have an opinion of his own, even if it be a wrong one. I suppose you know service well enough to understand that it is better in a commander to go wrong than to go nowhere. At all events, the Lord High Admiral couldn't command a yawl with dignity, if he consulted the cockswain every time he wished to go ashore. No, sir, if I sink, I sink! but hang me, I'll go down shipshape and with dignity."

"But, brother Cap, I have no wish to go down anywhere, unless it be to the station among the Thousand Islands, whither we are bound."

"Well, Sergeant, rather than ask advice—that is, direct, barefaced advice—of a foremast hand, or any other than a quarterdeck officer, I would go round to the whole thousand, and examine them one by one until we got the right haven. But there is such a thing as coming at an opinion without manifesting ignorance, and I will manage to rouse all there is out of these hands, and make them think all the while that I am cramming them with my own experience."

"I know we are steering in the right direction at present,"

returned the Sergeant; "but in the course of a few hours we shall be up with a headland, where we must feel our way with more caution."

"Leave me to pump the man at the wheel, brother, and you shall see that I will make him suck in a very few minutes."

Cap and the Sergeant now walked aft, until they stood by the sailor who was at the helm, Cap maintaining an air of security and tranquillity, like one who was entirely confident of his own powers.

"This is a wholesome air, my lad," Cap observed, in the manner that a superior on board a vessel sometimes condescends to use to a favoured inferior. "Of course you have it in this fashion off the land every night?"

"At this season of the year, sir," the man returned, touching his hat, out of respect to his new commander and Sergeant Dunham's connection.

"The same thing, I take it, among the Thousand Islands? The wind will stand, of course, though we shall then have land on every side of us."

"When we get farther east, sir, the wind will probably shift, for there can then be no particular land-breeze."

"Ay, ay; so much for your fresh water! It has always some trick that is opposed to nature. Now, down among the West India Islands, one is just as certain of having a land-breeze as he is of having a sea-breeze. In that respect there is no difference, though it's quite in rule it should be different up here on this bit of fresh water. Of course, my lad, you know all about these said Thousand Islands?"

"Lord bless you, Master Cap, nobody knows all about them, or anything about them. They are a puzzle to the oldest sailor on the lake, and we don't pretend to know even their names."

"I take it, John——" resumed Cap. "Your name is Jack, I believe?"

"No, sir; I am called Robert."

"Ay, Robert, it's very much the same thing, Jack or Bob. I say, Bob, it's good holding ground, is it, down at this same station for which we are bound?"

"Bless you, sir! I know no more about it than you do."

"Did you never anchor there?"

"Never, sir. Master Eau-douce always makes fast to the shore."

"But in running in for the town, you kept the lead going, out of question, and must have tallowed as usual."

"Tallow—and town, too! Bless your heart, there is no more town than there is on your chin, and not half as much tallow!"

The Sergeant smiled grimly, but his brother-in-law did not detect this proof of humour.

"No church tower, nor light, nor fort, ha! There is a garrison, as you call it hereaway, at least?"

"Ask Sergeant Dunham, sir, if you wish to know that. All the garrison is on board the *Scud*."

"But in running in, Bob, which of the channels do you think the best? the one you went last, or—or—or—ay, or the other?"

"I can't say, sir; I know nothing of either."

"You didn't go to sleep, fellow, at the wheel, did you?"

"Not at the wheel, sir, but down in the fore-peak in my berth. Eau-douce sent us below, soldiers and all, with the exception of the pilot, and we know no more of the road than if we had never been over it. This he has always done in going in and coming out; and for the life of me, I could tell you nothing of the channel, or the course, after we are once fairly up with the islands. No one knows anything of either but Jasper and the pilot."

"Here is a circumstance for you, Sergeant," said Cap, leading his brother-in-law a little aside; "there is no one on board to pump. How, then, am I to find the way to this station for which we are bound?

"Sure enough, brother Cap, your question is more easily put than answered. Is there no such thing as figuring it out by navigation? I thought you saltwater mariners were able to do as small a thing as that. I have often read of their discovering islands, surely?"

"That you have, brother; and this discovery would be the greatest of them all; for it would be discovering one island out of a thousand."

"Still the sailors of the lake have a method of finding the places they wish to go to."

"If I have understood you, Sergeant, this station or block-house is particularly private."

"It is, indeed, the utmost care having been taken to prevent a knowledge of its position from reaching the enemy."

"And you expect me, a stranger on your lake, to find this place without chart, course, distance, latitude, longitude, or soundings,— ay, hang me, or tallow! Allow me to ask if you think a mariner runs by his nose, like one of Pathfinder's hounds?"

"Well, brother, you may yet learn something by questioning the young man at the helm; I can hardly think that he is as ignorant as he pretends to be."

"Hum!—This looks like another circumstance. For that matter, the case is getting to be so full of circumstances that one hardly knows how to foot up the evidence. But we will soon see how much the lad knows."

Cap and the Sergeant now returned to their station near the helm, and the former renewed his enquiries.

"Do you happen to know what may be the latitude and longitude of this said island, my lad?" he asked.

"The what, sir?"

"Why, the latitude or longitude—one or both; I'm not particular which, as I merely enquire in order to see how they bring up young men on this bit of fresh water."

"I'm not particular about either myself, sir, and so I do not happen to know what you mean."

"Not what I mean! You know what latitude is?"

"Not I, sir! though I believe it is French for the upper lakes."

"Whe—e—e—w!" whistled Cap. "Hark'e, young man, do you know what longitude means?"

"I believe I do, sir; that is, five feet six, the regulation height for soldiers in the king's service."

"There's the longitude found out for you, Sergeant, in the rattling of a brace-block! You have some notion about a degree, and minutes and seconds, I hope?"

"Yes, sir; degree means my betters; and minutes and seconds are for the short or long log-lines. We all know these things as well as the saltwater people."

"Well, my lad, you understand the azimuth, and measuring distances, and how to box the compass."

"As for the first, sir, I can't say I do. The distances we all know, as we measure them from point to point; and as for boxing the compass, I will turn my back to no admiral in his Majesty's fleet. Nothe, nothe and by east, nothe, nothe-east, nothe-east and by nothe, nothe-east; nothe-east and by east, east-nothe-east, east and by nothe-east——"

"That will do. You'll bring about a shift of wind if you go on in this manner. I see very plainly, Sergeant," walking away again, and dropping his voice, "we've nothing to hope for from that chap. I'll stand on two hours longer on this tack, when we'll heave-to and get the soundings, after which we will be governed by circumstances.

To this the Sergeant made no objections; and as the wind grew lighter he made a bed of sail on deck, and was soon lost in the sound sleep of a soldier. Cap continued to walk the deck, and not once that night did he close his eyes.

It was broad daylight when Sergeant Dunham awoke, and the exclamation of surprise that escaped him, as he rose to his feet and began to look about him, was stronger than it was usual for one so drilled to suffer to be heard. He found the weather entirely changed, the view bounded by driving mist that limited the visible horizon to a circle of about a mile in diameter, the lake raging and covered with foam, and the *Scud* lying-to.

According to the account of Master Cap, the wind had died away to a calm about midnight, or just as he was thinking of heaving-to, to sound, for islands ahead were beginning to be seen. At one a.m. it began to blow from the north-east, accompanied by a drizzle, and he stood off to the northward and westward, knowing that the coast of New York lay in the opposite direction. At half-past one he stowed the flying-jib, reefed the mainsail, and took the bonnet off the jib. At two he was compelled to get a second reef aft; and by half-past two he had put a balance-reef in the sail, and was lying-to.

"I can't say but the boat behaves well, Sergeant," the old sailor added, "but it blows forty-two pounders. I had no idea there were any such currents of air up here on this bit of fresh water, though I care not the knotting of a yarn for it, as your lake has now somewhat of a natural look; and if the water had a savour of salt about it, one might be comfortable."

"How long have you been heading in this direction, brother Cap?" enquired the prudent soldier; "and at what rate may we be going through the water?"

"Why, two or three hours, mayhap, and she went like a horse for the first pair of them. Oh, we've a fine offing now! for, to own the truth, little relishing the neighbourhood of them said islands, although they are to windward, I took the helm myself, and run her off free for some league or two. We are well to leeward of them, I'll engage—I say to leeward; for though one might wish to be well to windward of one island, or even half a dozen, when it comes to a thousand, the better way is to give it up at once, and to slide down under their lee as fast as possible. No, no; they are there, up yonder in the dingle; and there they may stay, for anything Charles Cap cares."

"As the north shore lies only some five or six leagues from us, brother, and I know there is a large bay in that quarter, might it not be well to consult some of the crew concerning our position, if, indeed, we do not call up Jasper Eau-douce, and tell him to carry us back to Oswego? For it is quite impossible we should ever reach the station with this wind directly in our teeth."

"There are several serious professional reasons, Sergeant, against all your propositions. In the first place, an admission of ignorance on the part of a commander would destroy discipline. No matter, brother; I understand your shake of the head, but nothing capsizes discipline so much as to confess ignorance. I once knew a master of a vessel who went a week on a wrong course rather than allow he had made a mistake; and it was surprising how much he rose in the opinions of his people, just because they could not understand him."

"That may do on salt water, brother Cap, but it will hardly do on fresh. Rather than wreck my command on the Canada shore, I shall feel it a duty to take Jasper out of arrest."

"And make a haven in Frontenac. No, Sergeant; the *Scud* is in good hands, and will now learn something of seamanship. We have a fine offing, and no one but a madman would think of going upon a coast in a gale like this. I shall ware every watch, and then we shall be safe against all dangers but those of the drift, which, in a light low craft like this, without top-hamper, will be next to nothing. Leave it all to me, Sergeant, and I pledge you the character of Charles Cap that all will go well."

CHAPTER XVI

As yet the sea was not very high, from which it was inferred that the cutter was still under the lee of the islands; but it was apparent to all who understood the lake that they were about to experience one of the heavy autumnal gales of that region. Land was nowhere visible; and the horizon on every side exhibited that gloomy void, which lends to all views on vast bodies of water the sublimity of mystery. The waves were short and curling, breaking of necessity sooner than the longer seas of the ocean, while the element itself, instead of presenting that beautiful hue which rivals the deep tint of the southern sky, looked green and angry, though wanting in the lustre that is derived from the rays of the sun.

The soldiers were soon satisfied with the prospect, and one by one they disappeared, until none were left on deck but the crew, the Sergeant, Cap, Pathfinder, the Quartermaster, and Mabel. There was a shade on the brow of the last, who had been made acquainted with the real state of things, and who had fruitlessly ventured an appeal in favour of Jasper's restoration to the command. A night's rest and a night's reflection appeared also to have confirmed the Pathfinder in his opinion of the young man's innocence; and he, too, had made a warm appeal on behalf of his friend, though with the same want of success.

Several hours passed away, the wind gradually getting heavier and the sea rising, until the motion of the cutter compelled Mabel and the Quartermaster to retreat also. Cap wore several times; and it was now evident that the *Scud* was drifting into the broader and deeper parts of the lake, the seas raging down upon her in a way that none but a vessel of superior mould and build could have long ridden and withstood. All this, however, gave Cap no uneasiness; but, like the hunter that pricks his ears at the sound of the horn, or the warhorse that paws and snorts with pleasure at the roll of the drum, the whole scene awakened all that was man within him; and instead of the captious, supercilious, and dogmatic critic, quarrelling with trifles and exaggerating immaterial things, he began to exhibit the qualities of the hardy and experienced seaman which he truly was. The hands soon imbibed a respect for his skill; and, though they wondered at the disappearance of their old commander and the pilot, for which no reason had been publicly given, they soon yielded an implicit and cheerful obedience to the new one.

"This bit of fresh water, after all, brother Dunham, has some spirit, I find," cried Cap about noon. "The wind seems to be an honest old-fashioned gale, and the seas have a fanciful resemblance to those of the Gulf Stream. I like this, Sergeant, and shall get to respect your lake, if it hold out twenty-four hours longer in the fashion in which it has begun."

"Land, ho!" shouted the man who was stationed on the forecastle.

Cap hurried forward; and there, sure enough, the land was visible through the drizzle, at the distance of about half a mile, the cutter heading directly towards it. The first impulse of the old seaman was to give an order to "stand by, to ware off shore"; but the cool-headed soldier restrained him.

"By going a little nearer," said the Sergeant, "some of us may recognize the place. Most of us know the American shore in this part of the lake; and it will be something gained to learn our position."

"Very true; if, indeed, there is any chance of that, we will hold on. What is this off here, a little on our weather-bow? It looks like a low headland."

"The garrison, by Jove!" exclaimed the other, whose trained eye sooner recognized the military outlines than the less-instructed senses of his connection.

The Sergeant was not mistaken. There was the fort, sure enough, though it looked less dim and indistinct through the fine rain, as if it were seen in the dusk of evening or the haze of morning. The low, sodded, and verdant ramparts, the sombre palisades, now darker than ever with water, the roof of a house or two, the tall, solitary flagstaff, with its halyards blown steadily out into a curve that appeared traced in immovable lines in the air, were all soon to be seen, though no sign of animated life could be discovered. Even the sentinel was housed; and at first it was believed that no eye would detect the presence of their own vessel. But the unceasing vigilance of a border garrison did not slumber; one of the lookouts probably made the interesting discovery; a man or two were seen on some elevated stands, and then the entire ramparts next the lake were dotted with human beings.

"They see us," said the Sergeant, "and think we have returned on account of the gale, and have fallen to leeward of the port. Yes, there is Major Duncan himself on the north-eastern bastion."

"Sergeant, it would be worth standing a little jeering, if we could fetch into the river, and come safely to an anchor. In that case, too, we might land this Master Eau-douce, and purify the boat."

"It would indeed; but, as poor a sailor as I am, I well know it cannot be done. Nothing that sails the lake can turn to windward against this gale; and there is no anchorage outside in weather like this."

"I know it, I see it, Sergeant; and pleasant as is that sight to you landsmen, we must leave it. For myself, I am never so happy in heavy weather as when I am certain that the land is behind me."

The *Scud* had now forged so near in, that it became indispensable to lay her head off shore again, and the necessary orders were given. The storm-staysail was set forward, the gaff lowered, the helm put up, and the light craft, that seemed to sport with the elements like a duck, fell off a little, drew ahead swiftly, obeyed her rudder, and was soon flying away on the top of the surges, dead before the gale. While making this rapid flight, though the land still remained in view on her larboard beam, the fort and the groups of anxious spectators on its rampart were swallowed up in the mist. Then followed the evolutions necessary to bring the head of the cutter up to the wind, when she again began to wallow her weary way towards the north shore.

Hours now passed before any further change was made, the wind increasing in force, until even the dogmatical Cap fairly admitted it was blowing a thorough gale of wind. About sunset the *Scud* wore again to keep her off the north shore during the hours of darkness; and at midnight her temporary master, who, by questioning the crew in an indirect manner, had obtained some general knowledge of the size and shape of the lake, believed himself to be about midway between the two shores. The height and length of the seas aided this impression; and it must be added that Cap by this time began to feel a respect for fresh water which twenty-four hours earlier he would have derided as impossible. Just as the night turned, the fury of the wind became so great that he found it impossible to bear up against it, the water falling on the deck of the little craft in such masses as to cause it to shake to the centre, and, though a vessel of singularly lively qualities, to threaten to bury it beneath its weight. The people of the *Scud* averred that never before had they been out in such a tempest, which was true; for, possessing a perfect knowledge of all the rivers and headlands and havens, Jasper would have carried the cutter inshore long ere this, and placed her in safety in some secure anchorage. But Cap still disdained to consult the young master, determining to act like a mariner of the broad ocean.

It was one in the morning when the storm-staysail was again got on the *Scud*, the head of the mainsail lowered, and the cutter put before the wind. Although the canvas now exposed was merely a rag in surface, the little craft nobly justified the use of the name she bore. For eight hours did she scud in truth; and it was almost with the velocity of the gulls that wheeled wildly over her in the tempest, apparently afraid to alight in the boiling cauldron of the lake. The dawn of day brought little change; for no other horizon became visible than the little circle of drizzling sky and water already described, in which it seemed as if the elements were rioting in a sort of chaotic confusion. During this time the crew and passengers of the cutter were of necessity passive. Jasper and the pilot remained below; but, the motion of the vessel having become easier, nearly all the rest were on deck. The morning meal had been taken in silence, and eye met eye, as if their owners asked each other, in dumb show, what was to be the end of this strife in the elements. Cap, however, was perfectly composed, and his face brightened, his step grew firmer, and his whole air more assured, as the storm increased, making larger demands on his professional skill and personal spirit. He stood on the forecastle, his arms crossed, balancing his body with a seaman's instinct, while his eyes watched the caps of the seas, as they broke and glanced past the reeling cutter, itself in such swift motion, as if they were the scud flying athwart the sky. At this sublime instant one of the hands gave the unexpected cry of " A sail!"

The strange vessel was about two cables' length ahead of the *Scud*, standing by the wind athwart her bows, and steering a course to render it probable that the latter would pass within a few yards of her. She was a full-rigged ship; and, seen through the misty medium of the tempest, the most experienced eye could detect no imperfection in her gear or construction. The only canvas she had set was a close-reefed main-topsail, and two small storm-staysails, one forward and the other aft. Still the power of the wind pressed so hard upon her as to bear her down nearly to her beam-ends, whenever the hull was not righted by the buoyancy of some wave, under her lee. Her spars were all in their places, and by her motion through the water, which might have equalled four knots in the hour, it was apparent that she steered a little free.

"The fellow must know his position well," said Cap, as the cutter flew down toward the ship, with a velocity almost equalling that of the gale, "for he is standing boldly to the southward, where he expects to find anchorage or a haven. No man in his senses would run off free in that fashion, that was not driven to scudding, like ourselves, who did not perfectly understand where he was going."

"We have made an awful run, Captain," returned the man to whom this remark had been addressed. "That is the French king's ship, Lee-my-calm (*Le Montcalm*), and she is standing in for the Niagara, where her owner has a garrison and a port. We've made an awful run of it!"

"Ay, bad luck to him! Frenchman-like, he skulks into port the moment he sees an English bottom."

"It might be well for us if we could follow him," returned the man, shaking his head despondingly, "for we are getting into the end of a bay up here at the head of the lake, and it is uncertain whether we ever get out of it again!"

"Pooh, man, pooh! We have plenty of searoom, and a good English hull beneath us. We are no Johnny Crapauds to hide ourselves behind a point or a fort on account of a puff of wind. Mind your helm, sir!"

The order was given on account of the menacing appearance of the approaching passage. The *Scud* was now heading directly for the fore-foot of the Frenchman; and, the distance between the two vessels having diminished to a hundred yards, it was momentarily questionable if there was room to pass.

"Port, sir, port!" shouted Cap. "Port your helm and pass astern!"

The crew of the Frenchman were seen assembling to windward, and a few muskets were pointed, as if to order the people of the *Scud* to keep off. The water was dripping from the muzzles of two or three light guns on board the ship; the wind howled through her rigging, whistling the thousand notes of a ship; and the hails and cries that escape a Frenchman with so much readiness were inaudible.

"Let him halloo himself hoarse!" growled Cap. "This is no weather to whisper secrets in. Port, sir, port!"

The man at the helm obeyed, and the next send of the sea drove the *Scud* down upon the quarter of the ship, so near her that the old mariner himself recoiled a step, in a vague expectation that, at the next surge ahead, she would drive bows foremost directly into the planks of the other vessel. But this was not to be: rising from the crouching posture she had taken, like a panther about to leap, the cutter dashed onward, and at the next instant she was glancing past the stern of her enemy, just clearing the end of her spanker-boom with her own lower yard.

The young Frenchman who commanded the *Montcalm* leaped on the taffrail; and, with that courtesy which relieves even the worst acts of his countrymen, he raised his cap and smiled a salutation as the *Scud* shot past. But the Frenchman's *bonhomie* was lost on Cap, who shook his fist menacingly, and muttered to himself:

"Ay, ay, it's lucky for you I've no armament on board here or I'd send you in to get new cabin windows fitted."

"'Twas civil, brother Cap," returned the other, lowering his hand from the military salute which his pride as a soldier had induced him to return,—and that's as much as you can expect from a Frenchman. What he really meant by it no one can say."

"He is not heading up to this sea without an object, neither. Well, let him run in, if he can get there; we will keep the lake like hearty English mariners."

A few hours succeeded, and darkness came again to increase the perils of the *Scud*. A lull in the gale, however, had induced Cap to come by the wind once more, and throughout the night the cutter was lying-to as before, head-reaching as a matter of course, and occasionally waring to keep off the land.

During this night Cap slept soundly, and for several hours. The day was just dawning when he felt himself shaken by the shoulder; and arousing himself, he found the Pathfinder standing at his side. During the gale the guide had appeared little on deck, for his natural modesty told him that seamen alone should inter- fere with the management of the vessel; and he was willing to show the same reliance on those who had charge of the *Scud*, as he expected those who followed through the forest to manifest in his own skill; but he now thought himself justified in inter- fering, which he did in his own unsophisticated and peculiar manner.

"Sleep is sweet, Master Cap," said he, as soon as the eyes of the latter were fairly open, and his consciousness had sufficiently returned, "but life is sweeter still. Look about you, and say if this is exactly the moment for a commander to be off his feet."

"How now, Master Pathfinder?" growled Cap. "Are you, too, on the side of the grumblers? I little expected such a summons from you."

"As for myself, Master Cap, I feel I have my gifts, and I believe they'll interfere with those of no other man, but the case may be different with Mabel Dunham. It's on her account that I speak, and not on my own."

"I begin to understand. The girl is a good girl, my worthy friend; but she is a soldier's daughter and a sailor's niece, and ought not to be too tame or too tender in a gale. Does she show any fear?"

"Not she! Mabel is a woman, but she is reasonable and silent. Not a word have I heard from her concerning our doings; though

I do think, Master Cap, she would like it better if Jasper Eau-douce were put into his proper place, and things were restored to their old situation, like."

"I'll warrant it—girl-like, and Dunham-like, too. Anything is better than an old uncle, and everybody knows more than an old seaman. *This* is human natur', Master Pathfinder, and hang me if I'm the man to sheer a fathom, starboard or port, for all the human natur' that can be found in a minx of twenty. I've not been at sea forty years, to come up on this bit of fresh water to be taught human natur'. How this gale holds out! And what is all this to leeward?" (rubbing his eyes)—"land! as sure as my name is Cap—and high land, too."

The Pathfinder made no immediate answer; but, shaking his head, he watched the expression of his companion's face, with a look of strong anxiety in his own.

"Land, as certain as this is the *Scud*!" repeated Cap; "a lee shore, and that, too, within a league of us, with as pretty a line of breakers as one could find on the beach of all Long Island!"

"And is that encouraging? or is it disheartening?" enquired the Pathfinder.

"Ha! encouraging—disheartening!—why, neither. No, no, there is nothing encouraging about it; and as for disheartening, nothing ought to dishearten a seaman. You never get dis-heartened or afraid in the woods, my friend?"

"I'll not say that. When the danger is great, it is my gift to see it, and know it, and to try to avoid it; else would my scalp long since have been drying in a Mingo wigwam. On this lake, however, I can see no trail, and I feel it my duty to submit; though I think we ought to remember there is such a person as Mabel Dunham on board. But here comes her father, and he will naturally feel for his own child."

"We are seriously situated, I believe, brother Cap," said the Sergeant, when he had reached the spot, "by what I can gather from the two hands on the forecastle? They tell me the cutter cannot carry any more sail, and her drift is so great we shall go ashore in an hour or two. I hope their fears have deceived them?"

Cap made no reply; but he gazed at the land with a rueful face, and then looked to windward with an expression of ferocity, as if he would gladly have quarrelled with the weather.

"It may be well, brother," the Sergeant continued, "to send for Jasper and consult him as to what is to be done. There are no

French here to dread; and, under all circumstances, the boy will save us from drowning if possible."

"Ay, ay, 'tis these cursed circumstances that have done all the mischief. But let the fellow come; let him come; a few well-managed questions will bring the truth out of him, I'll warrant you."

This acquiescence on the part of the dogmatical Cap was no sooner obtained than Jasper was sent for. The young man instantly made his appearance, his whole air, countenance, and mien expressive of mortification, humility, and, as his observers fancied, rebuked deception. When he first stepped on deck, Jasper cast one hurried, anxious glance around, as if curious to know the situation of the cutter; and that glance sufficed, it would seem, to let him into the secret of all her perils. At first he looked to windward, as is usual with every seaman; then he turned round the horizon, until his eye caught a view of the high lands to leeward, when the whole truth burst upon him at once.

"I've sent for you, Master Jasper," said Cap, folding his arms, and balancing his body with the dignity of the forecastle, "in order to learn something about the haven to leeward. We take it for granted you do not bear malice so hard as to wish to drown us all, especially the women; and I suppose you will be man enough to help us to run the cutter into some safe berth until this bit of a gale has done blowing!"

"I would die myself rather than harm should come to Mabel Dunham," the young man answered.

"I knew it!" cried the Pathfinder, clapping his hand kindly on Jasper's shoulder.

"Humph!" ejaculated Cap. "Never mind, young man; we shall understand each other by talking like two plain seamen. Do you know of any port under our lee?"

"None. There is a large bay at this end of the lake, but it is unknown to us all, and not easy of entrance."

"And this coast to leeward—it has nothing particular to recommend it, I suppose?"

"It is a wilderness until you reach the mouth of the Niagara in one direction, and Frontenac in the other."

"Thank God! then, there can be no French. Are there many savages, hereaway, on the land?"

"The Indians are to be found in all directions; though they are nowhere very numerous."

"We must take our chance, then, as to the blackguards; but to be frank with you, Master Western, if this little unpleasant matter about the French had not come to pass, what would you now do with the cutter?"

"I am a much younger sailor than yourself, Master Cap," said Jasper modestly, "and am hardly fitted to advise you."

"Ay, ay, we all know that. But at all events, you can speak, and I can judge of your opinions, agreeably to my own experience."

"I think, sir, before two hours are over, the cutter will have to anchor."

"Anchor!—not out here in the lake?"

"No, sir; but in yonder, near the land."

"You do not mean to say, Master Eau-douce, you would anchor on a lee shore in a gale of wind?"

"If I would save my vessel, that is exactly what I would do."

"Whe—e—e—w!—this is fresh water, with a vengeance! I never yet heard of such a thing. I'd throw my ground-tackle overboard before I would be guilty of so lubberly an act!"

"That is what we do on this lake," modestly replied Jasper, "when we are hard pressed."

"No man induces me to commit such a sin against my own bringing-up. I should never dare show my face inside of Sandy Hook again, had I committed so know-nothing an exploit. You can go below again, Master Eau-douce."

Jasper quietly withdrew; still, as he passed down the ladder, the spectators observed that he cast an anxious look at the horizon to windward and the land to leeward.

CHAPTER XVII

As the soldier's wife was sick in her berth, Mabel Dunham was the only person in the outer cabin when Jasper returned to it; for, by an act of grace in the Sergeant, he had been permitted to resume his proper place in this part of the vessel. We should be ascribing too much simplicity of character to our heroine, if we said that she felt no distrust of the young man in consequence of his arrest; but we should also be doing injustice to her warmth of feeling and generosity of disposition, if we did not add, that this distrust was insignificant and transient. As he now took his seat near her, his whole countenance clouded with the uneasiness he felt concerning the situation of the cutter, everything like suspicion was banished from her mind, and she saw in him only an injured man.

"You let this affair weigh too heavily on your mind, Jasper," said she eagerly; "no one who knows you can, or does, believe you guilty."

"Then you, Mabel," returned the youth, "do not look upon me as the traitor your father believes me to be?"

"My dear father is a soldier, and is obliged to act as one. My father's daughter is not, and will think of you as she ought to think of a man who has done so much to serve her already."

"Mabel, I'm not used to talking with one like you, or saying all I think and feel with any. I never had a sister, and my mother died when I was a child, so that I know little what your sex most likes to hear——"

Mabel would have given the world to know what lay behind the teeming word at which Jasper hesitated; but the indefinable and controlling sense of womanly diffidence made her suppress her curiosity. She waited in silence for him to explain his own meaning.

"I wish to say, Mabel," the young man continued, after a pause which he found sufficiently embarrassing, "that I am unused to the ways and opinions of one like you, and that you must imagine all I would add."

Mabel had imagination enough to fancy anything, but there are ideas and feelings that her sex prefer to have expressed before they yield them all their own sympathies, and she had a vague consciousness that these of Jasper might properly be enumerated in the class. With a readiness that belonged to her sex, therefore, she preferred changing the discourse to permitting it to proceed any further in a manner so awkward and so unsatisfactory.

"Tell me one thing, Jasper, and I shall be content," said she, speaking now with a firmness which denoted confidence, not only in herself, but in her companion: "you do not deserve this cruel suspicion which rests upon you?"

"I do not, Mabel!" answered Jasper. "As I hope for mercy hereafter, I do not!"

"I knew it!" returned the girl warmly. "And yet my father means well;—but do not let this matter disturb you, Jasper."

"There is so much more to apprehend from another quarter just now, that I scarcely think of it,"

" Jasper !"

" I do not wish to alarm you, Mabel; but if your uncle could be persuaded to change his notions about handling the *Scud*; and yet he is so much more experienced than I am, that he ought, perhaps, to place more reliance on his own judgment than on mine."

" Do you think the cutter in danger?" demanded Mabel, quick as thought.

"I fear so; at least she would have been thought in great danger by us of the lake; perhaps an old seaman of the ocean may have means of his own to take care of her."

" Jasper, all agree in giving you credit for skill in managing the *Scud*. You know the lake, you know the cutter; you *must* be the best judge of our real situation."

" My concern for you, Mabel, may make me more cowardly than common; but, to be frank, I see but one method of keeping the cutter from being wrecked in the course of the next two or three hours, and that your uncle refuses to take. After all, this may be my ignorance."

"Think of my dear father, Jasper! Think of yourself; of all the lives that depend on a timely word from you to save them."

"I think of you, Mabel, and that is more, much more, than all the rest put together!" returned the young man.

Mabel's heart beat quickly, and a gleam of grateful satisfaction shot across her blushing features; but the alarm was too vivid and too serious to admit of much relief from happier thoughts.

" My uncle's obstinacy must not be permitted to occasion this disaster. Go once more on deck, Jasper; and ask my father to come into the cabin."

The minute or two which elapsed before the Sergeant came appeared an hour to Mabel, and she scarcely breathed when she saw him and Jasper descending the ladder in company. Quick as language could express her meaning, she acquainted her father with Jasper's opinion of their situation; and entreated him if he loved her, or had any regard for his own life, or for those of his men, to interfere with her uncle, and to induce him to yield the control of the cutter again to its proper commander.

" Jasper is true, Father," added she earnestly; " and if false, he could have no motive in wrecking us in this distant part of the lake at the risk of all our lives, his own included."

" Ay, this is well enough for a young woman who is frightened," answered the more phlegmatic parent; " but it might not be so excusable in one in command of an expedition. Jasper may think the chance of drowning in getting ashore fully repaid by the chance of escaping as soon as he reaches the land."

"Sergeant Dunham!"

"Father!"

These exclamations were made simultaneously, but in tones expressive of different feelings. In Jasper, surprise was the emotion uppermost; in Mabel, reproach. The old soldier continued as if neither had spoken. "Nor is brother Cap a man likely to submit to be taught his duty on board a vessel."

"But, Father, when all our lives are in the utmost jeopardy!"

"So much the worse. Charles Cap will not be likely to quit the helm because the ship is in danger. Besides, Jasper Eau-douce, he says your proposal in itself has a suspicious air about it, and sounds more like treachery than reason."

"He may think so; but let him send for the pilot and hear his opinion. I have not seen the man since yesterday evening."

"This does sound reasonably, and the experiment shall be tried. Follow me on deck then, that all may be honest and above-board."

Jasper obeyed, and so keen was the interest of Mabel, that she too ventured as far as the companion-way.

The pilot soon appeared, and there was no mistaking the look of concern that he cast around at the scene as soon as he was in the open air. He was allowed a few minutes to look about him, and then the question was put as to the course which he thought it prudent to follow.

"I see no means of saving the cutter but to anchor," he answered.

"What! out here in the lake?" enquired Cap.

"No: but closer in: just at the outer line of the breakers."

The effect of this communication was to leave no doubt in the mind of Cap that there was a secret arrangement between her commander and the pilot to cast away the *Scud*; most probably with the hope of effecting their escape.

"I tell you, brother Dunham," said he, in answer to the remonstrances of the Sergeant against his turning a deaf ear to this double representation, "that no seaman would give such an opinion honestly. To anchor on a lee shore in a gale of wind would be an act of madness that I could never excuse to the underwriters, so long as a rag can be set; but to anchor close to breakers would be insanity."

"His Majesty underwrites the *Scud*, and I am responsible for the lives of my command. These men are better acquainted with

Lake Ontario than we can possibly be, and I think their telling the same tale entitles them to some credit."

"Uncle!" said Mabel earnestly; but a gesture from Jasper induced the girl to restrain her feelings.

"We are drifting down upon the breakers so rapidly," said the young man, "that little need be said on the subject. Half an hour must settle the matter, one way or the other; but I warn Master Cap that the surest-footed man among us will not be able to keep his feet an instant on the deck of this low craft, should she fairly get within them. Indeed, I make little doubt that we shall fill and founder before the second line of rollers is passed."

"And how would anchoring help the matter?" demanded Cap furiously.

"By bringing the cutter head to sea we should lessen her drift," Eau-douce replied; "and even if we dragged through the breakers, it would be with the least possible danger. I hope you will allow the pilot and myself to *prepare* for anchoring, since the precaution may do good, and can do no harm."

"Overhaul your ranges, if you will, and get your anchors clear, with all my heart. We are now in a situation that cannot be much affected by anything of that sort. Sergeant, a word with you aft here."

Cap led his brother-in-law out of earshot; and then, with more of human feeling in his voice and manner than he was apt to exhibit, he opened his heart on the subject of their real situation.

"This is a melancholy affair for poor Mabel," said he. "You and I, Sergeant, are old fellows, and used to being near death, if not to actually dying, our trades fit us for such scenes; but poor Mabel!—she is an affectionate and kind-hearted girl, and I had hoped to see her comfortably settled before my time came. Well, well! we must take the bad with the good in every v'y'ge."

Sergeant Dunham was a brave man, and had shown his spirit in scenes that looked much more appalling than this. For himself he cared far less than for his daughter, feeling some of that self-reliance which seldom deserts a man who has been accustomed to personal exertions in moments of jeopardy; but as respects Mabel, he saw no means of escape, and, with a father's fondness, he at once determined that, if either was doomed to perish, he and his daughter must go together.

"Do you think this must come to pass?" he asked of Cap.

"Twenty minutes will carry us into the breakers; and what chance will the stoutest man among us have in that cauldron to leeward?"

By this time the *Scud* was within a mile of the shore, on which the gale was blowing at right angles, with a violence that forbade the idea of showing any additional canvas with a view to claw off. The small portion of the mainsail actually set, and which merely served to keep the head of the *Scud* so near the wind as to prevent the waves from breaking over her, quivered under the gusts, as if at each moment the stout threads which held the complicated fabric together were about to be torn asunder. Between the cutter and the shore the view was still more wild and appalling. The breakers extended nearly half a mile; while the water within their line was white with foam, the air above them was so far filled with vapour and spray as to render the land beyond hazy and indistinct.

While the Sergeant and Cap were gazing at this scene in silence, Jasper and his people were actively engaged on the forecastle. No sooner had the young man received permission to resume his old employment, than, appealing to some of the soldiers for aid, he mustered five or six assistants, and set about in earnest the performance of a duty which had been too long delayed. The two bowers were soon ready to be let go, ranges of the cables were overhauled, and then the party paused to look about them. No changes for the better had occurred, but the cutter was falling slowly in, and each instant rendered it more certain that she could not gain an inch to windward.

One long, earnest survey of the lake ended, Jasper gave new orders in a similar manner to prove how much he thought that the time pressed. Two kedges were got on deck, and hawsers were bent to them; the inner ends of the hawsers were bent, in their turns, to the crowns of the anchors, and everything was got ready to throw them overboard at the proper moment. These preparations completed, Jasper's manner changed from the excitement of exertion to a look of calm but settled concern. He quitted the forecastle, where the seas were dashing inboard at every plunge of the vessel, and walked to a drier part of the deck, aft. Here he was met by the Pathfinder, who was standing near Mabel and the Quartermaster.

"Jasper," commenced the guide, "I have been of no use this morning, for my gifts are of little account, as you know, in a vessel like this; but, should it please God to let the Sergeant's daughter reach the shore alive, my acquaintance with the forest may still carry her through in safety to the garrison."

"'Tis a fearful distance thither, Pathfinder!" Mabel rejoined. "I am afraid none of us could live to reach the fort."

"It would be a risky path, Mabel, and a crooked one; though some of your sex have undergone even more than that in this wilderness. But, Jasper, either you or I, or both of us, must man this bark canoe; Mabel's only chance will lie in getting through the breakers in that."

"I would willingly man anything to save her," answered Jasper; "but no human hand could carry that canoe through yonder breakers in a gale like this. I have hopes from anchoring, after all; for once before have we saved the *Scud* in an extremity nearly as great as this."

"If we are to anchor, Jasper," the Sergeant enquired, "why not do it at once? Every foot we lose in drifting now would come into the distance we shall probably drag when the anchors are let go."

Jasper drew nearer to the Sergeant, and took his hand.

"Sergeant Dunham," said he solemnly, "you are a good man, though you have treated me harshly in this business. You love your daughter?"

"That you cannot doubt, Eau-douce," returned the Sergeant.

"Will you give her the only chance for life that is left?"

"What would you have me do, boy? What would you have me do?"

"Support me against Master Cap for five minutes, and all that man can do towards saving the *Scud* shall be done."

The Sergeant hesitated, for he was too much of a disciplinarian to fly in the face of regular orders. He disliked the appearance of vacillation, too; and then he had a profound respect for his kinsman's seamanship. While he was deliberating, Cap came from his post at the side of the man at the helm.

"Master Eau-douce," said he, "do you know any spot near by where this cutter may be beached? The moment has arrived when we are driven to this hard alternative."

That instant of indecision on the part of Cap secured the triumph of Jasper. Looking at the Sergeant, the young man received a nod that assured him of all he asked.

"Shall I take the helm," he enquired of Cap, "and see if we can reach a creek that lies to leeward?"

"Do so," said the other. "Do so, Eau-douce, since, to be frank

with you, I can see nothing better to be done. We must beach
or swamp."

Jasper required no more; springing aft, he soon had the tiller in
his own hands. The pilot was prepared for what was to follow;
and, at a sign from his young commander, the rag of sail that had
so long been set was taken in. At that moment Jasper, watching
his time, put the helm up; the head of a staysail was loosened
forward, and the light cutter, as if conscious she was now under
the control of familiar hands, fell off, and was soon in the trough
of the sea. This perilous instant was passed in safety, and at the
next moment the little vessel appeared flying down toward the
breakers at a rate that threatened instant destruction. The distances had become so short, that five or six minutes sufficed for
all that Jasper wished, and he put the helm down again, when the
bows of the *Scud* came up to the wind, notwithstanding the turbu-
lence of the waters. A sign from Jasper set all in motion in the
forecastle, and a kedge was thrown from each bow. The fearful
nature of the drift was now apparent to even Mabel's eyes, for
the two hawsers ran out like towlines. As soon as they straight-
ened to a slight strain, both anchors were let go, and cable was
given to each, nearly to the better-ends. It was not a difficult
task to snub so light a craft with ground tackle of a quality
better than common; and in less than ten minutes from the
moment when Jasper went to the helm, the *Scud* was riding,
head to sea, with the two cables stretched ahead in lines that
resembled bars of iron.

"This is not well done, Master Jasper!" angrily exclaimed Cap,
as soon as he perceived the trick which had been played him.
"I order you to cut, and to beach the cutter without a moment's
delay."

No one, however, seemed disposed to comply with this order;
for so long as Eau-douce saw fit to command, his own people
were disposed to obey. Finding that the men remained passive,
Cap, who believed they were in the utmost peril, turned fiercely
to Jasper, and renewed his remonstrances.

"You did not head for your pretended creek," added he, "but
steered for that bluff, where every soul on board would have been
drowned, had we gone ashore."

"And you wish to cut, and put every soul ashore at that very
spot!" retorted Jasper.

"Throw a headline overboard and ascertain the drift!" Cap
now roared to the people forward. A sign from Jasper sustain-

ing this order, it was instantly obeyed. All on deck watched, with nearly breathless interest, the result of the experiment. The lead was no sooner on the bottom than the line tended forward, and in about two minutes it was seen that the cutter had drifted her length dead in towards the bluff. Jasper looked gravely, for he well knew nothing would hold the vessel did she get within the vortex of the breakers, the first line of which was appearing and disappearing about a cable's length directly under their stern.

"Traitor!" exclaimed Cap, shaking a finger at the young commander. "You must answer for this with your life! If I were at the head of this expedition, Sergeant, I would hang him at the end of the main-boom, lest he escape drowning."

"Moderate your feelings, brother. Jasper appears to have done all for the best, and matters may not be so bad as you believe them."

"Why has he brought us here, dead to windward of that bluff, and to a spot where even the breakers are only of half the ordinary width, as if in a hurry to drown all on board?"

"I headed for the bluff, for the precise reason that the breakers are so narrow at this spot," answered Jasper.

"Do you mean to tell an old seaman like me that this cutter could live in those breakers?"

"I do not. I think she would fill and swamp if driven into the first line of them. I hope to keep her clear of them altogether."

"With a drift of her length in a minute?"

"The backing of the anchors does not yet fairly tell, nor do I even hope that *they* will entirely bring her up."

"On what, then, do you rely? To moor a craft, head and stern, by faith, hope, and charity?"

"No, I trust to the undertow. I headed for the bluff because I knew that it was stronger at that point than at any other, and because we could get nearer in with the land without entering the breakers."

This was said with spirit, and its effect on Cap was marked, the feeling that was uppermost being evidently that of surprise.

"Undertow!" he repeated; "who ever heard of saving a vessel from going ashore by the undertow?"

"This may never happen on the ocean," Jasper answered; "but we have known it to happen here."

"The lad is right, brother," put in the Sergeant; "for, though I do not well understand it, I have often heard the sailors of the lake speak of such a thing."

Cap grumbled and swore; but, as there was no remedy, he was compelled to acquiesce.

The drift continued; though, as the kedges and hawsers with which the anchors were backed took the strains, it became sensibly less. At length the man at the lead announced the joyful intelligence that the anchors had ceased to drag, and that the vessel had brought up! At this precise moment the first line of breakers was about a hundred feet astern of the *Scud*, even appearing to approach much nearer as the foam vanished and returned on the raging surges. Jasper sprang forward, and, casting a glance over the bows, he smiled in triumph as he pointed exultingly to the cables. Instead of resembling bars of iron in rigidity, as before, they were curving downwards, and to a seaman's senses it was evident that the cutter rose and fell on the seas as they came in with the ease of a ship in a tides-way, when the power of the wind is relieved by the counteracting pressure of the water.

"'Tis the undertow!" he exclaimed with delight, fairly bounding along the deck to steady the helm, in order that the cutter might ride still easier. "Providence has placed us directly in its current, and there is no longer any danger."

"Ay, ay, Providence is a good seaman," growled Cap, "and often helps lubbers out of a difficulty. Undertow or uppertow, the gale has abated; and, fortunately for us all, the anchors have met with good holding ground."

Half an hour of uncertainty and doubt followed, it is true, during which period the lead was anxiously watched; but then a feeling of security came over all, and the weary slept without dreaming of instant death.

CHAPTER XVIII

It was near noon when the gale broke; and then its force abated as suddenly as its violence had arisen. In less than two hours after the wind fell, the surface of the lake, though still agitated, was no longer glittering with foam; and in double that time the entire sheet presented the ordinary scene of disturbed water, that was unbroken by the violence of a tempest.

As it was impossible to make head against the sea that was still up, with the light opposing air that blew from the eastward, all thoughts of getting under way that afternoon were abandoned. Jasper, who had now quietly resumed the command of the *Scud*, busied himself, however, in heaving up the anchors, which were lifted in succession, and everything was got in readiness for a prompt departure as soon as the state of the weather would allow.

As is common with those who are unused to the confinement of a vessel, Mabel cast wistful eyes towards the shore; nor was it long before she expressed a wish that it were possible to land. The Pathfinder was near her at the time, and he assured her that nothing would be easier, as they had a bark canoe on deck, which was the best possible mode of conveyance to go through a surf. After the usual doubts and misgivings, the Sergeant was appealed to; his opinion proved to be favourable, and preparations to carry the whim into effect were immediately made.

The party which was to land consisted of Sergeant Dunham, his daughter, and the Pathfinder. Accustomed to the canoe, Mabel took her seat in the centre with great steadiness, her father was placed in the bows, while the guide assumed the office of conductor, by steering in the stern. There was little need of impelling the canoe by means of the paddle, for the rollers sent it forward at moments with a violence that set every effort to govern its movements at defiance. More than once, before the shore was reached, Mabel repented of her temerity, but Pathfinder encouraged her, and really manifested so much self-possession, coolness, and strength of arm himself, that even a female might have hesitated about owning all her apprehensions. A few minutes sufficed for this excitement; for though the distance between the cutter and the land considerably exceeded a quarter of a mile, the intermediate space was passed in a very few minutes.

On landing, the Sergeant, taking his gun, announced his intention to pass an hour in quest of game.

"Pathfinder will remain near you, girl, and no doubt he will tell you some of his experiences with the Mingos."

The guide laughed, promised to have a care of Mabel, and in a few minutes the father had ascended a steep acclivity and disappeared in the forest. The others took another direction, which, after a few minutes of a sharp ascent, brought them to a small naked point on the promontory, where the eye overlooked an extensive and very peculiar panorama. Here Mabel seated herself on a fragment of fallen rock, while her companion stood at her side. Several minutes passed, and neither spoke; Mabel, in particular, being lost in admiration of the view.

The position the two had obtained was sufficiently elevated to command a wide reach of the lake, which stretched away towards the north-east in a boundless sheet, glittering beneath the rays of an afternoon's sun, and yet betraying the remains of that agitation which it had endured while tossed by the late tempest.

"We are very far here from human habitations!" exclaimed Mabel, after a long survey of the scene; "this is indeed being on a frontier."

"Have they more sightly scenes than this nearer the sea and around their large towns?" demanded Pathfinder.

"I will not say that: there is more to remind one of his fellow-beings there than here; less, perhaps, to remind one of God."

"Ay, Mabel, that is what my own feelings say. God is as near me, in this my home, as He is near the king in his royal palace."

"Who can doubt it?" returned Mabel. "One feels nearer to God in such a spot, I think, than when the mind is distracted by the objects of the towns."

"You say all I wish to say myself, Mabel, but in much plainer speech. I have coasted this lake in search of skins afore the war, and have been here already; not at this very spot, for we landed yonder, where you may see the blasted oak that stands above the cluster of hemlocks——"

"How can you remember all these trifles so accurately?"

"Remember them, indeed! I once made an appointment with the Big Sarpent to meet at twelve o'clock at noon, near the foot of a certain pine, at the end of six months, when neither of us was within three hundred miles of the spot."

"And did you meet at that very spot and hour?"

"When I reached the tree I found the Sarpent leaning against its trunk with torn leggings and muddied moccasins. No fear of Chingachgook when there is either a friend or an enemy in the case."

"And where is the Delaware now? why is he not with us?"

"He is scouting on the Mingo trail, where I ought to have been too, but for a great human infirmity."

"You seem superior to all infirmity, Pathfinder; I never yet met with a man who appeared to be so little liable to the weaknesses of nature."

"If you mean in the way of health and strength, Mabel, Providence has been kind to me; though I fancy the open air, long hunts, scoutings, forest fare, and the sleep of a good conscience may always keep the doctors at a distance. But I am human after all."

Mabel looked surprised, and her sweet countenance expressed a good deal of curiosity, though her tongue was more discreet.

"There is something bewitching in this wild life of yours, Path-finder," she exclaimed, a tinge of enthusiasm mantling her cheeks. "I find I'm fast coming to love all this grand silence of the woods; and, as my father will probably pass the remainder of his days here, where he has already lived so long, I begin to feel that I should be happy to continue with him, and not to return to the seashore."

"The woods are never silent, Mabel, to such as understand their meaning. Days at a time have I travelled them alone, without feeling the want of company."

"I believe you are happier when alone, Pathfinder, than when mingling with your fellow creatures."

"I will not say that. I have seen the time when I have thought that God was sufficient for me in the forest, and that I have craved no more than His bounty and His care. But other feelings have got uppermost, and I suppose natur' will have its way. All other creeturs mate, Mabel, and it was intended man should do so too."

"And have you never bethought of seeking a wife, Pathfinder, to share your fortunes?" enquired the girl. "To me it seems you only want a home to return to from your wanderings to render your life completely happy. Were I a man, it would be my delight to roam through these forests at will, or to sail over this beautiful lake."

"I understand you, Mabel; and God bless you for thinking of the welfare of men as humble as we are. We have our pleasures, it is true, as well as our gifts, but we might be happier."

"Happier! in what way, Pathfinder? In this pure air, with these cool and shaded forests to wander through, this lovely lake to gaze at and sail upon, with clear consciences, and abundance for all their real wants, men ought to be nothing less than as perfectly happy as their infirmities will allow."

"Every creetur' has its gifts, Mabel, and men have theirs," answered the guide, looking stealthily at his beautiful companion, whose cheeks had flushed and eyes brightened under the ardour of her feelings; "and all must obey them. Do you see yonder pigeon that is just alightin' on the beach?"

"Certainly; it is the only creature stirring, besides ourselves, to be seen in this vast solitude."

"Not so, Mabel; Providence makes nothing that lives to live quite alone. Here is its mate, just rising on the wing."

"I understand you, Pathfinder," returned Mabel, smiling sweetly. "But a hunter may find a mate, even in this wild region. The Indian girls are affectionate and true, I know; for such was the wife of Arrowhead."

"That would never do, Mabel, and good would never come of it. Kind must cling to kind, if one would find happiness. If, indeed, I could meet with one like you, who would consent to be a hunter's wife, and who would not scorn my ignorance and rudeness, then, indeed, would all the toil of the past appear like the sporting of the young deer, and all the future like sunshine."

"One like me! A girl of my years and indiscretion would hardly make a fit companion for the boldest scout and surest hunter on the lines."

"Ah, Mabel! I fear me that I have been improving a redskin's gifts with a paleface's natur'? Such a character would ensure a wife in an Indian village."

"Surely, Pathfinder, you would not think of choosing one so ignorant, so frivolous, so vain, and so inexperienced as I for your wife?"

"And why not, Mabel? If you are ignorant of frontier usages, you know more than all of us of pleasant anecdotes and town customs; and as for experience, that will come with years. Besides, Mabel, I fear men think little of these matters when they are about to take wives; I do."

"Pathfinder, your words — your looks: — surely you speak in pleasantry?"

"To me it is always agreeable to be near you, Mabel; and I should sleep sounder this blessed night than I have done for a week past, could I think that you find such discourse as pleasant as I do."

We shall not say that Mabel Dunham had not believed herself a favourite with the guide. This her quick feminine sagacity had early discovered; but the idea that he seriously sought her for his wife had never before crossed the mind of the spirited and ingenuous girl. Now, however, a gleam of something like the truth broke in upon her imagination, less induced by the words of her companion, perhaps, than by his manner. Looking earnestly into the honest countenance of the scout, Mabel's own features became concerned and grave; and when she spoke again, it was with a gentleness of manner that attracted him to her even more powerfully than the words themselves were calculated to repel.

"You and I should understand each other, Pathfinder," said she with an earnest sincerity; "nor should there be any cloud between us. Surely all this means nothing—has no other connection with your feelings than such a friendship as one of your wisdom and character would naturally feel for a girl like me?"

"I believe it's all nat'ral, Mabel. The Sergeant tells me he had such feelings towards your own mother. Yes, I dare say it's all nat'ral enough, and that makes it come so easy, and is a great comfort to me."

"Pathfinder, your words make me uneasy. You do not, cannot mean that——" even the tongue of the spirited Mabel faltered for a moment, but then she continued—"I mean, Pathfinder, that you do not wish me to understand that you seriously think of me as a wife?"

"I do, Mabel; that's just it. The Sergeant and I have concluded on the matter, if it is agreeable to you, as he thinks is likely to be the case; though I doubt my own power to please one who deserves the best husband America can produce."

Mabel's countenance changed from uneasiness to surprise; and then, by a transition still quicker, from surprise to pain.

"My father has thought of my becoming your wife, Pathfinder?"

"Yes, he has, Mabel. He has even thought such a thing might be agreeable to you, and has almost encouraged me to fancy it might be true."

"But you yourself—you certainly can care nothing whether this singular expectation shall ever be realized or not?"

"Anan?"

"I mean, Pathfinder, that you have talked of this match more to oblige my father than anything else?"

The scout looked earnestly into the beautiful face of Mabel, which had flushed with the ardour and novelty of her sensations, and it was not possible to mistake the intense admiration that betrayed itself in every lineament of his ingenuous countenance.

"I have often thought myself happy, Mabel, when ranging the woods on a successful hunt; but I now know that it has all been vanity compared with the delight it would give me to know that you thought better of me than you think of most others."

"I do, indeed, think better of you, Pathfinder, than of most others. I am not certain that I do not think better of you than of any other; for your truth, honesty, and courage are scarcely equalled by any of earth."

"Ah, Mabel, these are sweet and encouraging words from you! and the Sergeant, after all, was not so near wrong as I feared."

"Nay, Pathfinder, in the name of all that is sacred, do not let us misunderstand each other in a matter of so much importance. While I esteem, respect, nay reverence you, almost as much as I reverence my own dear father, it is impossible that I should ever become your wife——"

The change in her companion's countenance was so sudden and so great, that the moment the effect of what she had uttered became visible in the face of the Pathfinder, Mabel arrested her own words, notwithstanding her strong desire to be explicit, the reluctance with which she could at any time cause pain being sufficient of itself to induce the pause. Neither spoke for some time, the shade of disappointment that crossed the rugged lineaments of the hunter amounting so nearly to anguish as to frighten his companion, while the sensation of choking became so strong in the Pathfinder that he fairly griped his throat, like one who sought physical relief by physical suffering.

"Nay, Pathfinder," Mabel eagerly added, the instant she could command her voice—"I may have said more than I mean; for all things of this nature are possible. What I wish you to understand is, that it is not likely that you and I should ever think of each other as man and wife ought to think of each other."

"I do not — I shall never think in that way again, Mabel," gasped forth the Pathfinder. "No, no, I shall never think of you, or anyone else, again in that way."

"Pathfinder, dear Pathfinder, understand me; do not attach more meaning to my words than I do myself; a match like that would be unwise, unnatural, perhaps."

"Yes, unnat'ral—ag'in natur'; and so I told the Sergeant, but he *would* have it otherwise."

"Pathfinder! oh, this is worse than I could have imagined! Let me see that you do not hate me. For heaven's sake smile upon me again."

"Hate you, Mabel! Smile upon you! Ah's me!"

"Nay, give me your hand—both, Pathfinder! for I shall not be easy until I feel certain that we are friends again, and that all this has been a mistake."

"Mabel!" said the guide, looking wistfully into the face of the generous and impetuous girl, as she held his two hands in her own delicate fingers, and laughing in his silent manner, while anguish gleamed over lineaments which seemed incapable of deception, even while agitated with emotions so conflicting — "Mabel! the Sergeant was wrong!"

The pent-up feelings could endure no more, and the tears rolled down his cheeks like rain. His breast heaved, as if it possessed a tenant of which it would be rid, by any effort, however desperate.

"Pathfinder!" Mabel almost shrieked; "anything but this, anything but this! Speak to me, Pathfinder!"

"The Sergeant was wrong!" exclaimed the guide, laughing amid his agony, in a way to terrify his companion by the unnatural mixture of anguish and lightheartedness. "I knew it, and said it; yes, the Sergeant was wrong."

"We can be friends, though we cannot be man and wife," continued Mabel, almost as much disturbed as her companion; "we can always be friends, and always will."

"I thought the Sergeant was mistaken," resumed the Pathfinder, when a great effort had enabled him to command himself, "for I did not think my gifts were such as would please the fancy of a town-bred girl."

"If I thought any error of mine had raised false expectations in you, Pathfinder, I should never forgive myself; for, believe me, I would rather endure pain in my own feelings than you should suffer."

"That's just it, Mabel. I now see plainly, and begin to understand the difference between us better, and will strive to keep down thought, and to go abroad again as I used to do, looking for the game and the inimy."

"In a little while you will forget all this, and think of me as a friend, who owes you her life."

"This may be the way in the towns, but I doubt if it's nat'ral to the woods."

"You will forget it all, when you come to seriously recollect that I am altogether unsuited to be your wife."

"So I told the Sergeant; but he would have it otherwise. I knew you was too young and beautiful for one of middle age, like myself, and who never was comely to look at even in youth; and then your ways have not been my ways; nor would a hunter's cabin be a fitting place for one who was edicated among chiefs, as it were."

"Here comes my father," interrupted Mabel. "Let us look cheerful and happy, Pathfinder, as such good friends ought to look, and keep each other's secrets."

A pause succeeded; the Sergeant's foot was heard crushing the dried twigs hard by, and then his form appeared shoving aside the bushes of a copse just near. As he issued into the open ground, the old soldier said: "Mabel, child, you are young and light of foot — look for a bird that I've shot that fell just beyond the thicket of young hemlocks on the shore; and, as Jasper is showing signs of an intention of getting under way, you need not take the trouble to clamber up this hill again, but we will meet you on the beach in a few minutes."

Mabel obeyed, bounding down the hill with the elastic step of youth and health. But, notwithstanding the lightness of her steps, the heart of the girl was heavy, and no sooner was she hid from observation by the thicket, than she threw herself on the root of a tree and wept as if her heart would break. The Sergeant watched her until she disappeared, with a father's pride, and then turned to his companion with a smile as kind and as familiar as his habits would allow him to use towards any.

"She has her mother's lightness and activity, my friend, with somewhat of her father's force," said he. "Her mother was not quite so handsome, I think myself; but the Dunhams were always thought comely, whether men or women. Well, Pathfinder, I take it for granted you've not overlooked the opportunity, but have spoken plainly to the girl!"

"I believe Mabel and I understand each other at last, Sergeant," returned the other.

"So much the better. Some people fancy that a little doubt and uncertainty makes love all the livelier; but I am one of those who think the plainer the tongue speaks the easier the mind will comprehend. Was Mabel surprised?"

"I fear she was, Sergeant."

"Well, surprises in love are like an ambush in war, and quite as lawful. Mabel did not run away, did she?"

"No, Sergeant, Mabel did not try to escape; *that* I can say with a clear conscience."

"I hope the girl was not too willing, neither. But frankness, after all, is a recommendation in a man or woman."

"That it is, that it is; and judgment, too."

"You are not to look for too much judgment in a young creature of twenty, Pathfinder, but it will come with experience. A mistake

In you or me, for instance, might not be so easily overlooked; but in a girl of Mabel's years it is different."

The muscles of the listener's face twitched as the Sergeant was thus delivering his sentiments, though the former had now recovered a portion of that stoicism which formed so large a part of his character."

"You say true, Sergeant," Pathfinder answered; "a mistake in one like you is a more serious matter."

"You will find Mabel sincere and honest in the end; give her but a little time."

"Ah's me, Sergeant!"

"A man of your merits would make an impression on a rock, give him time, Pathfinder."

"Sergeant Dunham, we are old fellow-campaigners, and we have done so many kind acts to each other that we can afford to be candid—what caused you to believe that Mabel could ever fancy one so rude as I am?"

"What?—why, a variety of reasons—those same acts of kindness, perhaps, and the campaigns you mention."

"All this sounds well, so far as you and I are consarned; but they do not touch the case of your pretty daughter. Like loves like, I tell you, Sergeant; and my gifts are not altogether the gifts of Mabel Dunham."

"These are some of your old modest qualms, Pathfinder, and will do you no credit with the girl. Women distrust men who distrust themselves, and take to men who distrust nothing. Look at Lieutenant Muir; the man has had five wives already, they tell me, and there is no more modesty in him than there is in a cat-o'-nine-tails."

"Lieutenant Muir will never be the husband of Mabel Dunham, let him ruffle his feathers as much as he may."

"That is a sensible remark of yours, Pathfinder; for my mind is made up that you shall be my son-in-law."

"Sergeant, we must let Mabel follow her own fancy; she is young and light of heart, and God forbid that any wish of mine should lay the weight of a feather on a mind that is all gaiety now!"

"Have you conversed freely with the girl?" the Sergeant demanded quickly.

Pathfinder was too honest to deny a truth plain as that which the answer required, and yet too honourable to betray Mabel, and expose her to the resentment of one whom he well knew to be stern in his anger.

"We have laid open our minds," he said; "and though Mabel is one that any man might love to look at, I find little there, Sergeant, to make me think any better of myself."

"The girl has not dared to refuse you — her father's best friend!"

Pathfinder turned his face away to conceal the look of anguish that consciousness told him was passing athwart it, but he continued.

"Mabel is too kind to utter harsh words to a dog. I have not put the question in a way to be downright refused, Sergeant."

"And did you expect my daughter to jump into your arms before you asked her? She would not have been her mother's child had she done any such thing, nor do I think she would have been mine. Leave me to manage this matter for you, Pathfinder, and there shall be no unnecessary delay. I'll speak to Mabel myself this very evening.

"I'd rather not, Sergeant. Leave the matter to Mabel and me, and I think all will come right in the ind."

"On one condition I will, my friend; and that is, that you will promise me, on the honour of a scout, that you will put the matter plainly to Mabel the first suitable opportunity, and no mincing of words."

"I will ask her, Sergeant, on condition that you promise not to meddle in the affair—yes, I will promise to ask Mabel whether she will marry me, even though she laugh in my face at my doing so, on that condition."

Sergeant Dunham gave the desired promise very cheerfully; for he had completely wrought himself up into the belief that the man he so much esteemed himself must be acceptable to his daughter. He had married a woman much younger than himself, and he saw no unfitness in the respective years of the intended couple.

As Pathfinder and his friend descended the hill to the shore of the lake the discourse did not flag. The latter continued to persuade the former that his diffidence alone prevented complete success with Mabel, and that he had only to persevere in order to prevail. Pathfinder even began to think virgin coyness and ignorance of her own feelings might have induced Mabel to use the language she had.

CHAPTER XIX

MABEL was in waiting on the beach, and the canoe was soon launched. Pathfinder carried the party out through the surf in the same skilful manner that he had brought it in, and they reached the side of the *Scud* without having received even a drop of spray.

It was just sunset as the cutter's mainsail flapped and its stem began to sever the water. The air was light and southerly, and the head of the vessel was kept looking up along the south shore, it being the intention to get to the eastward again as fast as possible. The night that succeeded was quiet; and the rest of those who slept deep and tranquil.

Some difficulty occurred concerning the command of the vessel, but the matter had been finally settled by an amicable compromise. As the distrust of Jasper was far from being appeased, Cap retained a supervisory power, while the young man was allowed to work the craft, subject, at all times, to the control and interference of the old seaman. To this Jasper consented, in preference to exposing Mabel any longer to the dangers of their present situation; for, now that the violence of the elements had ceased, he well knew that the *Montcalm* would be in search of them. He had the discretion, however, not to reveal his apprehensions on this head; for it happened that the very means he deemed the best to escape the enemy were those which would be most likely to awaken new suspicions of his honesty in the minds of those who held the power to defeat his intentions. In other words, Jasper believed that the gallant young Frenchman, who commanded the ship of the enemy, would quit his anchorage under the fort at Niagara, and stand up the lake as soon as the wind abated, in order to ascertain the fate of the *Scud*, keeping midway between the two shores as the best means of commanding a broad view; and that, on his part, it would be expedient to hug one coast or the other, not only to avoid a meeting, but as affording a chance of passing without detection by blending his sails and spars with objects on the land. He preferred the south because it was the weather shore, and because he thought it was that which the enemy would the least expect him to take, though it necessarily led near his settlements, and in front of one of the strongest posts he held in that part of the world.

Of all this, however, Cap was happily ignorant, and the Ser-

geant's mind was too much occupied with the details of his
military trust to enter into these niceties, which so properly
belonged to another profession.   No opposition was made, therefore, and before morning Jasper had apparently dropped quietly
into all his former authority, issuing his orders freely, and meeting
with obedience without hesitation or cavil.

The appearance of day brought all on board on deck again;
and, as is usual with adventurers on the water, the opening horizon
was curiously examined, as objects started out of the obscurity,
and the panorama brightened under the growing light.   East,
west, and north nothing was visible but water glittering in the
rising sun; but southward stretched the endless belt of woods
that then held Ontario in a setting of forest verdure.   Suddenly
an opening appeared ahead, and then the massive walls of a
château-looking house, with outworks, bastions, blockhouses, and
palisadoes frowned on a headland that bordered the outlet of a
broad stream.   Just as the fort became visible, a little cloud
rose over it, and the white ensign of France was seen fluttering
from a lofty flagstaff.

Cap gave an ejaculation as he witnessed this ungrateful exhibition, and he cast a quick, suspicious glance at his brother-in-law.

"The dirty tablecloth hung up to air, as my name is Charles
Cap!" he muttered; "and we hugging this shore as if it were
our wife and children met on the return from an India v'y'ge!
Hark'e, Jasper, are you in search of a cargo of frogs, that you
keep so near in to this New France!"

"I hug the land, sir, in the hope of passing the enemy's ship
without being seen, for I think she must be somewhere down here
to leeward."

"Ay, ay, this sounds well, and I hope it may turn out as you
say; I trust there is no undertow here?"

"We are on a weather shore now," said Jasper, smiling; "and
I think you will admit, Master Cap, that a strong undertow makes
an easy cable; we owe all our lives to the undertow of this very
lake."

"French flummery!" growled Cap.   "Give me a fair, honest,
English-Yankee-American tow, above board, and above water,
too, if I must have a tow at all, and none of your sneaking
drift that is below the surface, where one can neither see nor
feel.   I dare say, if the truth could be come at, that this late
escape of ours was all a contrived affair."

"We have now a good opportunity, at least, to reconnoitre the enemy's post at Niagara, brother; for such I take this fort to be," put in the Sergeant. "Let us be all eyes in passing, and remember that we are almost in face of the enemy."

This advice of the Sergeant needed nothing to enforce it; for the interest and novelty of passing a spot occupied by human beings were of themselves sufficient to attract deep attention in that scene of a vast but deserted nature. The wind was now fresh enough to urge the *Scud* through the water with considerable velocity, and Jasper eased her helm as she opened the river, and luffed nearly into the mouth of that noble strait, or river, as it is termed. A dull, distant, heavy roar came down through the opening in the banks, swelling on the currents of the air, like the deeper notes of some immense organ, and occasionally seeming to cause the earth itself to tremble.

"That sounds like surf on some long, unbroken coast!" exclaimed Cap, as a swell, deeper than common, came to his ears.

"Ay, that is such surf as we have in this quarter of the world," Pathfinder answered. "There is no undertow there, Master Cap; but all the water that strikes the rocks stays there, so far as going back again is consarned. That is Old Niagara that you hear, or this noble stream tumbling down a mountain."

"No one will have the impudence to pretend that this fine broad river falls over yonder hills?"

"It does, Master Cap; and all for the want of stairs, or a road to come down by. This is natur', as we have it up hereaway, though I dare say you beat us down on the ocean. Ah's me, Mabel! a pleasant hour it would be if we could walk on the shore some ten or fifteen miles up this stream, and gaze on all that God has done there."

"You have, then, seen these renowned falls, Pathfinder?" the girl eagerly enquired.

"I have—yes, I have; and an awful sight I witnessed at that same time. The Sarpent and I were out scouting about the garrison there, when he told me that the traditions of his people gave an account of a mighty cataract in this neighbourhood, and he asked me to vary from the line of march a little to look at the wonder. I had heard some marvels consarning the spot from the soldiers of the 60th; but there are so many terrible liars in all rigiments that I hardly believed half they had told me. Well, we went; and though we expected to be led by our ears, and to hear some of that awful roaring that we hear to-day, we were disappointed, for natur' was not then speaking in thunder, as she is this morning. We came suddenly upon the stream, a short distance above the fall, and a young Delaware, who was in our company, found a bark canoe, and he would push into the current to reach an island that lies in the very centre of the confusion and strife."

"And what became of the poor wretch?" demanded Mabel.

"He went to the happy hunting grounds of his people."

A gun at this moment was discharged from a blockhouse near the fort, and the shot came whistling over the cutter's mast, an admonition to approach no nearer. Jasper was at the helm, and he kept away. The *Scud* was now in the current, and her outward set soon carried her far enough to leeward to avoid the danger of a repetition of the shot, and then she quietly continued her course along the land. As soon as the river was fairly opened, Jasper ascertained that the *Montcalm* was not at anchor in it; and a man sent aloft came down with the report that the horizon showed no sail. The hope was now strong that the artifice of Jasper had succeeded, and that the French commander had missed them by keeping the middle of the lake as he steered towards its head.

All that day the wind hung to the southward, and the cutter continued her course about a league from the land, running six or eight knots the hour in perfectly smooth water. When the sun was setting she was already a hundred miles on her route towards Oswego, into which river Sergeant Dunham now thought it his duty to go, in order to receive any communications that Major Duncan might please to make. With a view to effect this purpose, Jasper continued to hug the shore all night; and though the wind began to fail him towards morning, it lasted long enough to carry the cutter up to a point that was known to be but a league or two from the fort. Here the breeze came out light at the northward, and the cutter hauled a little from the land, in order to obtain a safe offing should it come on to blow, or should the weather again get to be easterly.

When the day dawned the cutter had the mouth of the Oswego well under her lee, distant about two miles; and just as the morning gun from the fort was fired, Jasper gave the order to ease off the sheets, and to bear up for his port, At that moment a cry from the forecastle drew all eyes towards the point on the eastern side of the outlet, and there, just without the range of shot from the light guns of the works, with her canvas reduced to barely enough to keep her stationary, lay the *Montcalm*, evidently in waiting for their appearance.

To pass her was impossible, for by filling her sails the French ship could have intercepted them in a few minutes; and the circumstances called for a prompt decision. After a short consultation, the Sergeant again changed his plan, determining to make the best of his way towards the station for which he had been originally destined, trusting to the speed of the *Scud* to throw the enemy so far astern as to leave no clue to her movements.

The cutter accordingly hauled upon a wind with the least possible delay, with everything set that would draw. Guns were fired from the fort, ensigns shown, and the ramparts were again crowded. But sympathy was all the aid that Lundie could lend to his party; and the *Montcalm*, also firing four or five guns of defiance, and throwing abroad several of the banners of France, was soon in chase under a cloud of canvas.

For several hours the two vessels were pressing through the water as fast as possible, making short stretches to windward, apparently with a view to keep the port under their lee, the one to enter it if possible, and the other to intercept it in the attempt.

At meridian the French ship was hull down, dead to leeward, the disparity of sailing on a wind being very great, and some islands were near by, behind which Jasper said it would be possible for the cutter to conceal her future movements. Although Cap and the Sergeant, and particularly Lieutenant Muir, to judge by his language, still felt a good deal of distrust of the young man, and Frontenac was not distant, this advice was followed; for time pressed, and the Quartermaster discreetly observed that Jasper could not well betray them without running openly into the enemy's harbour, a step they could at any time prevent, since the only cruiser of force the French possessed at the moment was under their lee, and not in a situation to do them any immediate injury.

Left to himself, Jasper Western soon proved how much was really in him. He weathered upon the islands, passed them, and on coming out to the eastward, kept broad away, with nothing in sight in his wake or to leeward. By sunset again the cutter was up with the first of the islands that lie in the outlet of the lake; and ere it was dark she was running through the narrow channels on her way to the long-sought station. At nine o'clock, however, Cap insisted that they should anchor; for the maze of islands became so complicated and obscure, that he feared, at every opening, the party would find themselves under the guns of a French fort. Jasper consented cheerfully, it being part of his standing instructions to approach the station under such circumstances as would prevent the men from obtaining any very accurate notions of its position, lest a deserter might betray the little garrison to the enemy.

The *Scud* was brought to in a small retired bay, where it would have been difficult to find her by daylight, and where she was perfectly concealed at night, when all but a solitary sentinel on deck sought their rest. Cap had been so harassed during the previous eight-and-forty hours that his slumbers were long and deep; nor did he awake from his first nap until the day was just beginning to dawn. His eyes were scarcely open, however, when his nautical instinct told him that the cutter was under way. Springing up, he found the *Scud* threading the islands again, with no one on deck but Jasper and the pilot, unless the sentinel be excepted, who had not in the least interfered with movements that he had every reason to believe were as regular as they were necessary.

"How's this, Master Western?" demanded Cap, with sufficient fierceness for the occasion; "are you running us into Frontenac at last, and we all asleep below, like so many mariners waiting for the 'sentry go'?"

"This is according to orders, Master Cap, Major Duncan having commanded me never to approach the station unless at a moment when the people were below; for he does not wish there should be more pilots in those waters than the king has need of."

"Whe—e—e—w! a pretty job I should have made of running down among those bushes and rocks with no one on deck!"

"I always thought," said Jasper, smiling, "you would have done better had you left the cutter in my hands until she had safely reached her place of destination."

"We should have done it, Jasper, had it not been for a circumstance. These circumstances are serious matters."

"Well, I hope there is now an end of them. We shall arrive in less than an hour if the wind holds, and then you'll be safe from any circumstances that I can contrive."

"Humph!"

Cap was obliged to acquiesce; and, as everything around him had the appearance of Jasper's being sincere, there was not much difficulty in making up his mind to submit. The islands might not have been literally a thousand in number, but they were so numerous and small as to baffle calculation, though occasionally one of larger size than common was passed. Jasper had quitted what might have been termed the main channel, and was winding his way, with a good stiff breeze and a favourable current, through passes that were sometimes so narrow that there appeared to be barely room sufficient for the *Scud's* spars to clear the trees, while at other moments he shot across little bays, and buried the cutter again amid rocks, forests, and bushes. The water was so transparent that there was no occasion for the lead, and, being of very equal depth, little risk was actually run, though Cap, with his maritime habits, was in a constant fever lest they should strike.

"I give it up, Pathfinder!" the old seaman at length exclaimed, when the little vessel emerged in safety from the twentieth of these narrow inlets through which she had been so boldly carried; "this is defying the very nature of seamanship."

"Nay, nay, Saltwater, 'tis the perfection of the art. My life on it, the lad brings us out right in the ind, as he would have done in the beginning had we given him leave."

"No pilot, no lead, no beacons, buoys, or lighthouses, no——"

"Trail," interrupted Pathfinder; "for that to me is the most mysterious part of the business."

"Hang me, if I believe there is even any compass!"

"Stand by to haul down the jib," called out Jasper, who merely smiled at the remarks of his companion. "Haul down—starboard your helm—starboard hard—so—meet her—gently there with the helm—touch her lightly—now jump ashore with the fast, lad—no, heave; there are some of our people ready to take it."

All this passed so quickly as barely to allow the spectator time to note the different evolutions, ere the *Scud* had been thrown into the wind until her mainsail shivered, next cast a little by the use of the rudder only, and then she set bodily alongside of a natural rocky quay, where she was immediately secured by good fasts run to the shore. In a word, the station was reached, and the men of the 55th were greeted by their expecting comrades, with the satisfaction which a relief usually brings.

None of the islands were high, though all lay at a sufficient elevation above the water to render them perfectly healthy and secure. Each had more or less of wood; and the greater number at that distant day were clothed with the virgin forest. The one selected by the troops for their purpose was small, containing about twenty acres of land, and by some of the accidents of the wilderness it had been partly stripped of its trees, probably centuries before the period of which we are writing, and a little grassy glade covered nearly half its surface.

At the eastern extremity of the island was a small, densely-wooded peninsula, with a thicket of underbrush so closely matted as nearly to prevent the possibility of seeing across it, so long as the leaves remained on the branches. Near the narrow neck that connected this acre with the rest of the island a small blockhouse had been erected, with some attention to its means of resistance. The logs were bulletproof, squared and jointed with a care to leave no defenceless points; the windows were loopholes, the door massive and small, and the roof, like the rest of the structure, was framed of hewn timber, covered properly with bark to exclude the rain. The lower apartment as usual contained stores and provisions; here indeed the party kept all their supplies; the second story was intended for a dwelling, as well as for the citadel, and a low garret was subdivided into two or three rooms, and could hold the pallets of some ten or fifteen persons. All the arrangements were exceedingly simple and cheap, but they were sufficient to protect the soldiers against the effects of a surprise. As the whole building was considerably less than forty feet high, its summit was concealed by the tops of the trees, except from the eyes of those who had reached the interior of the island. On that side the view was open from the upper loops, though bushes even there, more or less, concealed the base of the wooden tower.

The object being purely defence, care had been taken to place the blockhouse so near an opening in the limestone rock that formed the base of the island as to admit of a bucket's being dropped into the water, in order to obtain that great essential in the event of a siege. In order to facilitate this operation, and to enfilade the base of the building, the upper stories projected several feet beyond the lower, in the manner usual to blockhouses, and pieces of wood filled the apertures cut in the log flooring, which were intended as loops and traps. The communications between the different stories were by means of ladders.

But the situation of the island itself formed its principal merit as a military position. Lying in the midst of twenty others, it was not an easy matter to find it; since boats might pass quite near, and, by glimpses caught through the openings, this particular island would be taken for a part of some other. Indeed, the

channels between the islands which lay around the one we have
been describing were so narrow that it was even difficult to say
which portions of the land were connected, or which separated,
even as one stood in the centre, with the express desire of ascertaining the truth. The little bay in particular, which Jasper used
as a harbour, was so embowered with bushes and shut in with
islands, that, the sails of the cutter being lowered, her own people
on one occasion had searched for hours before they could find the
Scud, in their return from a short excursion among the adjacent
channels in quest of fish. In short, the place was admirably
adapted to its present objects, and its natural advantages had
been as ingeniously improved as economy and the limited means
of a frontier post would very well allow.

The hour which succeeded the arrival of the *Scud* was one of
hurried excitement. The party in possession had done nothing
worthy of being mentioned, and, wearied with their seclusion, they
were all eager to return to Oswego. The Sergeant and the officer
he came to relieve had no sooner gone through the little cere-
monies of transferring the command, than the latter hurried on
board the *Scud* with his whole party; and Jasper, who would
gladly have passed the day on the island, was required to get
under way forthwith, the wind promising a quick passage up the
river and across the lake, and in less than three hours from
the time when she had arrived the cutter was again in motion.

Mabel had taken possession of a hut; and with female readiness
and skill she made all the simple little domestic arrangements of
which the circumstances would admit, not only for her own comfort, but for that of her father. To save labour, a mess-table was
prepared in a hut set apart for that purpose, where all the heads of
the detachment were to eat, the soldier's wife performing the
necessary labour. The hut of the Sergeant, which was the best
on the island, being thus freed from any of the vulgar offices
of a household, admitted of such a display of womanly taste,
that, for the first time since her arrival on the frontier, Mabel
felt proud of her home. As soon as these important duties
were discharged, she strolled out on the island, taking a path
which led through the pretty glade, and which conducted to
the only point not covered with bushes. Here she stood gazing
at the limpid water, which lay with scarcely a ruffle on it at
her feet, musing on the novel situation in which she was placed,
and permitting a pleasing and deep excitement to steal over her
feelings, as she remembered the scenes through which she had

so lately passed, and conjectured those which still lay veiled in the future.

"You're a beautiful fixture, in a beautiful spot, Mistress Mabel," said David Muir, suddenly appearing at her elbow; "and I'll no engage you're not just the handsomest of the two."

"I will not say, Mr. Muir, that compliments on my person are altogether unwelcome," answered Mabel with spirit; "but I will say that if you would condescend to address to me some remarks of a different nature, I may be led to believe you think I have sufficient faculties to understand them."

"Hoot! your mind, beautiful Mabel, is polished just like the barrel of a soldier's musket, and your conversation is only too discreet and wise for a poor wretch who has been chewing birch up here these four years on the lines. But you are no' sorry, I take it, young lady, that you've got your pretty foot on *terra firma* once more."

"I thought so two hours since, Mr. Muir; but the *Scud* looks so beautiful, as she sails through these vistas of trees, that I almost regret I am no longer one of her passengers."

As Mabel ceased speaking, she waved her handkerchief in return to a salutation from Jasper, who kept his eyes fastened on her form until the white sails of the cutter had swept round a point, and were nearly lost behind its green fringe of leaves.

"There they go, and I'll no' say 'joy go with them'; but may they have the luck to return safely, for without them we shall be in danger of passing the winter on this island. Yon Jasper Eaudouce is a vagrant sort of a lad, and your worthy father, and almost as worthy uncle, have none of the best opinion of him."

"I am sorry to hear it, Mr. Muir, I doubt not that time will remove all their distrust."

"If time would only remove mine, pretty Mabel," rejoined the Quartermaster, "I should feel no envy of the commander-in-chief. I think if I were in a condition to retire, the Sergeant would just step into my shoes."

"If my dear father is worthy to step into your shoes, Mr. Muir," returned the girl, with malicious pleasure, "I'm sure that the qualification is mutual, and that you are worthy to step into his."

"You would not reduce me to the rank of a non-commissioned officer, Mabel?"

"No, indeed; I was not thinking of the army at all as you spoke of retiring. I was thinking how much you reminded me of my

dear father, by your experience, wisdom, and suitableness to take
his place as the head of a family."

"As its bridegroom, pretty Mabel, but not as its parent or
natural chief. I see how it is with you, loving your repartee.
Well, I like the spirit in a young woman, so it be not the spirit of
a scold. This Pathfinder is an extraordinair, Mabel, if truth may
be said of the man."

"Truth should be said of him or nothing. Pathfinder is my
friend, Mr. Muir, and no evil can be said of him in my presence
that I shall not deny."

"I shall say nothing evil of him, I can assure you; but, at the
same time, I doubt if much good can be said in his favour."

"He is at least expert with the rifle," returned Mabel, smiling.
"That *you* cannot deny."

"Let him have all the credit of his exploits in that way if you
please; but he is as illiterate as a Mohawk."

"He may not understand Latin, but his knowledge of Iroquois
is greater than that of most men, and it is the more useful language of the two in this part of the world."

"If Lundie were to call on me for an opinion which I admire
more, your person or your wit, Mabel, I should be at a loss to
answer. My admiration is so nearly divided between them, that
I often fancy this is the one that bears off the palm, and then the
other! Ah! the late Mrs. Muir was a paragon in that way also."

"The latest Mrs. Muir, did you say, sir?" asked Mabel, looking
up innocently at her companion.

"Hoot, hoot! That is some of Pathfinder's scandal. Now
I dare say that the fellow has been trying to persuade you
that I have had more than one wife already."

"In that case his time would have been thrown away as everybody knows that you have had four."

"Only three, as sure as my name is David Muir. The fourth is
pure scandal."

"Well, I'm glad I'm not that fourth person, as I should not like
to be a scandal."

"No fear of that, Mabel; for were you the fourth, all the others
would be forgotten, and your wonderful beauty and merit would
at once elevate you to be the first. No fear of your being the
fourth in anything."

"There is consolation in that assurance, Mr. Muir," said Mabel,
laughing, "for I confess I should prefer being even a fourth-rate
beauty to being a fourth wife."

So saying, she tripped away, leaving the Quartermaster to meditate on his success. David Muir, however, accustomed to rebuffs, and familiar with the virtue of perseverance, saw no reason to despair, though the half-menacing, half-self-satisfied manner in which he shook his head towards the retreating girl might have betrayed designs as sinister as they were determined. While he was thus occupied, the Pathfinder approached, and got within a few feet of him unseen.

"'Twill never do, Quartermaster," commenced the latter, laughing; "she is young and active, and none but a quick foot can overtake her. They tell me you are her suitor."

"And I hear the same of yourself, man, though the presumption would be so great that I scarcely can think it true."

"I fear you're right;—when I consider myself, what I am, how little I know, and how rude my life has been, I altogether distrust my claim, even to think a moment of one so tutored, and gay, and light of heart, and delicate——"

"You forget handsome," coarsely interrupted Muir.

"And handsome, too, I fear," returned the meek and self-abased guide; "for the young fa'n is not more pleasant to the eye of the hunter than Mabel is lovely in mine. I do indeed fear that all the thoughts I have harboured about her are vain and presumptuous."

"If you think this, my friend, my duty to you as an old fellow-campaigner compels me to say——"

"Quartermaster," interrupted the other, regarding his companion keenly, "you and I have lived together much behind the ramparts of forts, but very little in the open woods or in front of the enemy."

"Garrison or tent, it all passes for part of the same campaign, you know, Pathfinder; and then my duty keeps me much within sight of the storehouses, greatly contrary to my inclinations, as ye may well suppose, having yourself the ardour of battle in your temperament. But had ye heard what Mabel had just been saying of you, ye'd no think another minute of making yourself agreeable to the saucy and uncompromising hussy."

Pathfinder looked earnestly at the lieutenant, for it was impossible he should not feel an interest in what might be Mabel's opinion; but he had too much of the innate and true feeling of a gentleman to ask to hear what another had said of him. Muir, however, was not to be foiled by this self-respect; for he determined to practise on his credulity, as one means of getting rid of his rivalry.

"You ought to know her opinion, Pathfinder," he continued; "and I think every man ought to hear what his friends and acquaintances say of him; and so, by way of proving my own regard for your character and feelings, I'll just tell you in as few words as possible. You know that Mabel has a wicked malicious way with them eyes of her own, when she has a mind to be hard on one's feelings."

"To me her eyes, Lieutenant Muir, have always seemed winning and soft, though I will acknowledge that they sometimes laugh, and that right heartily, and with downright goodwill."

"Well, it was just when her eyes were laughing with all their might, as it were, that she broke out with an exclamation to this effect—I hope 'twill no' hurt your sensibility, Pathfinder?"

"I will not say, Quartermaster; Mabel's opinion of me is of more account to me than that of most others."

"Then I'll no' tell ye. Why should a man be telling another what his friends say of him, especially when they happen to say that which may not be pleasant to hear?"

"I cannot make you speak, Quartermaster, if you are not so minded, and perhaps it is better for me not to know Mabel's opinion, as you seem to think it is not in my favour."

"You noticed the manner in which she skipped off as you approached?"

"It was very observable," answered Pathfinder, drawing a long breath and clenching the barrel of his rifle as if the fingers would bury themselves in the iron.

"It was more than observable—it was flagrant. Well, you must know, Pathfinder, the minx bounded off in that manner in preference to hearing what I had to say in your justification."

"And what could you find to say in my behalf, Quartermaster?"

"Why, d'ye understand, my friend, I was preparing to meet particulars, as it might be, with particulars. If you were thought wild, half-savage, or of a frontier formation, I could tell her, ye know, that it came of the frontier wild and half-savage life ye'd led; and all her objections must cease at once, or there would be a sort of misunderstanding with Providence."

"And did you tell her this, Quartermaster?"

"I'll no' swear to the exact words, but the idea was prevalent in my mind, ye'll understand. The girl was impatient, and would not hear the half I had to say; but away she skipped, as if her opinion were fully made up, and she cared to listen no longer."

(M5)

"I fear such is the case, Quartermaster, and her father, after all, is mistaken."

"Well, man, why need ye lament, and undo all the grand reputation ye've been so many weary years making? Shoulder the rifle that ye use so well, and off into the woods with ye, for there's not the female breathing that is worth a heavy heart for a minute, as I know from experience. If you would really mortify Mabel, here is as glorious an occasion as any rejected lover could desire."

"The last wish I have, Lieutenant, would be to mortify Mabel."

"Well, ye'll come to that in the end, notwithstanding; for it's human nature to desire to give unpleasant feelings to them that give unpleasant feelings to us."

"Quartermaster, the last thing I could desire would be to give Mabel an uneasy moment."

"Ye say so, Pathfinder, and I dare say ye think so; but reason and nature are both against you, as ye'll find in the end. Now, listen to what is in your power to do. You know we occupy an exceedingly precarious and uncertain position here, almost in the jaws of the lion, as it were?"

"Do you mean the Frenchers by the lion, and this island as his jaws, Lieutenant?"

"Metaphorically only, my friend, for the French are no lions, and this island is not a jaw."

"The post is as well chosen as any I ever put foot in," said Pathfinder, looking round him as one surveys a picture.

The Quartermaster continued to reason with his companion, in order to induce him to quit the island without delay, using such arguments as first suggested themselves, sometimes contradicting himself, and not unfrequently urging at one moment a motive that at the next was directly opposed by another. The Pathfinder, simple as he was, detected these flaws in the Lieutenant's philosophy, though he was far from suspecting that they proceeded from a desire to clear the coast of Mabel's suitor. He did not exactly suspect the secret objects of Muir, but he was far from being blind to his sophistry. The result was that the two parted, after a long dialogue, unconvinced, and distrustful of each other's motives, though the distrust of the guide, like all that was connected with the man, partook of his own upright, disinterested, and ingenuous nature.

A conference that took place soon after between Sergeant Dunham and the Lieutenant led to more consequences. When it was ended, secret orders were issued to the men, and one accustomed to the movements of soldiers might have detected that an expedition was in the wind. In fact, just as the sun was setting, the Sergeant, who had been much occupied at what was called the harbour, came into his own hut, followed by Pathfinder and Cap; and as he took his seat at the neat table which Mabel had prepared for him, he opened the budget of his intelligence.

"You are likely to be of some use here, my child," the old soldier commenced, "as this tidy and well-ordered supper can testify; and I trust, when the proper moment arrives, you will show yourself to be the descendant of those who know how to face their enemies."

"Why, Father, I am not expected to fall in with the men, and to help defend the island?"

"And yet women have often done such things in this quarter of the world, girl. But lest you should be surprised at not seeing us when you awake in the morning, it is proper that I now tell you we intend to march in the course of this very night."

"*We*, Father? and leave me and Jennie on this island alone?"

"No, my daughter. We shall leave Lieutenant Muir, brother Cap, Corporal M'Nab, and three men to compose the garrison during our absence. Jennie will remain with you in this hut, and brother Cap will occupy my place."

"And Mr. Muir?" said Mabel, half unconscious of what she uttered, though she foresaw a great deal of unpleasant persecution in the arrangement.

"Why, he can make love to you, if you like it, girl; for he is an amorous youth, and, having already disposed of four wives, is impatient to show how much he honours their memories by taking a fifth."

The Sergeant nodded at the guide, as much as to say, You see how the land lies; and then he had sufficient consideration for his daughter's feelings to change the subject.

"Neither you nor Mabel, brother Cap," he resumed, "can have any legal authority with the little garrison I leave behind on the island; but you may counsel and influence. Strictly speaking, Corporal M'Nab will be the commanding officer, and I have endeavoured to impress him with a sense of his dignity, lest he might give way too much to the superior rank of Lieutenant Muir, who, being a volunteer, can have no right to interfere with the duty. I wish you to sustain the Corporal, brother Cap," for should the

Quartermaster once break through the regulations of the expedition he may pretend to command me as well as M'Nab."

"More particularly, should Mabel really cut him adrift while you are absent. Of course, Sergeant, you'll leave everything that is afloat under my care? The worst confusion has grown out of misunderstandings between commanders-in-chief, ashore and afloat."

"In one sense, brother, though in a general way, the Corporal is commander-in-chief. The Corporal must command; but you can counsel freely, particularly in all matters relating to the boats, of which I shall leave one behind to secure your retreat, should there be occasion. I know the Corporal well; he is a brave man and a good soldier. But then he is a Scotchman, and will be liable to the Quartermaster's influence, against which I desire both you and Mabel to be on your guard."

"But why leave us behind, dear Father? I have come thus far to be a comfort to you, and why not go farther?"

"You are a good girl, Mabel, but you must halt here. We shall leave the island to-morrow, before the day dawns, in order not to be seen by any prying eyes coming from our cover, and we shall take the two largest boats, leaving you the other and one bark canoe. We are about to go into the channel used by the French, where we shall lie in wait, perhaps a week, to intercept their supply-boats, which are about to pass up on their way to Frontenac, loaded, in particular, with a heavy amount of Indian goods. They contain the blankets, trinkets, rifles, ammunition, in short, all the stores with which the French bribe their savage allies. By cutting off these supplies we shall derange their plans, and gain time on them; for the articles cannot be sent across the ocean again this autumn."

Supper was no sooner ended than the Sergeant dismissed his guests, and then held a long and confidential dialogue with his daughter. He was little addicted to giving way to the gentler emotions, but the novelty of his present situation awakened feelings that he was unused to experience. Never before had Mabel struck him as so beautiful as she appeared that night. Possibly she never had displayed so many engaging qualities to her father; for concern on his account had begun to be active in her breast; and then her sympathies met with unusual encouragement through those which had been stirred up in the sterner bosom of the veteran. On the present occasion the conversation between the father and daughter became more confidential than usual, until Mabel rejoiced to find that it was gradually becoming endearing, a state of feeling that the warmhearted girl had silently pined for in vain ever since her arrival.

"Then mother was about my height?" Mabel said, as she held one of her father's hands in both her own, looking up into his face with humid eyes. "I had thought her taller."

"That is the way with most children who get a habit of thinking of their parents with respect. Your mother, Mabel, was as near your height as one woman could be to another."

"And her eyes, Father?"

"Her eyes were like thine, child, too; blue and soft, though hardly so laughing."

"Mine will never laugh again, dearest Father, if you do not take care of yourself in this expedition."

"Thank you, child; but I must do my duty. I wish I had seen you comfortably married before we left Oswego."

"Married?—to whom, Father?"

"You know the man I wish you to love. You may meet with many gayer, but with none with so true a heart and just a mind."

"None, Father?"

"I know of none; in these particulars Pathfinder has few equals."

"But I need not marry at all. You are single, and I can remain to take care of you."

"God bless you, Mabel! I know you would, and I do not say that the feeling is not right, for I suppose it is; and yet I believe there is another that is more so."

"What can be more right than to honour one's parents?"

"It is just as right to honour one's husband, my dear child."

"But I have no husband, Father."

"Then take one as soon as possible, that you may have a husband to honour. I cannot live for ever, Mabel, but must drop off in the course of nature ere long, if I am not carried off in the course of war. You are young, and it is proper that you should have a male protector."

"And do you think, Father," said Mabel, "that Pathfinder is just the man to do this? Is he not, within ten or twelve years, as old as yourself?"

"What of that? His life has been one of moderation and exercise, and years are less to be counted, girl, than constitution. Do you know another more likely to be your protector?"

Mabel did not; at least another who had expressed a desire to that effect, whatever might have been her hopes and her wishes.

"Nay, Father, we are not talking of another, but of the Pathfinder," she answered evasively. "If he were younger, I think it would be more natural for me to think of him for a husband."

"'Tis all in the constitution, I tell you, child; Pathfinder is a younger man than half our subalterns."

"He is certainly younger than one—Lieutenant Muir."

Mabel's laugh was joyous and light-hearted, as if just then she felt no care.

"That he is! God forbid, Mabel, that you should ever become an officer's lady, at least until you are an officer's daughter!"

"There will be little fear of that, Father, if I marry Pathfinder," returned the girl, looking up archly into the Sergeant's face.

"Not by the king's commission, perhaps, though the man is even now the friend and companion of generals. I think I could die happy, Mabel, if you were his wife."

"Father!"

"'Tis a sad thing to go into battle with the weight of an unprotected daughter laid upon the heart."

"I would give the world to lighten yours of its load, Father."

"It might be done," said the Sergeant, looking fondly at his child; "though I would not put a burthen on yours to do so."

The voice was deep and tremulous; never before had Mabel witnessed such a show of affection in her parent, and she yearned to relieve his mind.

"Father, speak plainly!" she cried, almost convulsively.

"Nay, Mabel, it might not be right; your wishes and mine may be very different."

"I have no wishes. Would you speak of my future marriage?"

"If I could see you promised to Pathfinder—know that you were pledged to become his wife, let my own fate be what it might, I think I could die happy. But I will ask no pledge of you, my child. Kiss me, Mabel, and go to your bed."

Had Sergeant Dunham exacted of Mabel the pledge that he really so much desired, he would have encountered a resistance that he might have found it difficult to overcome; but, by letting nature have its course, he enlisted a powerful ally on his side, and the warm-hearted, generous-minded Mabel was ready to concede to her affections much more than she would ever have yielded to menace. At that touching moment she thought only of her parent, who was about to quit her, perhaps for ever. One painful, rapid, almost wild gleam of thought shot across the brain of the girl, and her resolution wavered; but endeavouring to trace the foundation of the pleasing hope on which it was based, she found nothing positive to support it. Trained like a woman to subdue her most ardent feelings, her thoughts reverted to her father, and to the blessings that awaited the child who yielded to a parent's wishes.

"Father," she said quietly, "God blesses the dutiful daughter."

"He will, Mabel; we have the Good Book for that."

"I will marry whomever you desire."

"Nay, nay, Mabel, you may have a choice of your own——"

"I have no choice; none have asked me to have a choice, but Pathfinder and Mr. Muir; and between *them*, neither of us would hesitate. No, Father, I will marry whomever you may choose."

"Thou knowest my choice, beloved child; none other can make thee as happy as the noble-hearted guide."

"Well, then, if he wish it, if he ask me again—for, Father, you would not have me offer myself, or that anyone should do that office for me," and the blood stole across the pallid cheeks of Mabel as she spoke; "but if he seek me again, and, knowing all that a true girl ought to tell the man she marries, he then wishes to make me his wife, I will be his."

"Bless you, my Mabel! God in heaven bless you, and reward you as a pious daughter deserves to be rewarded."

"Yes, Father, put your mind at peace; go on this expedition with a light heart, and trust in God. For me you will have now no care. In the spring I will marry Pathfinder, if that noble-hearted hunter shall then desire it."

"Mabel, he loves you as I loved your mother. I have seen him weep like a child when speaking of his feelings towards you."

"Yes, I believe it; I've seen enough to satisfy me that he thinks better of me than I deserve; and certainly the man is not living for whom I have more respect than for Pathfinder."

"That is as it should be, child, and the union will be blessed. May I not tell Pathfinder this?"

"I would rather you would not, Father. Let it come of itself, come naturally." The smile that illuminated Mabel's handsome face was angelic, as even her parent thought, though one better practised in detecting the passing emotions, as they betray themselves in the countenance, might have traced something wild and unnatural in it. "No, no, *we* must let things take their course; Father, you have my solemn promise."

"That will do, Mabel; now kiss me. God bless and protect you, girl! you are a good daughter."

Mabel threw herself into her father's arms—it was the first time in her life—and sobbed on his bosom like an infant. The stern soldier's heart was melted, and the tears of the two mingled; but Sergeant Dunham soon started as if ashamed of himself, and, gently forcing his daughter from him, he bade her good-night, and sought his pallet.

CHAPTER XX

It was not only broad daylight when Mabel awoke, but the sun had actually been up some time. Springing to her feet and rapidly dressing herself, the girl was soon breathing the fragrance of the morning in the open air. For the first time she was sensibly struck with the singular beauties, as well as with the profound retirement, of her present situation. The day proved to be one of those of the autumnal glory so common to the climate, and its influence was in every way inspiriting and genial.

But the island seemed absolutely deserted; and our heroine had turned her eyes nearly around on every object in sight, before she caught a view of a single human being to remove the sense of utter solitude. Then, indeed, she beheld all who were left behind, collected in a group around a fire. The person of her uncle, to whom she was so much accustomed, reassured Mabel; and she examined the remainder with a curiosity natural to her situation. Besides Cap and the Quartermaster, there were the Corporal, the three soldiers, and the woman who was cooking. The huts were silent and empty; and the low but towerlike summit of the blockhouse rose above the bushes, by which it was half concealed, in picturesque beauty.

Perceiving that all the others were occupied with that great concern of human nature—a breakfast, Mabel walked, unobserved, towards an end of the island where she was completely shut out of view by the trees and bushes. Here she got a stand on the very edge of the water, by forcing aside the low branches, and stood watching the barely perceptible flow and reflow of the miniature waves which laved the shore; a sort of physical echo to the agitation that prevailed on the lake fifty miles above her.

While thus occupied, Mabel was suddenly alarmed by fancying that she caught a glimpse of a human form among the bushes that lined the shore of the island which lay directly before her. The distance across the water was not a hundred yards; and, though she might be mistaken, and her fancy was wandering when the form passed before her sight, still she did not think she could be deceived. Aware that her sex would be no protection against a rifle bullet, should an Iroquois get a view of her, the girl instinctively drew back, taking care to conceal her person as much as possible by the leaves, while she kept her own look riveted on the opposite shore, vainly waiting for some time in the expectation of the stranger. She was about to quit her post in the bushes and hasten to her uncle, in order to acquaint him of her suspicions, when she saw the branch of an alder thrust beyond the fringe of bushes on the other island, and waved towards her. The motion of the branch was such as she believed indicated amity; and, after a moment's hesitation, she broke off a twig, fastened it to a stick, and, thrusting it through an opening, waved it in return.

This dumb show lasted two or three minutes on both sides, when Mabel perceived that the bushes opposite were cautiously pushed aside, and a human face appeared. A glance sufficed to let Mabel see that it was the countenance of a redskin, while a second look satisfied her that it was the face of the wife of Arrowhead. During the time she had travelled in company with this woman, Mabel had been won by the gentleness of manner, and the mingled awe and affection with which she regarded her husband. Once or twice in the course of the journey she had fancied the Tuscarora had manifested towards herself an unpleasant degree of attention; and on those occasions it had struck her that his wife exhibited sorrow and mortification. As Mabel, however, had more than compensated for any pain she might in this way unintentionally have caused her companion, by her own kindness of manner and attentions, the woman had shown much attachment to her, and they had parted, with a deep conviction on the mind of our heroine that in the Dew-of-June she had lost a friend.

Hence, under the impression that this extraordinary visit was intended for her own good, Mabel felt every disposition to have a closer communication. She no longer hesitated about showing herself clear of the bushes, and was not sorry to see the Dew-of-June imitate her confidence, by stepping fearlessly out of her own cover. The two girls now openly exchanged signs of friendship, and the latter beckoned to her friend to approach. Dew-of-June, disappearing for a moment, soon showed herself again in the end of a bark canoe, the bows of which she had drawn to the edge of the bushes. Mabel was about to invite her to cross, when her own name was called in the stentorian voice of her uncle. Making a hurried gesture for the Tuscarora girl to conceal herself, Mabel sprang from the bushes and tripped up the glade towards the sound, and perceived that the whole party had just seated themselves at breakfast. That this was the most favourable instant for the interview flashed on the mind of Mabel; and, excusing herself on the plea of not being prepared for the meal, she bounded back to the thicket, and soon renewed her communications with the young Indian woman.

Dew-of-June was quick of comprehension; and with half a dozen noiseless strokes of the paddles, her canoe was concealed in the bushes of Station Island. In another minute, Mabel held her hand, and was leading her through the grove towards her own hut, which they both entered unseen. Hastily explaining to her guest the necessity of quitting her for a short time, Mabel, first placing the Dew-of-June in her own room, went to the fire and took her seat among the rest, with all the composure it was in her power to command.

"Late come, late served, Mabel," said her uncle, between two mouthfuls of broiled salmon; "it is a good rule, and keeps laggards up to their work."

"I am no laggard, Uncle; I have been stirring nearly an hour."

The discourse now became desultory, touching principally, however, on the probabilities of an invasion, and the best means of meeting it.

To most of this Mabel paid but little attention; though she felt some surprise that Lieutenant Muir, an officer whose character for courage stood well, should openly recommend an abandonment of what appeared to her to be doubly a duty, her father's character being connected with the defence of the island. Her mind, however, was so much occupied with her guest, that, seizing the first favourable moment, she left the table, and was soon in her own hut again. Carefully fastening the door, and seeing that the simple curtain was drawn before the single little window, Mabel next led June, as she was familiarly termed by those who spoke to her in English, into the outer room, making signs of affection and confidence.

"I am glad to see you, June," said Mabel, with one of her

sweetest smiles. "What has brought you hither, and how did you discover the island?"

"Speak slow," said June, returning smile for smile, "too quick."

Mabel repeated her questions.

"June, friend," returned the Indian woman.

"I believe you, June; what has this to do with your visit?"

"Friend come to see friend," answered June, again smiling.

"There is some other reason, June, else would you never run this risk, and alone. You are alone, June?"

"June wid you, no one else. June come alone."

"I hope so,—nay, I *know* so. You would not be treacherous with me, June? You would not give me to the French, to Arrowhead?"

June shook her head earnestly.

"You would not sell my scalp?"

Here June passed her arm fondly around the slender waist of Mabel and pressed her to her heart with a tenderness and affection that brought tears into the eyes of our heroine. Mabel returned the pressure, and then held the other off at the length of her arm, looked her steadily in the face, and continued her enquiries.

"If June has something to tell her friend, let her speak plainly," she said.

"June 'fraid Arrowhead kill her."

"But Arrowhead will never know it."

"He bury tomahawk in June's head."

"That must never be, dear June; say no more rather than run this risk."

"Blockhouse good place to sleep, good place to stay."

"Do you mean that I may save my life by keeping in the blockhouse, June?"

"Arrowhead wish no harm to handsome paleface," returned June, averting her face; "Arrowhead love paleface girl."

Mabel blushed, she knew not why. But it was necessary to know more, for her apprehensions had been keenly awakened, and she resumed her enquiries.

"Arrowhead can have no reason to love or to hate *me*," she said. "Is he near you?"

"Husband always near wife," said June.

"But tell me, June, ought I to keep in the blockhouse to-day—now?"

"Blockhouse very good: good for women—got no scalp."

"I fear I understand you only too well, June. Do you wish to see my father?"

"No here; gone away—all gone."

Anxious to learn how great the danger that impended over them might really be, Mabel rose from the camp-stool on which she had been seated; and, by assuming an attitude of less affectionate confidence, she hoped to hear more of that she really desired to learn.

"You know how much or how little you ought to tell me, June," she said; "and I hope you love me well enough to give me the information I ought to hear. My uncle, too, is on the island, and you ought to be his friend as well as mine; and both of us will remember your conduct when we get back to Oswego."

"Maybe, never get back; who know?"

"No one knows what will happen but God. Still, I think you are to be His instrument in saving us."

"Blockhouse very good," June repeated, laying strong emphasis on the last two words.

"Well, I understand this, June, and will sleep in it to-night. Of course I am to tell my uncle what you have said?"

"No, no!" she answered; "no good to tell Saltwater. Tell Arrowhead, and June die."

"You do my dear uncle injustice, for he would be as little likely to betray you as anyone."

"No understand. Saltwater got no eyes, no ears—not'ing but tongue!"

Mabel saw that Cap had not the confidence of the Indian woman, and that it was idle to expect she would consent to his being admitted to their interview.

"You appear to know our situation pretty well, June," Mabel continued; "have you been on the island before this visit?"

"Just come."

"How then do you know that what you say is true? my father, the Pathfinder, and Eau-douce may all be here within sound of my voice, if I choose to call them."

"All gone," said June positively, smiling good-humouredly.

"Nay, this is more than you *can* say certainly, not having been over the island to examine it."

"Got good eyes; see boat with men go away—see ship with Eau-douce."

"Then you have been some time watching us. I think, however, you have not counted them that remain."

June laughed, held up her four fingers again, and then pointed to her two thumbs.

"You think, then, June," Mabel continued, "that I had better live in the blockhouse?"

"Good place for woman. Blockhouse got no scalp. Logs t'ick."

"You speak confidently, June; as if you had been in it."

June laughed, though she said nothing.

"Does anyone but yourself know how to find this island?"

June looked sad, and she cast her eyes warily about her, as if distrusting a listener.

"Tuscarora everywhere—Oswego, here, Frontenac, Mohawk—everywhere. If he see June, kill her."

"But we thought that no one knew of this island, and that we had no reason to fear our enemies while on it."

"Much eye, Iroquois."

"Eyes will not always do, June. This spot is hid from ordinary sight, and few of even our own people know how to find it."

"One man can tell; some Yengeese talk French."

Mabel felt a chill at her heart.

"I understand your meaning, June," she said; "you wish me to know that someone has treacherously told your people where and how to find the island?"

June laughed, for in her eyes artifice in war was oftener a merit than a crime; but she was too true to her tribe herself to say more than the occasion required.

"Paleface know now," she added. "Blockhouse good for girl, no matter for men and warriors."

"But it is much matter with me, June; for one of these men is my uncle, and the others are my countrymen and friends. I must tell them what has passed."

"Then June be kill," returned the young Indian with concern.

"No; they shall not know that you have been here. Still, they must be on their guard, and we can all go into the blockhouse."

"Arrowhead know, see everything, and June be kill. June come to tell young paleface friend, not to tell men. June, woman, and tell woman; no tell men."

Mabel was greatly distressed at this declaration of her wild friend, for it was now evident the young creature understood that her communication was to go no farther. June now began to gather up the different little articles she had dropped in taking Mabel's hand, and was preparing to depart. To attempt detaining her was out of the question; and to part from her, after all she had hazarded to serve her, was repugnant to all the just and kind feelings of our heroine's nature.

"June," said she eagerly, folding her arms round the gentle being, "we are friends. From me you have nothing to fear, for no one shall know of your visit. If you could give me some signal just before the danger comes, some sign by which to know when to go into the blockhouse, how to take care of myself."

June paused, for she had been in earnest in her intention to depart; and then she said quietly: "Bring June pigeon."

"A pigeon! Where shall I find a pigeon to bring you?"

"Next hut; bring old one; June go to canoe."

"I think I understand you, June; but had I not better lead you back to the bushes, lest you meet some of the men?"

"Go out first; count men, one, two, t'ree, four, five, six"—here June held up her fingers, and laughed—"all out of the way—good; all but one, call him one side. Then sing, and fetch pigeon."

Mabel smiled at the readiness of the girl, and prepared to execute her requests. At the door, however, she stopped, and looked back entreatingly at the Indian woman. "Is there no hope of your telling me more, June?" she said.

"Know all now, blockhouse good, pigeon tell, Arrowhead kill."

The last words sufficed; for Mabel could not urge further communications, when her companion herself told her that the penalty of her revelations might be death by the hand of her husband. Throwing open the door, she made a sign of adieu to June, and went out of the hut. Mabel resorted to the simple expedient of the young Indian girl to ascertain the situation of the different individuals of the island. Having accounted for the whole party, Mabel now, affecting to have dropped something, returned nearly to the hut she had left, warbling an air, stooped as if to pick up some object from the ground, and hurried towards the hut June had mentioned. This was a sort of storehouse for the live stock. Among other things, it contained a few dozen pigeons, one of which Mabel had not much difficulty in catching; and, concealing it in her dress, she stole back towards her own hut with the prize. It was empty; and, without doing more than cast a glance in at the door, the eager girl hurried down to the shore. At the canoe she found June, who took the pigeon, and repeating the words, "blockhouse good", she glided out of the bushes and across the narrow passage, as noiselessly as she had come.

On returning from the shore, Mabel was struck with a little circumstance, that, in an ordinary situation, would have attracted no attention, but which, now that her suspicions had been aroused, did not pass before her uneasy eye unnoticed. A small piece of red bunting, such as is used in the ensigns of ships, was fluttering at the lower branch of a small tree, fastened in a way to permit it to blow out, or to drop like a vessel's pennant.

Now that Mabel's fears were awakened, June herself could not have manifested greater quickness in analysing facts that she believed might affect the safety of the party. She saw at a glance that this bit of cloth could be observed from an adjacent island; that it lay so near the line between her own hut and the canoe as to leave no doubt that June had passed near it, if not directly under it, and that it might be a signal to communicate some important fact connected with the mode of attack to those who were probably lying in ambush near them. Tearing the little strip of bunting from the tree, Mabel hastened on, scarcely knowing what her duty next required of her. June might be false to her, but her manner, her looks, her affection, and her disposition as Mabel had known it in the journey, forbade the idea. Then came the allusion to Arrowhead's admiration of the pale-face beauties, some dim recollections of the looks of the Tuscarora, and a painful consciousness that few wives could view with kindness one who had estranged a husband's affections. None of these images were distinct and clear, but they quickened Mabel's pulses, as they did her step, without bringing with them the prompt and clear decisions that usually followed her reflections. She had hurried onwards towards the hut occupied by the soldier's wife, intending to remove at once to the blockhouse with the woman, though she could persuade no other to follow, when her impatient walk was interrupted by the voice of Muir.

"Whither so fast, pretty Mabel?" he cried; "and why so given to solitude?"

"Surely, Mr. Muir, you must have some authority here?" Mabel suddenly arrested her steps to say.

"I don't know that," interrupted Muir, with an impatience and appearance of alarm that might have excited Mabel's attention at another moment. "Command is command; discipline, discipline; and authority, authority. Your good father would be sore grieved did he find me interfering to sully or carry off the laurels he is about to win; and I cannot command the Corporal without equally commanding the Sergeant. But what is that you're twisting round your slender finger as you may be said to twist hearts?"

"It is nothing but a bit of cloth — a sort of flag — a trifle. If——"

"A trifle! It's no' so trifling as ye may imagine, Mistress Mabel," taking the bit of bunting from her, and stretching it at full length with both his arms extended. "Ye'll no ha' been finding this, Mabel Dunham, in the breakfast?"

Mabel simply acquainted him with the spot where and the manner in which she had found the bit of cloth. While she was speaking, the eye of the Quartermaster was not quiet for a moment.

"We are not in the part of the world where our ensigns and gauds ought to be spread abroad to the wind, Mabel Dunham!" he said, with an ominous shake of the head.

"I thought as much myself, Mr. Muir, and brought away the little flag lest it might be the means of betraying our presence here to the enemy."

"This flag, if flag it can be called, belongs to a seaman's craft. It's surprisingly like the fly of the *Scud's* ensign. And now I recollect me to have observed that a piece had been cut from that very flag."

Mabel felt her heart sink, but she had sufficient self-command not to attempt an answer.

"It must be looked to," Muir continued, "and after all, I think it may be well to hold a short consultation with Master Cap."

"I have thought the warning so serious," Mabel rejoined, "that I am about to remove to the blockhouse, and to take the woman with me."

"I do not see the prudence of that, Mabel. The blockhouse will be the first spot assailed should there really be an attack; and it's no' well provided for a siege, that must be allowed. If I might advise in so delicate a contingency, I would recommend your taking refuge in the boat, which, as you may now perceive, is most favourably placed to retreat by that channel opposite. I've always been of opinion that Lundie hazarded too much in occupying a post so far advanced and so much exposed as this."

"It's too late to regret it now, Mr. Muir, and we have only to consult our own security."

"And the king's honour, pretty Mabel. Yes, his Majesty's arms and his glorious name are not to be overlooked on any occasion."

"Did you imagine, Mr. Muir, that two females could row that heavy boat in a way to escape the canoe of an Indian!"

"Ah, my pretty Mabel, love is seldom logical, and its fears and misgivings are apt to warp the faculties! I only saw your sweet person in the possession of the means of safety, and overlooked the want of ability to use them."

Mabel had heard enough. She took a hasty leave of her companion, and was about to trip away towards the hut of the other woman, when Muir arrested the movement by laying a hand on her arm.

"One word, Mabel," said he. "This little flag may, or it may not, have a particular meaning; if it has, now that we are aware of its being shown, may it not be better to put it back again, while we watch vigilantly for some answer that may betray the conspiracy?"

"This may be all right, Mr. Muir, though, if the whole is accidental, the flag might be the occasion of the fort's being discovered."

Mabel stayed to utter no more. The Quartermaster remained looking at the bit of bunting, which he still held before him in a way to denote indecision. His irresolution lasted but for a minute, however; for he was soon beneath the tree, where he fastened the mimic flag to a branch again, though, from his ignorance of the precise spot from which it had been taken by Mabel, he left it fluttering from a part of the oak where it was still more exposed than before to the eyes of any passenger on the river.

CHAPTER XXI

It seemed strange to Mabel Dunham, as she passed along on her way to find her female companion, that others should be so composed, while she herself felt as if the responsibilities of life and death rested on her shoulders. She saw, however, that she could not put her companions properly on their guard without letting them into the secret of her conference with June; and she found herself compelled to act cautiously and with a forethought to which she was unaccustomed, more especially in a matter of so much moment.

The soldier's wife was told to transport the necessaries into the blockhouse, and admonished not to be far from it at any time during the day. Mabel did not explain her reasons. She merely stated that she had detected some signs in walking about the island, which induced her to apprehend that the enemy had more

knowledge of its position than had been previously believed, and
that they two, at least, would do well to be in readiness to seek
a refuge at the shortest notice. As soon as Mabel believed that
her companion was sufficiently frightened to make her wary,
she threw out some hints touching the expediency of letting the
soldiers know the extent of their own fears. She determined to
render her uncle, the Corporal, and his men more cautious, by
adopting a different course. Unfortunately, the British army
could not have furnished a worse person for the particular duty
that he was now required to discharge than Corporal M'Nab, the
individual who had been left in command during the absence
of Sergeant Dunham.

After a few words, during which Mabel encountered his opinion-
ated obstinacy, she said: " My father expects the blockhouse in
particular to be strictly attended to."

"If he wishes to defend the honour of the 55th behind logs, he
ought to have remained in command himsel'; for, to speak frankly,
it goes against a Scotchman's bluid and opinions to be beaten out
of the field even before he is attacked."

"No true soldier despises caution. Even Major Duncan, than
whom there is none braver, is celebrated for his care of his men."

" Lundie has his weakness, and is fast forgetting the broadsword
and open heaths in his tree and rifle practice. We Scots come
from a naked region, and have no need and less relish for covers,
and so ye'll be seeing, Mistress Dunham——"

The Corporal gave a spring into the air, fell forward on his face,
and rolled over on his back, the whole passing so suddenly that
Mabel had scarcely heard the sharp crack of the rifle that had
sent a bullet through his body. Our heroine did not shriek ; for
the occurrence was too sudden, and too unexpected for that exhibition of weakness ; on the contrary, she stepped hastily forward,
with a natural impulse to aid her companion. There was just
enough of life left in M'Nab to betray his entire consciousness
of all that had passed.

" Ye'll be getting into the blockhouse as fast as possible," M'Nab
whispered, as Mabel leaned over him to catch his dying words.

Then came over the girl the full consciousness of her situation
and of the necessity of exertion. She cast a rapid glance at the
body at her feet, and fled. It was but a few minutes' run to the
blockhouse, the door of which Mabel had barely gained when it
was closed violently in her face by Jennie, the soldier's wife, who
in blind terror thought only of her own safety. The reports of

five or six rifles were heard while Mabel was calling out for admittance; and the additional terror they produced prevented the woman within from undoing quickly the very fastenings she had been so expert in applying. After a minute's delay, however, Mabel found the door reluctantly yielding to her constant pressure, and she forced her slender body through the opening the instant it was large enough to allow of its passage. Instead of yielding to the almost convulsive efforts of her companion to close the door again, Mabel held it open long enough to ascertain that none of her own party was in sight, or likely on the instant to endeavour to gain admission. Then she allowed the opening to be shut. But a single bar was crossed, and Jennie was directed to stand in readiness to remove even that at any application from a friend. Mabel then ascended the ladder to the room above, where by means of a loophole she was enabled to get as good a view of the island as the surrounding bushes would allow.

To her great surprise, Mabel could not at first see a living soul on the island, friend or enemy. The rifles had been discharged from the direction of the island whence June had come, though whether the enemy were on that island, or had actually landed on her own, Mabel could not say. Going to the loop that commanded a view of the spot where M'Nab lay, her blood curdled at perceiving all three of his soldiers lying apparently lifeless at his side. These men had rushed to a common centre at the first alarm, and had been shot down almost simultaneously by the invisible foe.

Neither Cap nor Lieutenant Muir was to be seen. With a beating heart Mabel examined every opening through the trees, and ascended even to the upper story of the blockhouse, where she got a full view of the whole island, so far as its cover would allow, but with no better success. She had expected to see the body of her uncle lying on the grass like those of the soldiers, but it was nowhere visible. Turning towards the spot where the boat lay, Mabel saw that it was still fastened to the shore; and then she supposed that by some accident Muir had been prevented from effecting his retreat in that quarter.

"For Heaven's sake, Mistress Mabel," called out the woman from below, "tell me if any of our friends are living! I think I hear groans that grow fainter and fainter, and fear they will all be tomahawked!"

Mabel now remembered that one of the soldiers was this woman's husband, and answered:

"We are in His holy keeping, Jennie. We must trust in Providence. Be careful with the door; on no account open it without my directions."

"Oh, tell me if you can anywhere see Sandy! If I could only let him know that I'm in safety, the guid man would be easier in his mind, whether free or a prisoner."

"There are some of our people gathered about the body of M'Nab," was the answer.

"Is Sandy amang them?" demanded the woman, in a voice that sounded appalling by its hoarseness and energy.

"He may be certainly; for I see one, two, three, four, and all in the scarlet coats of the regiment."

"Sandy!" called out the woman frantically; "why d'ye no' care for yoursal'? Come hither the instant, man, and share your wife's fortunes in weal or woe. Sandy! Sandy!"

Mabel heard the bar turn, and then the door creaked on its hinges. Expectation, not to say terror, held her in suspense at the loop, and she soon beheld Jennie rushing through the bushes in the direction of the dead. It took the woman but an instant to reach the fatal spot. So sudden and unexpected had been the blow, that she in her terror did not appear to comprehend its weight. Some wild and half-frantic notion of a deception troubled her fancy, and she imagined that the men were trifling with her fears. She took her husband's hand, which was still warm.

"Why will ye fool life away, Sandy?" she cried, pulling at the arm. "Ye'll all be murdered by these accursed Indians, and you no' takin' to the block like trusty soldiers! Awa'! awa'!"

In her desperate efforts, the woman pulled the body of her husband in a way to cause the head to turn completely over, when the small hole in the temple, caused by the entrance of a rifle bullet, and a few drops of blood trickling over the skin, revealed the meaning of her husband's silence. As the horrid truth flashed in its full extent on her mind, the woman clasped her hands, gave a shriek that pierced the glades of every island near, and fell at length on the dead body of the soldier. Thrilling, heart-reaching, appalling as was that shriek, it was melody to the cry that followed it so quickly as to blend the sounds. The terrific warwhoop arose out of the covers of the island, and some twenty savages, horrible in their paint and the other devices of Indian ingenuity, rushed forward, eager to secure the coveted scalps. Arrowhead was foremost, and it was his tomahawk that brained the insensible Jennie; and her reeking hair was hanging at his girdle as a trophy in less than two minutes after she had quitted the blockhouse. His companions were equally active, and M'Nab and his soldiers no longer presented the quiet aspect of men who slumbered.

All this did Mabel witness. She had stood riveted to the spot, gazing on the whole horrible scene, as if enchained by some charm. But no sooner did she perceive the place where the men had fallen covered with savages than it occurred to her that Jennie had left the blockhouse door unbarred. Her heart beat violently, for that defence alone stood between her and immediate death, and she sprang towards the ladder with the intention of descending to make sure of it. Her foot had not yet reached the floor of the second story, however, when she heard the door grating on its hinges, and she gave herself up for lost. Sinking on her knees, the terrified but courageous girl endeavoured to prepare herself for death, and to raise her thoughts to God. But when her ears heard the bars turning into their fastenings, not one, but all three, she started again to her feet, all spiritual contemplations vanishing in her actual temporal condition, and it seemed as if all her faculties were absorbed in the sense of hearing.

The thoughts are active in a moment so fearful. At first Mabel fancied that her uncle had entered the blockhouse, and she was about to descend the ladder and throw herself into his arms; then the idea that it might be an Indian, who had barred the door to shut out intruders while he plundered at leisure, arrested the movement. The profound stillness below was unlike the bold, restless movements of Cap, and it seemed to savour more of the artifices of an enemy. If a friend at all, it could only be her uncle or the Quartermaster; for the horrible conviction now presented itself to our heroine that to these two and herself was the whole party suddenly reduced, if, indeed, the two latter survived. This consideration held Mabel in check, and for full two minutes more a breathless silence reigned in the building. During this time the girl stood at the foot of the upper ladder, the trap which led to the lower opening on the opposite side of the floor; the eyes of Mabel were riveted on this spot, for she now began to expect to see at each instant the horrible sight of a savage face at the hole. She thought, too, that she heard a low rustling, as if one were ascending the lower ladder with an effort at caution so great as to betray itself by its own excess; then followed a creaking that she was certain came from one of the steps of the ladder. As yet, nothing was visible at the trap, but the girl's ears, rendered

exquisitely sensitive by intense feeling, distinctly acquainted her
that someone was within a few inches of the opening in the floor.
Next followed the evidence of her eyes, which beheld the dark
hair of an Indian rising slowly through the passage; then came
the dark skin and wild features, until the whole of the swarthy
face had risen above the floor. Mabel imagined many additional
horrors as she first saw the black, roving eyes and the expression
of wildness as the savage countenance was revealed, as it might
be, inch by inch; but when the entire head was raised above the
floor, a second and a better look assured our heroine that she saw
the gentle and anxious face of June.

CHAPTER XXII

It would be difficult to say which evinced the most satisfaction,
our heroine, on finding that her visitor was the wife of Arrowhead, and not Arrowhead himself; or June, at discovering that
her advice had been followed, and that the blockhouse contained
the person she had so anxiously and almost hopelessly sought.
They embraced each other, and the unsophisticated Tuscarora
woman laughed in her sweet accents as she held her friend at
arm's length, and made certain of her presence.

"Blockhouse good," said the young Indian; "got no scalp."

"It is indeed good, June," Mabel answered, with a shudder,
veiling her eyes at the same time, as if to shut out a view of
the horrors she had so lately witnessed. "Tell me, for Heaven's
sake, if you know what has become of my uncle! I have looked
in all directions without being able to see him."

"No here in blockhouse?" June asked, with some curiosity.

"Indeed he is not."

"Saltwater has boat; maybe he go on river."

"The boat is still on the shore, but neither my uncle nor the
Quartermaster is anywhere to be seen."

"No kill, or June would see. Hide away!"

"Your attack was awfully sudden, June!"

"Tuscarora!" returned the other, smiling with exultation at the
dexterity of her husband. "Arrowhead great warrior!"

"You are too good and gentle for this sort of life, June; you
cannot be happy in such scenes?"

" June's countenance grew clouded, and Mabel fancied there was some of the savage fire of a chief in her frown as she answered:

"Yengeese too greedy, take away all hunting grounds. Paleface very bad."

Mabel knew that there was much truth in this opinion. She felt the justice of the rebuke, therefore, too much to attempt an answer, and her thoughts naturally reverted to her own situation.

"And what am I to do, June?" she demanded. "It cannot be long before your people will assault this building."

"Blockhouse good—got no scalp."

"But they will soon discover that it has got no garrison too, if they do not know it already."

"Arrowhead know," answered June, holding up six fingers, to indicate the number of the men. "Four lose scalp already; two got 'em yet."

"Do not speak of it, June. Your people cannot know that I am alone in the blockhouse, but may fancy my uncle and the Quarter-master with me, and may set fire to the building, in order to dis-lodge them."

"No burn blockhouse," said June quietly.

"You cannot know that, June, and I have no means to keep them off."

"No burn blockhouse. Blockhouse good; got no scalp."

"But tell me why, June; I fear they will burn it."

"Blockhouse wet—much rain—no burn easy. Red man know it—fine t'ng—then no burn it to tell Yengeese that Iroquois been here. No, no; Indian too much cunning; no touch anything."

"I understand you, June, and hope your prediction may be true; for, as regards my dear father, should he escape—perhaps he is already dead or captured, June?"

"No touch fader—don't know where he gone—water got no trail. No burn blockhouse—blockhouse good; got no scalp."

"Do you think it possible for me to remain here safely until my father returns?"

"Don't know; daughter tell best when fader come back."

Mabel felt uneasy at the glance of June's dark eye as she uttered this; for the unpleasant surmise arose that her com-panion was endeavouring to discover a fact that might be useful to her people. She was about to make an evasive answer, when a heavy push at the outer door suddenly drew all her thoughts to the immediate danger.

"They come!" she exclaimed. "Perhaps, June, it is my uncle or the Quartermaster."

"Why no look? plenty loophole, made purpose."

Mabel went to one of the downward loops that had been cut through the logs in the part that overhung the basement, and caught a glance of what was passing at the door. The start and changing countenance told her companion that some of her own people were below.

"Red man," said June, lifting a finger in admonition to be be prudent.

"Four! Arrowhead is among them."

June had moved to a corner, where several spare rifles had been deposited, and had already taken one into her hand, when the name of her husband appeared to arrest her movements. It was but for an instant, however, for she immediately went to the loop, and was about to thrust the muzzle of the piece through it, when Mabel seized her arm.

"No, no, June!" said the latter; "not against your own husband."

"No hurt red man. No fire at 'em; only scare."

Mabel now comprehended the intention of June. The latter thrust the muzzle of the rifle through the loophole; and, taking care to make noise enough to attract attention, she pulled the trigger.

"You declared it was not your intention to fire," she said, "and you may have destroyed your own husband."

"All run away before I fire," returned June, laughing, and going to another loop to watch the movements of her friends. "See! get cover—every warrior. Think Saltwater and Quartermaster here."

"Heaven be praised! And now, June, I may hope for a little time to compose my thoughts to prayer, that I may not die like Jennie, thinking only of life and the things of the world."

June laid aside the rifle, and came and seated herself near the box on which Mabel had sunk. She looked steadily in our heroine's face, and the latter thought that her countenance had an expression of severity mingled with its concern.

"Arrowhead great warrior," said she. "All the girls of tribe look at him much. The paleface beauty has eyes too?"

"June!—what do these words imply? what would you say?"

"Why you so 'fraid June shoot Arrowhead?"

"Would it not have been horrible to see a wife destroy her own husband?"

"Very sure dat all?"

"That was all, June, as God is my judge! What other motive can you suspect?"

"Don't know. Tuscarora girl very foolish. Arrowhead talk of paleface beauty in his sleep. Great chief like many wives."

"Can a chief possess more than one wife, June, among your people?"

"Have as many as he can keep. Arrowhead got only June now; but he look too much, talk too much of paleface girl."

Mabel was conscious of this fact, which had distressed her not a little in the course of their journey; but, in addition to the pain and mortification she experienced at being the unwilling rival of a wife, she felt an apprehension that jealousy would be but an equivocal guarantee for her personal safety in her present situation. A closer look at June, however, reassured her; for, while it was easy to trace in the unpractised features of this unsophisticated being the pain of blighted affections, no distrust could have tortured the earnest expression of her honest countenance into that of treachery or hate.

"You will not betray me, June?" Mabel said, pressing the other's hand. "You will not give up one of your own sex to the tomahawk?"

"No tomahawk touch you. Arrowhead no let 'em. If June must have sister-wife, love to have you."

"No, June; my religion, my feelings, both forbid it."

June made no answer, but she looked gratified, and even grateful. She knew that few, perhaps no Indian girl within the circle of Arrowhead's acquaintance, could compare with herself in personal attractions; and, though it might suit her husband to marry a dozen wives, she knew of no one, beside Mabel, whose influence she could really dread. In a word, June, with a wife's keenness of perception, had detected Arrowhead's admiration of Mabel, and, instead of feeling that harrowing jealousy that might have rendered her rival hateful, as would have been apt to be the case with a woman unaccustomed to defer to the superior rights of the lordly sex, she had studied the looks and character of the paleface beauty, until, meeting with nothing to repel her own feelings, but everything to encourage them, she had got to entertain an admiration and love for her, which was scarcely less strong than her husband's. Arrowhead himself had sent her to warn Mabel of the coming danger, though he was ignorant that she had stolen upon the island in the rear of the assailants, and was now entrenched in the citadel along with the object of their joint care. On the contrary, he supposed, as his wife had said, that Cap and Muir were in the blockhouse with Mabel, and that the attempt to repel him and his companions had been made by the men.

"June sorry the Lily"—for so the Indian had named our heroine—"no marry Arrowhead. His wigwam big, and a great chief must get wives enough to fill it."

"I thank you, June, for this preference, which is not according to the notion of us white women," returned Mabel; "but I may not, probably never shall, marry at all."

"Must have good husband," said June.

"June! I would obtain some signs of my dear uncle's being alive and safe, if possible."

"June go see."

"Can you?—would it be safe for you to be seen on the island?"

Mabel had thought it extraordinary that June should be of the party, and, improbable as it seemed, she had fancied that the woman had covertly followed the Iroquois in her canoe, and had got in their advance, merely to give her the notice which had probably saved her life. But in all this she was mistaken, as June now found means to let her know.

Arrowhead, though a chief, was in disgrace with his own people, and was acting with the Iroquois temporarily, though with a perfect understanding. He had a wigwam, it is true, but was seldom in it; feigning friendship for the English, he had passed the summer ostensibly in their service, while he was, in truth, acting for the French, and his wife journeyed with him in his many migrations, most of the distances being passed over in canoes. Thus much having been explained to Mabel, it was soon settled between them that the Indian woman should quit the blockhouse with the object of ascertaining the fate of Cap the moment a favourable opportunity offered.

They first examined the island, as thoroughly as their position would allow, from the different loops, and found that its conquerors were preparing for a feast, having seized upon the provisions of the English and rifled the huts. Most of the stores were in the blockhouse; but enough were found outside to reward the Indians for an attack that had been attended by so little risk. A party had already removed the dead bodies, and Mabel saw that their arms were collected in a pile near the spot chosen for the banquet. None of the more prominent objects on the island, however, were disturbed, it being the desire of the conquerors to lure the party of the Sergeant into an ambush on its return. There did not appear to be any intention to attack the blockhouse immediately; but every indication, as understood by June, rather showed that it was the intention of the Indians to keep it besieged until the return of the Sergeant's party, lest the signs of an assault should give a warning to eyes as practised as those of Pathfinder. The boat, however, had been secured, and was removed to the spot where the canoes of the Indians were hid in the bushes.

June now announced her intention to join her friends, the moment being particularly favourable for her to quit the blockhouse. The process of unbarring the door was conducted with the utmost caution, and when the last bar was ready to be turned June took her station near the spot where the opening must necessarily be. The bar was just turned free of the brackets, the door was opened merely wide enough to allow her body to pass, and June glided through the space. Mabel closed the door again, and as the bar turned into its place she felt secure; the two other bars were then turned down, and when all was fast she ascended to the first floor, where alone she could get a glimpse of what was going on without.

Long and painfully melancholy hours passed. She heard the yells of the savages, for liquor had carried them beyond the bounds of precaution; occasionally caught glimpses of their mad orgies through the loops; and at all times was conscious of their fearful presence by sounds and sights that would have chilled the blood of one who had not so lately witnessed scenes much more terrible. Toward the middle of the day she fancied she saw a white man on the island, though his dress and wild appearance at first made her take him for a newly-arrived savage. A view of his face, although it was much darkened by exposure, left no doubt that her conjecture was true; and she felt as if there was now one to whom she might appeal for succour in the last emergency. Mabel knew little, alas! how small was the influence exercised by the whites over their savage allies, when the latter had begun to taste of blood.

The day seemed a month by Mabel's computation. She believed it highly probable that the blockhouse would be left unmolested until the return of her father, in order to entice him into an ambuscade, and she felt much less apprehension of immediate danger in consequence; but the future offered little ground of hope, and her thoughts had already begun to calculate the chances of her captivity.

While the light lasted Mabel's situation was sufficiently alarming; but as the shades of evening gradually gathered over the island, it became appalling. By this time the savages had wrought themselves up to the point of fury, for they had possessed themselves of all the liquor of the English; and their outcries and gesticulations were those of men truly possessed by evil spirits. All the efforts of their French leader to restrain them were entirely fruitless, and he had wisely withdrawn to an adjacent island, where he had a sort of bivouac, that he might keep at a safe distance from friends so apt to run into excesses. Before quitting the spot, however, this officer, at great risk to his own life, had succeeded in extinguishing the fire, and in securing the ordinary means to relight it. This precaution he took lest the Indians should burn the blockhouse, the preservation of which was necessary to the success of his future plans. This measure proved to be a most prudent one; for no sooner was the officer's back turned than one of the warriors in fact proposed to fire the blockhouse. Arrowhead had also withdrawn from the group of drunkards, as soon as he found they were losing their senses, and had taken possession of a hut, where he had thrown himself on the straw, and sought the rest that two wakeful and watchful nights had rendered necessary. It followed that no one was left among the Indians to care for Mabel, if, indeed, any knew of her existence at all; and the proposal of the drunkard was received with yells of delight by eight or ten more as much intoxicated and habitually as brutal as himself.

This was the fearful moment for Mabel. The Indians, in their present condition, were reckless of any rifles that the blockhouse might hold, and they approached its base whooping and leaping like demons. As yet they were excited, not overcome by the liquor they had drunk. The first attempt was made at the door, against which they ran in a body; but the solid structure, which was built entirely of logs, defied their efforts. Mabel's heart seemed to leap into her mouth as she heard the heavy shock at each renewed effort. At length, when she found that the door resisted these assaults as if it were of stone, her courage revived, and she seized the first moment of a cessation to look down through the loop, in order, if possible, to learn the extent of her danger.

Mabel found that two or three of the Iroquois had been raking the embers, where they had found a few small coals, and with these they were endeavouring to light a fire. The interest with which they laboured, the hope of destroying, and the force of habit, enabled them to act intelligently and in unison, so long as their fell object was kept in view. By the aid of a few dry leaves a blaze was finally kindled, and then the addition of a few light sticks made sure of the advantage that had been obtained. When Mabel stooped down over the loop the Indians were making a pile of brush against the door, and as she remained gazing at their proceedings, she saw the twigs ignite, the flame dart from branch to branch, until the whole pile was cracking and snapping under a bright blaze. The Indians now gave a yell of triumph, and returned to their companions, well assured that the work of destruction was commenced. Mabel remained looking down, scarcely able to tear herself away from the spot, so intense and engrossing was the interest she felt in the progress of the fire. As the pile kindled throughout, however, the flames mounted, until they flashed so near her eyes as to compel her to retreat. Just as she reached the opposite side of the room, to which she had retired in her alarm, a forked stream shot up through the loophole, the lid of which she had left open, and illuminated the rude apartment. Our heroine now naturally enough supposed that her hour was come; and she addressed herself, as she believed, for the last time, to her Maker in prayer. Her eyes were closed, and when they involuntarily opened again she perceived that the streak of flame was no longer flaring in the room, though the wood around the little aperture had kindled, and the blaze was slowly mounting under the impulsion of a current of air that sucked inward. A barrel of water stood in a corner; and Mabel caught up a vessel, filled it, and, pouring it on the wood with a trembling hand, succeeded in extinguishing the fire at that particular spot. The smoke prevented her from looking down again for a couple of minutes; but when she did her heart beat high with delight at finding that the pile of blazing brush had been overturned and scattered, and that water had been thrown on the logs of the door, which were still smoking, though no longer burning.

"Who is there?" said Mabel, with her mouth at the loop. "What friendly hand has Providence sent to my succour?"

A light footstep was audible below, and a gentle push at the door was heard.

"Who wishes to enter? Is it you, dear Uncle?"

"Saltwater no here," was the answer. "Open quick; want to come in."

The step of Mabel was never lighter than while descending the ladder and turning the bars. She thought only of her escape, and opened the door with a rapidity which did not admit of caution. Her first impulse was to rush into the open air, in the blind hope of quitting the blockhouse; but June repulsed the attempt, and entering, coolly barred the door again before she would notice Mabel's eager efforts to embrace her.

"Bless you, June!" cried the girl fervently; "you are sent by Providence to be my guardian angel!"

"No hug so tight," answered the Tuscarora woman. "Let June fasten door."

Mabel became more rational, and in a few minutes the two were again in the upper room, seated as before, hand in hand.

"Now tell me, June," Mabel commenced, "have you seen or heard aught of my poor uncle?"

"Don't know. No one see him; no one hear him; no one know anyt'ing. Quartermaster gone too. I look, and look, and look: but no see 'em, one, t'other, nowhere."

"Blessed be God! They must have escaped. I thought I saw a Frenchman on the island, June."

"Yes; French captain come, but he go away too. Plenty of Indian on island."

"Oh, June, are there no means to prevent my beloved father from falling into the hands of his enemies?"

"Don't know! t'ink warriors wait in ambush, Yengeese lose scalp."

"Surely, June, you, who have done so much for the daughter, will not refuse to help the father?"

"Don't know fader. June help her own people, help Arrowhead —husband love scalp."

"June, this is not yourself. I cannot, will not believe that you wish to see our men murdered!"

June turned her dark eyes on Mabel; and for a moment her look was stern, though it soon changed into one of compassion.

"Lily, Yengeese girl?" she said, as one asks a question.

"Certainly, and as a Yengeese girl I would save my countrymen from slaughter."

"Very good, if can. June no Yengeese; June Tuscarora—all over Tuscarora. Lily wouldn't run and tell French that her fader was coming to gain victory?"

"Perhaps not," returned Mabel, pressing a hand on a brain that felt bewildered,—"perhaps not; but you serve me, aid me—have saved me, June! Why have you done this, if you only feel as a Tuscarora?"

"Don't only feel as Tuscarora; feel as girl, feel as squaw. Love pretty Lily, and put it in my bosom."

Mabel melted into tears, and she pressed the affectionate creature to her heart.

"Let me know the worst, June," said she. "To-night your people are feasting; what do they intend to do to-morrow?"

"Don't know; afraid to see Arrowhead, afraid to ask question; t'ink hide away till Yengeese come back."

"Will they not attempt anything against the blockhouse?"

"Too much rum. Arrowhead sleep; French captain gone away, or no dare. All go to sleep now."

"And you think I am safe for this night, at least?"

"Too much rum. If Lily like June, might do much for her people."

"I am like you, June, if a wish to serve my countrymen can make a resemblance with one as courageous as yourself."

"No, no!" muttered June in a low voice; "no got heart, and June no let you, if had. June's moder prisoner once, and warriors got drunk; moder tomahawked 'em all."

"You say what is true," returned Mabel. "I cannot do that. I have neither the strength nor the will to dip my hands in blood."

"T'ink that too; then stay where you be—blockhouse good."

"You believe, then, that I am safe here, at least until my father and his people return?"

"Know so. No dare touch blockhouse in morning. Hark! all still now—drink rum till head fall down, and sleep like log."

"Might I not escape? Are there not several canoes on the island? Might I not get one, and go and give my father notice of what has happened?"

"Know how to paddle?" demanded June, glancing her eye furtively at her companion.

"Not so well as yourself, perhaps; but enough to get out of sight before morning."

"What do, then?—couldn't paddle six—ten—eight mile!"

"I do not know; I would do much to warn my father, and the excellent Pathfinder, and all the rest, of the danger they are in."

"Like Pathfinder?"

"All like him who know him—you would like him, nay, love him, if you only knew his heart!"

"No like him at all. Too good rifle—too good eye—too much shoot Iroquois and June's people. Must get his scalp if can."

"And I must save it if I can, June. In this respect, then, we are opposed to each other. I will go and find a canoe the instant they are all asleep, and quit the island."

"No can—June won't let you. Call Arrowhead."

"June! you would not betray me—you could not give me up after all you have done for me?"

"Just so," returned June, speaking with a warmth Mabel had never witnessed in her before. "Call Arrowhead. One call from wife wake a warrior up. June no let Lily help enemy—no let Indian hurt Lily."

"I understand you, June, and feel the nature and justice of your sentiments; and, after all, it were better that I should remain here, for I have most probably overrated my strength. But if my uncle comes in the night, and asks to be admitted, you will let me open the door of the blockhouse that he may enter?"

"Sartain—he prisoner here, and June like prisoner better than scalp. But Saltwater hide so close, he don't know where he be himself."

Here June laughed in her girlish, mirthful way, for to her scenes of violence were too familiar to leave impressions sufficiently deep to change her natural character. A long dialogue now followed, the substance of which may be summed up as follows.

Arrowhead had long been in communication with the French, though this was the first occasion on which he had entirely thrown aside the mask. He no longer intended to trust himself among the English, for he had discovered traces of distrust, particularly in Pathfinder; and, with Indian bravado, he now rather wished to blazon than to conceal his treachery. He had led the party of warriors in the attack on the island, subject, however, to the supervision of the Frenchman. The French had obtained their information of the precise position of the station but very recently; and Mabel felt a pang when she thought that there were covert allusions of the Indian woman which would convey the meaning that the intelligence had come from a paleface in the employment of Duncan of Lundie.

June did not hesitate to confess that she had been sent to the island to ascertain the precise number and the occupations of those who had been left on it, though she also betrayed in her *naïve* way that the wish to serve Mabel had induced her principally to consent to come. In consequence of her report, and information otherwise obtained, the enemy was aware of precisely the force that could be brought against them. They also knew the number of men who had gone with Sergeant Dunham, and were acquainted with the object he had in view, though they were ignorant of the spot where he expected to meet the French boats.

In this manner the hours passed away unheeded, for both were too much interested to think of rest. Nature asserted her rights, however, towards morning; and Mabel was persuaded to lie down on one of the straw beds provided for the soldiers, where she soon fell into a deep sleep. June lay near her, and a quiet reigned on the whole island as profound as if the dominion of the forest had never been invaded by man.

When Mabel awoke the light of the sun was streaming in through the loopholes, and she found that the day was considerably advanced. June still lay near her, but the movements of Mabel soon awakened one so accustomed to vigilance.

CHAPTER XXIII

THE tranquillity of the previous night was not contradicted by the movements of the day. Although Mabel and June went to every loophole, not a sign of the presence of a living being on the island was at first to be seen, themselves excepted. There was a smothered fire on the spot where M'Nab and his comrades had cooked; and all around the huts had been restored to former order and arrangement. Mabel started involuntarily when her eye at length fell on a group of three men, dressed in the scarlet of the 55th, seated on the grass in lounging attitudes, as if they chatted in listless security; and her blood curdled as, on a second look, she traced the bloodless faces and glassy eyes of the dead. They were very near the blockhouse, and there was a mocking levity in their postures and gestures, for their limbs were stiffening in different attitudes, intended to resemble life, at which the soul revolted. After carefully examining the shores of the island, June pointed out to her companion the fourth soldier, seated, with his feet hanging over the water, his back fastened to a sapling, and holding a fishing-rod in his hand. The scalpless heads were covered with the caps, and all appearance of blood had been carefully washed from each countenance.

Mabel sickened at this sight. She withdrew to a seat, and hid

her face in her apron for several minutes, until a low call from
June again drew her to a loophole. The latter then pointed out
the body of Jennie, seemingly standing in the door of a hut,
leaning forward as if to look at the group of men, her cap
fluttering in the wind, and her hand grasping a broom.

"June!" she exclaimed; "this exceeds all I have ever heard, or
imagined as possible, in the treachery of your people."

"Tuscarora very cunning," said June. "Do soldier no harm
now; do Iroquois good; got the scalp first; now make bodies
work. By and by, burn 'em."

This speech told Mabel how far she was separated from her
friend in character. But June set about preparing their simple
breakfast, in a way to show how insensible she was to feelings
in others which her own habits taught her to discard. Mabel
ate sparingly, her companion as if nothing had happened.
Then they had leisure again for their thoughts. Our heroine,
though devoured with a feverish desire to be always at the
loops, seldom went that she did not immediately quit them in
disgust, though compelled by her apprehensions to return again
in a few minutes, called by the rustling of leaves, or the sighing
of the wind.

Throughout the livelong day not an Indian nor a Frenchman
was to be seen, and night again closed over the frightful but
silent masquerade. The night was far more quiet than that
which had preceded it, and Mabel slept with an increasing confidence; for she now felt satisfied that her own fate would not
be decided until the return of her father. The following day
he was expected, however, and when the girl awoke, she ran
eagerly to the loops in order to ascertain the state of the
weather and the aspect of the skies. There lounged the fearful
group on the grass; the fisherman still hung over the water,
seemingly intent on his sport; and the distorted countenance
of Jennie still glared from out the hut. But the weather had
changed; the wind blew fresh from the southward, and though
the air was bland, it was filled with the elements of storm.

"This grows more and more difficult to bear, June," Mabel said.
"I could even prefer to see the enemy than to look any longer on
this fearful array of the dead."

"Hush! June thought hear a cry like a warrior's shout when
he take a scalp."

"What mean you? There is no more butchery!—there *can* be
no more."

"Saltwater!" exclaimed June, as she stood peeping through a loophole.

"My dear uncle? Thank God! he then lives! Oh, June, *you* vill not let them harm *him*?"

"June poor squaw. What warrior t'ink of what she say? Arrowhead bring him here."

By this time Mabel was at a loop; and, sure enough, there were Cap and the Quartermaster in the hands of the Indians, eight or ten of whom were conducting them to the foot of the block, for, by this capture, the enemy now well knew that there could be no man in the building. Mabel scarcely breathed until the whole party stood ranged directly before the door, when she was rejoiced to see that the French officer was among them. A low conversation followed, in which both the white leader and Arrowhead spoke earnestly to their captives, when the Quartermaster called out to her in a voice loud enough to be heard.

"Pretty Mabel!" said he; "look out of one of the loopholes, and pity our condition. We are threatened with instant death unless you open the door. Relent, then, or we'll no' be wearing our scalps half an hour from this moment."

Mabel thought there were mockery and levity in this appeal, and its manner rather fortified than weakened her resolution to hold the place as long as possible.

"Speak to me, Uncle," said she, with her mouth at a loop, "and tell me what I ought to do."

"Thank God!" ejaculated Cap; "the sound of your sweet voice, Magnet, lightens my heart of a heavy load, for I feared you had shared the fate of poor Jennie. You ask me what you ought to do, child, and I do not know how to advise you, though you are my own sister's daughter! The most I can say just now, my poor girl, is most heartily to curse the day you or I ever saw this bit of fresh water."

"But, Uncle, is your life in danger—do *you* think I ought to open the door?"

"I would counsel no one who is out of the hands of these wretches to unbar or unfasten anything in order to fall into them. As to the Quartermaster and myself, we are both elderly men, and not of much account to mankind in general; and it can make no great odds to him whether he balances the purser's books this year or the next; and as for myself, why, I can only say, that if I were behind that bit of a bulwark, it would take a good deal of Indian logic to rouse me out of it."

"You'll no' be minding all your uncle says, pretty Mabel," put in Muir, "for distress is obviously fast unsettling his faculties, and he is far from calculating all the necessities of the emergency. Our scalps may be lawful sacrifices to appease the manes of fallen foes, unless you save them by capitulation."

"I shall do wiser to keep within the blockhouse until the fate of the island is settled," returned Mabel.

"If nothing but your convenience were concerned, Mabel, we should all cheerfully acquiesce in your wishes, but these gentlemen fancy that the work will aid their operations, and they have a strong desire to possess it."

"No leave blockhouse," muttered June, who stood at Mabel's side. "Blockhouse good—got no scalp."

Our heroine might have yielded but for this appeal; for it began to appear to her that the wisest course would be to conciliate the enemy by concessions instead of exasperating them by resistance.

"No prisoner yet," whispered June; "let 'em make prisoner, before 'ey take prisoner—talk big; June manage 'em."

Mabel now began to parley more resolutely with Muir, and she plainly intimated that it was not her intention to yield the building.

"The honour of one of his Majesty's servants is concerned," said Muir; "and the honour of his Majesty through his servant."

"I know enough, Mr. Muir, to understand that you have no command in this expedition."

"You'll no' be persevering in your intentions, when your better judgment has had leisure to reflect."

"No mind what'e say," ejaculated June. "Blockhouse good—got no scalp."

"I shall remain as I am, Mr. Muir, until I get some tidings of my father. He will return in the course of the next ten days."

"Ah, Mabel, this artifice will no' deceive the enemy, who, by means that would be unintelligible, did not our suspicions rest on an unhappy young man with too much plausibility, are familiar with all our doings and plans, and well know that the sun will not set before the worthy Sergeant and his companions will be in their power."

"Mr. Muir, you appear to be deceived in the strength of this work. Do you desire to see what I can do in the way of defence, if so disposed?"

"I dinna mind if I do," answered the Quartermaster.

"What do you think of that, then? Look at the loop of the upper story?"

As soon as Mabel had spoken, all eyes were turned upward, and beheld the muzzle of a rifle cautiously thrust through a hole, June having resorted again to a *ruse* which had already proved so successful. The result did not disappoint expectation. No sooner did the Indians catch a sight of the fatal weapon than they leaped aside, and in less than a minute every man among them had sought a cover. The French officer kept his eye on the barrel of the piece in order to ascertain that it was not pointed in his particular direction, and he coolly took a pinch of snuff. As neither Muir nor Cap had anything to apprehend from the quarter in which the others were menaced, they kept their ground.

"Be wise, my pretty Mabel, be wise!" exclaimed the former. "In the name of all the kings of Albin, who have ye closeted with you in that wooden tower, that seemeth so bloody minded?"

"What do you think of the Pathfinder, Master Muir, for a garrison to so strong a post?" cried Mabel.

"Bear gently on the unfortunate, pretty Mabel. If Pathfinder be indeed in the blockhouse, let him speak, and we will hold our negotiations directly with him."

The reliance on Pathfinder's friendship did not extend beyond the Quartermaster and Cap, however, for even the French officer, who had hitherto stood his ground so well, shrank back at the sound of the terrible name, insisting that his two prisoners should follow him. Mabel was too glad to be rid of her enemies to lament the departure of her friends, though she called out to Cap in terms of affection as he moved slowly away.

The enemy now seemed disposed to abandon all attempts on the blockhouse for the present; and June, who had ascended to a trap in the roof, whence the best view was to be obtained, reported that the whole party had assembled to eat, on a distant and sheltered part of the island, where Muir and Cap were quietly sharing in the good things which were going. This information greatly relieved Mabel, and she began to turn her thoughts again to the means of letting her father know of the danger that awaited him. The Sergeant was expected to return that afternoon, and she knew that a moment gained or lost might decide his fate.

Three or four hours flew by. The island was again buried in a profound quiet, the day was wearing away, and yet Mabel had decided on nothing. June was in the basement, preparing their frugal meal, and Mabel herself had ascended to the roof, which was provided with a trap that allowed her to go out on the top of the building, whence she commanded the best view of surrounding objects that the island possessed; still it was limited and much obstructed by the tops of trees. Nevertheless, in the course of the afternoon, she made many surveys of the different channels about the island.

The sun had actually set; no intelligence had been received from the boats, and Mabel ascended to the roof to take a last look, hoping that the party would arrive in the darkness; which would at least prevent the Indians from rendering their ambuscade so fatal as it might otherwise prove. Her eye had turned carefully round the whole horizon, and she was just on the point of drawing in her person, when an object that struck her as new caught her attention. The islands lay grouped so closely, that six or eight different channels or passages between them were in view; and in one of the most covered, concealed in a great measure by the bushes of the shore, lay what a second look assured her was a bark canoe. It contained a human being beyond a question. Confident that if an enemy her signal could do no harm, and, if a friend, that it might do good, the eager girl waved a little flag towards the stranger, taking care that it should not be seen from the island.

Mabel had repeated her signal eight or ten times in vain, and she began to despair of its being noticed, when a sign was given in return by the wave of a paddle, and the man so far discovered himself as to let her see it was Chingachgook. Here, then, at last, was a friend; one, too, who was able, and she doubted not willing, to aid her. From that instant her courage and her spirits revived. The Mohican had seen her; must have recognized her, as he knew that she was of the party; and no doubt, as soon as it was sufficiently dark, he would take the steps necessary to release her. That he was aware of the presence of the enemy was apparent by the great caution he observed, and she had every reliance on his prudence and address. The principal difficulty now existed with June; for Mabel had seen too much of her fidelity to her own people, relieved as it was by sympathy for herself, to believe she would consent to a hostile Indian's entering the blockhouse, or indeed to her leaving it, with a view to defeat Arrowhead's plans. The half-hour which succeeded the discovery of the presence of the Great Serpent was the most painful of Mabel Dunham's life. She saw the means of effecting all she wished, as it might be within reach of her hand, and yet it eluded her grasp. At last she came reluctantly to the conclusion that there was no other way of attaining her end than by deceiving her tried companion and protector.

As soon as it was dark, Mabel's heart began to beat with increased violence; and she adopted and changed her plan of proceeding at least a dozen times in a single hour. June was always the source of her greatest embarrassment; for she did not well see, first, how she was to ascertain when Chingachgook was at the door, where she doubted not he would soon appear; and, secondly, how she was to admit him, without giving the alarm to her watchful companion. It would be too hazardous to the Delaware to remain long on the island; and it became absolutely necessary to determine on some course. After running over various projects, therefore, Mabel came to her companion, and said:

"Are you not afraid, June, now your people believe Pathfinder is in the blockhouse, that they will come and set it on fire?"

"No t'ink such t'ing. Blockhouse good; got no scalp."

"June, we cannot know. They hid because they believed what I told them of Pathfinder's being with us."

"Believe fear. Fear come quick, go quick. Fear make run away; wit make come back."

"I feel uneasy, June; and wish you would go up again to the roof and look out, to make certain nothing is plotting against us."

"June go, Lily wish; but very well know Indian sleep; wait for 'e fader. Warrior eat, drink, sleep, all time, when don't fight and go on wartrail. Den never sleep, eat, drink—never feel."

"God send it may be so; but go up, dear June, and look well about you. Danger may come when we least expect it."

June arose, and prepared to ascend the roof; but she paused, with her foot on the first round of the ladder. Mabel's heart beat so violently that she was fearful its throbs would be heard; and she fancied that some gleamings of her real intentions had crossed the mind of her friend. But after a pause she began slowly to mount the ladder.

Just as she reached the upper floor, a lucky thought suggested itself to our heroine; and, by expressing it in a hurried but natural manner, she gained a great advantage in executing her projected scheme.

"1 will go down," she said, "and listen by the door, June, while you are on the roof."

By these means Mabel was enabled to descend to the door, as

her friend ascended to the roof. The distance between the two was now too great to admit of conversation; and for three or four minutes one was occupied in looking about her as well as the darkness would allow, and the other in listening at the door.

June discovered nothing from her elevated stand; the obscurity indeed almost forbade the hope of such a result; but it would not be easy to describe the sensation with which Mabel thought she perceived a slight and guarded push against the door. Fearful that all might not be as she wished, and anxious to let Chingachgook know that she was near, she began, though in tremulous and low notes, to sing. So profound was the stillness of the moment that the sound of the unsteady warbling ascended to the roof, and in a minute June began to descend. A slight tap at the door was heard immediately after. Mabel was bewildered, but with unsteady hands she commenced unbarring the door. The moccasin of June was heard on the floor above her when only a single bar was turned. The second was released as her form reached halfway down the lower ladder.

"What you do?" exclaimed June angrily. "Run away—mad—leave blockhouse." The hands of both were on the last bar, and it would have been cleared from the fastenings but for a vigorous shove from without, which jammed the wood. June would probably have prevailed, had not another and more vigorous push from without forced the bar past the trifling impediment that held it, when the door opened. The form of a man was seen to enter; and both the women rushed up the ladder, as if equally afraid of the consequences. The stranger secured the door; and, first examining the lower room with great care, he cautiously ascended the ladder. June, as soon as it became dark, had closed the loops of the principal floor, and lighted a candle. By means of this dim taper, the two women stood in expectation, waiting to ascertain the person of their visitor. It would not be easy to say which was the more astonished on finding, when the stranger had got through the trap, that Pathfinder stood before them.

"God be praised!" Mabel exclaimed. "Oh, Pathfinder! what has become of my father?"

"The Sergeant is safe as yet, and victorious. Is not that the wife of Arrowhead skulking in the corner there?"

"Speak not of her reproachfully, Pathfinder; I owe her my life. Tell me what has happened and why you are here."

"Few words will do the last, Mabel. Everything turned out as we had hoped with the expedition; for the Sarpent was on the lookout, and he met us with all the information heart could desire. We ambushed three boats, druv' the Frenchers out of them, got possession and sunk them, according to orders, in the deepest part of the channel. We did not lose a man or have a skin barked; nor do I think the inimy suffered to speak of."

"Ah, Pathfinder, I fear, when Major Duncan comes to hear the whole of the sad tale, he will regret he ever undertook the affair."

"I know what you mean. As soon as the Sergeant found himself successful, he sent me and the Sarpent off in canoes to tell you how matters had turned out. I parted from Chingachgook this forenoon, it being agreed that he should come up one set of channels and I another, to see that the path was clear."

Mabel now explained the manner in which she had discovered the Mohican, and her expectation that he would yet come to the blockhouse.

"Not he! A regular scout will never get behind walls or logs, so long as he can keep the open air. I should not have come myself, Mabel, but I promised the Sergeant to look after your safety. Ah's me! I reconnoitred the island with a heavy heart this forenoon; and there was a bitter hour when I fancied you might be among the slain."

"By what lucky accident were you prevented from paddling up to the island and falling into the hands of the enemy?"

"By such an accident, Mabel, as Providence employs to tell the hound where to find the deer and the deer how to throw off the hound. These artifices with dead bodies may deceive the soldiers of the 55th and the king's officers; but they are all lost upon men who have passed their days in the forest. I came down the channel in face of the pretended fisherman; and, though the riptyles have set up the poor wretch with art, it was not ingenious enough to take in a practysed eye. The rod was held too high, for the 55th have learned to fish at Oswego, if they never knew how before; and then the man was too quiet for one who got neither prey nor bite. Neither the Sarpent nor myself would be likely to be taken in by these clumsy contrivances."

"Do you think my father may yet be deceived?" said Mabel quickly.

"Not if I can prevent it, Mabel; though it is by no means sartain by which channel the party may come."

"Pathfinder," said our heroine solemnly, "you have professed love for me, a wish to make me your wife?"

"I did ventur' to speak on that subject, Mabel, and the Sergeant has even lately said that you are kindly disposed; but I am not a man to persecute the thing I love."

"Pathfinder, I respect you, revere you; save my father from this dreadful death, and I can worship you. Here is my hand, as a solemn pledge for my faith."

"Bless you, Mabel; this is more than I desarve—more, I fear, than I shall know how to profit by as I ought. It was not wanting, however, to make me sarve the Sergeant."

"All that you do and say, Pathfinder, my reason approves, and the heart will, nay, it *shall* follow."

"These are sweet words, Mabel; but they were not wanting to make me do all that man can do in the present circumstances."

"Now we understand each other, Pathfinder," Mabel added hoarsely, "let us not lose one precious moment. Can we not get into your canoe and go and meet my father?"

"That is not the course I advise. I don't know by which channel the Sergeant will come, and there are twenty; rely on it, the Sarpent will be winding his way through them all. No! my advice is to remain here. The logs of this blockhouse are still green, and it will not be easy to set them on fire; and I can make good the place, bating a burning, ag'in a tribe. The Iroquois nation cannot dislodge me from this fortress, so long as we can keep the flames off it. The Sergeant is now 'camped on some island, and will not come in until morning. If we hold the block, we can give him timely warning, by firing rifles, for instance. No! my judgment says remain."

"Stay," murmured Mabel, "stay, for Heaven's sake, Pathfinder! Anything, everything to save my father!"

"Yes, that is natur'. Yes, Mabel, we must not only save the Sergeant's life, but we must save his reputation."

"No blame can rest on Father on account of the surprise of the island."

"There's no telling; military glory is a most unsartin thing. The parsons preach about humility in the garrison; but if humility would make Christians, the king's troops ought to be saints, for they've done little as yet this war but take lessons from the French, beginning at Fort du Quesne and ending at Ty."

"My father could not have suspected that the position of the island was known to the enemy," resumed Mabel.

"That is true; nor do I well see how the Frenchers found it out. There has been treachery, I fear."

"Oh, Pathfinder! can this be?"

"Nothing is easier, Mabel, for treachery comes as nat'ral to some men as eating."

"Jasper Western is not one of these," said Mabel impetuously.

"Jasper Western! No, no; I'll answer for Eau-douce's honesty with my own scalp, or, at need, with my own rifle."

"Bless you, Pathfinder!" exclaimed Mabel, pressing the iron fingers of her companion. "You are all that is generous, all that is noble! God will reward you for it."

"Ah, Mabel, I fear me, if this be true, I should not covet such a wife as yourself; but would leave you to be sued for by some gentleman of the garrison, as your desarts require."

"We will not talk of this any more to-night," Mabel answered in a smothered voice. "I rejoice from my soul that you believe Jasper innocent. Ought we not to release June?"

"I've been thinking about the woman. If we put her in the upper room, and take away the ladder, she'll be a prisoner at least."

"I cannot treat one thus who has saved my life. It would be better to let her depart; I think she is too much my friend to do anything to harm me."

"You do not know the race, Mabel. What is that?"

"It sounds like oars; a boat is passing through the channel."

Pathfinder closed the trap that led to the lower room, to prevent June from escaping, extinguished the candle, and went hastily to a loop, Mabel looking over his shoulder in breathless curiosity. By the time the eye of the scout had got a dim view of the things without, two boats had swept past and shot up to the landing. The obscurity prevented more from being seen; and Pathfinder whispered to Mabel that the newcomers were as likely to be foes as friends, for he did not think her father could possibly have arrived so soon. A number of men were now seen to quit the boats, and then followed three hearty English cheers, leaving no further doubts of the character of the party. Pathfinder sprang to the trap, raised it, glided down the ladder, and began to unbar the door. Mabel had followed, but she rather impeded than aided his exertions, and but a single bar was turned when a heavy discharge of rifles was heard. They were still standing in breathless suspense, as the warwhoop rang in all the surrounding thickets. The door now opened, and both Pathfinder and Mabel rushed into the open air. All human sounds had ceased. After listening half a minute, however, Pathfinder thought he heard a few stifled groans near the boats;

but the wind blew so fresh that he was far from certain. But Mabel was borne away by her feelings, and she rushed by him, taking the way towards the boats.

"This will not do, Mabel," said the scout in an earnest but low voice, seizing her by an arm. "Sartain death would follow, and that without sarving anyone. We must return to the block."

"Father! my poor, dear father!" said the girl wildly. "Pathfinder, if you love me, let me go to my father."

"This will not do, Mabel. It is singular that no one returns the fire from the boats."

At that moment the quick eye of Pathfinder caught an indistinct view of five or six dark crouching forms, endeavouring to steal past him, doubtless with the intention of intercepting the retreat to the blockhouse. Catching up Mabel, the sinewy frame of the woodsman was exerted to the utmost, and he succeeded in entering the building. Dropping his burden, he turned, closed the door, and had fastened one bar, as a rush against the solid mass threatened to force it from the hinges. To secure the other bars was the work of an instant.

Mabel now ascended to the first floor, relighted the candle mechanically, as her companion had desired, and returned with it below, where he was waiting her reappearance. No sooner was Pathfinder in possession of the light than he examined the place carefully, to make certain no one was concealed in the fortress, ascending to each floor in succession. When perfectly convinced on this material point, Pathfinder rejoined our heroine in the principal apartment, setting down the light and examining the priming of Killdeer before he seated himself.

"Our worst fears are realized!" said Mabel. "My beloved father and all his party are slain or captured!"

"We don't know that—morning will tell us all. Of one thing we may be sartain; if the inimy has really got the better, he will not be long in calling upon us to surrender. The squaw will let him into the secret of our situation; and, as they well know the place cannot be fired by daylight, so long as Killdeer continues to desarve his reputation, they will not be backward in making their attempt while darkness helps them."

"Surely I hear a groan!"

"'Tis fancy, Mabel."

"Nay, I am *not* deceived; there is surely one below, and in pain."

Pathfinder was compelled to own that the quick senses of

Mabel had not deceived her. He reminded her, however, that nothing was more likely than that the groans were feigned with a view to lure them from the blockhouse, or, at least, to induce them to open the door.

"No, no!" said Mabel hurriedly; "there is no artifice in those sounds, and they come from anguish of body, if not of spirit."

"Well, we shall soon know whether a friend is there or not. Hide the light again, Mabel, and I will speak the person from a loop."

Not a little precaution was necessary, according to Pathfinder's judgment, in performing even this simple act; he did not place his mouth to the loop itself, but so near it that he could be heard without raising his voice, and the same precaution was observed as regards his ear.

"Who is below?" Pathfinder demanded. "If a friend, speak boldly, and depend on our aid."

"Pathfinder!" answered a voice that both at once knew to be the Sergeant's—"Pathfinder, tell me what has become of my daughter!"

"Father, I am here, unhurt, safe! and oh that I could think the same of you!"

The ejaculation of thanksgiving that followed was distinctly audible to the two, but it was clearly mingled with a groan of pain.

"My worst forebodings are realized!" said Mabel with a sort of desperate calmness. "Pathfinder, my father must be brought within the block, though we hazard everything to do it."

"This is natur', and it is the law of God. All that can be effected for the Sergeant by human invention shall be done. Only be cool, Mabel."

"I am, Pathfinder. But remember how perilous may be every instant; for Heaven's sake, what we do, let us do without delay."

Pathfinder descended forthwith, and began to unbar the door. As he warily permitted the mass of timber to swing back on the hinges, he felt a pressure against it, that had nearly induced him to close it again. But, catching a glimpse of the cause through the crack, the door was permitted to swing back, when the body of Sergeant Dunham, which was propped against it, fell partly within the block. To draw in the legs and secure the fastenings occupied the Pathfinder but a moment.

Mabel, in this trying scene, conducted herself with the sort of unnatural energy that her sex, when aroused, is apt to manifest.

She got the light, administered water to the parched lips of her
father, and assisted Pathfinder in forming a bed of straw for his
body and a pillow of clothes for his head. All this time Mabel
had merely conjectured the condition of her parent. Pathfinder,
however, had shown greater attention to the physical danger of the
Sergeant. He had ascertained that a rifle ball had passed through
the body of the wounded man; and he was sufficiently familiar
with injuries of this nature to be certain that the chances of his
surviving the hurt were very trifling, if any.

CHAPTER XXIV

THE eyes of Sergeant Dunham had not ceased to follow the form
of his beautiful daughter from the moment that the light appeared.
He next examined the door of the block, to ascertain its security.
Then he sought the face of Mabel; for as life wanes the affections
resume their force, and we begin to value that most which we feel
we are about to lose for ever.

"God be praised, my child! you, at least, have escaped their
murderous rifles," he said. "Give me the history of this sad
business, Pathfinder."

"Ah's me, Sergeant! it *has* been sad. That there has been
treachery is now as sartain, in my judgment, as that we still hold
this block. But——"

"Major Duncan was right," interrupted Dunham.

"Not in the sense you mean, Sergeant—no, not in that p'int of
view! I know that natur' is weak—human natur' I mean—and
that we should none of us vaunt our gifts; but I do not think a
truer-hearted lad lives on the lines than Jasper Western."

"Bless you! bless you for that, Pathfinder!" burst forth from
Mabel's very soul, while a flood of tears gave vent to emotions
that were so varied while they were so violent. "The brave
should never desert the brave—the honest should sustain the
honest."

The father's eyes were fastened anxiously on the face of his
daughter, until the latter hid her countenance to conceal her
tears; and then they turned with enquiry to the hard features
of the guide. The latter merely wore their usual expression of
frankness and sincerity; and the Sergeant motioned to him to
proceed.

"You know the spot where the Sarpent and I left you, Sergeant," Pathfinder resumed. "It is now too late to regret what is gone; but I do think if I had stayed with the boats this would not have come to pass. I dare say poor Gilbert, who took my place, has suffered for his mistake."

"He fell at my elbow," the Sergeant answered in a low, melancholy tone. "We have, indeed, all suffered for our mistakes."

"No, no, Sergeant, I meant no condemnation on you; for men were never better commanded than yourn. I never beheld a prettier flanking; and the way you carried your own boat up ag'in their howitzer might have teached Lundie himself a lesson."

The eyes of the Sergeant brightened, and his face even wore an expression of military triumph.

"'Twas not badly done, my friend," said he; "and we carried their log breastwork by storm."

"'Twas nobly done, Sergeant; though, I fear, when the truth comes to be known, it will be found that the vagabonds have got their howitzer back ag'in. Well, well, put a stout heart upon it. If the inimy has got the howitzer ag'in, they've only got what belonged to them afore, and what we couldn't help. Well, Sergeant, the Sarpent and I separated about ten miles down the river. What has become of Chingachgook I cannot say, though Mabel tells me he is not far off, and I make no question the Delaware is doing his duty, although he is not now visible to our eyes. Well, as I came near the island I missed the smoke, and that put me on my guard; for I knew that the men of the 55th were not cunning enough to conceal that sign. This made me more careful, until I came in sight of this mock fisherman, as I've just told Mabel; and then the whole of their infernal arts was as plain before as if I saw it on a map. I need not tell you, Sergeant, that my first thoughts were of Mabel; and that, finding that she was in the block, I came here in order to live or die in her company."

The father turned a gratified look upon his child; and as the former held out his hand, Mabel took it in her own and kissed it. Then, kneeling at his side, she wept as if her heart would break.

"Mabel," said he steadily, "the will of God must be done. It is useless to attempt deceiving either you or myself; my time has come, and it is a consolation to me to die like a soldier. You do not forget our last conversation?"

"Nay, Father, my time has probably come too," exclaimed

Mabel. "I cannot hope to escape; and Pathfinder would do well to leave us, and return to the garrison with the sad news while he can."

"Mabel," said Pathfinder reproachfully, though he took her hand with kindness, "I have not desarved this. I know I am wild and ungainly——"

"Pathfinder!"

"Well, we'll forget it; you did not mean it. It is useless now to talk of escaping, for the Sergeant cannot be moved; and the blockhouse must be defended, cost what it will."

"Pathfinder—Mabel!" said the Sergeant, who had been writhing with pain until the cold sweat stood on his forehead; "come both to my side. You understand each other, I hope?"

"Father, say nothing of that; it is all as you wish."

"Thank God! Give me your hand, Mabel—here, Pathfinder, take it. I can do no more than give you the girl in this way. Do not wait on account of my death; there will be a chaplain in the fort before the season closes, and let him marry you at once. Mabel, your husband will have been my friend, and that will be some consolation to you, I hope."

"Trust this matter to me, Sergeant," put in Pathfinder; "leave it all in my hands as your dying request; and, depend on it, all will go as it should."

"I do, I do put all confidence in you, my trusty friend, and empower you to act as I could act myself in every particular. Mabel, child—hand me the water—you will never repent this night. Bless you, my daughter! God bless you and have you in His holy keeping!"

This tenderness was inexpressibly touching to one of Mabel's feelings; and she felt at that moment as if her future union with Pathfinder had received a solemnization that no ceremony of the Church could render more holy. Then followed a short pause, when the Sergeant briefly related what had passed since he parted with Pathfinder and the Delaware. The wind had come more favourable; and, instead of encamping, he had determined to continue, and reach the station that night. They had landed without the slightest suspicion of danger, though surprised at not finding a sentinel, and had actually left their arms in the boat, with the intention of first securing their knapsacks and provisions. The fire had been so close, that, notwithstanding the obscurity, it was very deadly. Every man had fallen, though two or three subsequently arose and disappeared. Sergeant Dunham fell with the others; and he had heard the voice of Mabel as she rushed from the blockhouse. This frantic appeal aroused all his parental feelings, and had enabled him to crawl as far as the door of the building, where he had raised himself against the logs in the manner already mentioned.

After this simple explanation was made, Pathfinder took occasion to reconnoitre from the loops and the roof, and to examine the condition of the rifles, of which there were a dozen kept in the building. Mabel never left her father's side for an instant; and when, by his breathing, she fancied he slept, she bent her knees and prayed.

The half-hour that succeeded was awfully solemn and still. Mabel's heart yearned to be in communication with the father she was so soon to lose, and yet she would not disturb his apparent repose. But Dunham slept not; he was in that state when the world suddenly loses its attractions, its illusions, and its power; and the unknown future fills the mind with its conjectures and its immensity. Meanwhile Mabel, who watched the slightest change in his breathing, heard a guarded knock at the door. Supposing it might be Chingachgook, she rose, undid two of the bars, and held the third in her hand, as she asked who was there. The answer was in her uncle's voice, and he implored her to give him instant admission. Without an instant of hesitation she turned the bar, and Cap entered. He had barely passed the opening, when Mabel closed the door again, and secured it as before.

The sturdy seaman, when he had made sure of the state of his brother-in-law, and that Mabel, as well as himself, was safe, was softened nearly to tears. His own appearance he explained by saying that he had been carelessly guarded, under the impression that he and the Quartermaster were sleeping under the fumes of liquor with which they had been plied with a view to keep them quiet in the expected engagement. Muir had been left asleep, or seeming to sleep; but Cap had run into the bushes on the alarm of the attack, and, having found Pathfinder's canoe, had only succeeded, at that moment, in getting to the blockhouse, whither he had come with the kind intent of escaping with his niece by water.

"If the worst comes to the worst, Pathfinder," said he, "we must strike, and that will entitle us to receive quarter. We owe it to our manhood to hold out a reasonable time, and to ourselves to haul down the ensign in season to make saving conditions. I wished Master Muir to do the same thing when we were captured by these vagabonds."

"You've found out their characters?" interrupted Pathfinder.

"Ay, ay! When these savages made the assault on us, killing Corporal M'Nab and his men as if they had been so many rabbits, Lieutenant Muir and myself took refuge in a hole, and there we remained stowed away like two leaguers in a ship's hold, until we gave out for want of grub. I desired the Quartermaster to make terms, for we could have defended ourselves for an hour or two in the place, bad as it was; but he declined, on the ground that the knaves wouldn't keep faith if any of them were hurt, and so there was no use in asking them to."

"Uncle," said Mabel in a mournful voice, "my poor father is sadly hurt!"

"True, Magnet; I will sit by him, and do my best at consolation. Are the bars well fastened, girl?"

"We are safe, I believe, from all but this heavy blow of Providence."

"Well then, Magnet, do you go up to the floor above and try to compose yourself, while Pathfinder runs aloft and takes a look-out from the crosstrees. Your father may wish to say something to me in private, and it may be well to leave us alone."

Although the idea of her uncle's affording religious consolation by the side of a deathbed certainly never obtruded itself on the imagination of Mabel, she thought there might be a propriety in the request with which she was unacquainted, and she complied accordingly. Pathfinder had already ascended to the roof to make his survey, and the brothers-in-law were left alone. After having been together thus for some time, Cap heard the guide descending, and said: "How now, Pathfinder! is there anything in the wind, that you come down the ladder like an Indian in the wake of a scalp?"

The guide raised a finger for silence, and then beckoned to Cap to ascend the first ladder, and to allow Mabel to take his place at the side of the Sergeant.

"We must be prudent, and we must be bold too," said he in a low voice. "The riptyles are in earnest in their intention to fire the block; for they know there is now nothing to be gained by letting it stand. I hear the voice of that vagabond Arrowhead among them, and he is urging them to set about the work this very night. Luckily there are four or five barrels of water in the block, and these are something towards a siege."

Cap did not wait for a second invitation; but, stealing away, he was soon in the upper room with Pathfinder, while Mabel took her post at her father's side. Pathfinder had opened a loop, and, expecting a summons, he stood with his face near the hole, ready to answer. The stillness that succeeded was at length broken by the voice of Muir.

"Master Pathfinder," called out the Scotchman, "a friend summons you to a parley. Come freely to one of the loops; for you've nothing to fear so long as you are in converse with an officer of the 55th."

"What is your will, Quartermaster? It must be a pressing errand that brings you under the loops of a blockhouse at this hour of the night, with the sartainty of Killdeer being inside of it."

"Oh, you'll no' harm a friend, Pathfinder, I'm certain. The enemy is too strong for us, my brave comrade, and I come to counsel you to give up the block, on condition of being treated as a prisoner of war."

"I thank you for this advice, Quartermaster; but I do not think it belongs to my gifts to yield a place like this while food and water last."

"Well, I'd be the last to recommend anything against so brave a resolution, did I see the means of maintaining it. But ye'll remember that Master Cap has fallen."

"Not he!" roared the individual in question through another loop; "and so far from that, Lieutenant, he has risen to the height of this here fortification, and has no mind to put his hair into the hands of such barbers again, so long as he can help it."

"If that is a living voice," returned Muir, "I am glad to hear it. But, Pathfinder, although ye're enjoying the society of your friend Cap, we've lost that of Sergeant Dunham, who has fallen, with all the brave men he led in the late expedition."

"You're wrong ag'in, Quartermaster," answered Pathfinder. "The Sergeant is safe in the block too, where one might say the whole family is collected."

"Well, I rejoice to hear it, for we had certainly counted the Sergeant among the slain. If pretty Mabel is in the block still, let her not delay an instant in quitting it, for the enemy is about to put it to the trial by fire. Ye will be acting more like the discreet warrior ye're universally allowed to be, in yielding a place you canna' defend, than in drawing down ruin on yourself and companions."

"I know the potency of fire, Quartermaster; but I make no doubt you've heard of the potency of Killdeer, and the man who indivours to burn this block over my head will find the fire squinched in his own blood."

"This is idle and romantic talk, Pathfinder, and ye'll no' maintain it yourself when ye come to meditate on the realities."

"As each of us seems to have made up his mind, Quartermaster, more words are useless. If the riptyles near you are disposed to set about their hellish job, let them begin at once. They can burn wood, and I'll burn powder."

"Pathfinder, ye'll no' be exposing Mabel to sic' a calamity!"

"Mabel Dunham is by the side of her wounded father, and God will care for the safety of a pious child. Not a hair of her head shall fall, while my arm and sight remain true."

Throughout this dialogue Pathfinder had kept his body covered, lest a treacherous shot should be aimed at the loop; and he now directed Cap to ascend to the roof in order to be in readiness to meet the first assault. Although the latter used sufficient diligence, he found no less than ten blazing arrows sticking to the bark, while the air was filled with the yells and whoops of the enemy. A rapid discharge of rifles followed, and the bullets came pattering against the logs in a way to show that the struggle had indeed seriously commenced.

These were sounds, however, that appalled neither Pathfinder nor Cap, while Mabel was too much absorbed in her affliction to feel alarm. As for her father, the familiar noises revived him; and Mabel perceived that his reason began slightly to wander.

"Order up the light companies," he muttered, "and let the grenadiers charge! Why does not the artillery open on them?"

At that instant the heavy report of a gun burst on the night; and the crashing of rending wood was heard as a heavy shot tore the logs in the room above, and the whole block shook with the force of a shell that lodged in the work. Pathfinder narrowly escaped the passage of this formidable missile as it entered; but when it exploded, Mabel could not suppress a shriek, for she supposed all over her head, whether animate or inanimate, destroyed.

"Mabel," said Pathfinder, with his head at the trap, "this is true Mingo work—more noise than injury. The vagabonds have got the howitzer we took from the French, and have discharged it ag'in the block; but fortunately they have fired off the only shell we had, and there is an ind of its use for the present. No one is hurt. Your uncle is still on the roof."

During the fearful minutes that succeeded, Mabel was so much occupied with the care of the invalid that she scarcely heeded the clamour that reigned around her.

Cap preserved his coolness admirably. When the shell passed through the logs below, the old sailor dropped his bucket, waved his hat, and gave three cheers; in which heroic act he was employed as the dangerous missile exploded. This characteristic feat probably saved his life; for from that instant the Indians ceased to fire at him, and even to shoot their flaming arrows at the block, having taken up the notion simultaneously, and by common consent, that the "Saltwater" was mad; and it was a singular effect of their magnanimity never to lift a hand against those whom they imagined devoid of reason.

The conduct of Pathfinder was very different. His person was kept carefully out of a line with the loops, and the spot that he selected for his lookout was one quite removed from danger. For the first ten minutes of the assault he never raised the breech of his rifle from the floor, except when he changed his own position, for he well knew that the bullets of the enemy were thrown away upon the massive logs of the work. There existed no reason, therefore, to dread the fire of the assailants, except as a casual bullet might find a passage through a loophole. But when he heard the sound of moccasined feet and the rustling of the brush at the foot of the building, he knew that the attempt to build a fire against the logs was about to be renewed. He now summoned Cap from the roof, and directed him to stand in readiness with his water at a hole immediately over the spot assailed.

One less trained than our hero would have been in a hurry to repel this dangerous attempt also, and might have resorted to his means prematurely; not so with Pathfinder. His aim was not only to extinguish the fire, about which he felt little apprehension, but to give the enemy a lesson that would render him wary during the remainder of the night. In order to effect the latter purpose, it became necessary to wait until the light of the intended conflagration should direct his aim, when he well knew that a very slight effort of his skill would suffice. The Iroquois were permitted to collect their heap of dried brush, to pile it against the block, to light it, and to return to their covers without molestation. All that Pathfinder would suffer Cap to do was to roll a barrel filled with water to the hole immediately over the spot, in readiness to be used at the proper instant. That moment, however, did not arrive, in his judgment, until the blaze illuminated the surrounding bushes, and there had been time for his practised eye to detect the forms of three or four lurking savages, who were watching the progress of the flames. Then, indeed, he spoke.

"Are you ready, friend Cap?" he asked. "The heat begins to strike through the crevices. Are you ready with the barrel? See that it has the right cut, and that none of the water is wasted."

"All ready!" answered Cap.

"Then wait for the word. Wait for the word."

While the Pathfinder was giving these directions, he was also making his own preparations. Killdeer was deliberately raised, pointed, and discharged. The whole process occupied about half a minute, and as the rifle was drawn in the eye of the marksman was applied to the hole.

"There is one riptyle the less," Pathfinder muttered to himself; "I've seen that vagabond afore, and know him to be a marciless wretch. One more of the knaves, and that will sarve the turn for to-night."

All this time another rifle was being got ready; and as Pathfinder ceased, a second savage fell. This indeed sufficed; for the whole band, ignorant of who was and who was not exposed to view, leaped from their covers and fled to different places for safety.

"Now, pour away, Master Cap," said Pathfinder; "we shall have no more fires lighted to-night."

"Scaldings!" cried Cap, upsetting the barrel, with a care that at once and completely extinguished the flames.

This ended the singular conflict; and the remainder of the night passed in peace. Pathfinder and Cap watched alternately, though neither can be said to have slept.

Mabel watched by her father's pallet, and began to feel how much our happiness in this world depends even on things that are imaginary.

CHAPTER XXV

As the light returned, Pathfinder and Cap ascended again to the roof, with a view to reconnoitre the state of things once more on the island.

The gale was still blowing very fresh at south; and there were places in the river where its surface looked green and angry, though the wind had hardly sweep enough to raise the water into foam. While they stood gazing anxiously about them, Cap cried out:

"Sail ho!"

Pathfinder turned quickly in the direction of his companion's face; and there, sure enough, was just visible the object of the old sailor's exclamation. The elevation enabled the two to overlook the low land of several of the adjacent islands; and the canvas of a vessel was seen through the bushes that fringed the shore of one that lay to the southward and westward. The stranger was under what seamen call low sail; but so great was the power of the wind, that her white outlines were seen flying past the openings of the verdure with the velocity of a fast-travelling horse.

"That cannot be Jasper," said Pathfinder in disappointment.

"This time you are out, friend Pathfinder, if you never were before," returned Cap. "Fresh water or salt, that is the head of the *Scud's* mainsail, for it is cut with a smaller gore than common; and then you can see that the gaff has been fished."

"I can see none of this, I confess," answered Pathfinder.

"No! Well, I own that surprises me, for I thought *your* eyes could see anything!"

"If Jasper is truly coming we can make good the block against the whole Mingo nation for the next eight or ten hours; and with Eau-douce to cover the retreat, I shall despair of nothing. God send that the lad may not run alongside of the bank, and fall into an ambushment, as befell the Sergeant!"

"Ay, there's the danger. If the lad fetches up, as you say, anywhere in the neighbourhood of this island, we may look upon the cutter as lost."

"We shall soon know, Master Cap; for there comes the cutter clear of the other island, and five minutes must settle the matter. It would be no more than fair, however, if we could give the boy some sign in the way of warning."

Anxiety and suspense, notwithstanding, prevented either from attempting to make any signal. The *Scud* came foaming through the channel, on the weather side of the island, at a rate that scarcely admitted of the necessary time. Nor was anyone visible on her deck to make signs to; even her helm seemed deserted, though her course was as steady as her progress was rapid.

Cap stood in silent admiration of a spectacle so unusual. But, as the *Scud* drew nearer, his practised eye detected the helm in play by means of tiller-ropes, though the person who steered was concealed. As the cutter had weather-boards of some little height, the mystery was explained, no doubt remaining that her people lay behind the latter, in order to be protected from the rifles of the enemy. As this fact showed that no force beyond that of the crew could be on board, Pathfinder received his companion's explanation with an ominous shake of the head.

"This proves that the Sarpent has not reached Oswego," said he, "and that we are not to expect succour from the garrison. I hope Lundie has not taken it into his head to displace the lad, for Jasper Western would be a host of himself in such a strait. We three, Master Cap, ought to make a manful warfare: you, as a seaman, to keep up the intercourse with the cutter; Jasper, as a laker who knows all that is necessary to be done on the water; and I, with gifts that are as good as any among the Mingos."

"That we ought," answered Cap heartily. "This Jasper is a young man of prudence, I find; for he keeps a good offing, and seems determined to know how matters stand on the island before he ventures to bring up."

"I have it!" exclaimed Pathfinder. "There lies the canoe of the Sarpent on the cutter's deck; and the chief has got on board, and no doubt has given a true account of our condition."

"That canoe may belong to the cutter," said the captious seaman. "Eau-douce had one on board when we sailed."

"Very true, friend Cap; but if you know your sails and masts, I know my canoes and my paths. That is the boat of the Sarpent, and the noble fellow has struck off for the garrison as soon as he found the block besieged, has fallen in with the *Scud*, and, after telling his story, has brought the cutter down here to see what can be done. The Lord grant that Jasper Western be still on board her!"

"Yes, yes; it might not be amiss; for, traitor or loyal, the lad has a handy way with him in a gale, it must be owned."

"And in coming over waterfalls!" said Pathfinder, nudging his companion. "We will give the boy his due, though he scalps us all with his own hand."

The *Scud* was now so near that Cap made no reply.

The gale was still blowing violently. Many of the smaller trees bowed their tops, as if ready to descend to the earth, while the air was filled with leaves, which, at that late season, were readily driven from their stems, and flew from island to island like flights of birds. Though the savages were taken entirely by surprise by the cutter, the sudden return of which was altogether unlooked-for, so inbred were their habits of caution while on the warpath, that the instant an alarm was given every man had taken to his cover with the instinct and cunning of a fox seeking his hole. Stillness reigned in the blockhouse; for though Pathfinder and Cap could command a view of the channel, they took the precaution necessary to lie concealed.

In the meantime the progress of the cutter was steady and rapid. Although under short canvas, her velocity was great, and there could not have elapsed ten minutes between the time when her sails were first seen glancing past the trees and bushes in the distance and the moment when she was abreast of the blockhouse. Cap and Pathfinder leaned forward as the cutter came beneath their eyrie, eager to get a better view of her deck, when, to the delight of both, Jasper Eau-douce sprang upon his feet and gave a hearty cheer. Regardless of all risk, Cap leaped upon the rampart of logs and returned the greeting. Pathfinder, however, kept in view the useful, and the moment he beheld his friend Jasper, he called out to him with stentorian lungs:

"Stand by us, lad, and the day's our own! Give 'em a grist in yonder bushes, and you'll put 'em up like partridges."

Only part of this reached Jasper's ears. By the time it was said, the *Scud* had driven past, and the next moment she was hid from view by the grove in which the blockhouse was partially concealed.

Two anxious minutes succeeded; but, at the expiration of that brief space, the sails were again gleaming through the trees, Jasper having wore, jibbed, and hauled up under the lee of the island on the other tack. The wind was free enough to admit of the manœuvre; and the cutter, catching the current under her lee bow, was breasted up to her course in a way that showed she would come out to windward of the island again without any difficulty. This whole evolution was made with the greatest facility, not a sheet being touched, the sails trimming themselves, the rudder alone controlling the admirable machine. When the *Scud* had made the circuit of the island, and had again got her weatherly position in the channel by which she had first approached, her helm was put down, and she tacked. The noise of the mainsail flapping when it filled, close-reefed as it was, sounded like the report of a gun, and Cap trembled lest the seams should open.

"His Majesty gives good canvas," muttered the old seaman; "and that boy handles his boat as if he were thoroughly bred! Hang me, Pathfinder, if I believe that this Mister Eau-douce got his trade on this bit of fresh water."

"He did. He never saw the ocean, and has come by his calling altogether up here on Ontario."

"There he comes round!" exclaimed Cap, the *Scud* at this moment filling on her original tack; "and now we shall see what the boy would be at; he cannot mean to keep running up and down these passages."

The *Scud* now kept so much away, that for a moment the two observers on the blockhouse feared Jasper meant to come-to. But Jasper had no such intention; familiar with the shore, and acquainted with the depth of water on every part of the island, he well knew that the *Scud* might be run against the bank with impunity, and he ventured fearlessly so near, that, as he passed through the little cove, he swept the two boats of the soldiers from their fastenings and forced them out into the channel, towing them with the cutter. As all the canoes were fastened to the two Dunham boats, by this bold and successful attempt the savages were at once deprived of the means of quitting the island, unless by swimming, and they appeared to be instantly aware of the very important fact. Rising in a body, they filled the air with yells, and poured in a harmless fire. While up in this unguarded manner, two rifles were discharged by their adversaries. One came from the summit of the block, and an Iroquois fell dead in his track; the other came from the *Scud*. The people of the *Scud* shouted, and the savages sank again to a man."

"That was the Sarpent's voice," said Pathfinder, as soon as the second piece was discharged. "I know the crack of his rifle as well as I do that of Killdeer."

As soon as the *Scud* had reached the end of the island, Jasper sent his prizes adrift, and then wore, and came stemming the current again, through the other passage. Those on the summit

could now perceive that something was astir on the deck of the
Scud; and just as the cutter came abreast of the principal cove,
on the spot where most of the enemy lay, the howitzer which
composed her sole armament was unmasked, and a shower of
case-shot was sent hissing into the bushes. A bevy of quail
would not have risen quicker than this discharge put up the
Iroquois; when a second savage fell by a messenger sent from
Killdeer, and another went limping away by a visit from the rifle
of Chingachgook. New covers were immediately found, but the
appearance of June, bearing a white flag, and accompanied by
the French officer and Muir, stayed the hands of all, and was the
forerunner of another parley.

The negotiation that followed was held beneath the blockhouse;
and so near it as at once to put those who were uncovered
completely at the mercy of Pathfinder's unerring aim. Jasper
anchored directly abeam; and the howitzer, too, was kept trained
upon the negotiators; so that the besieged and their friends had
no hesitation about exposing their persons.

"You've triumphed, Pathfinder," called out the Quartermaster,
"and Captain Sanglier has come himself to offer terms. I am
authorized to offer, on the part of the enemy, an evacuation of
the island and a mutual exchange of prisoners."

"What do you say to that, Jasper?" called out Pathfinder.

"What has befallen Mabel?" demanded the young man.

"She is safe below, nursing a dying parent, as becomes her
sex."

"She is here!" exclaimed the girl herself, who had mounted to
the roof the moment she found the direction things were taking,
—"and, in the name of our holy religion, let there be no more
bloodshed!"

"Tut, tut, Magnet!" put in Cap; "this sounds religious, perhaps, or like a book of poetry; but it don't sound like common
sense."

"Well," said Pathfinder, "I incline to Mabel's way of thinking.
So, Lieutenant Muir, let us know what your friends the Frenchers
and Indians have to say for themselves."

"My friends!" said Muir, starting; "you'll no' be calling the
king's enemies my friends, Pathfinder, because the fortune of war
has thrown me into their hands? Master Cap can testify whether
we did not do all that men can devise to escape the calamity."

"Ay, ay," drily answered Cap; "escape is the proper word.
You burrowed on that occasion, Quartermaster, as handily as a

fox; and how you knew so well where to find the spot is a matter
of wonder to me."

"And did ye no' follow? There are moments in a man's life
when reason ascends to instinct——"

"And men descend into holes," interrupted Cap, laughing.

This burst of merriment contributed largely towards keeping
the peace. After a short discussion, all the savages on the island
were collected in a body, without arms, at a distance of a hundred
yards from the block, and under the gun of the *Scud*; while Pathfinder descended and settled the terms on which the island was
to be evacuated by the enemy. The Indians were compelled to
give up all their arms, as a measure of precaution, their force
being still quadruple that of their foes. The French officer,
Monsieur Sanglier, as he was usually styled, remonstrated against
this act as one likely to reflect more discredit on his command
than any other part of the affair; but Pathfinder was obdurate.
The second stipulation was of nearly the same importance. It
compelled Captain Sanglier to give up all his prisoners, who
had been kept well guarded in the very hole or cave in which Cap
and Muir had taken refuge. When these men were produced,
four of them were found to be unhurt; and of the remainder,
two were so slightly injured as not to be unfit for service. This
addition to his force immediately put Pathfinder at his ease; for,
having collected all the arms of the enemy in the blockhouse, he
directed these men to take possession of the building, stationing
a regular sentinel at the door.

As soon as Jasper was made acquainted with the terms, he got
the *Scud* under weigh; and, running down to the point where the
boats had stranded, he took them in tow again, and brought them
into the leeward passage. Here all the savages embarked, when
Jasper took the boats in tow, and, running off before the wind,
he soon set them adrift full a mile to leeward of the island, the
young sailor well knowing that by keeping before the wind they
would land on the shores of Canada in the course of the morning

Captain Sanglier, Arrowhead, and June alone remained, the
former having certain papers to draw up and sign with Lieutenant
Muir; and the Tuscarora, preferring, for reasons of his own, not
to depart in company with his late friends, the Iroquois.

In the meantime, Pathfinder and Cap busied themselves with
preparing a breakfast; most of the party not having eaten for
four-and-twenty hours.

CHAPTER XXVI

As Pathfinder returned from the block, he was met by Muir, who led him aside in order to hold a private discourse. The manner of the Quartermaster had that air of supererogatory courtesy about it which almost invariably denotes artifice. Muir had much of this manner in common, mingled with an apparent frankness that his Scottish intonation of voice, Scottish accent, and Scottish modes of expression were singularly adapted to sustain. He owed his preferment, indeed, to a long-exercised deference to Lundie and his family; for, while the Major himself was much too acute to be the dupe of one so much his inferior in real talents and attainments, most persons are accustomed to make liberal concessions to the flatterer, even while they distrust his truth and are perfectly aware of his motives.

"My dearest friend," Muir commenced, "ye've just established yourself in this late transaction. I doubt if the commander-in-chief will carry away with him from America as much credit as will fall to yer share, and ye ought just to set down in content and enjoy yoursal' for the remainder of yer days."

"I feel your friendship, Quartermaster," said Pathfinder quietly.

"Ye'll understand that this expedition has been of a very peculiar nature; for here am I, bearing the king's commission, just a volunteer, as it might be; while a mere orderly has had the command. My blood has boiled to be in authority, while ye war' battling for the honour of the country and his Majesty's rights——"

"Quartermaster," interrupted the guide, "you fell so early into the enemy's hands that your conscience ought to be easily satisfied on that score; so take my advice, and say nothing about it."

"That's just my opinion, Pathfinder; we'll all say nothing about it. Sergeant Dunham is *hors de combat*——"

"Anan?" said the guide.

"Why, the Sergeant can command no longer, and it will hardly do to leave a corporal at the head of a victorious party like this; and I was just thinking I would claim the authority that belongs to one who holds a lieutenant's commission. As for the men, they'll no dare to raise any objection."

"As for commanding the 55th, Lieutenant, it is your right, I suppose, and no one here will be likely to gainsay it; though there are men who might stand out ag'in giving up their authority to a prisoner released by their own deeds."

"That's just it, Pathfinder; and when I come to draw up the report of our operations, including the capitulation, ye'll no find any omission of your claims and merits."

"Tut for my claims and merits, Quartermaster! Lundie knows what I am, and the General knows better than he. No fear of me; tell your own story, only taking care to do justice by Mabel's father."

Muir expressed his entire satisfaction with this arrangement, as well as his determination to do justice by all, when the two went to the group assembled round the fire. Here the Quartermaster began, for the first time since leaving Oswego, to assume some of the authority that might properly be supposed to belong to his rank.

All this time Captain Sanglier was looking after his own breakfast with the resignation of a philosopher.

The meeting between Pathfinder and Sanglier bore some resemblance to that celebrated interview between Wellington and Blücher which has been so often and graphically told. It took place at the fire; and the parties stood earnestly regarding each other for more than a minute without speaking.

After the two heroes had gazed at each other for some time in silence, Monsieur Sanglier touched his cap, and said:

"Monsieur le Pathfinder, *un militaire* honour *le courage, et la loyauté*. You speak Iroquois?"

"Ay, I understand the language of the riptyles, and can get along with it if there's occasion," returned the guide; "but it's neither a tongue nor a tribe to my taste. I've seen you often, though it was in battle. You must know most of our bullets by sight?"

"Nevvair, sair, your own; *une balle* from your honourable hand be sairtaine deat'. You kill my best warrior on some island."

"That may be; though I dare say, if the truth was known, they would turn out to be great rascals."

"Yes, sair," returned the Frenchman, who, comprehending with difficulty, was disposed to think he received a compliment, "you too good. What that mean? ha! what that *jeune homme* do?"

The hand and eye of Captain Sanglier directed the look of Pathfinder to the opposite side of the fire, where Jasper, just at that moment, had been rudely seized by two of the soldiers, who were binding his arms under the direction of Muir.

"What does that mean, indeed?" cried the guide, stepping forward and shoving the two subordinates away with a power of muscle that would not be denied. "Who has the boldness to do this before my eyes?"

"It is by my orders, Pathfinder," answered the Quartermaster, "and I command it on my own responsibility. Ye'll no' tak' on yourself to dispute the legality of orders given by one who bears the king's commission to the king's soldiers?"

"I'd dispute the king's words, if they came from the king's own mouth, did he say that Jasper desarves this. Has not the lad just saved all our scalps, taken us from defeat, and given us victory? No, no, Lieutenant; if this is the first use that you make of your authority, I, for one, will not respect it."

"This savours a little of insubordination," answered Muir; "but we can bear much from Pathfinder. It is true this Jasper has *seemed* to serve us in this affair, but we ought not to overlook past transactions. Did not Major Duncan himself denounce him to Sergeant Dunham before we left the post? Have we not seen sufficient with our own eyes to make sure of having been betrayed? and is it not natural, and almost necessary, to believe that this young man has been the traitor?"

Captain Sanglier shrugged his shoulders and looked earnestly from Jasper towards the Quartermaster, and from the Quartermaster towards Jasper.

"Jasper Eau-douce is my friend; Jasper Eau-douce is a brave lad, and a loyal lad; and no man of the 55th shall lay hands on him, short of Lundie's own orders, while I'm in the way to prevent it."

"*Bon!*" ejaculated Sanglier.

"Will ye no' hearken to reason, Pathfinder? Ye can see this bit of bunting; well, where should it be found but by Mabel Dunham on the branch of a tree on this very island, just an hour or so before the attack of the enemy; and if ye'll be at the trouble to look at the fly of the *Scud's* ensign, ye'll just say that the cloth has been cut from out it. Circumstantial evidence was never stronger."

"*Ma foi, c'est un peu fort, ceci,*"[1] growled Sanglier.

"Talk to me of no ensigns and signals when I know the heart," continued the Pathfinder. "No, no; off hands, or we shall see which can make the stoutest battle; you and your men of the 55th, or the Sarpent here, and Killdeer, with Jasper and his crew. You overrate your force, Lieutenant Muir, as much as you underrate Eau-douce's truth."

[1] My conscience, but this is a little strong.

" *Très bon!* "

"Well, if I must speak plainly, Pathfinder, I e'en must. Captain Sanglier here and Arrowhead have both informed me that this boy is the traitor."

" *Scélérat,* " muttered the Frenchman.

"Captain Sanglier is a brave soldier, and will not gainsay the conduct of an honest sailor," put in Jasper. "Is there any traitor here, Captain Flinty-heart?"

"Ay," added Muir, "let him speak out, then, since ye wish it, that the truth may be known. How is it, Captain; do ye, or do ye not, see a traitor amang us?"

" *Oui*—yes, sair—*bien sûr.* "

"Too much lie!" said Arrowhead in a voice of thunder, striking the breast of Muir with the back of his own hand in an ungovernable gesture; "where my warriors?—where Yengeese scalp?"

Muir wanted not for personal courage, nor for a certain sense of personal honour. The violence which had been intended only for a gesture he mistook for a blow; for conscience was suddenly aroused within him, and he stepped back a pace, extending his hand towards a gun. His face was livid with rage, and his countenance expressed the fell intention of his heart. But Arrowhead was too quick for him; with a wild glance the Tuscarora thrust a hand beneath his girdle, drew forth a concealed knife, and, in the twinkling of an eye, buried it in the body of the Quartermaster to the handle. As the latter fell at his feet, Sanglier took a pinch of snuff, and said in a calm voice:

" *Voilà l'affaire finie*; *mais,* " shrugging his shoulders, " *ce n'est qu'un scélérat de moins.* " [1]

The act was too sudden to be prevented; and when Arrowhead bounded into the bushes the white men were too confounded to follow. Chingachgook, however, was more collected; and the bushes had scarcely closed on the Tuscarora than they were again opened by the Delaware in full pursuit.

Jasper Western spoke French fluently, and the words and manner of Sanglier struck him.

"Speak, Monsieur," said he in English; " *am* I the traitor?"

" *Le voilà,* " answered the cool Frenchman, "dat is our *espion*—our *agent*—our friend—*ma foi—c'était un grand scélérat—voici.* "

While speaking, Sanglier bent over the dead body, and thrust his hand into a pocket of the Quartermaster, out of which he

[1] Behold the affair ended; but it is only one scoundrel the less.

drew a purse. Casting it from him in contempt, the soldier of fortune turned towards the soup he had been preparing with so much care, and, finding it to his liking, he began to break his fast with an air of indifference that the most stoical Indian warrior might have envied.

CHAPTER XXVII

THE reader must imagine some of the occurrences that followed the sudden death of Muir. While his body was in the hands of his soldiers, who covered it with a greatcoat, Chingachgook silently resumed his place at the fire, and both Sanglier and Pathfinder remarked that he carried a fresh and bleeding scalp at his girdle. With a view to ascertain the extent of Muir's treachery, as soon as the body was removed, Pathfinder began to question the Captain on the subject. The latter, having no particular motive for secrecy now that his agent was dead, revealed the following circumstances.

Soon after the 55th appeared on the frontiers, Muir had volunteered his services to the enemy. His terms had been accepted, and Monsieur Sanglier had several interviews with him in the vicinity of the fort at Oswego. Arrowhead, however, was the usual channel of communication; and the anonymous letter to Major Duncan had been originally written by Muir, transmitted to Frontenac, copied, and sent back by the Tuscarora, who was returning from that errand when captured by the *Scud*. It is scarcely necessary to add that Jasper was to be sacrificed in order to conceal the Quartermaster's treason, and that the position of the island had been betrayed to the enemy by the latter. An extraordinary compensation—that which was found in his purse—had induced him to accompany the party under Sergeant Dunham, in order to give the signals that were to bring on the attack. He would have married Mabel, or any one else who would accept his hand; but his admiration of her was in a great degree feigned, in order that he might have an excuse for accompanying the party without sharing in the responsibility of its defeat, or incurring the risk of having no other strong and seemingly sufficient motive.

"*Touchez-la*," said the cold-blooded partisan, holding out his hand to Pathfinder, when he ended his explanations; "you be *honnête*, and dat is *beaucoup*. We tak' de spy as we tak' *la médecine,* for de good; *mais, je les déteste!*"

"I'll shake your hand, Captain; for you're a lawful and nat'ral inimy," returned Pathfinder, "and a manful one; but the body of the Quartermaster shall never disgrace English ground. I did intend to carry it back to Lundie, but now it shall lie here on the spot where he acted his villainy, and have his own treason for a headstone. Jasper, boy, a word with you aside, for a single minute."

Pathfinder now led the young man apart; and, squeezing his hand, he continued:

"You know me, Eau-douce, and I know you," said he, "and this news has not changed my opinion of you in any manner. I never suspected you for a minute, for I know your gifts don't lie that-a-way; but, I must own, I didn't suspect the Quartermaster neither."

"And he holding his Majesty's commission, Pathfinder!"

"It isn't so much that, Jasper Western. He held a commission from God to deal fairly with his fellow-creeturs, and he has failed awfully in his duty."

"To think of his pretending love for one like Mabel, too, when he felt none."

"That was bad, sartainly; the fellow must have had Mingo blood in his veins. The man that deals unfairly by a woman can be but a mongrel, lad; for the Lord has made them helpless on purpose that we may gain their love by kindness and sarvices. Here is the Sergeant, poor man, on his dying bed; he has given me his daughter for a wife, and Mabel, dear girl, she has consented to it. Ah's me, Jasper, I sometimes feel that I'm not good enough for that sweet child!"

Eau-douce had nearly gasped for breath when he first heard this intelligence; and, though he succeeded in suppressing any other outward sign of agitation, his cheek was blanched nearly to the paleness of death. Still he found means to answer not only with firmness, but with energy:

"Say not so, Pathfinder; you are good enough for a queen."

"Ay, ay, boy, according to your idees of my goodness; that is to say, I can kill a deer, or even a Mingo at need, with any man on the lines; or I can follow a forest-path with as true an eye, or read the stars, when others do not understand them."

"If you pass for your value, Pathfinder, the greatest lady in the land would be happy with you."

"Now, Jasper, I dare to say *you* think so, nay, I *know* you do; for it is nat'ral, and according to friendship, for people to look over-favourably at them they love. I wonder, Jasper, that Mabel never took a fancy to you, now, rather than setting her mind on me."

"Take a fancy to me, Pathfinder!" returned the young man, endeavouring to clear his voice without betraying himself; "what is there about me to please such a girl as Mabel Dunham? I have all that you find fault with in yourself, with none of that excel-lence that makes even the generals respect you."

"Well, well, it's all chance, say what we will about it. Here have I journeyed and guided through the woods female after female, and consorted with them in the garrisons, and never have I even felt an inclination for any until I saw Mabel. I'm tough, Jasper; yes, I'm very tough; and yet I think it would quite break me down, now, to lose Mabel!"

"We will talk no more of it, Pathfinder," said Jasper, returning his friend's squeeze of the hand, and moving back towards the fire, and in the manner of one who cared little where he went.

By this time they were so near the fire that it was necessary to change the conversation. Luckily, at that instant, Cap, who had been in the block in company with his dying brother-in-law, now appeared, walking with a meditative and melancholy air towards the group.

"This death, gentlemen," said he, when he had got sufficiently near, "is a melancholy business, make the best of it. Now, here is Sergeant Dunham, about to slip his cable; and yet he holds on to the better end of it, as if he were determined it should never run out of the hawse-hole; and all because he loves his daughter, it seems to me."

"You wouldn't kill the Sergeant before his time!" Pathfinder reproachfully answered.

Nothing had been further from Cap's real thoughts than the wish to hasten his brother-in-law's end. A little shocked, there-fore, at the interpretation that had been put on his words, he rejoined with some of the asperity of the man, though rebuked by a consciousness of not having done his own wishes justice. "You are too old and too sensible a person, Pathfinder," said he, "to fetch a man up with a surge, when he is paying out his ideas in distress, as it might be. Sergeant Dunham is both my brother-in-law and my friend—that is to say, as intimate a friend as a soldier well can be with a seafaring man,—and I respect and honour him accordingly. I make no doubt, however, that he has lived such a life as becomes a man, and there can be no harm, after all, in wishing any one well berthed in heaven. Death is a circumstance, after all, Master Pathfinder, and one of a very general character too, seeing that we all must submit to it, sooner or later."

"You say truth, and for that reason I hold it to be wise to be always ready. As to myself, when the order comes to march I shall be ready at a minute's warning; and, let me tell you, Master Cap, that's what I call a circumstance too."

"'Tis just so with me," answered the sailor, as the two walked towards the block; "that's just my way of feeling and reasoning. How often have I felt, when near shipwreck, the relief of not owning the craft! Hang me, Pathfinder, if I think a man without a heart any better than a fish with a hole in his air-bag."

"I don't know how that may be, Master Cap; but a man without a conscience is but a poor creetur', take my word for it. I can easily believe, by what I've seen of mankind, that if a man *has* a chest filled with coin, he may be said to lock up his heart in the same box; and if I have consarn in marrying Mabel, it is that I may get to love such things too well, in order to make her comfortable."

"You're a philosopher, that's clear, Pathfinder; and I don't know but you're a Christian."

"I should be out of humour with the man that gainsayed the last, Master Cap. I have not been Christianized by the Moravians, like so many of the Delawares, it is true, but I hold to Christianity and white gifts. The Sarpent and I talk these matters over often, for he has a hankerin' after Christianity——"

"And what does he intend to do in a church with all the scalps be takes?"

"Don't run away with a false idee, friend Cap. These things are only skin-deep, and all depend on edication and nat'ral gifts. Tell me why you see a red warrior here, a black one there, and white armies in another place? No, no; each colour has its gifts, and its laws, and its traditions; and one is not to condemn another because he does not exactly comprehend it."

"You must have read a great deal, Pathfinder, to see things so clear as this," returned Cap. "It's all as plain as day to me now, though I must say I never fell in with these opinions before. I think a word from you might lighten the Sergeant over the shoals of death, Master Pathfinder."

They were now so near the building that neither thought of pursuing the subject any further; but each prepared himself for the final scene with Sergeant Dunham.

CHAPTER XXVIII

Sergeant Dunham was a brave man; but he was departing for a country in which resolution could avail him nothing; and as he felt himself gradually loosened from the grasp of the world, his thoughts and feelings took the natural direction; for if it be true that death is the great leveller, in nothing is it more true than that it reduces all to the same views of the vanity of life.

Pathfinder, though a man of peculiar habits and opinions, was always thoughtful, and disposed to view the things around him with a shade of philosophy, as well as with seriousness. In him, therefore, the scene in the blockhouse awakened no very novel feelings. But the case was different with Cap: rude and dogmatical, the old sailor was little accustomed to view even death with any approach to the gravity which its importance demands; and notwithstanding all that had passed, his first thought on entering the room of the dying man was to commence a narration of the events which had just led to the deaths of Muir and Arrowhead. "Both tripped their anchors in a hurry, brother Dunham," he concluded; "and you have the satisfaction of knowing that others have gone before you in the great journey."

June arose at this intelligence, and stole from the blockhouse with a noiseless step. Dunham listened with a vacant stare, for life had already lost so many of its ties that he had really forgotten Arrowhead, and cared nothing for Muir; but he enquired in a feeble voice for Eau-douce. The young man was immediately summoned, and soon made his appearance. The Sergeant gazed at him kindly, and the expression of his eyes was that of regret for the injury he had done him in thought. The party in the blockhouse now consisted of Pathfinder, Cap, Mabel, Jasper, and the dying man. Mabel kneeled at his side, now pressing a clammy hand to her head, now applying moisture to the parched lips of her father.

"Your case will shortly be ourn, Sergeant," said Pathfinder, "and I make no question we shall meet ag'in hereafter. You have done your duty in life; and when a man does that, he

may start on the longest journey with a light heart and an
actyve foot."

"I hope so, my friend: I've tried to do my duty."

"Ay, ay," put in Cap; "intention is half the battle, no one
here doubts that you meant all for the best, and no one anywhere
else, I should think, from what I have seen of this world and read
of t'other."

"I did; yes. I meant all for the best."

"Father! Oh, my beloved father!"

"Did you speak, Mabel?" Dunham asked, turning his eyes in
the direction of his daughter.

"Yes, Father; rely on nothing you have done yourself for mercy
and salvation; trust altogether in the blessed mediation of the
Son of God!"

"The chaplain has told us something like this, brother. The
dear child may be right."

"Ay, ay, that's doctrine, out of question. I do believe Mabel
is right; but then you need not be concerned, as no doubt the
account has been fairly kept."

"Uncle!—dearest Father! this is a vain illusion! Oh, place all
your trust in the mediation of our Holy Redeemer! There is no
hope for any but in the mediation of Christ."

"This is what the Moravians used to tell us," said Pathfinder to
Cap in a low voice; "rely on it, Mabel is right."

"I have heard this before," Dunham at length replied. "Ah,
Mabel! it is strange for the parent to lean on the child at a
moment like this!"

"Put your trust in God, Father; lean on His holy and com-
passionate Son. Pray, dearest Father; pray for His support."

"I am not used to prayer, brother. Pathfinder—Jasper, can
you help me to words?"

"Father," said Mabel, wiping her eyes, and endeavouring to
compose features that were pallid, and actually quivering with
emotion, "*I* will pray with you, *for* you, for *myself*, for us *all.*
The petition of the feeblest and humblest is never unheeded."

There was something sublime, as well as much that was su-
premely touching, in this act of filial piety. The quiet but
earnest manner in which this young creature prepared herself
to perform the duty; and the holy calm into which her grief
was compressed, rendered her, for the moment, an object of
something very like awe and veneration to her companions.

When she kneeled at the bedside of her father, the very reverence of her attitude and manner prepared the spectators for what was to come; and as her affectionate heart prompted her tongue, and memory came in aid of both, the petition and praises that she offered up were of a character which might have worthily led the spirits of angels.

But when our heroine came to touch upon the situation of the dying man, she became the most truly persuasive, for then she was the most truly zealous and natural. The beauty of the language was preserved, but it was sustained by the simple power of love; and her words were warmed by a holy zeal that approached the grandeur of true eloquence. We might record some of her expressions, but doubt the propriety of subjecting such sacred themes to a too familiar analysis, and refrain.

Sergeant Dunham laid his hand feebly on the head of Mabel as she ceased, and buried her face in his blanket.

"Bless you, my beloved child!" he rather whispered than uttered aloud; "this is truly consolation: would that I too could pray!"

"Father, you know the Lord's Prayer; you taught it to me yourself while I was yet an infant."

The Sergeant's face gleamed with a smile; he was then silent for several minutes, and all present believed that he was communing with God.

"Mabel, my child!" he at length uttered, in a voice which seemed to be reviving,—"Mabel, I'm quitting you. I'm quitting you, my child; where is your hand?"

"Here, dearest Father—here are both—oh, take both!"

"Pathfinder," added the Sergeant, feeling on the opposite side of the bed, where Jasper still knelt, a..d getting one of the hands of the young man by mistake, "take it—I leave you as her father —as you and she may please—bless you—bless you both!"

At that awful instant, no one would rudely apprise the Sergeant of his mistake; and he died a minute or two later, holding Jasper's and Mabel's hands covered by both his own. Our heroine was ignorant of the fact until an exclamation of Cap's announced the death of her father; when, raising her face, she saw the eyes of Jasper riveted on her own, and felt the warm pressure of his hand. But a single feeling was predominant at that instant, and Mabel withdrew to weep, scarcely conscious of what had occurred. The Pathfinder took the arm of Eau-douce, and he left the block.

The two friends walked in silence past the fire, along the glade, and nearly reached the opposite shore of the island in profound silence. Here they stopped, and Pathfinder spoke.

"'Tis all over, Jasper," said he. "Poor Sergeant Dunham has finished his march. Well, we never know what is to happen, and his luck may be yourn or mine to-morrow or next day!"

"And Mabel? What is to become of Mabel, Pathfinder?"

"You heard the Sergeant's dying words; he has left his child in my care, Jasper; and it is a most solemn trust, it is; yes—it is a most solemn trust."

"It's a trust, Pathfinder, of which any man would be glad to relieve you," returned the youth, with a bitter smile.

"I've often thought it has fallen into wrong hands. I'm not consaited, Jasper, but if Mabel Dunham is willing to overlook all my imperfections and ignorances like, I should be wrong to gainsay it, on account of any sartainty I may have myself about my own want of merit."

"No one will blame you, Pathfinder, for marrying Mabel Dunham, any more than they will blame you for wearing a precious jewel in your bosom that a friend had freely given you."

"Do you think they'll blame Mabel, lad? I've had my misgivings about that too; for all persons may not be so disposed to look at me with the same eyes as you and the Sergeant's daughter."

Jasper Eau-douce started as a man flinches at sudden bodily pain: but he otherwise maintained his self-command. "And mankind is envious and ill-natured, more particularly in and about the garrisons. I sometimes wish, Jasper, that Mabel could have taken a fancy to you; and that you had taken a fancy to her; for it seems to me that one like you, after all, might make her happier than I ever can."

"We will not talk about this, Pathfinder," interrupted Jasper hoarsely; "you will be Mabel's husband, and it is not right to speak of anyone else in that character. As for me, I shall take Master Cap's advice, and try what is to be done on the salt water."

"You, Jasper Western!—you quit the lakes, the forests, and the lines; and this, too, for the towns and wasty ways of the settlements, and a little difference in the taste of the water! I counted on you, Jasper, and thought, now that Mabel and I intend to dwell in a cabin of our own, that some day you might be tempted to choose a companion too, and come and settle in our neighbourhood."

"You forget, my friend," answered Jasper, taking the guide's hand and forcing a friendly smile, "that I have no one to love and cherish; and I much doubt if I ever shall love any other as I love you and Mabel."

"Thank'e, boy; I thank you with all my heart: but what you call love for Mabel is only friendship like, and a very different thing from what I feel. Now, instead of sleeping as sound as natur' at midnight, as I used to could, I dream nightly of Mabel Dunham, and the bitterest moments I've ever known were them in which Satan, or some Mingo conjuror, perhaps, has just put into my head to fancy in dreams that Mabel is lost to me by some unaccountable calamity either by changefulness or by violence."

"Oh, Pathfinder! if you think this so bitter in a dream, what must it be to one who feels its reality, and knows it all to be true? So true as to leave no hope; to leave nothing but despair!"

These words were uttered involuntarily, almost unconsciously, but with a truth and feeling that carried with them the instant conviction of their deep sincerity. Pathfinder started, gazed at his friend for a full minute like one bewildered, and then it was that, in despite of all his simplicity, the truth gleamed upon him. Our hero was so confiding by nature, so just, and so much disposed to imagine that all his friends wished him the same happiness as he wished them, that, until this moment, a suspicion of Jasper's attachment for Mabel had never been awakened in his bosom. He was, however, now too experienced in the emotions which characterize the passion; and the burst of feeling in his companion was too violent and too natural to leave any further doubt on the subject. The feeling that first followed this change of opinion was one of deep humility and exquisite pain. He bethought him of Jasper's youth, his higher claims to personal appearance, and all the general probabilities that such a suitor would be more agreeable to Mabel than he could possibly be himself. Then the noble rectitude of mind asserted its power; it was sustained by his rebuked manner of thinking of himself, and all that habitual deference for the rights and feelings of others which appeared to be inbred in his very nature. Taking the arm of Jasper, he led him to a log, where he compelled the young man to seat himself, and where he placed himself at his side.

The instant his feelings had found vent, Eau-douce was both alarmed at, and ashamed of, their violence. He would have given all he possessed on earth could the last three minutes be recalled; but he was too frank by disposition and too much accustomed to deal ingenuously by his friend to think a moment of attempting further concealment, or of any evasion of the explanation that he knew was about to be demanded.

"Jasper," Pathfinder commenced, in a solemn tone, "this *has* surprised me! You have kinder feelings towards Mabel than I had thought; and, unless my own mistaken vanity and consait have cruelly deceived me, I pity you, boy, from my soul I do! This matter must be cleared up, Eau-douce, until there shall not be a cloud atween us."

"What clearing up can it want, Pathfinder? I love Mabel, and Mabel does not love me; she prefers you for a husband; and the wisest thing I can do is to go off at once to the salt water, and try forget you both."

"Forget me, Jasper! That would be a punishment I don't desarve. But how do you know that Mabel prefars *me*? how do you know it, lad?"

"Is she not to marry you, and would Mabel marry a man she does not love?"

"She has been hard urged by the Sergeant; and a dutiful child may have found it difficult to withstand the wishes of a dying parent. Have you ever told her that you bore her these feelings?"

"Never, Pathfinder. I would not do you that wrong."

"I believe you, lad, and I think you would now go off to the salt water, and let the scent die with you. But this must not be. Mabel shall hear all, and she shall have her own way, if my heart breaks in the trial, she shall. No words have ever passed atween you, then, Jasper?"

"Nothing of account. Still, I will own all my foolishness, Pathfinder. You know how young people understand each other, or think they understand each other, without always speaking out in plain speech, and get to know each other's thoughts by a hundred little ways."

"Not I, Jasper," truly answered the guide. "I know nothing of all this. Mabel has always treated me fairly, and said what she has had to say in speech as plain as tongue could tell it."

"You have had the pleasure of hearing her say that she loved you, Pathfinder?"

"Why, no, Jasper, not just that in words. She has told me that we never could, never ought to be married; that *she* was not good enough for *me*, though she *did* say that she honoured me and respected me. But then the Sergeant said it was always so with the youthful and timid; and that I ought to be satisfied if she would consent on any terms to marry me, and so I have concluded that all was right."

In spite of all his friendship for the successful wooer, in spite of all his honest, sincere wishes for his happiness, we should be unfaithful chroniclers did we not own that Jasper felt his heart bound with an uncontrollable feeling of delight at this admission.

"Tell me more of this manner of talking without the use of the tongue," continued Pathfinder. "I can and have conversed with Chingachgook; but I didn't know that young girls practysed this art, and, least of all, Mabel Dunham."

"'Tis nothing, Pathfinder. I mean only a look, or a smile, or a glance of the eye, or the trembling of an arm or a hand when the young woman has had occasion to touch me. I never spoke plainly to Mabel myself, and now there is no use for it, since there is clearly no hope."

"Jasper," returned Pathfinder simply, with dignity, "we will talk of the Sergeant's funeral and of our own departure from this island. After these things are disposed of, it will be time enough to say more of the Sergeant's daughter. This matter must be looked into, for the father left me the care of his child."

Jasper was glad to change the subject, and the friends separated, each charged with the duty most peculiar to his station and habits.

That afternoon the dead were interred, the grave of Sergeant Dunham being dug beneath the shade of a huge elm. Mabel wept bitterly at the ceremony, and she found relief in thus disburthening her sorrow. The night passed tranquilly, as did the whole of the following day, Jasper declaring that the weather was too severe to venture on the lake. This circumstance detained Captain Sanglier also, who did not quit the island until the morning of the third day after the death of Dunham.

CHAPTER XXIX

THE morning of the third day was set for that on which the *Scud*
was to sail. Jasper had made all his preparations; the different
effects were embarked, and Mabel had taken leave of June, a
painful and affectionate parting. In a word, all was ready, and
every soul had left the island but the Indian woman, Pathfinder,
Jasper, and our heroine. The former had gone into a thicket to
weep, and the three last were approaching the spot where three
canoes lay, one of which was the property of June, and the other
two were in waiting to carry the others off to the *Scud*. Pathfinder
led the way, but, when he drew near the shore, instead of taking
the direction to the boats, he motioned his companions to follow,
and proceeded to a fallen tree, which lay on the margin of the
glade and out of view of those in the cutter. Seating himself
on the trunk, he signed to Mabel to take her place on one side
of him and to Jasper to occupy the other.

"Sit down here, Mabel; sit down there, Eau-douce," he commenced, as soon as he had taken his own seat. "I've something
that lies heavy on my mind, and now is the time to take it off,
if it's ever to be done. Sit down, Mabel, and let me lighten my
heart while I've the strength to do it."

The pause that succeeded lasted two or three minutes, and both
the young people wondered what was to come next.

"Mabel," our hero at length resumed, "we must talk plainly
to each other afore we join your uncle in the cutter. Ah's me!
I try to be pleasant, and to feel lighthearted, but the power of
man can't make water run up stream. Mabel, you know that
the Sergeant, afore he left us, had settled it atween us two
that we were to become man and wife, and to love one another
as long as the Lord was pleased to keep us both on 'arth; yes,
and afterwards too?"

Mabel's cheeks had regained a little of their ancient bloom in
the fresh air of the morning; but at this unlooked-for address
they blanched again. Still, she looked kindly, though seriously,
at Pathfinder, and even endeavoured to force a smile.

"Very true," she answered; "this was my poor father's wish,
and I feel certain that a whole life devoted to your welfare could
scarcely repay you for all you have done for us."

"I fear me, Mabel, that man and wife needs be bound together by a stronger tie than such feelings. You have done

nothing for me, or nothing of any account, and yet my very heart yearns towards you; and therefore it seems likely that these feelings come from something besides saving scalps and guiding through woods."

Mabel's cheek had begun to glow again; and though she struggled hard to smile, her voice trembled as she answered:

"Had we not better postpone this conversation, Pathfinder?" she said; "nothing is so unpleasant to a listener, they say, as family matters in which he feels no interest."

"It's because Jasper is with us, Mabel, that I wish to talk of this matter. The Sergeant believed I might make a suitable companion for you, and, though I had misgivings about it, he finally persuaded me into the idee, and things came round atween us, as you know. But when you promised your father to marry me, Mabel, and gave me your hand so modestly, but so prettily, there was one circumstance that you didn't know; and I've thought it right to tell you what it is, before matters are finally settled."

"You speak in a way, Pathfinder, that is difficult to be understood."

"Well then, Mabel, I've been thinking it was quite likely, when you gave in to the Sergeant's wishes, that you did not know the natur' of Jasper's feelings towards you?"

"Pathfinder!" and Mabel's cheeks now paled to the livid hue of death, while her whole frame shuddered. Pathfinder, however, was too intent on his own object to notice this agitation; and Eau-douce had hidden his face in his hands.

"I've been talking with the lad; and, on comparing his feelings with my feelings, and his wishes with my wishes, I fear we think too much alike consarning you for both of us to be very happy."

"Pathfinder, you forget; you should remember that we are betrothed!" said Mabel hastily, and in a voice so low that it required acute attention in the listeners to catch the syllables.

"Anan?"

"You forget that we are to be married; and such allusions are improper as well as painful."

"Everything is proper that is right, Mabel; and everything is right that leads to justice and fair dealing; though it *is painful* enough. Now, Mabel, had you known that Eau-douce thinks of you in this way, maybe you never would have consented to be married to one as old as I am."

"Why this cruel trial, Pathfinder? To what can all this lead? Jasper Western thinks no such thing: he says nothing, he feels nothing."

"Mabel!" burst from out of the young man's lips, in a way to betray the uncontrollable nature of his emotions.

Mabel buried her face in both her hands; and the two sat like a pair of guilty beings. At that instant, perhaps, Jasper himself was inclined to deny his passion, through an extreme unwillingness to grieve his friend; while Mabel, on whom this positive announcement of a fact that she had rather unconsciously hoped than believed, came so unexpectedly, felt her mind momentarily bewildered; and she scarcely knew whether to weep or to rejoice. Still she was the first to speak, since Eau-douce could utter nought that would be disingenuous, or that would pain his friend.

"Pathfinder," said she, "you talk wildly. Why mention this at all?"

"Well, Mabel, if I talk wildly, I *am* half wild, you know." As he said this, he endeavoured to laugh in his usual noiseless way, but the effort produced a strange and discordant sound. "Yes, I *must* be wild."

"Dearest Pathfinder! you *cannot, do not* think I intended to say that!" interrupted Mabel. "If courage, truth, and nobleness of soul and conduct can render any man respectable, esteemed, or beloved, your claims are inferior to those of no other human being."

"What tender and bewitching voices they have, Jasper!" resumed the guide, laughing. "Yes, natur' seems to have made them on purpose to sing in our ears, when the music of the woods is silent. But we must come to a right understanding, we must. I ask you again, Mabel, if you had known that Jasper Western loves you as well as I do, or better perhaps, though that is scarcely possible, would you then have consented to marry me?"

Mabel could not have answered this question if she would; but, though her face was buried in her hands, there was a single instant when the astonished girl stole a glance at Jasper, read the truth of all he said in that furtive look, and instantly concealed her face again, as if she would hide it from observation for ever.

"Take time to think, Mabel," the guide continued, "for it is a solemn thing to accept one man for a husband while the thoughts and wishes lead to another. Jasper and I have talked this matter over, and, though I always knowed that we viewed most things pretty much alike, I couldn't have thought that we regarded any particular object with the very same eyes, as might be, until we opened our minds to each other about you. Nay, the lad has even acknowledged that he often weeps at the thought that you are likely to spend your days with another, and not with him."

"Jasper!"

"It's solemn truth, Mabel, and it's right you should know it. Now stand up, and choose atween us. The Sergeant left me your protector, and not your tyrant. I told him that I would be a father to you as well as a husband, and it seems to me no feeling father would deny his child this small privilege. Stand up, Mabel, therefore, and speak your thoughts as freely as if I were the Sergeant himself, seeking your good, and nothing else."

Mabel dropped her hands, arose, and stood face to face with her two suitors, though the flush that was on her cheeks was feverish, the evidence of excitement rather than of shame.

"What would you have, Pathfinder?" she asked. "Have I not already promised my poor father to do all you desire?"

"Then I desire this. Here I stand, a man of the forest and of little larning, though I fear with an ambition beyond my desarts, and I'll do my endivours to do justice to both sides. When all is remembered, age, looks, learning, and habits, Mabel, conscience tells me I ought to confess that I'm altogether unfit for you, if not downright unworthy; and I would give up the hope this minute, I would, if I didn't feel something pulling at my heart-strings which seems hard to undo."

"Pathfinder! noble, generous Pathfinder!" cried our heroine, seizing his hand and kissing it with reverence; "you do yourself injustice—you forget my poor father and your promise—you do not know *me*!"

"Now, here's Jasper," continued the guide, "with *him* the case is different. In the way of providing, as in that of loving, there's not much to choose atween us; for the lad is frugal, industrious, and careful, and can understand you at all times, which, perhaps, is more than I can say for myself."

"What of all this?" interrupted Mabel impatiently; "why speak of it now?"

"Then the lad has a manner of letting his thoughts be known, that I fear I can never equal. He fairly made my blood warm, when he spoke of your having beauty without seeming ever to delicacy and flavour that might have tempted the appetite of an epicure. This species of intercourse lasted a month, June obstinately refusing to abandon the grave of her husband all that time, though she still accepted the friendly offerings of her protector. Occasionally they met and conversed, Pathfinder sounding the state of the woman's feelings; but the interviews were short, and far from frequent. June slept in one of the huts, and she laid down her head in security, for she was conscious of the protection of a friend, though Pathfinder invariably retired at night to an adjacent island, where he had built himself a hut.

At the end of the month, however, the season was getting to be too far advanced to render her situation pleasant. The trees had lost their leaves, and the nights were becoming cold and wintry.

At this moment Chingachgook reappeared. He had a long and confidential interview on the island with his friend. June witnessed their movements, and she saw that her guardian was distressed. Stealing to his side, she endeavoured to soothe his sorrow with a woman's gentleness and with a woman's instinct.

"Thank you, June!" he said; "'tis well meant though it's useless. But it is time to quit this place. To-morrow we shall depart. You will go with us, for now you've got to feel reason."

In the morning the three departed. They went in two canoes; Chingachgook led the way, and Pathfinder followed, the course being up stream. Two days they paddled westward, and as many nights they camped on islands. Fortunately the weather became mild, and when they reached the lake it was found smooth and glassy as a pond. It was the Indian summer, and the calms, and almost the blandness of June, slept in the hazy atmosphere.

On the morning of the third day they passed the mouth of the Oswego, where the fort and the sleeping ensign invited them in vain to enter. Without casting a look aside, Chingachgook paddled past the dark waters of the river, and Pathfinder still followed in silent industry. The ramparts were crowded with spectators; but Lundie, who knew the persons of his old friends, refused to allow them to be even hailed.

It was noon when Chingachgook entered a little bay where the *Scud* lay at anchor, in a sort of roadstead. A small ancient clearing was on the shore; and near the margin of the lake was a log dwelling, recently and completely, though rudely fitted up. There was an air of frontier comfort and of frontier abundance around the place, though it was necessarily wild and solitary. Jasper stood on the shore; and when Pathfinder landed, he was the first

to take him by the hand. The meeting was simple, but very
cordial. No questions were asked, it being apparent that Chin
gachgook had made the necessary explanations. Pathfinder never
squeezed his friend's hand more cordially than in this interview;
and he even laughed cordially in his face as he told him how well
and happy he appeared.

"Where is she, Jasper? where is she?" the guide at length whis
pered, for at first he had seemed to be afraid to trust himself with
the question.

"She is waiting for us in the house, my friend, where you see
that June has already hastened before us."

"And so, lad, you found the chaplain at the garrison, and all
was soon settled?"

"We were married within a week after we left you, and Master
Cap departed next day."

"Did the child smile or did she weep when the ceremony was
over?"

"She did both, my friend; but——"

"Yes, that's their natur', tearful and cheerful. And do you
think, Jasper, that she thought of me at all on that joyful occasion?"

"I know she did, Pathfinder; and she thinks of you and talks
of you daily, almost hourly. None love you as we do."

"I know few love me better than yourself, Jasper. Well, there's
no use in putting it off any longer; it must be done, and may as
well be done at once; so, Jasper, lead the way, and I'll endivour
to look upon her sweet countenance once more."

Jasper did lead the way, and they were soon in the presence of
Mabel. The latter met her late suitor with a bright blush, and
her limbs trembled so, she could hardly stand; still her manner
was affectionate and frank. During the hour of Pathfinder's visit
(for it lasted no longer), one who was expert in tracing the working of the human mind might have seen a faithful index to the
feelings of Mabel in her manner to Pathfinder and her husband.
With the latter she still had a little of the reserve that usually
accompanies young wedlock; but the tone of her voice was kinder
even than common; the glance of her eye was tender, and she
seldom looked at him without the glow that tinged her cheeks
betraying the existence of feelings that habit and time had not
yet soothed into absolute tranquillity. With Pathfinder, all was
earnest, sincere, even anxious.

At length the moment came when Pathfinder must go his way

Chingachgook had already abandoned the canoes, and was posted on the margin of the woods, where a path led into the forest. Here he calmly waited to be joined by his friend. As soon as the latter was aware of this fact, he rose and took his leave.

"I've sometimes thought that my own fate has been a little hard," he said; "but that of this woman, Mabel, has shamed me into reason."

"June remains, and lives with me," interrupted our heroine.

"So I comprehend it. If anybody can bring her back from her grief, and make her wish to live, you can do it, Mabel; though I've misgivings about even your success."

"Pathfinder," asked Mabel, "when shall we see you again?"

"I've thought of that, too; yes, I've thought of that, I have. If the time should ever come when I can look upon you altogether as a sister, Mabel, or a child, depend on it I'll come back; for it would lighten my very heart to witness your gladness. But if I cannot,—farewell—farewell,—the Sergeant was wrong,—yes, the Sergeant was wrong!"

This was the last the Pathfinder ever uttered to the ears of Jasper and Mabel. He turned away as if the words choked him, and was quickly at the side of his friend. Mabel, her husband, and June all watched the form of the Pathfinder, in the hope of receiving a parting gesture, but he did not look back; and a tread, whose vigour no sorrow could enfeeble, soon bore him out of view, and he was lost in the depths of the forest.

Neither Jasper nor his wife ever beheld the Pathfinder again. They remained for another year on the banks of Ontario; and then the pressing solicitations of Cap induced them to join him in New York, where Jasper eventually became a successful and respected merchant.